CIRCUMSTANCE

CIRCUMSTANCE

BY

S. WEIR MITCHELL, M.D.

LL.D. HARVARD AND EDINBURGH

NEW YORK

THE CENTURY CO.

1901

THE DE VINNE PRESS.

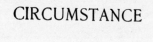

CIRCUMSTANCE

On a hilltop of an island endeared to me by many memories, the ocean wind has permanently bent pine, fir and spruce.

Here and there a single tree remains upright, — stanchly refusing to record the effect of circumstance on character.

CIRCUMSTANCE

I

IT was nearly full moon on Long Island Sound—a night so faultless that almost all of the few passengers on the steamer were out upon deck. High in air above them the dark walking beams swung up and down, and, quivering with their power, the huge bulk of the steamer hurled on through the snow-white lift of water cast from her cleaving bow.

A young girl and a man leaned over the rail, gaily chatting, unsubdued by the radiant beauty of a windless, moonlit night which, by degrees, had brought to unexplained silence most of the groups scattered here and there along the decks.

From the level of the upper deck a woman of some thirty-six years watched the couple on the bow. Once or twice she looked at her watch, and at last, seeing them move, went down to the lower deck, where she met them walking aft.

"My dear Miss Morrow," she said, "I have been looking for you everywhere. I was told you were on board. Imagine my surprise! I am sure Mr. Masters must want a cigar, and will let me have you for a walk on deck."

Mr. Masters was entirely willing, and, with a civil word of conventional protest, left them, saying he would look after them at the pier in New York next morning.

Miss Morrow's greeting of the older woman had been warm and honest. As he turned away Mrs. Hunter said:

"Were I in Mr. Masters's place I should hate Mrs. Hunter; but the fact is I do want to have you to myself."

Miss Morrow remarked that it was "awfully nice."

"I was greatly surprised," said her friend, "to find that you had left Newport, and to know that I was on the boat with you did seem better fortune than life usually provides for me."

"I called to tell you I was going," said Miss Morrow; "you were out—"

"Come to the stern." They gave up the suggested walk, and sat down by themselves where they could see the white wake of the steamer melt into the distant darkness. The mysterious beauty of sea and sky affected neither of them.

"I cannot help repeating," Mrs. Hunter began, "what luck it is to find you on board." (She had taken care to arrange that this fortunate meeting should occur.)

Miss Morrow again explained: she had meant to write, but, really, there was too much to do; her maid was to remind her and never did—

"And," said the elder woman, "we might never have met again."

"Oh, but we should! I should have written to New York—you know I have your address."

"Ah, dear child! You would have quite forgotten me in the joys of a happier life."

"Oh, no, no!"

"Pardon me. No, you would not. How a night like this sets one to thinking. This sad world is full of broken friendships. One meets a woman like you, a person of force and character, and then—the accidents of life part them and they meet no more—" she paused—"no more on earth."

Miss Kitty sat up, conscious of a form of appreciative consideration to which she was not elsewhere accustomed. Her appetite for flattery was boundless. She had the avarice of praise, and was willing to pay for it in her own feebler coinage.

"Oh, to have *you* say so," she said; "a woman like you, Mrs. Hunter—"

"I felt, my dear, when we first met that—well, there is such a thing as friendship at first sight, just as, alas! there is such a thing as love without second sight."

"Oh, what a clever idea, Mrs. Hunter."

"Why must you call me Mrs. Hunter? In the colder world of misapprehending people it may be as well, but when we are alone, dear, alone, let it be Lucretia. It seems to bring two kindred hearts more near together." Much amused, she smiled under the veil of shadows.

Miss Morrow murmured:

"Lucretia! I will try; but you do seem so far above me, so much older—"

Whether she was quite able to believe anyone her mental superior may be doubted, but she made believe to herself to believe it, being, like many people of thin intellect, an actress in a small way—and with one's self for sole audience this answers well enough.

"And now, my dear," said Mrs. Hunter, "tell me more of your own life. What can be as interesting as a life? It remains always, to some extent, unknown. Its residue of mystery is its charm. The novelists are the fools of their fancies. Tell me about yourself. Rational talk is quite impossible in these social camps we absurdly call 'watering-places.'"

"Just as if we were horses," said Miss Morrow.

"How witty!" exclaimed Mrs. Hunter. "How delightful! I must remember that. If ever you hear me use it, don't betray me."

"Oh, no!" said Miss Morrow, well pleased and serious.

"But I do want to hear all about you, and of that cousin of whom everyone speaks with admiration. I suspect Mr. Masters is a little afraid of her—and I do want to hear of your uncle, too. Mr. Wentworth describes him as a most interesting talker."

Kitty was too well trained to pour herself out, as yet, with entire frankness, but she soon allowed the shrewd woman at her side to understand that she felt herself the victim of an exacting old man, and that she was scarcely appreciated, as she thought she had a right to be, by this cousin, Miss Fairthorne. Mrs. Hunter's hand sought that of the girl, and for a moment expressed thus, and by silence, the sympathy she meant to offer.

"My friend," she said at last, "I, too, have the deeper experience of sorrow which no years can bury. If the thought and tenderness of an older woman can ever help and guide you, they are yours. It is not rare that a stranger should best understand a soul as peculiar as yours."

"Thank you," said Miss Kitty, feeling more intensely than ever how completely she had been underestimated at home. Here, at last, was one who comprehended her. She had been made to feel this before when she had met Mrs. Hunter at Newport. That lady had said to her:

"You should not permit yourself to be called Kitty, and I hope that you spell Katherine with a 'K.'"

Katherine was delighted.

"I shall always hate to hear you called Kitty. Katherine—Katherine with a K seems to suit you— to be really fitting."

Here again was insight truly remarkable. People do not very eagerly investigate the source of flattery, and even if Miss Kitty had known how easily Mrs. Hunter had gathered her material it is still likely that the willing receiver would have been more pleased than critically curious. Any one of the young women who were, for the time, of Miss Morrow's circle, could smilingly have given all the foreknowledge which Mrs. Hunter required, and now made use of so cleverly.

"*My* cousin Margaret," said Miss Morrow, "says

'people are so often injudiciously labelled.' How just you are, Mrs. Hunter.''

"Lucretia, dear," corrected the elder woman; "Lucretia, love."

Mrs. Hunter had come from Wiesbaden with the Wenhams, had made herself useful to an invalid daughter, and so agreeable to everybody that an invitation to spend a month with them at Newport had ended in its extension for another like term. Then her hosts went away to their city home and Mrs. Hunter felt that a promising campaign had ended without practical results. The Wenhams had parted with her civilly but without sign of deep regret, except in the case of their daughter, who, in her hysterical craving, foresaw the loss of demonstrative sympathy. Mrs. Hunter, considering in turn the sons, the father, and finally the mother, said to herself at last:

"I ought to have cultivated that doctor." She had enjoyed the game and now, regretting a partial defeat, was ready to play again.

After a while she began: "How one is tempted by a friendly heart and the silent confessional of night! If ever I tell my life story, dear, to you, it will be thus—alone, in the night, when you cannot see my face. You, also, I know have suffered. It is eloquently written on a too expressive brow; a tender riddle, my dear, which few know how to read."

If Kitty had been able to purr, it is probable that she would have vibrated with that instinctive signal of feline satisfaction. She was young, pretty, vain, greedy of all forms of homage. She had been, for her, unusually quiet. Now she spoke:

"How good you are, and you have, as Mr. Knellwood once said of my cousin Mary, 'that reserve of the high-minded which adds a mysterious interest to life.'"

Mrs. Hunter smiled anew under the partial mask of moonlight shadows.

"Fine, very fine; that—and, I hope, true!" she exclaimed. "But who is Mr. Knellwood?"

"My rector," replied Kitty; "my confessor," she added, under her breath.

Mrs. Hunter made mental note of it.

"Well, I shall soon be in your city; I shall hope to know him. I have a letter from my own dear old rector at Umstead. I had a Sunday-school class there. Ah, the quiet of that life of peace! Ah, the dear little old village! Well, well! Shall we walk, Katherine, or shall it be bed?"

Miss Kitty, yawning under her hand, thought the latter preferable. Mrs. Hunter had given her so much to think about.

When, in the early morning, Mrs. Hunter parted from Miss Morrow on the pier in New York, it was with a solemn promise not to fail to let Miss Katherine know when she, Mrs. Hunter, would have a chance to see her in her own city and home.

"You will be most welcome, most welcome! And be sure to write to me. I know how busy you are, but do find a little time for poor me."

It seemed that there was an article—Mrs. Hunter had not decided what title to give it—it was for the

"Atlantic" magazine. It would keep her occupied in New York for a while. At last they kissed and parted. Miss Kitty said amiable good-byes to a group of summer friends, men and women, and then turned to Mr. Masters, who was watching with interest Miss Kitty's performance. She was the only woman he had ever loved, whom he did not afterward regard with the kindliest of liking. He would gladly have avoided her on the steamer, but her people were old friends, and she herself was not easy to avoid.

He waited patiently and at last saw the young woman and her maid into their carriage. As he set foot on the step of his own cab he looked back at Mrs. Hunter, as she stood bargaining with a hackman.

"Well," said an elderly man, who was to share his carriage, and was already seated, "do you know that lady? What a figure! I noticed her on the boat. She walks well!"

"I cannot say I know her," said Mr. Masters. "I have talked to her pretty often. I rather think I ought to say she has talked to me."

"That is all we know of most people," said his friend; "get in, I want my breakfast."

As they drove up-town, he asked where Mrs. Hunter came from. Mr. Masters said, with a lift of his brow, that he had never asked her, but that someone had said she gave the impression of an actress of distinction who had retired from the stage. His companion, a shrewd old leader of the bar, returned:

"Actress? Yes—but retired? No! She is still in business."

Mr. Masters, summing up, remarked that she was handsome, had a neat figure, dressed well and not too much, as to all of which Mr. Masters was as good an authority as on pigeon-shooting or salmon-fishing.

II

IT was afternoon of a mild October day. The open windows of a large room on the second floor of a house on Fourth Street, near to Spruce, in the city of Penn, looked out on a broad garden, which extended about one hundred and fifty feet westward and was now carpeted with the fallen red and gold of a wide-spreading maple. Here and there were a few late roses, amid a more seasonable growth of asters, scarlet sage, and marigolds. The room was empty. A wood fire blazed on the hearth. Presently a large, yellow Angora cat leaped into the window from the roof of the veranda. The miniature tiger trod with care over the account books and inkstand of a well-ordered table. Lightly moving, the cat reached a cushioned easy-chair, and, coiling herself into a mound of dark orange-tinted fur, went peacefully to sleep, undisturbed by the entrance of a girl of some twenty-three years of age.

Miss Fairthorne looked about her with an air of relief, pleased to find a place where she could be alone. She gently lifted the cat and took her place near the window, in the sunshine of the fading day.

"If," she murmured—"if ever I have a home of my own I shall have a hermit-room on the roof."

Thus musing, she sat down, took a pen from the table, and, unlocking the clasp of a rather large diary, was soon busily engaged in the transfer of her thoughts to its pages.

A few minutes later her lips parted with a slight expression of annoyance. A much younger and very pretty girl announced her presence by a merry laugh as she stood in the doorway.

"Ah!" she cried, "I have been looking for you everywhere. You told me you had to talk to the cook." The tone was reproachful.

"It was true, Kitty; but, also, I have now and then to talk to myself, and really, dear, in this house, what with my uncle's wants and the endless procession of people who waste my time and their own, I find it hard to get leisure to read a page, or to think in peace."

"But," said the girl, with excess of emphasis, "my dear Mary, what is there to think about? I have so much to tell you. There was Long Branch, and then Newport—"

"But, Kitty, you really wrote a good deal, and I lay awake last night until one o'clock, while you sat on the bedside and told me no end of things about people in whom I have less interest than in Felisa, the cat."

"But I did not nearly finish," said Miss Morrow; "I met Mr. Masters on the boat."

"That must have been interesting—I should say, exciting. Well, go on, Kitty."

Miss Fairthorne gave up in despair and shut her diary with a sharp movement.

"I do not see, Mary, why you are so cross," said Kitty.

"Am I cross, dear?"

"Yes, you are; you shut up that tiresome diary the way Uncle John slams a door."

"I do not mean to be cross." As she spoke she rose, a strongly-built young woman, whose rather large features and unusual height would acquire new esthetic values as she came to middle age. She kissed her cousin and petted her with tender touches, saying pleasant things of her gown and her looks, knowing well her appetite for such food. The younger woman, satisfied with tributes to which she was well accustomed, regained her lost temper and began again to pour out her flood of quite harmless gossip.

As they stood, Mary Fairthorne looked down on the rosy, vivacious little cousin with now a kindly caressing touch, and now an uninterested but positive "Ah!" or "Really!" "Is that so, dear?" and the like.

This girl of twenty-three years was engaged in the construction of character out of strong but not very plastic material. The cousin known to her intimates as Kitty was as nearly an instinctive creature as evolutionary forces and educational training permit a young woman of her class to be. Life seemed as easy to her ready acceptances as it was difficult to the larger nature, which possessed far wider horizons both past and future. More womanly than her cousin Kitty, she was less obviously feminine, and was a person about whom people were apt to express decisive opinions of rather varied character. Her patience seemed to be near to its reward when Kitty said:

"Now I must go and see Margaret Swanwick."

She turned at the doorway:

"What were you writing in your diary?"

Miss Fairthorne smiled.

"Do you really want very much to know, Kitty?"

"Oh, yes, yes!"

"And you will never tell?"

"Never."

Mary opened her diary and read:

"Mahomet says, 'When one of you getteth angry, he must sit down, and if his anger still endure, let him lie down.'"

"I don't think," said Kitty, "that there was any need to promise secrecy if that's all."

She was as nearly without sense of humor as the slumbering Angora on the hearth-rug.

"Try it when Uncle John is at his worst," laughed Mary.

"But I never get angry without cause, and then, as Mr. Knellwood says, 'There is a righteous anger and an unrighteous anger.'"

This sort of vagueness, the quoting of other folk's wisdom and the lack of sense of the comic, were apt to exasperate the tall cousin. Now she merely said:

"Well, by-by, dear. Try Mahomet's receipt."

As she spoke she playfully pushed Kitty through the doorway. Then she stood for a moment, and reopened her diary.

"I forgot," said Kitty, turning back, "I forgot

to ask you to remind me to tell you about Mrs. Hunter.''

Mary Fairthorne sat down. She had stood Kitty's amiable and too merry volubility for a large part of the day and had given up to the girl more hours than she cared to waste. She was, to tell the truth, again on the verge of vexed and futile remonstrance when, instinctively obedient to Mahomet, she sat down.

As she dropped into the chair Kitty's rosy face grew serious—she had a faint gleam of enlightenment as she said:

''Are you resorting to Mahomet's remedy?''

Mary laughed.

''I? No!'' It was hardly true. ''What else is there, dear?''

''I forgot to tell you, you would like her. Oh, you will be sure to like her. Mr. Masters knows her; he says she has charm—''

''He says that about everything that wears a petticoat,'' said Mary, resolute to control any sign of impatience. ''But whom are you talking about, Kitty?''

''I told you, Mary—Mrs. Hunter. She is so gentle, so wise, so learned, and she carries her knowledge *so* lightly—'' Here Mary recognized a phrase which Mr. Knellwood had with justice applied to Margaret Swanwick.

''But I must go, and I know you are tired of me. I really had to tell you.''

''I tired of you, my dear Kit? You must not say such things—''

"But you are tired of me," repeated the girl, with dull persistency; "and yet, Mrs. Hunter is so like you—in some ways, I mean—that—"

"Then I shall surely hate her," exclaimed Mary, laughing.

"Oh, no! You must like her for my sake; and now, we will leave the rest until to-morrow. Don't look so resigned."

"My dear child," said Miss Fairthorne, "I have some right to be tired to-day, but I am not tired of you, only of these numberless people who interest you and do not in the least interest me."

"There is nothing human that should fail to interest us, Mary; we are all the children of one Father."

"*Vide* somebody," thought Mary. A touch of the comic always cured her mild attacks of impatience and the young cause was pretty sure, soon or late, to supply the remedy. She was a trifle disappointed that Kitty had not answered her crossly. It would have seemed to excuse her own brief failure of temper.

Kitty's weaknesses appealed to the stronger girl, who had an unusual charity for moral defects and who found in her cousin what everyone found—the attractiveness which childlike and too natural women possess. Despite nearness of years, Mary Fairthorne was more mother than cousin to this self-spoiled, unstable beauty, who was now pouting a little, and feeling, as she was apt to say, that she was not sufficiently considered. Turning again to go, she said:

2

"I suppose you very superior people think me foolish. Mrs. Hunter says I have an analytic mind."

"What!" exclaimed Mary Fairthorne; "you have many, many gifts, dear, but—"

"Oh, don't scold me!" cried Kitty. "I do not mind Margaret, but I do love you, and when you lecture me, I—I am getting to be too old to be lectured by the entire family. Kiss me, and don't scold." She was herself demonstrative in her affection, and was prone to take as evidence of want of it her cousin's disinclination to physical expressions of a very real attachment. It was real, but the nobler woman would have found it hard to explain why she liked this girl. Few of us can sufficiently analyze many of our attachments, perhaps because they are attachments, the offspring of habit, propinquity, and the claims which weakness makes on the higher nature.

Kitty had that surface amiability which is a little uncertain and very far from the self-sacrificing heroism of really good temper.

"You shall tell me all about Mrs. Hunter, dear, another time," said Mary; "it is I who was foolish." She did not say how or why. Rising, she kissed the girl tenderly.

"I think I hear Uncle John."

"Then I must run; I shall go down the back-stair. He has been at me all day—my first day at home—to arrange those new autographs, such stupid, tiresome trash."

"Run, dear," cried Mary, laughing, and, gathering her skirts, Kitty fled as ordered. This sort of mild vexation was a more frequent thing in her life than Mary Fairthorne liked. While outspoken anger was rare with her and like a storm in its physical and moral consequences, her daily encounters with two antagonistic and unsympathetic natures merely resulted in irritation and never disturbed her long. She looked up at the clock, closed and locked her diary, and sat down to resolute work on the task from which Kitty had fled.

The table at which she seated herself was of unusual size, and was nearly covered with portfolios, each carefully labelled and numbered. She laid aside one after another, lingering with interest over the labels and contents. At last she found the one she was looking for; on it lay a sheet of note-paper upon which was written, "Arrange chronologically, J. F." They were letters of Lord Byron, a dozen or more, some to women, an angry missive to Lord Carlisle, etc. As she ended her simple task, she said to herself:

"He needed a woman friend who was not in love with him. He must have been interesting. I should like to have known him. I suppose there never was a thoughtful woman who has read his letters who did not wish she had known him." As she closed the portfolio, and wrote under the label, "Arranged in order of years," she heard a step, and, rising, said:

"I hope you are feeling better, Uncle John."

"There is nothing the matter with me," he replied. "I hope you have been careful as to those dates."

"I have been so," she returned. "Is there anything else, sir?"

"Where is Kitty? I have had no account of her expenditures while she was away. She is very careless. Send her here."

"She has gone to Margaret Swanwick's."

"She ought to have been here; I told her to be here."

Mary made no reply, and he added:

"I am constantly neglected. I shall have to hire a secretary, and that with two idle girls in the house." Again receiving no answer from the tall girl, who stood beside his chair, he said:

"Why the devil don't you say something?"

"I should only have to repeat, sir, what I say every day."

He did not reply to this, but asked again to have Kitty sent to him, and again his niece said:

"She is out. I think I mentioned that she has gone to see Madge."

"I suppose," he replied, "that you think I am losing my memory."

"Hardly, uncle; it is altogether too good." It was for all causes of irritation, but for other matters it had become, of late, irregularly uncertain. He was a slowly failing old man.

"Well," he said, "that will do just now. See if this account be correct. Write to Mr. Pilgrim that I should like, at his leisure, to talk to him about the Kanawha coal lands. Ask when he will be in the city. I shall dine in my room, Mary. I am going to lie down now. As to Kitty— Oh, I forgot!

Damn everything! One ought to be shot at forty-
five—no, at fifty.'' And so concluding, he left her
to her toil over a complicated account. As he went
out, he turned.

"Who the deuce is this Mrs. Hunter Kitty is rav-
ing about? Hunter? Hunter? A good name in
Virginia and Rhode Island.'' The old man's memory for genealogical details was remarkable and at
times perilously competent.

"I do not know,'' returned Mary. "Kitty has
many sudden enthusiasms about people. They do
not last long.''

"You would be better for a few,'' he said sharply,
and so left her.

"Now I wonder if that be true,'' thought Mary
Fairthorne, as she turned to her task. "No, it is
not true. Kitty's accounts! He will never see
them, or I am much mistaken.'' After very carefully revising her arithmetical results, she wrote
"Correct'' on a slip of paper, and pinned it to the
account.

Next she took a fresh sheet, and began to write to
Mr. Pilgrim, but, perceiving that the paper bore her
own monogram, she tore it up, took a sheet from the
other table, and, after a few moments of reflection,
wrote to the rising engineer a very formal letter
with the signature, "John Fairthorne, per M. F.''

III

IN the year 1782 John Fairthorne, the youngest son of a small squire of County Essex, emigrated to Pennsylvania. The Fairthornes had lived and died among their turnips in tranquil decency, with no distinguishing excess of vices or virtues. They were small gentlefolk and contented, neither rising nor falling in the social scale. The younger sons were, by custom and of necessity, tumbled out of the home nest and disposed of in the army or navy or, more rarely, in business. Generally they did well, but no Fairthorne was ever spoken of as a man of distinction. The women had notable beauty, and the race was tall and sturdy.

John Fairthorne, the emigrant, was a serious youth, and pleased Mr. Penn, the proprietary, although he never gave up the Church of England. He had of Penn, for one hundred pounds, five thousand acres in and about the Welsh barony in Chester County, then by no means so important or valuable a possession as it looks to the modern view. Fairthorne soon sold his land, became a trader in furs, and by and by had coasters and trafficked with the other colonies. He became rich, and had sons and daughters. In their new environment, that happened to the Fairthornes which happened to many children of English race whose people had made no mark in the older land.

From the time John Fairthorne landed in Pennsylvania the Fairthornes became and remained people of signal importance. In every generation some one of them rose to distinctive place. They had a hand in every war and in time of peace won success at the bar or in the ventures of East Indian commerce. They were notably few in number, long livers, and well-built, handsome folk. Calmly assured of their own position, they were generally sensitive as to familiar approach, and had been, perhaps because of a certain gravity and good sense, fortunate in their marriages. In early colonial days they were of Penn's council. Later they became rebellious subjects of the crown; still later, stanch Federalists, and when the great Civil War broke out they were sturdy republicans. John and Mary were favored names among them, but no one of them was ever known as Jack or Molly.

John, the eldest of the few Fairthornes left in Pennsylvania—for they had scattered widely—was a man who had added largely to inherited wealth. This John married, when young, a wife who, dying, left him childless. As sometimes chances, one of the minor qualities of a strong breed rose in his case into disabling power, so that, as life went on, his dislike of democratic familiarities and close contacts with men gradually caused his withdrawal from all forms of public usefulness. He became a self-centered man, uselessly learned, and with a fondness for rare books and autographs. He had, too, in an extreme degree the liking for method which all his people possessed. By descent and training a very courteous and formal man to those he did not know well, he was too often otherwise in his own home. Nature, latent gout, and having outlived the time of balanced faculties made him irritable and exacting, even to those he loved the best, or, perhaps I should say liked the best. He had preferences, but lacked affections. He had been left the guardian of the persons and moderate estates of the orphan children of a brother and sister; Mary represented the finer qualities of his race and was a woman of wide intellectual and human sympathies, while her uncle's were languid or had dwindled, owing to the atrophy of disuse. Kitty, despite her lightness, was apparently the person he came most near to loving, but she had not her cousin's power to influence his decisions. He was now beginning to feel the dependency of breaking health and was bitterly resenting it. As to what else he was, or became, this story may show.

The house which Kitty entered to visit her cousins, the Swanwicks, was far away from that Fourth Street neighborhood, which fashion was slowly giving up to commerce and finance. It was not large, and was built in a way peculiar to the city, with back buildings which left room for side-light and some space for the garden area behind it.

Kitty, who knew well her cousin Margaret's dislike to being pursued up-stairs, sat down in the parlor and looked about her. The room was too severely furnished with inherited claw-toed tables and straight-backed chairs to suit Miss Morrow's views, and indeed an antique disregard for comfort was in every line of the inhospitable seats. A few important pieces of old Dresden and two portraits by Sully in his rather thin manner, were all that there was to relieve the hardness of the furnishings; and yet the room had an air of distinction, and there was no lack of taste in curtain, carpet, or wall-paper. Several miniatures stood on the mantel. Its cool, gray marble and the brass fender and firedogs, aglow with the light of a hickory-wood fire, gave to the room a look of being in habitual use. Kitty looked about her with critical comment, disliking the old-fashioned furniture.

But nothing pleased or displeased her very long. As she rose at the sound of coming steps, a slightly built, rather small woman appeared in the doorway. She wore a simple gray linen gown and carried a basket of keys.

"Oh, you dear thing," cried Kitty, kissing her again and again.

The older woman submitted to Kitty's caresses with faint internal protest, and then, holding her off, said:

"How pretty you are, dear. Oh, if I were a man I should—"

"Marry me?"

"I do not know about that," said Mrs. Swanwick: "certainly I should make love to you. What a fine gown!"

"I have come for a good long talk," said Kitty.

"I ran away when Uncle John came in, and I have so many things to tell you. Imagine it, he wanted to see my accounts."

"Is it so, dear?" said Margaret, as if it were a novelty. "But not to-day, dear; I cannot talk to you now. Harry has some men to dine, and I am busy." It was true, but, besides this, Margaret well knew that Kitty's desire to pour out her flow of disconnected social items would lessen after she had sufficiently repeated them to others. Margaret, who had an orderly and trained mind, hated few things so much as Kitty's mild flow of gossip.

"I think," she once said, "that I could stand it better if it were even a bit wicked; but Kitty is good because she is not bad." Margaret was herself valuably and variously sweet tempered. Seeing Kitty's look of disappointment, she said:

"Come up to the library and see Harry. If I let you go without seeing him I shall hear of it. How is Mary? I have not seen her for nearly a week."

Miss Kitty said that Mary was quite useless as sister or cousin; that between Uncle John and charities and this and that it was impossible to get her to listen to the most serious things.

"Such as— ?" asked Mrs. Swanwick, demurely.

"Oh, last night, about a question of dogma. Mr. Knellwood wrote to me—you see, I had asked him about it before I went away."

"Dogma!" said Mrs. Swanwick, vastly amused. Miss Kitty assumed an air of gravity and related at length that the question of dogma concerned the

proper material for candles to be used on the altar.
Mrs. Swanwick was not rash enough to inquire if
she had put the question to her rector in this shape;
she imagined her sister Mary's amusement, and since
she was wise enough to know her cousin for one of
the many daughters of Sir Forcible Feeble, she
wasted no mental ammunition in intellectual con-
tests with Kitty. Not listening to Kitty, who followed her, she went along the hall thinking of what
the girl would be at forty and only recovered consciousness of what Kitty was saying when she asked
about the children. She had toys for them, and
might she not return to dine? Margaret said no,
that it was a man's dinner, a lot of old army com-
rades; nothing but war talk; she herself would be
the only woman, and her table was full. Kitty,
laughing, declared that she would come and sit at a
side table, and who could she have with her? Then,
feeling that she had been very witty, she asked if
Margaret had any errands down-town. As she lingered on the stair, a masculine voice called out, as
its owner descended:

"Halloa! Kitty Sunshine! Why did n't you call
me, Margaret?" His wife made no reply. "Come
up-stairs," he said.

They went up to the second story of the back
building.

"I like this better," said Miss Morrow. "I hate
your parlor."

The room was full of books; on one wall were law
reports and treatises, on the other all manner of
books. A half dozen good prints filled the vacant

spaces on the walls; a single small spring landscape by Inness hung over the mantel, and beneath it a cavalry saber. Below the windows were two very business-like tables.

Harry Swanwick picked up his still lighted pipe from the pile of leather-clad law-books.

"Well, Kitty, what is the news? Tom Masters told me you had returned. He says you have a new idol. I thought he was himself pretty well captured."

"Oh, that is an old affair," said Miss Kitty.

"Bother! I don't mean you. Tom is a lot too good for you, or any woman except one who is unattainable. Tom was radiating praise, the material for which he seemed to have absorbed at Newport."

"She is certainly worthy of it," said Miss Morrow, with emphasis of the nodded head; "a most remarkable woman, Harry; really, a woman with that rare quality of charm it is so impossible to define." Margaret cast a look of quickly controlled mirth at her husband, who knew better than to betray his own sense of amusement.

"Who the deuce is your charmer, Kit?"

"Mrs. Hunter," said Kitty. "Lucretia Hunter."

"Did she ask you to call her Lucretia?" said Margaret, with one of those too efficient glimpses of insight which, except for her husband, she rarely put in words, but with which she sometimes surprised people.

"How did you know that?" said Kitty, a trifle sharply.

"I did not know, I guessed," laughed her cousin.

"Who is she?" asked Harry.

"Now that is just the kind of thing," said Kitty, with severity, "which makes people in New York say we are provincial."

"Well, Kit," he returned, "we still have quality and distinctiveness, a civic soul, if that is to be provincial."

"I do not think I understand you, Harry. Mary and you are so vague sometimes."

"Mary vague!" cried Mr. Swanwick. "Good heavens! But really, my dear Kit, what with you and Tom I am becoming curious. Is she handsome?"

"Ye-es," said Kitty.

"The witness seems in doubt," said Margaret.

"Oh, but she is," cried Kitty; "and so intellectual—"

"A widow?" asked Swanwick.

"Yes, I believe so, and she has had so much sorrow in her life."

"Did you see her often?" asked Margaret.

"Often? Yes, ever so often—at Newport. She was staying with the Wenhams. They met her in Europe—and then she was on the boat with us. They adore her. You will see her. She is coming here soon. Bless me, what time is it? I forgot to wind my watch. Not after five! Really! I must go."

IV

HEN husband and wife were left alone together in the library they gladly shared in common, Margaret took up a freshly arrived number of Dickens's last book and, seated beside the smoldering wood fire, continued to talk as she cut the leaves with careful respect for neatness. Presently she said to her husband, who was at his own table:

"Are you busy, Harry?"

"I—not if you want anything, Madge."

"Do you know what day it is?"

"Do I, indeed? Do you, Madge?"

"Yes. It reminds me of how young and foolish I was."

"And me of how clever I was to get my head in the way of a saber, in order to decide what answer I should get to a letter. It was rash, but it won the trick."

As he turned from his table she smiled, and met his seeking blue eyes with a look which somehow made a smile interpret love, respect, and thankfulness.

In 1862, at the close of a short leave, Captain Swanwick had returned to the Sixth Pennsylvania

Cavalry just in time to stop a revolver bullet and to receive a saber cut from a South Carolina gentleman in the gallant mellay known as the fight at Brandy Station. Two days later, a young girl in Philadelphia, anxiously reading the list of killed, wounded, and missing, looked up and said faintly:

"Mother! Harry Swanwick is wounded—mortally. I must go to him at once—at once."

Mrs. Fairthorne, who was one of the Maryland Grays, and as brave as the rest of them, said:

"You were in doubt, dear, yesterday."

"I was—now I am not."

Then the mother, being wise enough never to believe a newspaper until it had said the same thing for three days, said: "You must stay at home. We do not do that kind of thing. I will go. If he is to die I will wire you to come."

The young woman, who was very white and longing to scream with the pain of it, said quietly:

"Yes, but go soon—at once! I will write a letter for him if he be able to read it."

Captain Swanwick was very ill when Mrs. Fairthorne came down to the hospital camp at Flourtown, and, acting on the advice of the young surgeon, Sydney Archer, ventured to carry North a man in deadly peril. He was put in the officers' hospital in Camac's woods, and, slowly mending, found that for him active service was over.

The day he read Miss Margaret Fairthorne's letter had been ever since kept by them as an anniversary of which they spoke to no one. Now he said:

"It was ten minutes to nine when I read it. If

you can't wait, Madge, even that long, go down to the parlor, and under the big Dresden bowl—''

Before he could finish she was out of the room and on the stair. Moods of childlike joy and gaiety were a part of the pleasantness of this woman, who had also the grave good sense of the Fairthornes, with more sentiment, wit, intellect, and definiteness of mind than ever a one of the breed since John, the first, sat in the house cave he had dug on the banks of the Delaware. Unlike the rest of her race, she was slight and small.

Mr. Swanwick was invalided, unfit for war and, after declining a brevet as he had before refused promotion, he married this Margaret Fairthorne, the much elder sister of Mary. She nursed him into sound health, and in the two years it required, as he meant to go to the bar, she began to read law-books to him. She soon found satisfaction in the lofty reason and equity on which the great structure has risen. She enjoyed the accuracy of it, of what she startled Harry one day by calling the mathematics of right and wrong. When, at last, he could use his eyes and task his head, she quietly let the study drop, and for wise reasons of her own made believe to have quite forgotten Kent and Blackstone. It was a sacrifice firmly made. She had readily assimilated the law, and surprised herself by the ability with which she anticipated the judgments and decisions of great jurists, as she and her husband read and talked. About the time that she began to suspect she possessed a better legal mind than Harry Swanwick he had regained his usual vigorous health.

He was straightforward, upright, industrious, and of good sense and fair intelligence. The wife was of ampler mind. A great affection united them. At times he had had, ever since his wound, severe headaches, when he was apt to be irritable and hasty. As years went on his and her connections and the deaths of middle-aged seniors at the bar, pushed him forward. Men liked this courteous gentleman, and they prospered. How much the woman was or stood for in the partnership she hid even from him, magnanimous as only love can be. Perhaps he knew, better than she thought, the largeness of the mental and moral capital thus lovingly invested. Only a masculine mind so great as not to have needed her help could have fully seen and thanked it, and yet— he listened.

She came back, swift and graceful, holding up the hand on which a ruby shone, and crying:

"Oh, thank you, Harry! What an extravagance!" and, leaning over as he sat, she kissed the red scar which crossed cheek and temple. There was some pretty, tender talk, which I shall not report, and at last she said:

"Did you ask Dr. Archer to come in and see my Jack?"

"Yes, he dines here. I asked him to replace Weston, but he will come in before dinner. I had a little talk with him about your Uncle John."

"Well, Harry?"

"He thinks that he is breaking up, not here or there, in any one organ, but a general—well, what he described as a slackening of all the complicated

3

gearing of mind and body; perhaps, too, a weak heart.''

"How like him, Harry. How fond he is of illustration! I wish he cared for Mary rather than for Kitty. But ten men—oh, of the best of you!—would ask for Kitty, where one would ask for Mary."

"I am glad," he said, laughing, "that I am not of the best."

"Foolish fellow! Come and see the children—and, oh! You were interrupted last night—what did you conclude as to the Stoneville railroad? Shall you ask to have a receiver appointed?"

"We have not decided. The Republic Trust Company—I mean its officers—are in doubt. They hold largely for themselves and others of its securities—bonds, of course."

"Was it you, Harry, who thought it might be best to wait until the eastward movement of grain, and see if the bonds would be lifted in value?"

"And then get rid of them, Madge. Receiverships are disastrous. I did not say that, or did I? I will think it over—"

"Isn't that trust company paying unusual dividends?"

"Yes, dear; too large, I think. I sold all our stock when we bought our house. Mr. Fairthorne must be a heavy owner of its stock; but, really, I know little of their condition; I am only their counsel, and not always consulted—as I should be."

"Indeed!" she said, and went with him up-stairs

to the nursery, thoughtful.   Jack was riding to battle on a chair, and Retta, which was short for Margaret, was, from the dignity of four-year-old maternity, entreating Jack not to wake the baby—a large
rag-doll, preferred before a family of dolls lovely
and accomplished.

V

HE October days went by, and the leaves, drifting down, marked like the sands in an hour-glass the failing hours of autumn. Kitty, who professed to feel, and perhaps did feel, the gentle sadness of the fall, kept up a voluminous correspondence with Mrs. Hunter. She was fond of letter-writing, and wrote in brief childlike sentences, which, however, gave her new friend, by degrees, and in answer to her guarded questions, all that she desired to learn of Kitty's relatives and their surroundings.

Mrs. Hunter had found a room at the top of an unfashionable hotel in New York, and now, as she stood with a letter of Kitty's in her hand, she looked at the soiled carpet, the not over-clean furniture, and the whitewashed wall, dotted with red splotches where uneasy lodgers in the past had revenged themselves on the gorged mosquito. Mrs. Hunter was a lover of luxury, and herself neat by nature. The room smelled musty. She lifted a sash and let in the cool evening air.

Thinking to find from Kitty's letter what day it was, she turned to the first page. Kitty had forgotten to date it, a not rare omission on her part. She wrote "private" at the top of all of her letters, even the most trivial notes, and sacredly guarded them by a fold of white paper from inquisitive eyes. She wrote:

"DEAR LUCRETIA: I have just been arranging, for my uncle, some letters of my great-grandfather."

"Ah!" exclaimed Mrs. Hunter, and stopped to make a memorandum in a note-book, "Mem. Jn. F., member Constitutional Convention of 1787—to read of him—mem. autographs?" Then she returned to the letter:

"Mary does not approve of my writing to you. I do not know why. I am the best judge. I have bought the sweetest little ring for you. I know Mary would not like this, but it is because she does not know you. When she does, I shall be jealous. I hope you will never speak of the ring. My uncle insists on seeing my accounts every month. I do not believe he goes over them. This time I could not find them. I suppose when I go to confession I must tell. That is another thing about which Mary and I differ. I go to St. Agnes's and she likes that stuffy old Christ Church. The seats are very uncomfortable. How can anyone attend to her soul if the pews are uncomfortable?"

"How, indeed?" thought Mrs. Hunter.

"What you say about self-discipline is so true. I asked Uncle John about the book you spoke of—I mean 'Feuchtersleben's Psychology of the Soul' (I don't believe I spell it right). He has read everything. He said it was pretentious and commonplace. That seems strange! Mr. Knellwood said he had read it, but that he could not as a churchman recommend it."

"I shall be on thin ice," murmured Mrs. Hunter, who had once read a review of the book.

"I hope you will soon come. When I told Uncle John that you were interested in autographs, he said I must get him to show you his collection. It is very large."

Mrs. Hunter smiled as she sat in her small room at the top of the dingy hotel, and slowly refolded Kitty's letter.

She said to herself: "I do not yet get at the love affairs of this tall Mary Fairthorne." As to these Miss Morrow was decently reticent, and would not, as yet, have easily betrayed any knowledge she might have possessed. She had her suspicions, but when once she had flippantly intruded on this ground she had been warned off as a trespasser in a manner which left an impression as permanent as it was possible to make on a nature so briefly sensitive.

Mrs. Hunter wrote in reply:

" DEAREST KATHERINE : It is years since I read Feuchtersle-ben, but I know it well. It was in a day of sorrow. Whether as a whole I should like it now, I do not know; but I feel, and shall always feel, that I can trust your judgment to assimilate what is best. Perhaps I might even more readily accept, as a good churchwoman, Mr. Knellwood's opinion, and may some-time be able to discuss it with him.

" In regard to confession—of which you speak so often with the innocent sweetness of a pure soul—I have always had but one opinion. To you, were it kind to burden you, I could easily confess the griefs of a life which has been a long and sorrowful struggle against a nature too readily given to trusting others. Since I have known you life has seemed a brighter thing and I am trying to forget the past and to look forward with re-newed hope.

"Remember, dear, that, while to you I write from an open heart, these intimate revelations are for you and you only. I hope to be with you, and able to see you often, in a week or two. As my means are limited, I have to be careful. No, I cannot let you help me, as you say you would wish to do. God bless you!   Yours ever and always,
                              "LUCRETIA."

"My article is nearly done. These editors are so impatient."

(A statement which would probably have amused the gentlemen in question.)

Mrs. Hunter read this letter with care, and at last inclosed and directed it.

"And now," she said, "if Lionel does not make any new claims I shall be able to live for three months. 'After that the deluge,' but even then one can go a-fishing." She felt a little weary, but smiled at her jest. As she moved to the open window and looked over the great city to where on the East River the lights were beginning to appear on tug or steamer, a hawk hovered high above her, set dark against the violet glow of the eastward sky. She wondered how and where he fed himself? Then she turned to a long cheval-glass, which, because of a crack, had been transferred to this upper story.

What she saw reassured her. She had the art of dress, was skilful in its arrangement, apt with her fingers. She could meet that difficulty; for the rest —she saw a tall woman of fine figure, still handsome, with something Oriental in the ivory-like tint of skin, the red, thin lips, the somewhat too black and distinct eyebrows over very dark eyes, deep-set and large.

The twilight darkening, she turned away, went to her trunk, and came back with two half candles, which she set in the tilted, battered candlesticks on each side of the glass. Next, she lighted the single gas-jet, and, returning, again faced the mirror. Something in the situation called upon her imagination and it became fertile. She tilted the long mirror and stood still, wondering how many girls, brides, the newly married, the old, the wretched, had confessed themselves with joy, wonder, fear, despair, to this long-abandoned confidant. Then she started back with a cry. Something behind her in the dimly lighted room took the shape of a gaunt face, seen over her shoulder in the glass. It was a cap, hung on a nail. She said: "Pshaw!" but took it down, and again looked into the mirror. Some one of her imaginings became a memory, and suddenly she dropped on the floor, her face in her hands, her dark hair tumbled about her.

"What a fool I was!" The candles, set awry, dripped. The gas-jet flared sideways in the sea wind, and still she sat, the hostess of more thoughts than she cared to entertain. A knock startled her. She went to the door. It was the laundress with her linen. Having paid and dismissed her, she went back to the mirror.

"It will do," she said, and, gathering her dress, curtsied with admirable grace, saying in a low, clear voice, in which there was at times a hardly perceptible foreign accent:

"Mr. Fairthorne, I am sure; only a Fairthorne could bow like that. One must have had traditions,

ancestors—'' She laughed. "We must be alone
for that. It is pretty strong. How shall I manage
it? Or else—or else, if that sugary little bon-bon
is with me—'I have looked forward, sir, to this so
long.' I must be mildly fluttered, afraid, and—a
little flattery in rising doses. The old bear it well.
As time ceases to flatter they like it from anyone.
And how for a moment to make a man forget his
years? There are ways—ways; yes, for men, but
not for women. Ah! Madame Lucretia, best to trust
to the inspiration of opportunity. Yes," she cried,
"I am more than handsome; I have power, attraction—what that commonplace man called 'charm.'
He might prove manageable. I wonder if he is
caught in the sugar-plum's net? Well, some day
she will tell me.''

VI

N the afternoon in which Mrs. Hunter had taken account of her munitions of war, Sydney Archer rang the door-bell of John Fairthorne's home. As he waited, Mrs. Harry Swanwick came up the steps.

"I hope Uncle John is not ill," she said. "I have been away for two days."

"No," he replied. "Mr. Fairthorne likes now to see me daily; but, as a rule, we talk autographs or the last book. You know how interesting he can be when he is interested. He loses me a good deal of time."

"I suppose that can't be helped."

"Oh, no! If one could go from bed to bed, and simply be the technical engineer of human machines, it would be easy; but these machines have mothers, and wives, and notions. One has to listen and prescribe for anxieties, and splint broken hopes."

"The servants must be deaf or asleep," she said, as she rang again; "they are as uncertain as"—she laughed—"well, as the art of medicine."

"I admit the uncertainty," he returned pleasantly; "that is part of its interest."

"Oh, it is bad enough," she said, "to be the wisely

ignorant patient, but I should hate to follow so illogical a profession.''

"It is not that, but—shall I ring again?"

"Please." He pulled the bell as only a doctor can.

"They are usually prompt," he said.

"It is really too bad. Doesn't Uncle John's autograph mania bore you?"

"Only when I am busy, and have to let him talk. It is a privilege of age to bore people."

The door was thrown open in competitive haste by the old black butler and a maid, who muttered profuse apologies. As they turned to enter the house a man passed on the far side of the street. The doctor returned his salutation.

"Who is that?" asked Mrs. Swanwick.

"Mr. Grace."

"Ah! Roger Grace, the banker! Now, that is a man I am quite curious about. He has taken a very useful fancy to Harry. Do you know him?"

"Yes. What I have seen of him I like. He is a son of the soil—what people call a 'self-made man.' "

She laughed.

"The soil must have been rich." They were now in the wide hall at the foot of the stairs.

"Yes, Mrs. Swanwick, I suppose that man makes more in a year than I shall save in a lifetime. He deserves it, too. Money never fell into kinder hands, as I once had reason to know."

Meanwhile the two old blacks were blaming one another, and explaining volubly that Miss Kitty had sent the other servant on an errand.

"That will do, Peter," said Mrs. Swanwick. "I have heard all this before. Come into the parlor, Dr. Archer. And would you change lives with Mr. Grace?"

"I! No, indeed," he laughed, "not I!"

"Tell my uncle that Dr. Archer is here, Peter. Harry speaks of Mr. Grace as very generous, and says he is taken of late with social ambitions. That does seem to me a belated fancy for a man of forty, who has had a mere business life—"

"There is more in that man than business talent. If you knew him even as slightly as I do you would not think his ambition unreasonable. You and I, who are born to it, having it without effort, may undervalue it."

"You may be right." As she spoke, Miss Fairthorne came into the room.

"Good morning, Dr. Archer; my uncle will see you. When he lets you go, I should like to see you a moment. My uncle is at times very hard to keep to your orders. You doctors ought to supply moral remedies."

"Well, there are love philters," said Madge.

"Oh, I want temper philters. Please not to keep him waiting. My cousin Katherine is with him; please to tell her Mrs. Swanwick is here."

Archer went up-stairs, thinking pleasantly of Kitty. Mary Fairthorne looked after him a moment, and then followed her sister into the back parlor, which, to the westward, overlooked the garden.

The rooms had been furnished when changing

taste had sent the fine old colonial furniture to the attic, and put in its place hideously scrolled chairs and tables of mahogany, ottomans of chenille work, and black hair-cloth sofa and chair covers. The fireplace was closed by a white marble slab, through which opened what we absurdly call the register of the hot-air furnace. A wall-paper of Chinese landscapes decorated pictureless walls, and on the mantel were a clock and candelabra in the worst taste of the era of the Directory.

"I shudder, Mary, whenever I enter these rooms," said Mrs. Swanwick; "but I am glad grandfather Fairthorne made them hideous, otherwise I should not have captured all that beautiful Sheraton suite. Let us go to your room."

"No, dear; I must wait here to see Dr. Archer. I once spoke of this furniture to uncle; but he hates change, and as we give neither balls nor dinners it does not matter. We are very well here. Kitty will not come down; after Uncle John is through with Dr. Archer, Kitty will take him into my little sitting-room to ask about my uncle's health, etc.. This will last twenty minutes or more. After that, Dr. Archer will give me my five minutes, while you call on Uncle John."

"Does this happen daily?"

"Yes, if you mean the consultation with Kitty," said Mary, glancing at her sister.

"Is not this anxiety about her dear uncle of rather recent growth?"

"How can you ask, Madge? You know Kitty." She spoke with a note of impatience in her voice,

which none who did not know her well would have
observed. She was always a little on her guard
when with Margaret. The sisters were aware of
their power to see into each other, and were at times
uneasily conscious of the fact. This gift of insight
arose from no self-interpretative resemblance, since
they were as unlike in mind as in body. When Mary
replied, Madge said:

"Well, I hope it is not one of Kit's comedies. I
should not like to see Sydney Archer served as Tom
Masters has been. If it be a real thing—oh, I should
hate it! Harry and I would have to make believe a
good deal."

"It is not a real thing, Madge."

"It may be too good an imitation, Mary. I suppose Nemesis will overtake Kitty some of these
days."

"Poor little Kitty! Nemesis seems large for
her."

"Poor Kit! You are wasting your charity. Poor
little Kitten, if you like. She has neither sense nor
compassion. Life for her, my dear sister, is a toy
to play with. It has troubled Harry and me. The
wisest of men could not influence or educate Kitty;
she is a grown-up child. I am longing to say a word
of warning—"

"To Kitty? You would repent it."

"No—to Archer," said Madge.

"What man was ever stopped in a love affair by
reason? And yet—"

"Could a woman be, Mary? Could you?"

"What a question! Yes; but I predict that

Kitty's wiles will not wear well. He must, soon or late, find her out. The man's character is too wholesome to be long satisfied by a woman like Kitty. Why I love her I do not know. Even her sugar of amiability is only outside like that of a pill. To think of such an ending for a man like him does seem sad. But I am sure that it will not be.''

"I hope you may prove to be right," said her sister; "and of course no one can be of any use. He will find our light-headed Kitty a costly toy, and only a toy. But why does she capture people? Why do you love her, and Uncle John? If he loves any one, it is Kit. Frankly, I do not love her.''

"It is as hard to explain likes as dislikes, Madge; and, after all, although I think I love Kitty, I am not sure that I like her.''

"What a droll distinction! That sounds more like Luke Pilgrim than like you.''

"What does Harry say?'' asked Mary.

"He laughs and says nothing, except that advice lent unasked loses both self and friend. Of course, dear, Harry is worried. You know what Archer was to us when Harry was wounded, and what he has been ever since.''

"Oh, yes, I know. Sometimes I want to give Kit a good shaking. She has more power to make me angry than ten Uncle Johns. Whenever you touch Kitty she gets small.''

"What do you mean?''

"Well, she shrinks like some insect, or those queer sea things.''

"I see what you mean, but for me she begins

small and ends small, and Archer is really a large personality.''

''I think he so impresses most people. When Mr. Pilgrim said he had an 'open-air mind' I thought it well said.''

''Open-air mind! I hate his roundabout English, Mary; but when you folks of poetic temperament and Emersonian expressions vow that you understand one another, what can a poor outsider say? In my poor way, I should call Sydney Archer a high-minded gentleman who has too much intellect for the professional uncertainties of medicine.''

''He would not agree with you,'' said Mary, smiling.

''No. He is piously devoted to one mistress, and also to Kitty.''

''Well, *che sarà sarà*,'' said Mary.

''Not if I can help it,'' thought Mrs. Swanwick. ''I want to see him about Jack, and I have but ten minutes. Could you not disturb that tête-à-tête with Kitty?''

''No,'' said Mary, ''not I.'' She was vexed to feel that she was flushing slightly. ''No, you do not live with our dear Kitty; go and do your own errand, Madge; I shall not help you, my dear.''

''Well, I must go myself, I suppose. If I say, 'Pretty Kitty,' she will come like a cat. If you flatter Kit she will do what you want. Try it.''

''Not I.''

''Why not? I say to Jack, 'Here, take this dose, and you shall have this nice bon-bon.' I give Kitty the bon-bon first, and the dose afterward. It does not answer always. I am just a little fearful that this Mrs. Hunter may have won Kitty's heart by my own base means; but why any woman as clever as she must be thinks it worth while to cultivate our empty-headed Kit, I do not see.''

''Nor I. They write like two lovers.''

''Indeed!''

''Yes, and twice Kitty, with an air of mysterious importance, has mentioned letters to Mr. Knellwood which Mrs. Hunter asked her to forward. Why the woman cannot write direct to a man so well known I cannot see.''

''Because, dear,'' said Madge, ''you are direct; and as to Kitty—Mrs. Hunter won't last. If you would flatter Kitty you would have an easier time.''

Mary Fairthorne, smiling, shook her head.

''I do not know. When I try it I feel as if I were fibbing, and I am, too, in a way.''

''I think,'' said Madge, ''I shall ask Dr. Soper to attend you for hypertrophied conscience; or perhaps,'' she added, with meek malice, ''you may prefer Dr. Archer. Here he comes; I am saved my perilous errand.''

''He is not my M.D.,'' laughed Mary.

''How is uncle to-day?'' asked Madge, as the doctor, hearing their voices, entered the somber drawing-room. Archer laughed as at some humorous recollection:

''He has three new symptoms and four new autographs. One is a letter of William Harvey, the discoverer of the circulation. I am sure it is a forgery, but I did not say so.''

4

Mary looked up.

"That was wise and well. It would only annoy him."

"Yes," he said; "one must praise whatever he has or acquires. Then he will do what I want, Miss Mary, and I do assure you he has good need to obey me."

"And this man does not see through Kitty!" thought Mary.

Mrs. Swanwick cast an amused glance at her sister, who seemed unready to reargue the point of conscience. Dr. Archer continued:

"I used to fight some of his queer theories as to education, religion, or morals. Now I listen and act as chorus. It is sad to stand by and watch the crumbling of a strong intellect; but he is still very interesting—very."

"You will come to see him every day, please," said Mrs. Swanwick; "Jack is better. There is no need to call to-day."

"Thank you," he returned. "What a pleasant dinner that was!"

"Yes," she said; "I liked the war talk and that story Mr. Masters told of Harry. I had never heard it. I must tell it to you, Mary."

"I saw how it pleased you," returned Archer, "and so did Tom Masters." Archer had a vast admiration for Margaret Swanwick's combination of strength, tact, and goodness, and he was one of the men who profess to believe that women make the best friends.

"Good-bye," he said. As he spoke, tall, fair, blue-eyed, he looked down on his friend's graceful slightness, and then at the nobly modeled girl, whose too cold hand awakened his professional instincts, and made him consider her with brief attention. He concluded, as he drove away, that this uneasy household was enough to account for her look of care. Or was it care? With characteristic self-study, he began to ask himself why Miss Kitty was so attractive. It was fast becoming a serious question, and somehow went and came in his mind with the contrasted thought of this other woman, Mary Fairthorne, whom he called "friend"; her unstirred serenity—people spoke of her as "cold"—her calm endurance; and then again he saw the rosebud Kitty, with her pretty ways, her vivacity, and—here his thought was checked by something reminiscent. He had listened with a sense of shock when Tom Masters, long before, had said:

"Yes, Sydney, Miss Morrow is as agreeable as a woman can be who has no conception of the value of repose of mind or body. Perhaps she is just a trifle common." Then he had added: "But I should not have said that." And yet, later, Masters had proved an easy victim. Archer had made no reply, but the criticism stuck in his head like a memorial bur. He had, of late, in Mr. Fairthorne's interest, been obliged to see Miss Fairthorne often, for Miss Kitty generally avoided duties which exacted length of service, and made up for this neglect by a certain affectation of interest which she contributed as her share of the business of caring for a querulous invalid.

After one of his talks with Kitty, Archer could never remember what she had said, but a talk with Mary left a strong and valid impression of a thoughtful and imaginative mind. Once her uncle had said to him that Mary Fairthorne would be an old maid, that she was cold by nature, and that if men did sometimes fancy themselves in love with a statue, the statue was not very apt to contribute opportunity. Archer had disliked the comment—he did not know why. He was dimly aware that Miss Fairthorne cut short the necessary interviews which Kitty, for herself, managed to lengthen; and yet he felt that his friendliness of relation with the elder girl increased as time went on, while with Kitty he was conscious of an attraction which he did not incline to analyze, and when with or away from Mary Fairthorne he was aware of an attraction which he found it less hard to explain. Her calm reserve was like a challenge. Men, in general, dislike to think that there is any woman who cannot be captured. This is the fragmentary survival of an animal instinct. If love could begin both in heart and head, Sydney Archer was in double danger.

He was driven to his out-clinic, and gave himself head and heart to a business which requires ideal patience, perfect sweetness of character, and sympathetic insight. He was far from thought of the girl who stood at the window, unable to escape from importunate reflections as to the man who had just left her. She was deeply troubled. The modest reserve of a self-contained nature recoiled from self-confession.

Her days, since at eighteen she had begun to live, an orphan, with her uncle and cousin, had not been happy. Now she was resolutely taking stock of her life. Yes, she had friends—women, two or three. Her uncle, who could be royal company, was often, for a week at a time, increasingly capable of wearing out the sweetest temper. And now she was even wrathfully becoming aware that she was too constantly thinking of one man. Her peril lay in his character, and the completeness with which it satisfied her ideals and tempted her imagination.

Archer was a South Carolinian whose mother had come to the North to educate her children. When the war broke out he had just finished his medical studies. He elected to stand by his country, to the rage of all whom he loved best. For four years he served as a surgeon, and then, having made many friends, settled in the Northern city. He had had a hard struggle to keep himself afloat and to help brothers and sisters left ruined by the war. It had been difficult, but useful. Perhaps in his early life his sense of his own mental powers had made him a little too positive, even a trifle vain. All that had gone, or was going. He was of those who prosper morally in the sunshine of success. He, too, was imaginative, fond of music, and ready with brush or pencil. If any one now knew of his skill, it was when he lectured and the ready hand on the blackboard made clear to the eye what he was eagerly striving to teach.

This habitual giving of the tithes of life to the ward and the clinic, so common that we forget how large is the gift, made it natural and easy for Mary Fairthorne to use his contact with the poor as a channel for her generous use of a moderate income. It had brought them more together, and in the paucity of human intercourse to which her reserved nature inclined her, the constant, every-day company of a man as genial as Archer had full chance to affect a woman generously capable of appreciation.

He was a man of quick sympathies, nor is it true that to be effective these require the schooling of personal sorrow. He had known only one deep grief, when he had decided to stand by his country and saw his mother leave him to go south, refusing his parting kiss. But that was far in the past. Certainly he had the gift of understanding the nervously disordered and the mother anguished beside the cot of her child.

The woman he had left rebelled in all her nature at these too intrusive thoughts of a man who was nominally but a friend. At last, hearing her uncle's bell, she went up-stairs.

When Mary entered, Kitty was seated on the arm of his chair. She held one of his hands in her lap, and with the other was gently playing with his hair, which he wore in thick gray curls above the strongly marked features of his race. It was one of his good days, or Kitty would have been otherwise occupied. He had the fondness of some very old men for agreeable women and was at times well pleased when Kitty was, as now, in one of her caressing moods. As he turned at the sound of Mary's step, Kitty kissed him and a letter fell from her lap on to the floor unnoticed.

"Are you going out this afternoon, Mary?" he said.

"Yes," she replied; "I ride at four. What can I do for you?"

"Stop at the library and ask them to send me Hakewill's 'Apologia.' I want to show Archer a passage about bleeding in the reign of Elizabeth. You might walk there before you ride." As usual, Mary had her hands over-full.

"Very well, sir; but, Kitty, could n't you go?"

"I have an engagement, and letters I really must write."

"I will get you the book," said Mary.

"Talking of letters, Mary, Katherine"—he never called her Kitty—"has had a very interesting letter from Mrs. Hunter. She must be a remarkable woman. She has asked to have my views on a passage in Catullus. I shall write to her, and, by the way, get down the three editions and put them on the table. Katherine could not find them. I have always said you ought to have learned Latin. It will be a pleasure to talk to a woman who reads Catullus. I should like to have his autograph. I should like, by the way, to know what is the oldest autograph extant."

Kitty was outside of this kind of talk. Mary's imagination began to wander in the past.

"Perhaps," she said, "the scrawled name of some Roman soldier upon the walls of the temples on the Nile."

"Oh, no! The Assyrian tablets would be older." They went on talking. Kitty, a little bored, declared that she must go, and remembering that she wanted a novel, said she would order the book her

uncle had asked for as soon as she had written her
letters. Mary thanked her. Sad to say, when Kitty
reached the library she had forgotten all about the
title, except that it was somebody's "Apology."
This resulted in Barclay's "Apology" being sent,
of which Mary Fairthorne heard next day to her cost.

After a pleasant talk with her uncle, such as was
becoming rare of late, Mary left Catullus on his
table, and as she reminded him that it was time for
his afternoon nap, saw on the floor the letter Kitty
had let fall. She picked it up and seeing that it
was addressed to her cousin took it to Kitty's room
and said as she entered:

"Here is a letter you dropped."

Kitty flushed, and said quickly:

"Did you read it?"

"I? My dear Kitty, I do not read other people's
letters."

"But it was open. I am sure you read it."

"I did not, and never, never again"—and she
laid a strong hand on the little woman's shoulder
as she sat—"never do you dare to say such a thing
to me! I neither lie nor read letters not meant
for me."

"I—I—did n't mean that," said Kitty, who had
been well scared, and began to cry.

"Well, never, never **try** me in this way again,"
and, despite Kitty's sobs, she went out, tall, stately,
angry with her cousin, and beginning to be vexed
with her own want of self-command.

Kitty rose, shut the door, rubbed her plump shoulder, for the grip had been strong, and cast an eye

over the letter. She knew that under like circumstances she herself might have read the letter, and it was characteristic that a residuum of doubt still possessed her mind. At last she reflected, with relief, that had Mary really read it she would have been even more angry, for this was a part of what Mrs. Hunter wrote:

"But enough of the fashions—not the most earnest-minded woman can afford to neglect them—you have the good sense to know that [Kitty felt the force of this remark]. Sad experience has made me cautious in friendship, but more and more do I feel that to you and with you I can be frank.

"I can see why, as you say, you are not considered in your uncle's house as you should be. You should assert yourself, and when we are more together I may help you with advice. You are too mature to be governed incessantly by your cousin, and I can well understand why you should resent these petty criticisms of dress and manner. I do not see how either could be improved.

"Remember, dear, to ask your uncle about the passage in Catullus. Perhaps he will honor me with a word of reply. I am detained here a few days, but hope soon to be with you, and some day to introduce to you my brother Lionel, the best and the handsomest of men."

Kitty reread this letter, and gave brief thought to Lionel as she locked it up and went out on her uncle's errand.

Meanwhile Mary Fairthorne rode through the roads of the low-lying Neck-lands at a rate which astonished her old black groom. The ride did her good, body and soul, and care sat less heavily behind the rider as she turned to walk her horse homeward over the paved streets.

VII

HE Reverend Cyril Knellwood was the
rector of the small church of St. Agnes, which a few wealthy parishioners
and his own means enabled him to sustain with due attention to the High-
Church forms which seemed to him essential. He
was from conviction celibate. Honest, cautious, and
in some ways narrow, he was devoted to his work,
and gave himself thoroughly to such unending labor
among the poor as would have been more easy if he
had fasted less and given his large frame the dis-
used tonic of healthful exercise. At his church Miss
Kitty lightly professed her creed and said her
prayers once a day on Sundays, finding the music
and the ceremonial service much to her taste. At
times Kitty was religious, as at times she was several
other things; but her brief periods of seriousness
were usually in some relation to the Reverend Cyril,
whose gaunt largeness, ascetic, firmly lined face, and
melancholy eyes she greatly admired. Her deliciously rosy, gay girlhood was in some way pleasing
to the unsuspicious, tired, worn man of middle age;
as for Kitty, she would have coquetted with St.
Paul. The rector, as yet unaware of his peril,
waited for Miss Morrow in the drawing-room, and

consulted at intervals a note-book, which he put in his pocket as Miss Kitty entered. She had lingered to change a neck ribbon and to set in order the wilful masses of her flaxen hair.

"God's peace be with you, child," he said, as she came in, rosy, radiant, smiling.

She said: "Good morning, Father," and went on to ask a number of needless questions as to the music and the services. He answered patiently, in a rather low voice, pleasingly modulated.

Kitty had seated herself on the black hair-cloth sofa beside him. Presently, moving a little, he said that he had come on a small matter of business, and, rising, went to the window, remarking that his sight was not good. Perhaps it was not; he was slightly near-sighted. He took out his glasses and considered his note-book, after which, returning, he sat down in a chair. This ripe, eager, material beauty disturbed him. He looked up and as it were past her, and felt a momentary sensation of half-explained emotion.

"You look pale, Father," said Kitty. "Mary says you fast too much." As she spoke she put a hand on his arm. "Let me get you a glass of wine."

"No, no," he said, drawing away; "I am very well." It was not quite true. He was underfed and overworked—just in the condition when emotions are apt to get out of control. He felt the weakness, and resented the fact that it had been visible to the girl.

"Perhaps a little cologne," said Kitty, with a gentle note of real anxiety in her tones.

"I am in no need of it," he said, almost sharply. "I have had, as you know, letters from a Mrs. Hunter, who, it seems, intends to spend the winter here. She incloses a letter of warm praise, given, it appears, some years ago by her former rector at Umstead. He is now dead. She writes very intelligently as to her desire to assist in the church work, and refers to you as her friend."

"Oh, yes, she is a friend of mine, and so good, and so—so attractive."

"I desire to know rather more of her, and of what she wants. Her letters are a little vague."

"Oh, she can do anything," said Kitty.

"And still I should like to know more." He was careful, perhaps over-cautious, for not all the women who had asked for his guidance or proffered help had proved to possess the single-minded devotion which accepted the noble-looking priest as one shut out from the world of feminine allurements. Just now, when Kitty had said that Mrs. Hunter was attractive, and later that she had such a perfect figure, he reasonably thought it irrelevant and said as much. At last, seeing that Kitty was unable materially to aid his quest, he rose: "Mrs. Hunter spoke of having corresponded with your uncle. I have to see him about another matter. Is he at home?"

Kitty said yes; would he come up to the library? As they crossed the room, she took a rose from a vase.

"Let me put it in your button-hole."

"I do not wear flowers."

"Then you must carry it," she cried, gaily. "I cannot have my gifts slighted." He put out an open palm. Her touch, lingering, as she laid the rose on his hand, again disturbed him, while Kitty went on cheerfully:

"I am afraid I have rather neglected confession of late. I—"

"No matter," he broke in; "we will talk of that another time." He was sternly asking himself if he were a fit confessor for this rosy girl, with her pretty ways.

Her uncle had always liked the broad-shouldered clergyman, although they had scarcely one opinion in which they were agreed. Once, when he had been asked by Mary why he liked Mr. Knellwood, he had answered:

"Well, Mary, he is a gentleman, which is rare nowadays. Also, we are at one about nothing, and that adds interest to human interviews; and finally, my dear, he is very definite, which I like."

Mary laughed; she respected Mr. Knellwood, but did not wholly like, perhaps did not understand him.

"I do not think him definite at all, Uncle John. He has been wobbling feebly for years between two churches, if you call that definite."

"He does not admit that," and in fact it was not true. "About the churches, I do not care. He is definite enough while it lasts."

"Ah!" exclaimed Mary, laughing, "I like that!"

"And 'wobble' is an objectionable word."

"But expressive, sir."

When the servant said "Mr. Knellwood is in the parlor," Mr. Fairthorne, who heard imperfectly, asked:

"What was that? Who is it?"

Mary replied: "Mr. Knellwood. He is talking to Kitty. He will ask you for money; he told me yesterday that he would."

"They all do that—I mean ask for money. I gave him some help last year. The charity is a good one—at least you said so."

"I do not fancy him, uncle; but as an intelligent engine of charity he is unequaled."

"He is as wasteful as other engines," said Fairthorne; "between him and your other mendicants and that blank doctor I am being impoverished. I won't give him a dime."

"Yes, you will."

"I hate to give away money and see no results. When you become old you will know that the virtue, the goodness, represented by giving money grows with the years; the older you are, the harder to give, and the greater credit, I presume."

"I see no credit in it at all," said Mary, leaning over his chair; "it is the easiest of all duties. I hear Mr. Knellwood; now, a good large check." As she was about to leave him, Mr. Knellwood entered, Kitty saying:

"Here is Father Knellwood, uncle." Mary waited, while Kitty sat down and taking Felisa, the cat, on her lap, began to make her uncomfortable by blowing on her ears. Mr. Fairthorne greeted the rector warmly. Meanwhile, Mr. Knellwood, with his hat on his knees, was glancing with eager longing at the thousands of brilliantly bound volumes about him. Mary Fairthorne leaned against the mantel, looking down from her fair height on the two men, resolute, now that she had not escaped in time, to see that her uncle did not refuse to give.

"Well, your reverence," said Fairthorne, "is it money or books—or theological advice?"

"Oh!" cried Kitty, as Felisa's temper failing her, she laid a sharp claw on Kitty's white hand and leaped to the floor.

"The beast!" cried Kitty.

"You are rightly served," said John Fairthorne, while the girl wrapped a handkerchief about the hand and Cyril Knellwood looked up in wonder that any one could scold her. Kitty pouted for a minute and then, as she was never at rest very long, arose and standing beside her uncle's chair, began to pose, laying the uninjured hand on his shoulder and patting him tenderly.

"Damn it!" he said, "let me alone." When weak or ill and alone with her he liked her caressing ways, but at times, or when he felt well, as plainly disliked them.

"I do not think you ought to swear before clergymen," said Miss Morrow.

"Go to the devil, you goose!" Then he turned to Mr. Knellwood, and with the utmost courtesy said: "Pardon me, it was purely exclamatory."

Mr. Knellwood, embarrassed, returned:

"It is of no moment. I did not make the decalogue."

Kitty, indignant, walked across the room, sat down at a window, and considered her offended dignity and the garden.

"Well," asked Fairthorne, "are you coveting your neighbor's goods, Mr. Knellwood?"

"I am," said the rector; "but it is not I, it is my Master who asks."

"And how much, pray? Out with the whole villainy."

"The St. Agnes orphanage is in debt, and the interest on the mortgage is in arrears."

"How much do you want?"

"We need five hundred dollars. Miss Mary has given me one hundred."

"Did you not say there were other needs?" said Mary.

"Yes," he returned, hesitating.

"Hold your tongue, miss, and give me my check-book. There, will that do?"

"I thank you in the name of my Master."

"Well, don't come back soon."

Mary moved over to his side and saw that he had given eight hundred dollars. She said, smiling:

"You are very grasping, Mr. Knellwood. Eight hundred! Thank you, uncle."

"The Lord knows why I was such a fool!"

"Yes, he knows," said Cyril. "I wish your kind of folly were common."

Kitty, who was as usual in debt, and had lately loaned Mrs. Hunter a modest sum, had early in the day been refused relief by her uncle. Now she rose and left the room without a word—a rather unusual exit for her. Seeing Mr. Knellwood about to express his feelings further in some form of thankful statement, Fairthorne said:

"Let us drop this matter. Yes, I know; but if there be one thing I hate more than giving money, it is being thanked for it. Console me by taking—no, let me send you some of these new books. Here is a life of Servetus and Random's 'Theories of Divine Methods.' I am keeping this 'History of the Council of Trent' to bait you about celibacy. Mr. Random has hit on my favorite idea that the imperfection of this world suggests imperfection in the immediate Creator."

"Indeed!" said the rector.

"Yes, considering the ingenuity of Nature and the unlimited possibilities at her disposal, she seems to have bungled pretty badly."

"But were they unlimited?"

"Take care, Mr. Knellwood!" cried Mary, laughing.

"He thinks," continued Fairthorne, "that the task of creation may have been relegated to inferior creative individualities. If each had a world so assigned, star travel would be interesting." Fairthorne's deep-set gray eyes—the gray eyes which the years leave always young—twinkled with mirth. Mr. Knellwood sat up, and, as usual, accepted battle, never suspecting the enjoyment which the old gentleman got out of the earnestness with which the clergyman considered his gay inventions.

"Mr. Fairthorne," he returned, "what you say is interesting. I will think it over. As the angels, we are told, are God's ministers, he may have chosen to use them thus."

"Oh, Mr. Knellwood!" said Miss Mary, much

5

amused, "you are getting into trouble. Never begin by admitting my uncle's premises."

"Thank you, Miss Mary; but my good friend cannot tempt me to-day. His check is a solid argument against the completeness of this earth's imperfection. There is one good man in it." It was pleasantly said, with the courtesy which made Knellwood a likable man, despite his obvious limitations. Mary clapped her hands joyously.

"A hit! A very palpable hit!"

"And yet," said Cyril, "you will let me say, too, Mr. Fairthorne, that however curious such varieties of speculation may be, I do not think they ought to be cast in the way of the young."

"By George! Knellwood, that is fine. Mary riots in skeptic delights."

"I do not, sir. Do not trust him."

"And as to Katherine, she is as supremely incapable of thought as Felisa, my cat."

"I am glad," said the clergyman, "to think you do not know as I do my good little parishioner. But my time is up. I had another small errand; I have had letters from a Mrs. Hunter, who speaks of knowing Miss Morrow and mentions you as a correspondent."

"Well, we have exchanged letters. She is, I take it, a remarkable woman. What of her?"

"She is coming here, and wants to assist in my parish work. My experience in the past makes me careful."

"I recommend Mrs. Hunter," said Fairthorne, lightly; "she is handsome and clever. What more can the church ask? Katherine, as you must know, is an unfailing judge of human character. I am told that she adores her.''

Mr. Knellwood smiled. He knew that he was not being seriously considered; nevertheless, he said as he rose: ''Many thanks, Mr. Fairthorne; I must wait to see her, I suppose. Pardon my troubling you, and again, thank you.'' Miss Fairthorne went down-stairs with Mr. Knellwood, saying:

''You must not take my uncle too literally. He knows nothing of Mrs. Hunter.''

''Miss Morrow tells me she is a woman of serious views. That ought to suffice; but I am perhaps over-cautious.''

When Mary returned to the library she found her uncle asleep in his chair. This had been common of late. He disliked to be reminded of it and accordingly Mary sat down noiselessly to make a copy, in her clear hand, of letters in Lord Burleigh's crabbed script recently added to her uncle's collection. As he would buy letters only, she often found them such as to excite her interest. Presently John Fairthorne sat up.

''That theological idiot has gone?'' he asked.

''Mr. Knellwood has gone, delighted with your generosity.''

''What? what? Generosity!'' He had forgotten. Mary was too kindly to insist on this lapse of memory. She said, however:

''Uncle John, you should not have left him with the belief that you can indorse this Mrs. Hunter.

Kitty's enthusiasms are not always wisely placed. I hope you will not—"

"Will not what? Confound it, Mary, I shall do as I please." He looked flushed and angry. "Damn Mrs. Hunter! Every one tries to manage me. Katherine is the only comfort I have."

Mary was in no wise disturbed by these sudden fits of unreason.

"The letters are copied, sir, I think, clearly." She set the portfolio on his desk, and left the room.

"I had better not have tried to counsel Uncle John," she said to herself; but for Mary duties were very insistent creditors.

VIII

I T was the end of November before Mrs.
Lucretia Hunter was able to go to Philadelphia. When at last the time of her
quarterly paid income arrived she no
longer delayed. Mr. Knellwood, with
whom she had exchanged several letters, had at her
desire mentioned a reputable boarding-house, and
Miss Morrow had secured for her the desired room.
Meanwhile, Fate had dealt harshly with this gallant free-lance. The brother suddenly appeared.
He was now out of employment for the third time.
After his early boyhood he had been sustained at
school and then at a Western college for two years,
by work and self-sacrifice on the part of his sister. He was always just going to succeed, was capable of brief effort in any novel pursuit, and then
was as sure to give up or be given up. School,
college, an art school, law studies, a business college,
and last a clerkship, all in turn ended in some form
of failure. He was the constant burden she carried,
and she carried it bravely, loving him, proud of his
singular beauty, lavish to him alone, hopeful always,
with a strange satisfaction in self-immolation, due
perhaps in part to the fact that the years between

them gave her sisterly relation the effect of motherhood. It is doubtful if perfect physical beauty is
ever unselfish. This man, though small and slight,
was more beautiful than a man should be. He knew
it, and the sister counted on it as a part of her
capital.

This time he had come upon her again a little too
early for her plans, having lost his clerkship by reason of ignorance and unpunctuality. He told her
that he had left because he was tired of it. She
was fully aware that he was lying, but that investigation was useless waste of time. After thinking
it all over she said that she would write for him to
the house where a room had been taken for her.
She might perhaps go elsewhere. She hoped he
would keep quiet and behave himself. He spoke of
his desire to pay certain debts, but when she learned
that they were owing in Boston she smiled at the
simple artifice, said they must wait, and kissed him,
adding:

"I should like, Lionel, to ask you to be good; failing that, may I ask you to be prudent? I must feel
at ease; and remember, as I told you, we are still the
orphan children of an English clergyman—Halifax,
please don't forget. I was a teacher, which is true.
I have always taken care of you. We are Craigs,
and I am the widow of the principal of the St. Jude
Academy near Halifax. You have been unable to
bear the harsh climate of Canada. As concerns my
life, bury it and be careful. This is our last chance.
It may prove a good one, and it is all very simple;
only I am a little afraid of you."

He did not see why, but, promising all things, he went away to Philadelphia by the noon train.

This man—he was now twenty-five, but looked quite boylike—was of a nature the reverse of complex; a mild animal with male instincts, with crude appetites, lazy in mind and body—a man without thought of to-morrow, and for whom yesterdays were valueless. He was attached to his sister by habit and necessity. He had come by degrees to understand her and her ways, and indeed knew more of them than she liked. He laughed as he left her.

"I wonder what she is up to now," he said.

No one who writes or has written of men has ever completely unraveled to perfect clearness the tangle of one human life. Even the lesser task of describing the face and form so as to identify an individual is no easy task. As a rule, the greater masters have left these personal details to the hearer's imaginative helping. For some people there was repulse and not invitation in the curiously faultless features of Lionel Craig. It was a face on which time did not readily write its records, good or bad, and which it had so far left uncharactered.

John Fairthorne once said to Mary that the world was a fleeting show and all of us merely its more or less well-trained animals. When she replied, being then of the age of sixteen, that she was not an animal, he advised her to adjourn opinion until she was a mother, which sent her away reflective.

Lionel Craig was certainly an animal, but nearly incapable of assimilative use of training, moral or mental. He had the cunning of his kind.

IX

I F we be the sport of chance-bred circumstance, it is no more strange than any uninfluential fact that beside Lionel Craig there were on the noon train two persons who would in time gravely affect each other's fates.

When Sydney Archer, returning from a consultation in New Jersey, caught the express at Elizabeth, he found no seat except in a rather crowded smoking-car. His custom was to smoke only after the day's work was over, but now, accepting the joy of breaking a dutiful habit, he found, as the tempted do, an ally in a cigar forgotten in his waistcoat pocket. He bent over the seat in front of him and asked a light. A sun-darkened young man replied:

"I have no match. Won't my pipe do?" Archer said:

"Yes, but it is quite a bit of art to get a light from a pipe." The owner of the pipe said he had n't noticed that, and it could n't hurt the pipe. Said Archer, smiling:

"But it can put it out, and the man, too." The young fellow did not rise to this small joke, and made no reply, which pricked Archer into continuing an aborted talk. Leaning over the half-occupied seat, he got a side look at an ugly, rugged, resolute face.

"Pardon me," he said, with the soft tongue and courteous ways of his Southern breed; "I see that I have actually put out your pipe—I thought I should. You must pardon me."

"Well, I am not any put out." He stated it as a fact, not in any relation to Archer's mild jest. "I have smoked all I want." Then he looked out of the window at the cheerful landscape of New Jersey. Archer tried again:

"Queer phrase, that of a man being put out."

"I don't know. Is it?"

Archer gave up. The man must be stupid. He was not, though he was a slow thinker, and socially to be defined as a strong, untrained creature, crude, capable, observant—a man who had led a rather lonely life. After a full half-minute of silence he turned and showing in full the big-featured face and somewhat tender eyes, said slowly:

"To say you are put out can't mean that you are pushed out of temper, as if a fellow put you out of a quiet place you were in."

Archer sat up, attentive. He was a student of his kind.

"Why not?" he asked.

"Because no man can shove me out of my temper if I want to stay there."

Archer, delighted, was about to take the vacant seat beside his comrade of the minute, when he was anticipated by an over-dressed young man who said to the sun-burned one, "Sorry to trouble you," and

sat down beside him. The other made room, but did
not speak. Presently, however, he became interested
in his neighbor, who, to make things easier to state,
we may say was Lionel Craig. The new-comer unlocked a large bag which he had set at his feet. It
was a rather luxuriously furnished dressing-case, and
at once excited the curiosity of the other young man.
Craig turned over its untidy contents, opened a sil-
ver-topped cologne bottle, put a little on his handkerchief, selected a large cigar from a foolishly heavy
silver case, and asked his neighbor for a match.
Finding that he had none, Craig tumbled over the
gloves and brushes and coming upon a little gold
match-safe, shut up his bag and smoked in silence,
while he looked over the society news and comments
of the "Daily Gossip." At last, that edifying
amusement failing, he turned toward the sun-burned
man. Archer saw the two contrasted side faces, the
large, well-clad head, the big features, with hardly
enough of facial space, and beside him the richly
colored, clean-shaven delicacy of the new-comer, with
a thinner crop of black hair. It was easy to hear
their talk.

"Not a strong face," thought the doctor. "I
would bet on the brown paws and dirty nails against
the gloves." They were too fine for travel and mere
protective use.

The sun-burned man seemed to talk easily enough
to Craig. At last he said:

"Do you know Philadelphia well enough to tell
me where I could get cheap board?"

"No, I am a stranger. I have the address of a

house where I have taken rooms. I prefer a hotel, but this is—well, a rather unusual kind of boarding-house. You see, in this city ladies who have lost means sometimes resort to this way of earning a living. But it is not at all cheap.''

''Then it won't suit me.''

''You might try,'' said Craig, ''the Misses Markham, 290 Pine Street. Here is their card; queer for boarding-house keepers to have visiting-cards.''

''Why not?'' said the other. ''I never had one myself, but there is no law against it, I suppose.''

''No, of course not.'' By and by the other asked casually:

''Are you traveling?'' Most of the over-dressed men he had met in smoking-cars had been drummers. Mr. Craig said shortly, yes, he was traveling, of course.

''In what line?'' asked the other.

''Oh, damn it! I 'm not in trade.''

''I guessed you were.'' Then it seemed to him natural that, having asked, he should give. He added:

''My name 's Martin Blount. I am going to study medicine at the university.''

Mr. Craig said:

''It must be rather an unpleasant business,'' and with no more words, having smoked his cigar, he picked up his bag and went back to the car he had left. Archer took his vacant seat, saying:

''You puzzled me, Mr. Blount. I am Dr. Sydney Archer.'' A large smile occupied the young fellow's face.

"Why, now, I 'm right pleased, sir, to see you," and he wrung the offered hand with too efficient cordiality. "I took your advice."

"Well, and pray what was it? I forget."

"I guess you might forget a good lot of kindness, and remember enough for nest-eggs." Archer, amused, repeated his query:

"But, really, what was it?"

"Well, sir,—don't you remember?—I came to see you last spring. I wanted a scholarship in the university, and you said that required one foreign language besides the other qualifications. So I learned German this summer—I had some Latin. I came on early in September and got in number two."

"But you are late at the work; the session begins in October."

"That 's so. I was keeping hotel books at Old-field, and my time was n't out till November. I shall make it up."

"Where do you mean to live in the city?"

"I guess I can get a garret somewhere."

"I think that if you will go and see the Misses Markham and give them my card they will contrive to make a place for you—at least for the time needed to look about you. I will see them later."

"Why, that is the same house that fellow—that fellow with the bag—was going to." Archer saw the obvious, unuttered difficulty.

"Take what they offer. I shall see them in a day or two. They are good women, and, I chance to know, have at present a half-empty house. Here is my card." He wrote a few lines upon it. "It was

Dr. Bergwynn sent you to me, I remember now. He said you were the son of an Andover professor, an orphan.''

"Yes, sir; I never saw my father or mother.''

"And how is it as to money? With the help of the scholarship can you manage?'' The brown, good-humored face set hard.

"I 've got to manage.'' Archer was too tactfully wise to say more.

"Come and see me. Ah, here we are,'' he said, as they ran into the station. "Be sure to go to Miss Markham's.''

In the mid-afternoon Mr. Lionel Craig was left in the front parlor of a large, old-fashioned Georgian house on Pine Street. He was somewhat surprised, and for a little while thought he had mistaken the number. It was a paneled room, painted white. There were portraits by the elder Peale, Copley, and two by Jarvis, set against wall-paper which was laid on in squares, each a gay-tinted fox-hunt. The wooden mantel held four tall Wedgwood vases. A corner cupboard was filled with Dresden cups, with a background of buff-and-gold Nankin plates, and on top stood a huge china punch-bowl, with the name "Robt. Markham, 1783,'' and a coat of arms. Craig sat down in one of the dignified arm-chairs of old mahogany, and began to look about him at the rather grim gentlefolks who would have seemed to any one else to suit so well the room and its furniture. He had an uneasy sense of being in the wrong place.

He meant to be particular about his room. That was desirable, in order to make people feel at once the position and wants of a gentleman. Of course, there must be a bath-room near it, and sun was desirable. He would ask about that. He had again a slight shock of surprise as he rose on the entrance of two ladies.

The elder woman wore over her gray hair a lace cap. A closer observer than Craig would have seen that her delicate features wore the look of fatigue and care. The sister was slighter. She was possibly near to thirty, and might once have been a very pretty girl. Trouble, work, and anxiety had not spared her, but the somewhat critical look she turned on Craig, who had brought in with him his precious bag, was not devoid of either intelligence or a subdued expression of amusement. Except for the elder sister's cap, they were dressed precisely alike in some soft, gray, silken stuff. The younger woman had opened the door and stepped back to let her sister enter the room.

"I am Mr. Craig," said Lionel. Miss Markham put up a pair of gold eye-glasses, as she returned:

"Quite so. We expected you. Mrs. Hunter wrote to us, and as Miss Morrow is her friend we consented to receive you."

"Yes," said the younger lady, "we consented."

"Pardon me, I should have said I am Miss Markham," said the elder woman; "my sister, Miss Clementina—you will kindly show Mr. Craig his room. We are sure you will be comfortable. Miss Clementina will tell you our meal hours. You will excuse us if we say, as you are young and we rarely have young people with us, that we like them to be punctual. In fact, and you will pardon me, we rather insist on it.''

''Yes, certainly,'' said Mr. Craig, somewhat embarrassed.

''And of course, sister,'' said Miss Clementina, ''Mr. Craig will understand that we are old-fashioned folks and particular—''

''We hope,'' said Miss Markham, ''that you do not use tobacco—of course, I mean smoke, Clementina.''

''Yes, we mean smoke,'' said that lady; ''or, at least not in our house.''

Craig said:

''Oh, no!'' feeling that he was by no means dictating terms. Then, rallying his forces, he thought it desirable to put these boarding-house women in their proper places. He said:

''I will look at your rooms before I decide, and of course there must be a bath-room on the same floor.''

''Mr. Wilson has our only bath-room,'' said Miss Markham; ''you will of course have a bath-tub in your room. We have given you a room because Mrs. Hunter is commended to us by Miss Morrow. There is no choice of rooms, as we have but one for you and one for Mrs. Hunter.''

Mr. Craig, somewhat disconcerted, said:

''Oh, I suppose it will be all right.''

''May I ask you to follow me?'' said Miss Clementina.

The exquisite neatness of the third-story back room, into which he was shown, pleased his taste, and he refrained from further critical inquiry.

''I think I shall be quite satisfied, Miss Markham.''

"Miss Clementina," she corrected, pleasantly smiling.

"What time do you have supper?"

"We dine at half after six. Our friend Mr. Wilson, on the second floor, dines at his club. You will have time to change your clothes before dinner, but if your trunk does not arrive we shall not mind it for to-day."

"Good heavens!" exclaimed Craig.

"I beg pardon," said Clementina, thinking what a pretty, self-important little man he was. "You will find the clock on the stair correct. My sister is particular as to the hours of meals. I will have your trunk sent up."

When Miss Clementina found Miss Markham in the parlor, that lady said:

"Well, dear, will he suit us?"

"I fear not. An underbred young man and pretentious," returned the sister.

"I was not favorably impressed," said Miss Letitia. "I do not like these girl-faced men. He will have to be kept in his place, Clementina."

"Yes, we must keep him in his place, Letitia. It is unfortunate. Perhaps we may have to send him away."

"We must hope, Clementina, that Mrs. Hunter may be nicer. Plain people are well enough, but common people cannot be endured."

"Do you suppose Katherine Morrow knows this young man?"

"Perhaps not. We may have been hasty, Clementina."

As she spoke, Martin Blount entered. He had walked across the great city, carrying his not too heavy portmanteau. He had paused to look through the iron gate of St. Peter's at the crumbling tombstones. He had seen the tall form of Mary Fairthorne on a big thoroughbred and wondered why she was followed by a groom. He had used his eyes well. That he was dusty and begrimed with travel did not trouble him, as it had done Lionel Craig.

"I am Martin Blount," he said, "and here is a card, ma'am, from Dr. Archer. I hope," and he looked with wistful doubt about the parlor, "I do hope you can take me in."

"Take him in!" murmured Miss Letitia, as she read the card. "I—do suppose we must manage." She was somewhat annoyed. Dr. Archer had been a faithful, helpful friend, but the last-comer had tried the little gentlewoman shrewdly. She said:

"Sit down, while I talk to my sister. You will excuse us—"

"Why, of course; I am not in any hurry."

The two ladies went out. Then he began to use his eager eyes. When they returned he was looking at a portrait over the mantel. For the minute this alone interested him. He did not wait to hear their conclusion, but said:

"Now, that's a right strong face." He could have said nothing better. Miss Markham returned:

"Yes, that is Major-General Markham, and this is his grandson, who was killed in the action between the *Constitution* and the *Java*."

"And that?" said Mr. Blount, with increasing in-

6

terest, pointing out a miniature which hung below the general.

"That is our brother. He fell at Fredericksburg."

"At Fredericksburg. He was our only brother," echoed the sister.

"Let us talk of what we can do for you," said Miss Markham.

"I think I just ought to say right at once I can't afford to have a room in a house like yours. I can afford to pay five dollars a week. It 's too like a home, miss—I can't afford a home. I just want a room and breakfast. I guess I 'll have to eat dinner somewhere near the college."

"Miss Clementina and I have consulted, and we know that Dr. Archer meant us to take you, or at least for a time. We can give you breakfast and an attic. We are sorry it must be only an attic. Dr. Archer says you will be satisfied with that."

"And a stove," said Clementina.

"And a stove," repeated Miss Markham, "and breakfast. You will take your other meals outside, you say. We think you said so?"

"Yes, the college is far from here." He found in that an excuse.

"Then Miss Clementina will show you your room." He was overjoyed, gratefully satisfied with the old house and the two women.

"Thank you," he said, and followed the neat little lady.

When again Clementina came back she said:

"It is getting to be dreadfully like keeping a

boarding-house. We have been making believe to—''

"And we will still make believe, till we, too, change our lodgings, dear, for a better. The young man is plain, but not common.''

"He is very uncommon, sister. Is it too late for service?''

"Yes.''

For the next few days Mr. Craig idled about the city, waiting. Martin Blount threw himself eagerly into the early studies of his profession. He used his days, and sat up so late that Miss Clementina, troubled about candles, put a lamp in his room.

Clementina had long been accustomed to accept the position of a younger sister, and to yield to the will and ways of Letitia, who was always too weary to talk, and read little except her Bible. She was not strong, and sometimes submitted to having her breakfast sent up to her little room in the "back building,'' as Philadelphians call it.

Craig ate fast, and went out as soon as he could to smoke. He rarely returned until after dinner. Martin Blount was apt to linger over his breakfast. With his shrewd, observant ways and varied interests, he pleased Clementina, who loved books and good talk, and had small leisure for visits. He soon told her his story, and the kindly heart of the woman began to take pleasure in helping the courageous young fellow. She went over his clothes, and mended shirts and darned socks or sewed on buttons. At last she bought him handkerchiefs. He told black Judith that there was some mistake, and wished to pay her for the astonishing repair of a collar. The old negress laughed and said no one could mend like Miss Clementina. "But he was n't to know about the handkerchiefs, not on no account." The thoughtful kindness touched him as few things had done.

His life had been hard and had hardened the man a little. Now, having fallen among friends he found it strange.

The winter began. Dr. Archer saw him twice, but was too busy to think much of one of many struggling students.

A week after Lionel Craig arrived, his sister wrote to Miss Markham that she preferred to go to a hotel, and should not need the room reserved for her. Her offer to pay was declined. Her brother remained with the two ladies, and, now that his sister was near, was kept in reasonable order by the promise of better things and by contributions of money she could ill spare.

X

"ARE you not late, Harry?" said Mrs. Swanwick to her husband.

"Yes," he said, looking up from his paper and then at his watch, "but I have had a note from Mr. Grace. He wants to see me here before I go to the office."

"I, too, have an appointment," she cried, gaily. "Mr. Masters wishes to consult me."

"Indeed, I shall be jealous. Might I ask—"

"No, you may not. I never reveal professional secrets. By the way, Harry, are you altogether satisfied about the Republic Trust? You talked of it last month."

"I did. I think I said, also, that by accident I found out that Mr. Underwood had been twice consulted by Thurston."

"Without your knowledge?"

"Yes."

"Isn't that unusual?"

"Yes. It is sometimes done, but not secretly. I should be consulted first."

"Is he a reputable lawyer?"

"Well, yes, of late years. Not altogether—very able—sharp, I should say."

"Then, as you observed, Harry, there must be

something wrong, very wrong—more than those bonds. You said they were improving. Uncle John must hold a good deal of the Republic stock. If they are doing things their counsel is not to know, I—'' and she paused.

"Quite true, dear. It does look suspicious. What made you talk of it?"

"Yes. What was it? Oh, yes, Dr. Archer said something about it. Perhaps, as uncle is wrapped up in himself and his autographs, you might, as you said, look into the matter before you speak to him. Why not ask Mr. Grace?"

"He is a director. It would never do."

"Oh, indeed!" She knew it very well, and knew also that her husband was amply able to learn all that was needed and only required to be made a little anxious.

"Don't resign in a pet, Harry; not yet, anyhow. They cannot make you aid any wrong, and no matter what happens you are above reproach. Wait at least until there is something more definite. Besides, being counsel enables you to ask questions and learn what may be of value to uncle."

"How did you know, Madge, that I thought of resigning?"

"Oh, you innocent dear!" she cried. "How long have we been married? There, go; I hear the bell. If Tom Masters comes, send him up to me, and, Harry, do let me see the paper book in the Bridge case.—Ah!" she sighed as he went down-stairs, "I should like to argue that case." Then she said to herself, "I have a half-hour," and whistled gaily, at which signal Jack and the "Kid," as he called her, made tumultuous descent from the nursery into her arms and were chased into the library, where the three rolled about in undignified joy until at last the little lady, gay, glad, and very red, cried as Masters came in:

"Shoo! Shoo! Run, off with you! Ah! I would rather be a mother, Tom, than chief-justice. Pardon me, I have been the prey of those children. I am not fit to be seen. Sit down. Are the ducks in yet at Carroll's Island?"

"Yes, I am off to-morrow. You shall have your share and lend me Harry next week."

"Not I; he must work for his living. How are the old aunts, the ladies you dare to call the white mice?"

"Well, are n't they white mice? That house always seems to me like a mild little peep-show. Aunt Letitia is like a gentle ancestral breeze out of the country of long ago, and Aunt Clementina, so dainty, and so gentle—"

"And sometimes so pretty, in spite of her absurd notion of dressing to look old. I wonder if Letitia does really like that?"

"Possibly. Now and then she is severe with our young and inexperienced Clementina. You should hear it."

"They must have a rather hard struggle at times."

"Yes, I know, Margaret, but you can't help them. I could manage Clementina, but Aunt Letitia— never! The last time I ventured Aunt Letitia returned my check in a formal note, and actually in the third person."

"Not really?"

"Yes, and they loathe it all, and make believe, like Miss What's-her-name in Dickens, and won't take a cent. Now they have a fellow there like a small, painted Apollo, and another like a rather nice kind of Caliban. Aunt Clementina is in love with him. It is her first. Once a man got as far as—I do not know how far, but I was told that Miss Markham ordered him out of the house. They are more celibatic than old Knellwood. By the way, Margaret, I think the reverend bachelor is fairly on the way to trouble—"

"What! Cyril Knellwood! I have long suspected it; but how can she? Oh, Kitty!"

"The meshes of that net are small. No fish escape." He spoke bitterly for him, but he was now talking to his nearest friend as he talked to no other. Usually he took his defeats sweetly, but Kitty had gone far and he was hurt; as he said to himself, "pretty badly net-marked, like an old salmon."

He was a man few understood. Mary Fairthorne said of him that he took in more and gave out less than any one she knew. Men who had been with him in the Wilderness fighting spoke of him with pleased remembrance. He read immensely, and few suspected it; he gave, and none knew; and used to be called the club grandfather, because to him the young fellows always came for advice or aid. In fact, he was genially constructed, had clear notions as to duties and honor, and after the war was left stranded without distinct ambitions except to be a first-rate shot. Why no woman had ever said yes to this gentleman Margaret Swanwick did not know. In her case, Harry had blocked the way. Mary said it was his excessive reverence for women. Margaret laughed, and admitted that there was something in that, but that it did seem to her a malady easily cured.

When Tom Masters spoke with decent reserve of the sad ways of the ever-impenitent Kitty, Margaret touched his arm kindly:

"We are none of us good enough for you, Tom. Certainly not Katherine Morrow."

"Please don't," he said.

"Yes, but I must. You shall never marry. Are n't you my Jack's godfather, and everybody's uncle?"

Margaret Fairthorne had once been on the boundary of a love affair with Mr. Masters. That was long ago. She had yet a real if faintly felt dislike to his marrying, although had he declared himself engaged she would have joyfully welcomed the news.

"Well, I want your help, Madge," he said; and when she replied, confidently:

"Of course, Tom," he added that it was n't very easy.

"The fact is, Margaret, Roger Grace is afflicted with social ambition. You do not know him—of course not."

"But I do," she said; "I went to his banking-office yesterday to ask if he would help our farm-home reformatory. He was very nice about it, and said he would think it over."

"Oh, is that so? He is talking to Harry now, down-stairs, about some law question."

"And what," said Margaret, "can I do for this man of millions, poor little me?"

"What he wants is to be put on the Assembly list. Why, heaven knows. He is a bachelor of forty or thereabouts. He is a kindly, generous, plain man, without pretence. Where he came from he will tell you or any one frankly, but he does not boast about his rise from farmer folk in the Alleghanies. I advised him to ask Harry Swanwick. He said no, that Mr. Swanwick was his counsel, and might feel obliged to say he would do it. Well, anyhow, Madge, he said that he saw no objection to my speaking to you—I said I would. But why do our newly rich folk want this kind of thing?"

"They ought to want it, Tom. I am glad they do. Because we have always had it, it seems of no moment. There is no reason why Mr. Grace should not have the subscription book sent to him. I am one of the patronesses this year, and Harry has been a manager. He hated it, and I am sure to have so often to say no, without giving a reason, must make needless enmities. I will speak to Harry. No, if I do and he gives—I mean if Mr. Grace gives me what I asked, will it not seem as if—"

"Yes, perhaps. Don't do it, Madge; I will say a word to some of the other managers. He will not get in this year, but millions win at last, and this man is quite unobjectionable. Let us leave it. How is Jack? Ah, here is Harry—"

"Mr. Grace, Madge. I suppose it is about that farm school. Take care, Grace, she is greedy."

"Yes, it is that. I want to know a little more about it," said the banker. Roger Grace was a compactly built man in the early forties; a strong, clean-shaven face carried the jaw and chin of power, with some unanalyzable look of sadness in the eyes. He had the money-making talent, and enjoyed its use. Of late he had found out that the pleasure of giving was worth the attentive care he soon spent upon it. A stainless commercial character had led to friendships which in turn taught a receptive nature the taste for things undreamed of in the busy years of laborious effort. With ample leisure, he began to desire, he hardly asked himself why, the life of a class into touch of which he had come by degrees.

Mrs. Swanwick fell at once into easy talk with the banker after Masters and her husband went away. He asked many questions, and she soon knew that the whole matter of the discipline, education, and care of the morally imperfect was familiar to him. As he rose, he said:

"But there must be also flower culture. I think that of use—of real use. When I am tired or troubled"—Mrs. Swanwick looked up—"I go out to my flower-farm, and if that does not help me I am past remedy." He was curiously near to a desire to make the only confession of his guarded life. She was in fact one of the women to whom the heavily burdened and those weary of struggle turn, assured of aid and comprehension.

This woman, with her well-bred kindliness and her intelligent compassion, pleased and attracted a man who was slowly finding new pleasures of heart and mind, and discovering in his own nature unused resources of happiness. He looked up at the landscape by Inness, and spoke of its having sentiment. Then he laid an envelope on the table, and said:

"I should like to come and see you again, and to visit the school. I have a high regard for your husband, Mrs. Swanwick. I suppose you do know what a good fellow he is?" Margaret laughed, pleased at the blunt praise.

"Yes, I know," she said, "but I like others to know and to say so."

"By the by," he said, laying a large hand on the envelope, "I wrote a check at once after you left. I shall send you another to-morrow. That will be for the flowers. I want also to say, Mrs. Swanwick, that I asked Mr. Masters to speak to you about the Assembly. Curious old thing that—ever since 1740, I hear. That interests one in our land of uneasy change. Mr. Masters says it is difficult. I hope you won't bother about it. I shall get there. I always get what I want. I would n't like you to think that I am buying my way. I should dislike any one to say that."

"Please don't," said Margaret, "no one—no one could think that. May I use your name as the giver?"

He said yes, if it would be serviceable. After this she told him that late in the afternoons she was likely to be at home, and would be glad to see him. When he had gone she eagerly opened the envelope, and found in it a check for five thousand dollars.

The Assembly business was, of course, discussed, and as usual the new candidate was laid aside for the year. Almack's had never been more uncertain, nor at times more unreasonably difficult.

Mr. Grace was shrewdly observant, and was getting to understand this small and exacting social life, which with reluctance admitted the claims of mere money. He reflected a little on his way to his office. He felt that even the appearance of being willing to buy his way into the life he desired to enter was not to his taste. Accordingly, when he wrote to Mrs. Swanwick, inclosing a second check, he said that, on the whole, he preferred not to have his name associated with his gift to the farm home. Mrs. Swanwick, however, had already mentioned it to Mary, and now asked her why he had so changed his mind about the use of his name? To this Mary replied that he must be a nice man and when Madge still wondered, declared that if her elder sister only possessed as much imagination as intellect this would not seem a hard riddle.

"Put yourself in his place, dear," she added, "and you will know. I think I should like to see the man."

Madge said neither she nor any one could put themselves in any other person's place.

OR a brief time Mr. Lionel Craig was capable of self-restraint, and as the funds supplied by his sister barely sufficed for his board he had been reasonably punctual and decently behaved. Moreover, he had acquired a certain respect for the ladies in whose card-basket he recognized the names of people he would have been most glad to visit.

Meanwhile, Mrs. Hunter was biding her time in New York, and frequenting libraries where she could learn all about these people with historic stories and, what she valued more, long purses. Kitty's letters had begun to be brief, and to betray less eagerness. It was time to exert a nearer influence and to be within reach of her brother, who was getting, as he reported, anxious to obtain employment. Mrs. Hunter knew well what that meant.

Meanwhile, Miss Morrow had a variety of interesting occupations. The old city was becoming gay with its usual moderation, and Miss Morrow danced as few dance. With this she combined frequent late services at St. Agnes's, and a suddenly developed interest in a variety of matters relating to the ritual. Mr. Knellwood found himself constantly consulted by Miss Kitty, who, with other young women, had organized an altar fund, and found it needful to be guided to its employment.

Mr. Knellwood was becoming as uneasy as St. Anthony. How could he, even to a brother priest, confess a trouble which was fast becoming temptation? He was terrified at times by his own peril. If Mrs. Swanwick and her sister Mary saw what Kitty was about they took no step to interfere. They had been thus tempted once when Mr. Masters, having recovered from unrequited devotion elsewhere, had been wickedly taken in hand by Kitty, who assumed the fatal rôle of consoler, and ended by doing more mischief to a heart hospitable to affection than she was capable of imagining. Mary had on this occasion expressed herself freely to Kitty, who sulked like a child reproved for breaking a too valuable toy. Tom Masters came nearer to hate than he had ever done in his life, and, indeed, said "some certain things" to Kitty which for a day made her uncomfortable, and that amiable gentleman still more so, until he had written and apologized for his intemperate language. All of this he had confided to Margaret Swanwick, who said something in high wrath about pearls which filled him with amazement. He had very meek views as to Tom Masters's value, and was shocked when Madge said Kitty was a vulgar coquette. Indeed, she had small affection for her cousin, and was bored to the limit of patience by her mindless chatter.

One afternoon this mischief-making bit of pretty instinctivity called on Miss Markham to bring the letter in which Mrs. Hunter said she should not need the room kept for her. When she entered the paneled parlor, Miss Clementina was seated by the fire near Martin Blount. Mr. Craig was wearily looking out of the window at the red brick and the white snow-drifts which made up the wintry prospect of a November day. He blew a mist of breath on the pane, and traced figures upon it. He took mild interest in the way the old wrinkled glass of the window distorted the figures of men shoveling snow from the sidewalk.

He had gone out to walk and been repelled by the brisk company of the north wind, for he liked warmth as did his sister, but had no such pleasure as she found in mere exercise.

Martin Blount had a sore throat, and had been reluctantly compelled by Miss Clementina to remain at home. He was busy with a leather-covered text-book of physiology and now and then looked up, with his difficult smile, to say to his anxious hostess that indeed he could not have flannel around his neck—no, not even red flannel. No, he should be all right to-morrow; but to lose a day of lectures was too bad. He really could not have opodeldoc and his neck rubbed. Craig became for a moment an amused listener.

"What a ridiculous, fussy old maid," he thought.

The other man saw again the white waste of a New England winter, the relentless farm life, the scenes of hard labor and temptation in lumber-camps, his friendless youth. A sense of pleasant amaze came over him as the gentle voice recalled him from these sad remembrances. How freshly delightful to have a home, to know that others had kind thought of and for him! It was a constant novelty. He had never seen a relative, and had never made a friend outside of the books for which he had an inherited liking. He had come of a breed which for two centuries of colonial and national life had been well known and socially of the best and had at last gotten back to the soil whence it came. Now, under this fostering providence of interest and kindness, the qualities of his race began to feel its sunshine. The man was fast becoming gentled.

Miss Morrow came in, a double-rose from the healthy stinging of the driven snow. Blount got up at once, and Craig, after a glance at the new-comer, also stood up. Miss Clementina said:

"I am glad to see you, Katherine. Come up-stairs with me."

Miss Kitty was in no haste. She glanced at the ugly, good-humored face of Blount, who stood a-gaze at the wonderful prettiness of the girl. Then, as she saw Craig turn from the window, she knew at once that he must be the brother of whose beauty and accomplishments Mrs. Hunter had written so much. As he moved forward, he hastily thrust in his pocket the caricature he had been making of Miss Clementina's placid face. Miss Kitty said promptly, in reply to Miss Clementina:

"I have only a moment. I have a letter from Mrs. Hunter." Miss Clementina had small liking for the over-dressed lodger with the too exact fea-

7

tures and had no mind to present him to Miss Morrow. She rejoined:

"My sister is up-stairs."

Mr. Craig saw his chance. He had fairly good
surface manners, which at times he shed.

"Pardon me," he said; "Miss Morrow, I am sure,
will excuse me if I present myself to my sister's
friend. I am Mr. Craig."

Miss Morrow was glad to see Mr. Craig, "who,"
she said, "perhaps knew that Mrs. Hunter would
arrive next day," and with a word or two more she
followed Clementina, thinking a little as she went
up-stairs of the singular resemblance between the
brother and sister. Craig said, as the door closed:

"By George, she 's a pretty girl! Got a look of
breeding, of distinction." It was just that which
Kitty lacked. As he went on talking, Blount said,
as he opened his book:

"Oh, shut up! I can't get these heart-valves
clear. Don't bother me!" He, too, disliked this
pretentious young fellow, who came up to his attic
and borrowed quarters and half-dollars and had to
be asked to return them. When, the night before,
he had shown Blount Miss Markham cleverly cari-
catured on a postal card, Martin had angrily torn
up the drawing, and said it was a shame. Craig,
surprised at his wrath, hoped he would not speak of
it. Blount asked if he thought him a fool. Craig
laughed, having no other reply, and took out a cigar,
on which Blount said:

"Can't smoke here. You have done it twice, and
Miss Markham made a row. I said I would not do

it any more, and now please to leave me with these confounded bones. You would make a lovely skeleton," he added, grimly. "You will, some day." This was obvious. Craig said:

"Great George! you 're darned unpleasant sometimes," and left him.

This chanced the night before, and now, when Craig found no idle talk was to be had, he, too, went up-stairs, vaguely hoping to meet Miss Morrow, who, however, had done her friend's errand and gone. As Blount wrestled with the heart movements in the gathering dusk, he heard Dr. Archer enter.

"Why, halloa, Blount! From Miss Clementina's note I supposed you almost past hope or medicine."

"I am sorry, sir, Miss Clementina troubled you. It is really only a slight cold. It 's just all of a piece, her kindness. I can't tell you, sir, how I thank you for sending me here. It is the only home I have ever had; and as for Miss Clementina's goodness—"

"The good God so made her. Now that I am here, let us see what is wrong." He went on to study seriously the young fellow's condition, saying finally that it was in fact of small moment. Miss Clementina had written that he *would* go out without an overcoat, and why was that?

Martin replied that he and another student, who boarded near by, had only one overcoat between them, and wore it day about. Archer made no comment, but asked where Blount lunched.

It appeared that the ladies every day put up a small basket of food, having heard with dismay how and where he had taken this meal.

"And what of dinner?" queried Archer, curious. "You stay away late."

Blount laughed.

"Well, sir, West—that 's my overcoat friend—he markets one week and I the next. When he markets, that week I cook. It 's a great waste of time, but it is fine and cheap."

"And where do you cook?"

"Well, West has a grate-stove, and the people don't mind the smell of fried things. It would n't do here, sir, you see."

"Hardly," said Archer. "Stay in to-morrow—that will be Saturday. Come and lunch with me at one on Sunday. We shall be alone. I want to talk to you."

As Archer drove away, he said to himself:

"I think that boy wants a woman friend, and for the rest, I must tap somebody's purse; my own is rather low. He is having a needlessly hard time."

When Sydney Archer set his mind on anything worth doing it was characteristic of the man that he kept it in view until it was in some way disposed of. It is one of the factors of success. If the matter were small, it recurred to him in his few intervals of leisure. Any larger subject fastened itself upon him so that to escape it or leave it unsettled was quite impossible.

When he said to himself that Martin Blount was worth helping he had in mind the fact he well understood, that, for success in life, Blount needed in some way to be socially educated. It was very like Archer to make so unusual a reflection. He knew that tact and good manners in his own profession enormously assist the essential qualities of mind which he was sure the young student possessed.

As Archer, bent on finding an ally, thought over the available women he knew well enough to ask of them an unusual favor, one constantly presented herself. The nature of Miss Fairthorne was one to which the social evolution of a man like Blount, with good ancestry but untrained taste for the refinements of life, would surely appeal. She was more imaginative than her sister Margaret; but Archer knew, of course, that what he required was a married woman who could be made to share his own interest in this very intelligent waif.

Before his lunch with Blount was over he made up his mind that his guest had a rare combination of the mental and moral qualities needed in the physician's life—a man whom it would be both a duty and a pleasure to help.

"Take a cigar," he said.

"No, sir, thank you. Miss Markham does n't like tobacco, so I gave it up for the time, and if I don't smoke at all it is easier."

"Then you are happily one of what I call the 'unhabituals,' an awkward word for the people who can make and break at will a custom of the body."

"It does not seem to take much will."

"Not for you, or for me. By the by, I spoke of you to a friend of mine, a great banker, and he was so interested that he would like to talk with you a little. To be open with you, Mr. Grace helps a great many people who need help."

"Oh, but I don't want it, and I—"

"Wait a little. You wear an overcoat only on alternate days; you will ruin your stomach with bad food; you are losing time—at least, such habits will in the end lose you time."

"That is so; but—"

"One moment. Grace will lend you money enough to enable you to live a wholesome life. I have an overcoat I bought which is too big for my breadth. Do you mind taking it?" Martin saw through the kindly device, but said at once:

"I! No, sir, I shall be glad; but about the money? Do you think I shall be right? I—I might never repay it."

"I am asking you to do what I did myself. I paid easily. So will you."

"Yes," said Blount, smiling, "but I am not Sydney Archer."

"No, but you are Martin Blount; and if I understand character aright you are going to be among the winners on that front bench folks talk about. Take my advice and take the money. Go to see Mr. Grace to-night. I set nine as the time."

"I will go."

"And so must I," said his host; "sorry to turn you out. Don't study on Sundays."

"I never do. I have too much preacher blood for that. Miss Markham takes me to St. Peter's in the mornings. When I said I had been a Congregationalist for two hundred years she said that she did not know what that was, but that it certainly was an exaggerated mode of stating the case. I would go to a mosque if she asked me. In the afternoon on Sundays I walk all over the country."

The rest of his friendly scheme Archer set aside for the time, until he could interest Mrs. Swanwick.

When, that evening, Martin Blount found Mr. Grace in his own home, that gentleman said to him:

"I wanted to see you, after what Dr. Archer told me. I help a lot of incapables, and it is a pleasure to find a man who does n't want help and ought to have it. I am going to bet on your success, that is all. No, don't interrupt me. It is only a pleasant little gamble. You will call to-morrow at my office, and then the first of each month, and give them my card and your name. You will receive a check for fifty dollars. My clerks will know nothing about it."

"But—"

"Ah, do keep quiet! You are terribly fond of 'buts.' You will give a receipt. This will go on until June."

"I said I would take it," said Blount, flushed and embarrassed. "But, O Lord—"

Grace rose.

"I want to say to you, finally, that if you took this help easily it would lessen the pleasure I have in a simple duty. You have had, as I had, a hard life; let me feel that I am saving a good man from needless risks. And now good-bye; I 'm very, very much obliged to you."

Martin looked up at the clean-shaven, vigorous face, and saw, as Mrs. Swanwick had done, something pathetic in the look which met his own filling eyes. He could not speak. He simply wrung the offered hand and went down-stairs with a choky feeling in his throat. He was still unused to kindness and within the sturdy young fellow was the tender heart of a child and a rare talent for gratitude.

XII

N the afternoon of that Sunday a very different meeting took place. Mrs. Hunter had arrived in the city on Saturday and Lionel Craig called to see her in the evening at the hotel she had preferred to the house of the Misses Markham. She had learned from Lionel's letters enough to make the oversight of two shrewd maiden ladies seem to her an undesirable element in her campaign.

Lionel, in his inefficient way, had been trying to secure some kind of clerkship, but, having only certain mildly worded certificates from the college of business and from a former cautious employer, he had so far failed. As usual, his sister's hopefulness sent him away with the belief that she would readily find him friends and a fresh mood of elation produced in him as usual the feeling that he could now afford luxuries. He stopped at the hotel bar and bought a dozen high-priced cigars. Whatever made his weak nature hopeful, at once made him extravagant.

Mrs. Hunter slept late, with a mind at ease. After her morning bath she lay down on a lounge in her wrapper. For her, also, the probability of success had its effect. She rang, and ordered breakfast in

her room. Despite vigor of mind and body, she was
prone to yield to moods of self-indulgence. Rich
food and all forms of luxurious rest she found pleasant, and would have used strong scents, such as
musk, if she had not been sure that to do so sub-
jected her to disagreeable comment. She was, however, capable of much temporary sacrifice of her
desires. Power she liked for itself, as well as for
any practical values it might have, as people like
food without reference to its nutrient possibilities,
and here was one source of weakness which she
could not resist and did not always apprehend.

She had a fondness for social adventure and a
pleasure in small intrigue such as many men have
in field sports, but she was at present a little tired
of this uncertain existence. When first she met Miss
Morrow she had no distinct views as to her own
future, until as the girl became the ready victim of
her flattery and she heard more and more of her
expectations, she began to think how she could make
use of so easy a capture. The possibility of also
preying upon an old man came to her by degrees.
It was for her no novel game, but it seemed as yet
only an experiment worth a trial.

She read lazily ''La Cousine Bette,'' being a good
French scholar, or lay at rest with half-closed eyes,
dreaming her favorite day-dream of an apartment
in Paris, the Bois, and the opera. She had seen
Paris for a month, and longed for it again.

In the afternoon she dressed with care and found
her way to John Fairthorne's house. Miss Morrow
had gone to Christ Church, St. Agnes's being under

repair, as Mrs. Hunter knew. Enjoying the dry, frosty air, she walked up Second Street, and finding it still too early, turned up Arch Street to the grave-yard of Christ Church. It was open for a burial. She wandered about for a half-hour, looked at the grave of Franklin, smiled at the odd epitaphs, and glad thus to have escaped a part of the service, at last went thence to the old church in Second Street.

She sat down in a back pew, and soon saw amid the scant congregation our devout Kitty. At the close of the service she hastened to a side door, and when Kitty came out was bending over the queerly worded epitaph in which Elizabeth Ferguson is commemorated.

"Dear Mrs. Hunter!" cried Kitty.

"My dearest Katherine! How long it has been, and how pretty you are, child! And who was Elizabeth Ferguson? I shall like to think that when I die you will thus remember me." She pointed to the tombstone.

"Don't talk about dying," said Kitty. "I hate tombstones, and as for Mrs. Ferguson you must ask uncle."

Mrs. Hunter knew all about that unlucky and captivating maker of mischief in a far-away time.

"Come," said Kitty; "you must go home with me. If uncle is not lying down, you must see him. Mary is out in the country with Cousin Margaret, at a farm school. She goes there sometimes on Sunday to teach. It must be an awful bore. I hate dirty boys—poor boys."

"Yes," said Mrs. Hunter, "that is one of the

trials of a refined nature," and they walked on, talking, until they reached Kitty's home. The ample house impressed Mrs. Hunter agreeably. Yes, Mr. Fairthorne was in the library, and without pause Kitty led her friend up-stairs, saying, rapturously, as she entered:

"Oh, Uncle John! Here is Mrs. Hunter!"

It was one of his better days. Fixing his keen eyes on the new-comer, he rose and, with old-fashioned courtesy, made her welcome. He liked handsome women. She caught at once the note of his formal manner, and curtsied slightly as he took her hand and bade her be seated, saying:

"A fine day, madam, a fine day."

"A red-letter day for me," she replied. "I have long hoped for the pleasure of seeing Miss Katherine's relations." A smile, hardly perceptible, indicative of some latent amusement, put Mrs. Hunter on her guard. She had just sat down when Felisa, the cat, moving daintily about, suddenly leaped upon her lap. She liked cats, and said:

"What a compliment, Mr. Fairthorne." Again he smiled.

"Perhaps, madam, perhaps. It is certainly an unusual compliment on the part of Felisa. I am the only Fairthorne she cares for. She has occasional uncertain flirtations with Kitty. But Kitty is not a Fairthorne. We are of other make."

"I was for half an hour in the company of Fairthornes to-day, as I wandered in Christ Church graveyard. I should be afraid if I owned a name like yours that I never could live up to it." He liked the implied flattery.

"I have never troubled myself much as to that," he said. "I have no genealogical conscience, or, at least, no conviction that I must live up to ancestral virtues. They were uneasy, urgent folk. I am making up a human average of repose, an example to my restless countrymen. I produce nothing."

"Oh, Mr. Fairthorne! You may like to say so, but the mind that produced, years ago, that interesting series of papers on the influence of occupation on handwriting and on the effect of different languages on forms of script—" The old man was again pleased.

"Forgotten stuff, madam! You must let me give you a copy."

"Oh, thank you; and with your autograph, please. I am very much interested in autographs. May I not some day hope to be shown your collection?"

"Most gladly, and come soon. There are among them some letters of unusual interest. I am rearranging them now in epochs."

"How delightful!"

"My difficulty lies in the fact that no one method of classifying them suits me." He had, in fact, that excessive desire for method which sometimes defeats its own purpose.

Mrs. Hunter rose, well satisfied.

"I shall take you at your word, Mr. Fairthorne."

He urged her to stay longer. She was too wise, and excusing herself went away with Kitty to her room, while the old man sat still, with a pleasant sense of having had an appreciative visitor. Then he fell asleep.

When, an hour later, Mary and her sister Margaret Swanwick entered he woke up. He did not like to be told he had been asleep, so that, mindful of this, Margaret said:

"Have you had any visitors, uncle?"

"Yes, she has just gone—a most remarkable woman, most intelligent, most appreciative."

"And who was it?" said Mary.

"I told you. How stupid you are, Mary."

"Thank you," said she, laughing; "but as you did not tell us—"

"Oh, well, I thought I did. It was Mrs. Hunter."

"And so we have our Kitty's paragon here at last," said Margaret. "I am a trifle curious."

"She seems to have an interest in autographs that is rather remarkable. I think I may get some ideas from her as to methods of classifying."

Mary glanced at her sister. John Fairthorne had never been easy of approach and his first judgment of strangers was apt to be tinged with cynical dispraise.

"Is she handsome, uncle?" asked Margaret. He said cautiously:

"Well, rather," and then, rising, he said he thought it was time for his nap, and so left them. It was now near dusk.

"He has forgotten his drive and his nap," said Mary; "that is unusual for uncle."

"A total stranger—a woman Kitty has picked up, heaven knows why! It is unlike him, altogether unlike him. Why should she have taken to Kitty so abruptly? Do you know anything about the woman? Tom Masters says she is intelligent. That is hardly descriptive. When he added that she dressed well and had a neat figure, he seemed to feel that he had said enough.''

''Did you ask him, like a good Philadelphian, who she was?''

''I did not, but Harry did. Tom, I am given to understand, said he 'd be-something if he knew—and what did that matter?''

''Certain it is that she has captured Kitty, interested Mr. Knellwood and now has pleased Uncle John. I wish I could, dear; it is pretty hard here at times.''

''Well, we ought to be glad that he has found one human being who interests him. I hope she will help to keep him in a good humor. Does she stay long in town?''

''I do not know; very likely Kitty does.''

XIII

HE winter had begun early in stormy earnest, with unusually heavy falls of snow. Archer was busy and made short visits to Mr. Fairthorne, and secondary visits of varying length to Kitty. Mr. Knellwood was absent while his chapel was under repair. The mild gaieties of the cold season went on to Kitty's satisfaction. Mr. Grace dropped in now and then at Mrs. Swanwick's. Lionel Craig grumbled in a small way and idled, a purposeless man, unless to crave unearned luxuries may be called a purpose.

For a few days Mrs. Hunter contented herself with Kitty. They drove together, for it was Kitty who commonly monopolized her uncle's carriage when bad weather forbade his driving. Her cousin Mary preferred a walk or a ride, defying all weather.

Mrs. Hunter waited. Mr. Fairthorne seemed to have forgotten her, but at last she moved the pawn.

"Kitty, I am a little hurt, dear," she said, "that your cousins have not called on me." Kitty felt that her own society ought to satisfy her friend, but when that lady said that it was really not very respectful to Kitty, the latter saw fit to act on a hint from Mrs. Hunter, and finding her uncle one day in the state in which Kitty's demonstrative attentions were agreeable, she said, as she played with his hair:

"Don't you think Mary ought to call on Mrs. Hunter, uncle? I think she would like to come often to see you, and me, too; but, of course, she feels, you know—" here Kitty's memory failed her. She paused.

"Well, what the deuce does she feel?"

"Oh, she does admire you so much. She says you are the best talker she ever knew."

The old man smiled feebly. He was this day a little inert, a little weary of a life he had made monotonous. At another time he might have turned on her, cynically critical of her ill-played game.

"Quite right," he said. "Remind me, and I will see to it. I shall insist on her being treated with respect. Where is Mary? Send her to me."

Kitty, pleased, but a little dubious, found Mary busy in her room.

"Uncle wants you," she said.

"What, already?" said Mary, rising. "It is hardly ten." She followed Kitty, who was too curious and too eager not to desire to see how her suggested scheme would work. Mrs. Hunter really cared little that Miss Fairthorne should call. Kitty was, as yet, enough her friend; but what she also desired was to establish some closer relation with the uncle and yet to seem in no haste. Miss Fairthorne, however, had seen fit not to call on her, and Mrs. Hunter could not resist the wish to make her do so. She

8

had been wiser to have refrained from the use of power which could do her no good.

Mr. Fairthorne had recovered the memory of a handsome, appreciative woman. Kitty kissed and caressed him and bored him. Mary had too positive views, and many interests. As for Madge, she was "too damned logical for a woman." As he grew more feeble, his self-esteem cast off the garments of his training and the crude appetite for praise grew upon him. He had also the old man's hidden fear of loss of consideration. He said to Kitty, as her cousin followed:

"What was it I wanted Mary for?" This was more than Kitty had expected. She said promptly:

"I do not know, sir," but she colored a little as she told her lie, and this did not escape her cousin's eye.

"Why do you lie," said Fairthorne, "you little cat! You want Mary to call on Mrs. Hunter. Quite right, too, quite right. I wish you to call, Mary; I desire you to ask her to dine. I need intelligent society. I am neglected by everybody."

"If," said Mary, "you want me to call upon Mrs. Hunter I will do so."

"Yes, to-day."

"Kitty asked me, but I saw no reason why I should call, and the little I know of her—" She checked herself. "I did not know that Kitty really cared whether I went or not. The fact is, I forgot all about it. I am sorry she thought it necessary to appeal to you. I will call on Mrs. Hunter—"

"And ask Margaret to call," he said.

"That," said Mary, "I must ask you to do, uncle. Is there anything else?"

"No, that is all."

That afternoon she went, but she was not eager to find Mrs. Hunter, and was relieved to hear that she was out. Happy to be done with it, she walked up Walnut Street, rejoicing in the snow and the blue sky. Glad of a change of human company, she went on to her sister's house. Her uncle had twice recalled her, and had kept her occupied for many hours of the morning, but now, tingling with the wholesome freshness of the winter air, she felt renewed in mind and temper, and went gaily up-stairs. As she entered, Madge said:

"Mr. Grace, Mary." Tom Masters also greeted her, and she sat down, well pleased to know the banker of whom Dr. Archer had said enough to excite her curiosity and secure her esteem.

"I see you ride," he said, "and in all weathers, Miss Fairthorne, and are fond, too, of my own favorite resort—the meadows of the Neck."

They talked of how much it was like Holland and of how bad the roads were, and at last he said:

"I used to see your uncle on horseback, but I suppose he is now too old; a pity he has become such a hermit, I might say an intellectual hermit; I fancy he never did take any large interest in the life and politics of the city."

"Nor of the nation, I am sorry to say. He voted for Lincoln, but has never voted since, and what political principles he has he inherited. He says he is a Federalist."

"So was Washington, and I think would not have been on the side of his State had he lived in those sad sixties."

"Do you yourself take any keen interest in politics, Mr. Grace?"

"I?—of course. It is a duty."

Mary Fairthorne liked the imperative way in which he spoke.

"I wish all the younger men shared your conviction; to feel as strongly as I do and to be absolutely without voice or influence is most unpleasant."

"And would you like to vote?" he asked.

"I do not see why I should not." At this moment Kitty entered, and Mary, amused at the thought her coming suggested, added: "But I should like to choose the female voters."

"And I the men," he cried.

Miss Kitty sat down between Mr. Masters and Margaret.

"Oh, Mr. Masters, I am glad to see you. I saw you at the Assembly, but we had not even one dance." He felt this to be brutal. He was still sore with a very real pain, but Miss Kitty was like a cat which, having left a captured mouse, returns at intervals to see if there be any life worth sporting with. Margaret watched her, half sorry, half disgusted.

"I wish," she thought, "that Kitty was not so obvious."

Meanwhile, Mr. Grace asked Miss Fairthorne if she chanced to know a Mrs. Lucretia Hunter.

"Pardon my question. She has brought her brother to me, and wants a place for him in my office. I ask you because she gave me to understand that she knew you all. A clever woman, I thought. The brother did not impress me very favorably. I rather think the sister has had a hard life.''

Mary was at once on her guard.

"She is a friend of my cousin, Miss Morrow. I personally do not know her well.''

"Then I must ask Miss Morrow,'' he said. "How very pretty she is.'' He was feeling with all the force of his natural but untrained refinement the pleasantness of the society into which he was slowly finding his way. Of course he overestimated what to him was so freshly agreeable and when Miss Kitty, as Masters moved away, turned upon him the fatal artillery of youth and physical loveliness, he accepted without reserve Miss Kitty's estimate of her friend. When he spoke of the brother with some doubt Miss Morrow said it would be a real charity at least to give him a chance. This decided him, and he readily assented.

"Now, how nice it would be if I could tell my friend that you would oblige her—and me,'' she added, turning her childlike blue eyes upon the strong face of Roger Grace. They had done, in their time, much wilful mischief, but never ignorantly so much as now.

"I am glad to oblige you. I will give him a chance.''

Kitty thanked him warmly, and, after further talk, he went away with Miss Morrow, as Dr. Archer entered.

"Your uncle is very wilful to-day, Miss Mary," said the doctor. "Do you see how fast he is changing?"

"I do. His love of method is at times really a mania and no method suits him long. He used to be courteous and to apologize for his irritability. Now he never does. My cousin Kitty has a love affair with him one day and the next drives him frantic."

"He must be easily vexed. How any one can quarrel with so gentle a being as Miss Katherine I do not see."

Mrs. Swanwick smiled to herself. Mary did not smile.

"It is strange that at times he should yet be his old interesting self," continued Archer. "He talked to me very long about Mrs. Hunter, Miss Katherine's friend."

"Indeed," said Mrs. Swanwick, "I suppose we should be glad that she is willing to amuse him."

Mary was silent, and, after some less personal talk, Archer asked if Mr. Swanwick was at home. No, he was not. The women discussed the Farm School Home and minor matters, while Archer sat still. At last Madge said: "You are quiet, Sydney. Are you tired?"

"No," he said, "I was only indulging in the privilege of giving my tongue a holiday. I talk all day; no one has to talk as much as a doctor."

"And yet," said Miss Fairthorne, laughing, "people say women will not make good doctors."

"They can be anything," said Margaret, decisively; "if they should be is quite another matter. As I see it, celibacy is essential to a woman doctor. You cannot compromise with this tremendously natural business of motherhood."

"You touch the true question," said Archer. They went on to discuss eagerly other questions then maturing in regard to the need to enlarge the education of women. When presently he and Madge spoke of nurses and of their want of a fuller preliminary education, Mary, who had listened with interest, said:

"I should like to be a nurse." The craving for some exacting rôle of duty had of late been much in her mind.

"You would make a good one," said Archer.

"I am not sure," she returned. "I might fancy hospital work. Do you yourself prefer ward work to private practice?"

"Oh, both—both; but the wards for study. By the way, when you go to the Farm School of a Sunday your readings in our men's ward are greatly missed."

"Are they indeed?" She flushed joyously. "Thank you, but you fail to really answer us."

"Yes, you must not get me on to my hobby. Take the best and ablest of men, give him the heart of St. John, give genius, every accomplishment, and he will never rise to the ideal level of the perfect physician. There is no life fit to compare to it."

"The clergyman's?" asked Margaret.

"Oh, no! That has too many limitations. No! Ah, see how you have trapped me."

He was waiting for Miss Fairthorne to go. She lingered, half unwillingly. This man affected her as no other had ever done. Secure in her modestly guarded secret, she was now yielding to the mere pleasure of being in Archer's company.

Seeing, at last, that Miss Mary was for some reason of no mind to leave, he said to himself:

"Why, after all, may I not talk myself out before her?" He set about his kindly business artfully.

"Do you not think Grace an interesting specimen of the best kind of our self-made men?"

"Oh, yes," said Miss Fairthorne. "I saw several of the species last year in Washington, but none like Mr. Grace. Usually they were handicapped by some commonplace wife."

"The man who means to rise," said Mrs. Swanwick, "who means to make himself, ought to marry at forty. The woman partner is very important. It is amazing how some men who rise from the soil assimilate all that is best in life. I do not think that the same class of woman has this power."

"Has she ever a man's opportunities?" asked Mary.

"No, perhaps not," returned Archer. "Speaking of Grace reminds me of a young fellow who just now interests me a good deal." He went on to tell very cleverly of the partnership in the overcoat and of the domestic economies of the two young men, sketching at last with much adroitness the sad, homeless life and the strong mental and moral character of Martin Blount.

"And so our dear white mice, the Markhams, are

caring for him!'' said Miss Fairthorne. ''Clementina spoke of him to me. If you need any help—if he needs money—you might let me do my share.''

Archer laughed, well pleased.

''No, that is provided for. He won a scholarship, and the rest is assured.

''Ah!'' said Mary. ''I envy him the battle of life.''

''He will win, but just now the man needs something else. He is socially untrained, and, alas! where is there a college for manners? He is unneat, careless as to dress, and you will shudder at his nails. In fact, he ate with his knife until Miss Markham mildly mentioned the desirability of using the fork. But, really, he is worth polishing. He is only by the accidents of misfortune a son of the soil.''

''Why not bring him here?'' said Mrs. Swanwick.

''I wanted you to say that. And now I may tell you what is strange, that he and I have a common descent, as we both share the blood of Edward Fitz Randolph, who came to Massachusetts in 1640. My people finally went to Carolina; Blount's were a race of New England clergymen, governors, and soldiers. He has some of their grimness. Of course, this far-away kinship interests me. Will you help him?''

''Bring him here on Sunday night, and I will see.''

''Very good,'' and he left. Then Mary said: ''Uncle made me call on Mrs. Hunter, but I refused to ask you to do so. He will ask you himself, unless he forgets it. I have seen her twice with Kitty, and I still marvel why a woman of education and so clever should take a fancy to Kit. I suppose Kitty will drop her as she does friends and lovers. There is something about the woman I do not fancy. What it is I cannot tell, but I can usually predict my dislikes.''

"How feminine that is, Mary!"

"Well, it is none the worse for that."

"But you must have some grounds. What are they?"

"She is—well, she is furtive."

"The synonym for stealthy, dear."

"There are no such things as synonyms. She is furtive and may be stealthy. Furtive I insist upon. However, we shall see. Meanwhile, good or bad, she is interesting."

"And so is Sydney Archer. How well he told his little story. I wish Kitty would let him alone. He is quite too good for her."

"I hope you will not interfere." She knew Madge well. "Please do not. It would be useless, quite useless, Madge, and he will never marry Kitty."

"Why do you think so?"

"I know, I do not think."

"Some time ago, Mary, I had a suspicion that—"

"Nonsense! Oh, there is Harry. It is late and he must walk home with me. By-by, dear," and she went down to capture her brother-in-law in the hall, while Margaret said to herself:

"I was foolish to talk to Mary." Nevertheless, she knew herself so well that she was sure she should some day yield to the temptation to warn or advise

Sydney Archer. She was sometimes too much inclined to interfere in other folk's affairs, not, like Mrs. Hunter, from mere love of rule, but because, being a warm friend, the desire to help and her belief in her own judgment were apt to conquer in the end.

XIV

FEW days later Mrs. Hunter, walking to and fro under the bare trees in what we still call the State-House yard, talked to her brother.

"Lionel, you now have a good place and the best chance you have ever had. I know you will try hard." She had her doubts.

Of course he would try, but the salary was very small, and those old ladies very disagreeably particular.

"And yet, you must stay," she said. "I am making friends for you and for myself." She said no word as to what her schemes were. As far as possible she hid from him what might appear too crooked in a rather seamy life. She wished the only person she loved to think well of her. But far more did she desire him to be all that she was not. Her own cravings were for ease, luxury, dress, music. Her ambitions for him were far higher. With his looks and manners, for here she lost power to be critical, what might he not do and be? She promised him that before long he should see Kitty, and perhaps, who knows— They both laughed. But, above all, he must satisfy Mr. Grace, and now he must go. It was time he went to the office.

She herself had lingered for this talk on her way to visit Mr. Fairthorne, who had asked for her again and again. She had pretended occupation, and waited.

Kitty was, as usual, delighted to see her. No one else listened to her good-humored prattle as did Mrs. Hunter. They kissed a good deal, and Kitty said: "Uncle expects you to-day, and I hope, too, you will see Mary. Father Knellwood will be here to make an appointment about the meeting of the altar society. You must join it. I was sure you would."

Mrs. Hunter was happy at the thought of meeting him, and would do whatever her dear Kitty desired. What a pleasure to see that the decorations of the altar were all that they should be. There was ordinarily so much bad taste in religion. Kitty treasured the phrase for future use.

As Mary Fairthorne was continually taking herself to task for something done or thought, it was natural for her to feel that on too small grounds she had harshly judged her cousin's friend. Certainly Miss Morrow was injudicious in her unfaltering admiration of her new friend, and had never learned that excess of praise is apt, for obvious reasons, to provoke a tendency toward suspicious undervaluing of the thing praised. Mary thought of this and of the injustice it may occasion. When she was told that Mrs. Hunter had come to see Mr. Fairthorne, she rose in the freshness of self-condemnation, resolved to be very pleasant to Mrs. Hunter.

As she went down-stairs she remembered that Mr. Masters had once asked Margaret Swanwick what would happen if folks tired of themselves could have a character auction and sell out and buy in.

"What," thought Mary, "would Kitty's fetch? or Mrs. Hunter's?" The idea had amused and also a little surprised her, until Masters had said it was Pilgrim's wisdom. Meeting Mrs. Hunter on the stairs, she addressed her with a graciousness which gained something from her unusual height and made her greeting seem like a generous compliment to the guest of the hour.

"I am glad to see you," she said, as she turned to reascend the stair. "I was not so fortunate as to find you at home."

Mrs. Hunter, who was prepared by self-knowledge to expect a hostile, or at least a cool reception, at once became cordial.

"You were very good to call on me, Miss Fairthorne. I know how full your life is and how little leisure you must have."

A mildly critical comment arose in Mary's mind, an instinctive sense that this lady, with her good taste in dress and her intelligence, was not an entirely well-bred woman. She said:

"I hope to be more fortunate in future. My uncle sees very few people, but he has been asking for you, and is very well to-day, which is not always the case. Mrs. Hunter, Uncle John." She set a chair near him, as he said: "I am very glad to see you. Sit down; excuse my not rising. I am not very strong to-day, but I can always talk. If that confounded doctor did not dose me I should be better. I have no faith in his tribe."

Mary laughed.

"But if he misses seeing you every day you do not like it."

"Mere habit! A question of habit. He is intelligent enough, and talks well. If I do not take his stuff he stays away and then I miss the talk. We all believe in drugs, sort of fetich—a survival of the medicine man."

"That depends," said Mrs. Hunter. "From all I hear, Dr. Archer is an unusual man and a very original thinker. I have long wished to see him."

"Then you can have a consultation presently," said Kitty, who was restlessly moving about, while Felisa again made herself comfortable on Mrs. Hunter's lap, to the surprise of Miss Fairthorne. She, herself, did not like cats, and now she fancied this woman a little less because of Felisa's sudden friendliness. She said to herself:

"How ridiculous of me!"

Her uncle, rather amused, went on talking of cats and of Washington's aversion to them and of the odd fact that cats are not mentioned in the Bible.

"Perhaps that was because the Egyptians worshiped cats," said Mrs. Hunter.

"Or perhaps," returned Mary, "because there are so few mice in the Bible."

Mrs. Hunter knew a woman who fainted when a cat was in the room, and wondered why to see a caged tiger did not kill her outright. She talked well and had read enough to sustain the delusion of having read more. She asked questions and received the replies of Fairthorne with an air of surprise and satisfaction; but playing to this double audience tasked all her power and she was relieved when Miss Fairthorne rose.

Mary had remained long enough to feel assured that her uncle was for that hour well pleased and that she might without discourtesy escape. She said, when for a moment there was a pause:

"You will pardon me if I leave you with my uncle."

A few minutes later, Kitty, who was never long at rest, said she too must be excused for a few minutes, and thus, at last, Lucretia found herself alone with her host, a coveted chance.

The woman who sat beside John Fairthorne more than satisfied his exactions as to face and figure, for, like a greater philosopher of his own city, he is said to have remarked that in women he liked best moderate intelligence, capacity to listen, and a good figure; and as for the face, that was of less moment. In his narrowing life he had grown to be observant of things which escape the inattentively busy and, in fact, liked to waste in the futile study of handscripts a mind which, although once capable enough, had suffered from lazy disuse and later from personal dislike of the competitions of life.

After a half-hour of chat, Mrs. Hunter suddenly rose and, with the joyousness of a girl, cried:

"Oh, Mr. Fairthorne, is not that a portrait of General Wayne? Pardon me, I must look at it." The picture, a Kitcat portrait, was framed by the bookshelves around it, and was the only picture in the library, a room which extended across the sixty-feet width of the house. Mrs. Hunter stood with hands behind her back.

"What a virile face," she said.

Meanwhile, John Fairthorne watched her, and, excited by this new visitor, talked on as she gazed at the great soldier or turned her animated face toward her host. He was in the presence of an actress so great that she was sometimes for the moment the person she was acting.

"I am glad you like it," he said. "The artist is unknown. Some day you must come to our country home. Most of my family portraits are there. We will drive over to St. David's, where Wayne lies buried. My great-uncle was on his staff at Stony Point."

"Yes, I know," she said; "George Fairthorne."

She remained before the portrait, while her host, more critically considering her, said to himself:

"What an ivory-like skin—yes, a pearl hue." He was pleased to have found the right word. "Interesting face, noticeable face." Strongly pronounced eyebrows, large, deeply-set eyes, passionless and rather thin, very red lips contributed to her general expression something which inevitably attracted, but did not quite satisfy.

"Devilish handsome," he concluded. Perhaps that did describe her and was a better summary than he guessed it to be.

"Sit down," he said. "I cannot hear well at a distance, but I hear your voice unusually clearly." He did.

She moved a chair close to his, and slowly, with

9

purpose, drew off her gloves, saying, as if the act suggested the remark:

"What pretty hands Miss Kitty has!"

"Hands!" he returned. "No character in them —none! No character in them; you may see that in her writing. I could describe her hand from the abominable scrawl she writes."

"Indeed? That is beyond my skill. You must pardon a stranger if I say that you have the ideal masculine hand, the hand of intellect and refinement." She had heard of this as one of his small vanities.

"Ah!" he said, with his old-world manner, "the value of flattery lies in the flatterer."

"No, no," she cried. "It would be true if Münchhausen had said it. But could you from my hand tell how I write? See, sir," and she set forth for inspection her most faultless possession, a nearly perfect hand. The old gentleman took it in his, looked it over and retained it, as if forgetful.

"Yes, I could tell."

"But you have seen my writing."

"Yes, yes, very true," he laughed; "that assists one," and still he kept his prisoner.

Mrs. Hunter, hearing some one coming up the stairs, said:

"Do you not think, sir, you have sufficiently inspected my hand?" She laughed gaily, gently setting herself free, and rising as she added: "I fear you are not always to be trusted in these studies. Bad people do say that you were very fatal to my sex."

"Chut, chut!" he cried, much delighted. "I am past all such follies—a broken old man. Age has—"

"Age!" she broke in. "Time has taken with one hand and given with the other."

"Very pretty that, madam; very neat, but damned nonsense. Pardon me, I have the bad ways of the men of my day."

"But they were men!" she cried. "And now, good-bye, and may I, may I say I have a good deal of leisure? Miss Fairthorne is busy, Miss Katherine otherwise occupied," and she smiled. "If ever you have any work on your autographs you could let me do at home, I should feel honored."

"Thank you. I may take you at your word; but you would have to work here. I could not trust my autographs out of my house—not even with you, madam."

"Oh! I beg pardon, of course not. How could I have ventured to think of such a thing!" She never had believed that he would, and when he returned: "But perhaps you will come and look over them with me," she said that would be an added pleasure, and asked when it would suit him.

"Why not to-morrow?" he said.

"How delightful! And about this hour? About eleven?"

"Yes, that would do. We shall be quite alone then. Ah! Do not go. Here is my daily nuisance, my doctor. Archer," he rose with some effort, "permit me to present you to Mrs. Hunter."

Archer took her hand, and, interested by what he

had heard of her, looked her over quickly with an eye trained to observe, and trained also not to seem to observe. He thought her appearance singular— an unusual type—but she was Miss Morrow's friend. Nevertheless, he vaguely felt the serpent-like power of this woman to attract and still to be what he hesitated to call repellent.

"I was about to leave, Dr. Archer," she said, "but I am glad to see you, if only for a moment. You will hardly believe me, but I have read your essay in the 'Atlantic' on the 'Medical Organization of the Roman Armies.'" It was a little bit of the literary by-play of a busy life and the one of his minor essays which had given him the most pleasure. Needless to say, she knew it by title only. He did not see why he ought to feel surprise at her having read it, but he did. He disliked to be the subject of discussion, so that when she asked Mr. Fairthorne if he had read Dr. Archer's book on the "Psychology of Childhood," he turned the talk, saying:

"Oh, no one reads that but mothers, and they do not understand it. How are you to-day, Mr. Fairthorne?"

Mrs. Hunter accepted the hint and, hoping she might soon have the pleasure of a longer talk, went away to the library Franklin founded and spent an hour over the book last in question. She thought, as she closed it:

"A strong man, that. He may be in the way. Shall he marry Kitty or not? I think not. I want her. I must know Mary Fairthorne better. Yes," she said, "that will do; I must make her life easier, and I can."

Here her confidence in her own capacity misled her. Her love of rule was certain to be the successful foe of her politic wish.

XV

RS. HUNTER wrote next day and excused herself to Mr. Fairthorne. She had some literary work to do. He was vexed, and made both his nieces feel his disappointment. The day after Kitty reported that Mrs. Hunter had a headache. Even Mary began to think that a visit from Kitty's friend might be desirable, but what with one excuse and another Lucretia failed to appear. She was playing her fish with patient skill.

When, after some days, Mary Fairthorne came in about noon, she found Mrs. Hunter busy over a table covered with portfolios of autographs. Her uncle, hearing her, let fall the hand he had laid on Mrs. Hunter's shoulder, as he stood beside her chair.

"Come in, Mary," he said cheerfully. "Mrs. Hunter has given me a hint as to how to cross-catalogue. We are going to try it on the reign of Anne. Authors and the subject of their letters. Will you give Mrs. Hunter some lunch? We are through for to-day."

Mary, who always found it hard to believe ill of anybody, although by no means drawn to Mrs. Hunter, had no valid suspicions of evil against Kitty's friend and was for a while a little amused and considerably relieved by her frequent visits to John Fairthorne. She had put aside as without foundation the impression that lady had made upon her and now pleasantly insisted upon her coming down to lunch.

Mrs. Hunter was here on new ground. The old silver and the buff-and-gold Nankin china pleased her, as did the bowl of roses on the table, the ease of her hostess. She talked quietly and well of the latest books, of her pleasure that her brother was with Mr. Grace, and altogether made a good impression. When at last Mary asked if she meant to remain long in the city she said two or three months; that she was doing some magazine work on which she was, to some extent, dependent. That she picked up a little money by writing items for a New York journal she did not state. She went on to add that she was in Philadelphia chiefly to use the library of the Historical Society.

"I envy you work that you must do," said Mary.

"It is pleasant to find in my life anything that a woman like you can envy. I am to write a series of articles on the women of colonial times."

"I am sure that my uncle could help you. He knows—oh, wickedly well!—everybody's family history."

"Yes, he has already given me useful hints; and will you pardon me if I say something unusual?"

"Certainly," said Mary, smiling. "What is it?"

"He has asked me—you heard what he said—to aid him in the cataloguing of his collection; but I did feel, Miss Fairthorne, I do feel that, as it would make me a frequent visitor, I could not say frankly yes, until I learned whether it would be entirely agreeable to you. Katherine thinks that it would really relieve you. I think you must understand my very reasonable hesitation. I have the time, and, frankly, it will be of more or less use to me in a variety of ways. Mr. Fairthorne has such remarkable literary sympathies—'' She felt she had made a mistake. Something in Mary's look told her this as the girl replied a little coldly:

''I really can see no objection.'' After all, it was her uncle's affair, not hers; and it would at least relieve her in a measure. She added, more cordially: ''I think my uncle enjoys your assistance. Whatever pleases him pleases us.''

Mrs. Hunter felt that for the time this was enough and, the lunch being over, they rose, as a servant announced that Mr. Knellwood was in the drawing-room to see Miss Morrow, but that Miss Katherine was out. She had an easy way of forgetting engagements. Mary said:

''Perhaps he will wait. I have an engagement. I must go out. You will excuse me.''

''If you will allow me, I will join Mr. Knellwood and wait for your cousin.''

''Certainly, if you like,'' and Mrs. Hunter was shown into the dismal drawing-room.

Mr. Knellwood had been out of town, as we have said, and on his return had found several notes from Miss Kitty. He had penitently schooled himself while absent and returned serious and full of self-reproach and his usual fervor. Miss Kitty's notes were of no moment; but he had now another errand. He wanted money. He always wanted money, and it was hard to resist him. Roger Grace simply asked "How much?" and John Fairthorne, who was indifferent about the poor, gave because giving was a traditional family habit, and because, as he said, when Mary grew curious about motives: "Well, I do not go to church—must do something, and, besides, I like Knellwood." Margaret Swanwick said this was vague; and Mary replied that a very fair amount of human goodness was vague and not always to be explained.

Miss Kitty was a person who made tremendous confidences and now Lucretia was her advisory confessor and knew as well as a shrewd woman could know the veering winds of Kitty's mind. Herself cold and passionless, she could not fully apprehend the influence which this self-indulgent beauty exerted over so many men. It was the force which in all ages has mocked the rivalry of every other feminine influence—mere bodily perfection, with the animal instinct of desire to capture. It is apt in the end to make passionate surrender to some coarse athlete, or, at least, to fall sense-wakened before some man of athletic build. Women like Kitty are ruled by their instincts.

Mrs. Hunter, without clearly understanding why, soon saw that for Kitty the nobly built clergyman was a heart-risk larger than the more accomplished physician. She meant, however, to own Kitty body and soul, and, looking far ahead, intended that neither man should marry her. The game grew difficult, but this player enjoyed it.

"Father Knellwood," she said, as she noted with surprise the upright carriage of the athletic priest, and his drawn, ascetic features, "allow me to present myself—I am Mrs. Hunter, and I am more glad to see you than I can say."

She saw his failure to put out his hand. He avoided this manual greeting like a nun, and Mrs. Hunter knew it in time.

"Miss Morrow has spoken much of you, and I have had, too, your very interesting letters. I am glad of the chance of learning what kind of work you desire. I have been away for a while."

She replied that she had already joined the altar society. He smiled a kindly, gradual smile, and said:

"That is hardly work, you know, Mrs. Hunter."

"Oh, no! But I thought I would wait a little and see." She was not quite free enough to visit among the poor. Her magazine work left her tired and she was not yet strong enough.

The rector considered briefly the compact figure and the clear, ivory-like tint of her face, and said:

"I find, myself, that helping Christ's poor is a marvelous tonic."

"Soon or late," she returned, "you shall have all there is of me to give."

"Not I, but another, my dear lady. Now I must leave you. I came to beg a little from Miss Katherine. She is generous, indeed lavish, when she has means, but as she is still under age she has not as much to give as Miss Mary."

"Let me help you, Mr. Knellwood. That the little I can offer is of my own making may give it value. Do you think the widow had earned the mite she gave? I often wonder."

The rector took the five-dollar note, and said:

"A gift thanks the giver, they say in Syria; and what an interesting thought about the widow's mite! Perhaps it had been given to her. Ah, well, I seem always to get what I want."

"One moment, Mr. Knellwood," she said, as they both rose; "you must let me call you Father. It makes possible so much that otherwise—but you understand."

"I shall hope to do so." He bowed slightly, a little on guard, and for that reason the more courteous.

"May I ask that what I am about to say be considered as a confidence? I do not mean that the knowledge may not be used but—but that— Oh! I am so troubled! It is about my friend, Katherine Morrow. The girl has become very dear to my childless life." Mr. Knellwood's hand went up to the cross on his broad chest, and then, dropping it, fell to buttoning a neglected button of his long coat.

"Pray go on," he said. Then Mrs. Hunter felt secure, and, speaking with well-acted embarrassment, said:

"If you are Katherine's confessor" (she knew he had been) "you must, as the friend of her soul, feel as I do that this dear child is in some danger of giving her heart to a man without distinct beliefs, to one to whom all that we hold dearest is—not what it is to us—to you—to me."

"Do you mean Sydney Archer?" he said, faintly.

"Yes," she said, surprised at his directness.

"But," and he straightened himself, seeing with honest scorn a temptation in his path, "I think you are mistaken as to his opinions."

"I may be; but Kitty, who spoke of it, was herself shocked. Perhaps in my spiritual distress I have done wrong, but I thought that if some one— if you, her confessor, could add your warning to aid the small influence I possess— Oh, Father Knellwood, it is so hard to do right—to be sure one is right."

"That is true for all of us. We can only prayerfully consider a course of action and then do as seems right. God asks no more of us."

"Thank you. I did fear so much that you might not understand me."

"What you have said to me is a very grave matter. I suspect that both you and Miss Morrow are wrong as to Dr. Archer's opinions. But no matter what they are, I can do nothing, and my advice to you, if you asked it, would be to let the matter drop —I said if you asked my advice."

"I do, I do indeed. That is why I spoke."

"Then, have you asked for wiser guidance than mine? Have you done this?"

Something out of the past, out of her youth, made her hesitate to lie about prayer. She said:

"No."

"Then you know what to do. With Miss Katherine you can, of course, talk freely. You may be doing her and Dr. Archer incalculable wrong."

"I am glad to know that I may be mistaken, but, in any case, I shall never forget your kindness."

He had done what he thought right and said what he thought true. Now he stood nervously grasping the cross he wore.

"I ought to say further, Mrs. Hunter, that on my return, in rearranging our parish work, it has appeared better to assign the confessions of some of my parishioners to an older man than I." Here he felt that he was needlessly self-explanatory.

"He is hard hit," thought Mrs. Hunter. "He is afraid of her."

"Pardon me. You are no doubt right. I abide by your decision," she said meekly, "and I do hope you feel that in speaking to you I could have but one motive." He smiled pleasantly.

"Rest easy as to that." Indeed, he was a man who thought ill of no one and moved with charitable tenderness of explanation amid the crimes and follies of the poor and the rich.

He went away, saying to himself:

"Here is a good woman ignorantly tempting me. Oh, let her marry whom she will!" and then the fair face and figure filled his soul with yearning, and he thought of a home and Kitty, of children, and how he loved them. He went up the street, tramping down the gathering snow and praying as he went. He was the victim of a self-made, revocable vow, and the strong, natural man was in revolt.

Mrs. Hunter waited, smiling as she looked out of the window after him. She had no entire faith in any one.

"If," she said, "he does something—speaks to that other priest—it will do no harm. If he does not? Well, I know now that he loves the girl. He is the very person to attract her, and he will never marry her—never; but he will kill the doctor's chance."

Kitty did not come in and Mrs. Hunter went home to the company of a French novel.

XVI

IME went its lavish way. The weeks passed and Mrs. Hunter gradually became more and more important to John Fairthorne. Several things helped her. Many disliked the uninteresting work of mere cataloguing, but did it at need with the honesty and dutifulness she brought to all the tasks of life. Kitty hated and did not do it—in fact, was incompetent. She caressed and kissed her uncle and slyly fled. Mrs. Hunter relieved them both.

One day Dr. Archer came in and found Mrs. Hunter reading aloud to Mr. Fairthorne Landor's "Imaginary Conversations." She read well, but not better than Mary, who liked to read to him because he usually fancied the English classics and on his better days was interestingly critical. Archer was a little surprised. He paused a moment, pleased with the voice as it rose and fell.

"You read admirably," he said. Mrs. Hunter started a little.

"Thank you. Let me detain you a moment as you go out."

When this occurred, she said to him in the drawing-room:

"Mr. Fairthorne's left arm has been twitching all day."

"Yes, I noticed it—an old symptom. Where is Miss Mary?"

"She is lying down."

"Not ill?" he said, quickly.

"I do not know. She has sent for Dr. Soper. Rather an old-fashioned kind of M.D., I fancy." Archer contributed no comment and she went on: "If you will kindly tell me what you want done, I will see to it until Miss Mary can do so. Miss Katherine is out. Is Mr. Fairthorne very ill? Is he in any danger?" The service she was performing Archer had of course observed. The question seemed natural.

"He may live a year or two, or die at any hour. The family know what is my opinion."

"He has been very good to me. I shall be at your orders."

Archer gave her the needed directions, which involved some changes. She pleased him by her accuracy and the intelligence of her questions and he went away well satisfied. Nor was Mrs. Hunter less pleased. To do full justice to these new duties made it needful that she should return in the afternoons. What could have been more lucky! She was not eager for Miss Fairthorne's recovery.

But no human sky is long cloudless. There was Lionel. She was thinking of him when, returning, she found Mr. Fairthorne dozing over a book. She sat down as if to work, but really for a chance to consider tranquilly certain too urgent questions. Usually, when new to a place, Lionel was sure to be for a little while attentive to his work, and to make no serious claims upon her purse; but now, although he had been only a few weeks in Grace's office, he was every few days asking her for loans which were such only in name. Worse still, she had received a curt note from the banker's partner stating that Lionel was so unpunctual that he must either reform or leave the office.

As if to emphasize her annoyance, Craig was bored, tired of the little ladies, and was picking up idle company, for want of better, as he said. Mrs. Hunter felt him to be a sad encumbrance, but he was the one thing on earth she loved better than she loved Lucretia Hunter.

She put him aside for the time, and turned over the autographs. She had been well educated, and, more lazy in body than in mind, had found in her present surroundings a great deal that honestly interested and much about which she pretended interest. Above all, there were ease and luxury. Just now a portfolio of musical autographs attracted her. She looked them over carelessly. There were scores or portions of them by Schubert, Haydn, Mendelssohn, a song with Beethoven's setting. Each was in a cover with the date and place of purchase and the price. She read their values with amazement and with a sudden sense of temptation and an idea that here, in case of need, might be a valuable resource. The risk would be small. She was capable of long-continued use of evil means, but had never stolen, and had a certain fear of definite crime. Hearing some one on the stair, she closed the portfolio and went down.

10

It was Dr. Soper, who had been to visit Miss Fairthorne.

"Dr. Soper, I believe. I am Mrs. Hunter, Mr. Fairthorne's—" She hesitated and added: "Mr. Fairthorne's amanuensis. Since Miss Mary's indisposition I have been taking care of her uncle. For three days now she has been off duty and her uncle desires me to ask when she will be up."

"Oh, very soon."

"And will she then be fit to read to him, write his letters, attend to his diet? You understand. He exacts a good deal."

He seemed to reflect, and then said:

"That is another matter, quite. I shall think of it. There is no haste. Perhaps, later, a brief absence might be desirable before, I may say, resuming her duties."

"What an admirable counselor!" thought Lucretia. "May I ask what is wrong with Miss Fairthorne?"

He had the long-since acquired affectation of seeming to pause for reflection before replying to even a simple question. Mrs. Hunter was keenly considering him.

Dr. Soper was fat, rosy, gray of head, and wore the old-fashioned side whisker. He had a look of mellow prosperity. Mentally, he was competent enough when alone in a case, but was apt to yield to a colleague's opinion, and, in the face of a patient's obstinacy, to give way or modify an unpleasant order. Perhaps this contributed with many kindly qualities to make him popular. Unfortunately, the confusing in-rush of novel ideas and new medicines found him unable to select or to sit in judgment, so that he lazily accepted and hopelessly failed to digest or assimilate the new knowledge. It was Dr. Soper's belief that he must always be up to the hour, and he liked to say so. Dimly conscious of indecisiveness, he disliked consultations.

He stood handling the bunch of seals on his watch-guard as he answered her very simple request to know what was wrong with his patient.

"My dear Mary," he replied, "is a little tired—overworked; perhaps, too, a touch of the prevalent influenza. Nothing worse." Mary was never tired, but this doctor said every one was overworked.

"Miss Katherine," he continued, "remarked that you thought Atlantic City might be advisable when her cousin was better."

"Yes, yes, I may have said so. A very good idea, but it was Miss Katherine who suggested it, not I. I never meddle."

"Well, I will bear it in mind. Good morning; you do not look as if you would ever profit my profession, Mrs. Hunter."

"Ah, Dr. Soper, I am glad you reminded me. I was about to ask if you thought that in insomnia small doses of chloral would do harm."

"No, no; but certainly only under advice."

"And are not bromides safer?"

"Oh, decidedly! You are quite safe with them."

"I am often sleepless. Some time I must ask you to advise me at length."

"With pleasure. Fine woman!" he murmured.

"What a medical Polonius!" laughed Mrs. Hunter. "A nice old weather-cock. He may answer in case of need."

Mary was with difficulty kept in bed for three or four days. When, in Dr. Soper's opinion, she was able to move about he advised with unusual emphasis a fortnight's rest by the sea. To the surprise of Mrs. Hunter, Mary eagerly assented. Kitty generously insisted that she should take with her the maid whose service they were supposed to share equally. When, also, her uncle bade her good-bye and gave her a very ample check and hoped she would enjoy the ocean, Mary felt that every one was good to her, and spent no thought upon the causes of such unanimous helpfulness.

In fact, she was glad to go. Kitty's too evident transgressions troubled her and she saw with regret that she, who alone of the family had been able to influence the wilful beauty, was losing control; so that now it was Mrs. Hunter to whom Kitty referred the many small questions of a petty existence. Moreover, Mrs. Hunter was becoming more essential to John Fairthorne than was pleasant to his niece, who found awkward the changing relations which were fast developing. Feeling the strain of it all, she confessed her own inability to supply remedies. Then, too, there was a more intimate question which at times urgently asked the hospitality of attention.

She went away, glad of escape. When Madge promised that in a day or two she should have Jack as company she was altogether delighted. She left without the slightest suspicion that she owed her holiday to Mrs. Hunter's provident care and to that lady's desire to be alone for a season with Mr. Fairthorne and Kitty.

When Miss Morrow received her rector's note, stating that he could no longer act as her spiritual director, she promptly declared to Mrs. Hunter that she had of late become doubtful as to the wisdom of confession, and could not consent to be coldly transferred to some one who would not comprehend her spiritual wants. Mrs. Hunter, on the whole, agreed with her. Kitty ceased to go to confession, but assiduously attended Mr. Knellwood's services at St. Agnes's.

For a week after her sister's departure Margaret made it a daily duty to visit her uncle, but very soon found that there was little for her to do. Mrs. Hunter usually left her free to talk with Mr. Fairthorne, but he was apt, shortly, to ask:

"Where is Mrs. Hunter?"

Margaret began to feel uneasy at this growing attachment.

"It is so sudden," she thought, but, being a person who prided herself on not acting without reasons, she was not embarrassed, like Mary, by the predictions of an active imagination.

The absolute control Mrs. Hunter was gaining over Kitty was also becoming too obvious to escape Margaret's observation. She did not like it, and liked it less because she did not understand it. It annoyed her, though not as it did Mary, because, unlike her sister, she had neither affection nor respect for Katherine Morrow.

A larger experience might have explained the cause of Lucretia's conquest of a girl so difficult to attach. It was due in part, as has been said, to her power to feed Kitty's vanity with very gross flattery, and in part to that singular influence of an older woman over one younger, which has caused much mischief and is difficult to explain.

Nearly a fortnight had gone by, and one morning just before Mary was expected to return Mr. Fairthorne said to Margaret:

"I am going to secure Mrs. Hunter's full services as my secretary. Mary is absent."

"But she is coming home at once."

"Yes, I know, I know," he replied, irritably. "Kitty is valueless. I must get more efficient help."

"You must do as you think best," she said, coldly. "Mary will be hurt, and is by no means valueless."

He made no comment on this, but said:

"I want you to ask Mrs. Hunter to your house, my dear."

Margaret was annoyed.

"My dear uncle," she said, "of course what you want I will do. You know that both Mary and I try in all ways to carry out your wishes. But we know nothing of this woman, except that suddenly you announce her as your secretary. She is simply a clever woman Kitty has picked up, and whom she pesters me to present to our friends." Margaret spoke with unusual heat. She meant to yield, but not until she had had her say. She was surprised that her uncle did not show any sign of the anger which contradictory objections to his will were pretty sure to awaken. Having, however, been well schooled, he replied quietly and with but slight impatience in his tone:

"My dear Margaret, I have long wanted more regular help. I hoped to relieve Mary. She has made no complaint. So much for the secretary, and now let me say I have done my duty by you two girls and your estates. I never have asked of you a favor. Now I do, and you say no."

"I did not say no."

"Well, you made it plain enough." He was losing his temper. She looked at the excited old man, with his handsome, well-bred face, now irregularly red, and saw the tremor of the left hand as it rapped in a kind of spasm on the arm of his chair. She was alarmed.

"My dear uncle, I will do anything you want."

"I knew you would. Mary fights and argues and contradicts me, and I am a broken old man and failing fast." To hear him plead weakness was strange. As she again assured him of her willingness, the servant said:

"Mr. Masters." Margaret rose.

"No, do not go yet. Harry has been away very long. I suppose we shall soon hear more from him about those coal-lands. When do you look for him?"

She thought in about a week; that would be on Monday, and Mary seemed to be enjoying Jack and the sea.

She rose to speak to her old friend Masters, saying gaily, as her uncle greeted him:

"What, no ducks at Currituck or the Island! I hoped for a brace or two of canvasbacks."

"It is no joking matter. It is getting to be serious. The ducks are disappearing. Some rascals in Canada or Alaska are stealing the eggs for Lord knows what!"

"You should represent the matter at Washington, Tom," said Fairthorne, laughing. "I foresee international complications."

"It is awful," said Tom. Madge sympathized, and again rose to go.

"No, do not go, Madge. Sit down. How have you been, Tom? What do you want? No one comes here who does not want something."

"For shame!" cried Margaret.

"My wants are few," said Masters. "If I could have another big war and decent cause for it, I should be happy. As it is, I kill things and loll about clubs. Don't look at me, Madge, with that look of suggested duties. How are the brats?"

"Oh, well. Come in on Saturday, after dinner."

"One minute," he said, "and I will walk with you. I want to ask Mr. Fairthorne a question. It may concern you and Harry."

Then he went on to say that he had a moderate amount of stock of the Republic Trust Company, and thought he would like to ask Mr. Fairthorne if it still enjoyed his confidence. He had heard, of late, unpleasant rumors. There was nothing definite. Fairthorne had once been a shrewd adviser, and, as often happens to the old, his keenness as to business was rather increased by that fear of poverty which is one of the haunting apprehensions of declining life. He said:

"Why not sell? Why risk the holding of your stock?"

"But, by George, it pays ten per cent."

"Does it? I had forgotten that. You sold your stock, Madge? Harry is their counsel, I believe."

"Yes, yes, he is their counsel."

"And yet he sold? I hold a good deal of it myself. Harry ought to have told me."

"We wanted the money for the house. He did not then distrust it."

"And does now?" said her uncle, quickly. "Where is my property book? Call Mrs. Hunter, Madge."

"Cannot I find it, Uncle John?"

"Call Mrs. Hunter." When she appeared, he asked her to bring the book with a schedule of personal property. She said: "Yes, the red cover," and promptly set it on the table. Madge sat still, confounded. He usually kept these books locked up and rather jealously guarded from other eyes than his own.

"Turn to the stock index and find the Republic Trust stock." Madge watched her, as she seemed in doubt and unable to find it. At last she said as much.

"Can't find the index!" he cried. "You made it a week ago."

It was found at last. He looked at the page and said: "It stood well when I bought it. You had better ask Harry Swanwick or one of the directors. Who are they?"

When Tom named several of them, Mr. Fairthorne said:

"Oh, Grace! Decent sort of fellow, I hear. Manage to see him; put it in business shape—you think of selling to reinvest. Ask what he advises. Don't ask him directly whether this stock is good to hold as a permanent investment. As a director, he might be disinclined to advise. Put it the other way." Tom was amused at a form of over-shrewdness he himself did not possess and was little likely to utilize, being as straightforward a man in his way as the able master of finance to whom he was advised to apply.

Tom rose, thanking Mr. Fairthorne, to whom, as his father's executor, he was apt to turn for counsel. In fact, he had made the investment in question long before by Mr. Fairthorne's advice, but was careful not to say so.

As he went down the stairway with Mrs. Swanwick he said:

"Has your uncle much of that stock?"

"I do not know. He is very secretive as to all his property. Harry does not know. Uncle often asks Harry's advice as to affairs, but he never mentions amounts."

"This Mrs. Hunter appears to know," said Tom, with a queer, half-puzzled look made up of a mild frown and a smile.

"Yes, so it seems."

"What is she doing here, Madge?"

"She is my uncle's secretary."

"Indeed! I should have chosen a man were I you, or a woman with a worse figure."

"I did not choose her."

"I fancy she chose herself, Madge."

"That is too true, Tom. Wait a minute. I have to ask her to my house. I promised my uncle, I suppose I must do it."

"Ask me, too. She is very amusing."

"Well, that is as may be. My uncle wants me to ask her. I could not refuse."

"Refuse! Why should you, Madge? She went everywhere in Newport and was really liked in Boston."

"Newport is not my house. Well, no matter. Wait a minute." Margaret went back to the library. Mrs. Hunter, standing beside Mr. Fairthorne, was holding his hand and talking. Madge caught a phrase or two, as Mrs. Hunter said:

"I am afraid, sir, you will hardly be as comfortable when Mary comes home."

"But you won't leave me—"

"Mary!" murmured Mrs. Swanwick.

Lucretia moved in haste, taken by surprise as Margaret entered. Mrs. Swanwick was acquiring distinct enough reasons for not liking the secretary. Nevertheless, she had no mind to disoblige her uncle.

"I came back, Mrs. Hunter, to ask you to come in on Saturday night, after nine, please. I am usually at home on that evening, and this time you will be sure to find a few pleasant people. It is quite informal." Having resolved to please her uncle, she delivered her invitation with as much cordiality as she could command.

Mrs. Hunter would have the "utmost pleasure." She was a little embarrassed, wondering if she had been overheard. She swiftly concluded, from Mrs. Swanwick's pleasant ease of manner, that she had not. It is not well to underrate other actresses.

Margaret went down-stairs furious, and Mrs. Hunter had an enemy added and one neither to be despised nor readily dealt with.

"Do not forget me on Saturday night, Tom. Harry may not be at home, but Mary will be, so she writes me." She left him at his club, and walked on to her own house, deep in thought.

"Mary, indeed! What insolence!"

XVII

HE next morning Mrs. Hunter complained that there were evil odors about the house, and Kitty was easily persuaded that a slight leakage of gas was really some defect in the drainage. John Fairthorne, always anxious about health, sent at once for Archer, who naturally prescribed a resort to the plumber. Then Mrs. Hunter saw Dr. Soper, and he, in turn, advised Mary by letter to remain away until the house was set in order. Mary replied that she thought she would go for a week to her sister's, which suited Mrs. Hunter very nearly as well.

One morning, a day or two before her cousin's expected return, Kitty complained that she needed exercise, and that Dr. Soper had said that she ought to ride. Mrs. Hunter asked why, as Miss Mary was away, she did not use her horse. Kitty, who rode in summer a quiet little mare, replied that her cousin would not like it.

"My dear," said Lucretia, "she really should be obliged to you. The horse ought to be exercised more." Kitty, over persuaded, tried it twice, and then gave it up in terror, and none too soon, for Mary telegraphed Madge on Saturday morning that she would return that evening and remain with them a week. She had concluded that she had had quite enough of the ugliest seaside town on the coast.

The day after Mr. Masters saw John Fairthorne he called on Mr. Grace, just at the close of his business hours, and sent in his card. As he passed into the banker's office Lionel Craig came out. He was flushed and angry, Mr. Grace having told him that his books were badly kept, and that but for the fact that he had promised his sister to give him another trial he would have at once dismissed him. Craig was more hurt than helped by the warning, but for a time it proved effectual. The well-dressed, well-built gentleman glanced with approval at the figure, and with surprise at the dress, of the clerk, and wondered whom he resembled.

Mr. Grace, who had long had a club acquaintance with Masters, and knew very well who he was, said:

"Sit down. How can I oblige you?"

Quite neglecting Fairthorne's advice, Tom said:

"I want to ask you, if I may, whether the Republic Trust stock is a safe investment, or should I sell and invest in something else? Kindly consider this as a matter of business."

The banker smiled.

"It is a rather uncommon form of question. Usually my upper clerks or juniors answer such questions or do not; for, really, Mr. Masters, it is not usual to give advice in the form you desire. If you wish us to sell for you and to advise as to investment we will do so."

Tom laughed.

"Suppose, sir, I ask if I shall invest in the Republic?"

Grace, much amused, replied:

"Mr. Masters, I was a director of the Trust. I have lately resigned. I do not altogether like their ways. I can give no advice—at least, no direct advice."

"Thank you."

"And if you act on what I have said, kindly consider what has passed here as absolutely confidential. Can I further serve you? No? Well, you will find Mr. Owens outside. I think you will see your stock," he added, smiling.

"I will," said Tom. Then he paused, and said:

"I have an old friend, Mr. John Fairthorne, who holds, I suspect, a good deal of this stock."

"Then it is held by a man quite fit to take care of himself. I have, Mr. Masters, a weakness for you men who were deep in the war while I was grubbing for dollars. It is one of the regrets of my life that I was not in it. Generally, I should have declined to answer in any shape. You are wise enough to know that I did answer."

"Well," said Tom, "that is the first good I ever got out of the war."

"Oh, no, Mr. Masters; you got a great deal besides. By the way, is your friend Swanwick at home yet?" He was well aware of their intimacy. "Mrs. Swanwick expected him within a day or two."

"I do not know."

"I am going to Mrs. Swanwick's on Saturday night," said Grace. It was irrelevant, but the banker was pleased to have been asked and liked to speak of it. Tom, perfectly understanding him, said:

"Before I go I want to say how much I thank you." Grace smiled, pleased with himself and Masters.

Tom sold his stock at no loss, as it was still far over par, but falling and rising again, being, as a rule, firmly held and long thought to be secure.

When Masters left, Mr. Grace asked to see his partner. They talked gravely awhile, and then Grace, left alone, walked up and down his office reflecting. At last he sat down and wrote:

" [Private.]

"DEAR SIR: You know that my dissatisfaction with the recent management of your company caused me to resign my seat in your board. I have excused myself, outside of it, as having too many such offices. You know how frankly I urged on the finance committee my utter disapproval of some of their Western investments. I need not further remind you of what more I said. I am constantly hearing unpleasant rumors, and observe that the stock is going down by degrees. We are, I think, in a bad way just now, and for this reason I do not care to throw my own large holding on the market. I greatly fear money troubles in the spring. If you are in, or get into, real difficulties, it will be needful to support so old and important an institution. Let me hear frankly and soon. Do not leave it until help is useless.

"Yours truly,

"ROGER GRACE."

"To CYRUS THURSTON, ESQ."

He read it over and said to himself:

"That will answer. They will pull through if we

have no abrupt mischief in the Western banks.''
Then he rang.

When the clerk appeared, he said: ''Mr. Jones,
see that Mr. Thurston gets this letter as you go to
lunch.''

Jones was just going out for his midday meal, and
walked up-town with Craig, to whom he said, as they
came near to the Trust office: ''You run in and give
this to Mr. Thurston. See that he gets it. I am in
a hurry. See you at lunch. I guess it 's important.''

Craig replied, ''All right,'' and his friend left
him.

Craig looked at the letter and felt that the closing
mucilage was still damp. He had a sudden and
childlike desire to know what was within. He knew,
as did others, that the brokers felt a little suspicious
as to this company. It might be useful to know.
Stocks were moving uneasily. He stepped aside
into another street and tried the envelope to see if
the adhesive paste had made it too secure. It opened
readily. He read it with dull interest, not seeing
that it was or could be of any value to him to know
its contents.

He found Mr. Thurston and delivered it, seeing,
although of a not very alert intelligence, that the
Trust's president was discomposed as he read and
reread the letter. ''No, there was no answer.''

When, that evening, he sat with his sister, who
was in high spirits and was glad of a cigarette, he
gaily related this exploit. Strange to say, it seriously troubled her that he had opened the letter.

11

She herself would have done so without the least hesitation, but she wanted this man to be what she was not, and scrupulously hid from him whatever of actual wrong-doing she had put into her own life. As they had usually lived apart, this had been easy.

"Oh, Lionel!" she said. "How could you do such a thing?" That he should so calmly have confessed it to her as rather a good joke on the banker seemed to her acuteness evidence that Lionel believed she would show no disapproval. Did he think that of her? She wanted him to love her, to think well of her, even to respect her. She was so severe that he felt he had been a fool to tell her. He weakened, as he always did under her hand, and at last promised, as usual, all manner of good behavior.

After this they talked of the theaters, and finally of Kitty. He had, of course, enjoyed his walk on Sunday with his sister and Miss Katherine. When he had gone, Mrs. Hunter sat down to think. So far she had done well. She had become necessary to Mr. Fairthorne; Miss Fairthorne was out of the way for a time; Mrs. Swanwick had asked her to her house. She was in a fair way to make mischief between Mary and Kitty Morrow. The doctor was in her road, and for some reason was coldly civil and no more. He had said that his orders must be carried out, and Mrs. Hunter, who had ideas of her own as to treatment, had been reminded most distinctly that he was to be obeyed. He was altogether impervious to flattery and neither to be cajoled nor bullied. Mrs. Hunter lacked the talent for letting things alone. She need not have interfered with Archer, but the desire for petty rule was deeply set in her nature, and made her incline to cross swords needlessly with a man of whom she had better not have made a foe.

He had begun, soon after Miss Fairthorne left, to feel continually that there was some interference, some excuse for a failure to carry out orders; or if he forbade the usual drive Mr. Fairthorne must have misunderstood, because Mrs. Hunter had said that was only in case the east wind continued. This sense of a hostile atmosphere, of inexplicable and intangible opposition, began to annoy Archer. Every physician must, at some time, have been made to feel as he now did, and few things are harder to bear.

As to Archer's intermittent attention to Kitty, Mrs. Hunter was easy. He had but little leisure, and she herself was well informed as to Kitty's sentiments. The real peril was in the clergyman, of whom, Mrs. Hunter observed, the girl, for some latent cause, no longer spoke as Father Knellwood.

"I must live in that house," thought Mrs. Hunter; "but how am I to manage it?" It would be pleasant and save money for that endless drain, Lionel. A dozen plans amused her leisure, as she sat smoking cigarettes in her hotel chamber, with a *petit verre* of cognac—only one, for she was prudent and sober as to some things. Of course, cigarettes would have to go for the time, but, save for this, there was comfort in the idea of a home in that luxurious house. Her day-dreams were queer enough. If just a trifle of something were to make Kitty ill, and she would have no nurse save Lucretia, or if Mr. Fairthorne were to be worse—well, just for a while. She had become used to living on the margin of serious crime.

"Once there," she said, "I should stay."

Meanwhile she used her present advantages with energetic industry.

While Mary was away she spent her mornings in Fairthorne's library, intelligently busy with the catalogue, or when not so occupied suggestive, amusing, with now and then a caressing touch, a soothing hand. Well, something would turn up, or she must make it turn up. She had the adventurer's belief in her luck. Meanwhile she received from Fairthorne seventy-five dollars a month. The contents of that letter to Thurston occupied her busy brain for a few minutes, as she recalled the fact that Mr. Fairthorne was a large holder of the stock. Above all, was a feeling of satisfaction in the tangle she was making. She undressed and slept the sound sleep of wholesome health.

The guests who chanced to appear on Saturday nights at Mrs. Swanwick's were not always, or indeed generally, such as pleased Miss Morrow. She rarely did what she did not want to do, and now, in the afternoon, told Mrs. Hunter that the rides on that brute of Mary's had left her stiff and sore. She really could not go to Margaret's, and the horse was lame and his back was sore—as if that was any one's fault. But what a row there would be! Yes, Mrs. Hunter thought there might be trouble, some people were so selfish.

Mrs. Hunter did not mean to go alone to Mrs. Swanwick's. She made no direct reply to Kitty's statement of her bodily ills, but mentioned casually that Mr. Knellwood would be disappointed, an inference which Kitty's vanity eagerly accepted. She presently said: "If you would really like me to go with you I will certainly try to do so; but, dear me, it is dull, and I am stiff from head to foot."

When, in the evening, Mr. Fairthorne's carriage brought Mrs. Hunter from her hotel to the Fourth Street house, she was not surprised to find Kitty in her room and ready. It was one of the girl's errors of taste to be rather over-dressed, and as she stood before her glass, Mrs. Hunter admired her white neck. Kitty admired it no whit less and as she turned from the glass, said with a sigh: "I do wish I could wear Mary's pearls. She never has worn them, not once. When she was going she asked me to have her box of trinkets put in uncle's safe. I forgot all about it."

"Let me see them, dear." Kitty brought the box, and taking a costly pearl necklace from its worn morocco case placed it in Mrs. Hunter's hand. Lucretia said:

"How beautiful they are, but they would not suit Mary's complexion. I know where they belong," and she clasped them around Kitty's neck, crying: "Now they are where they ought to be. Oh, Katherine, how they become you!"

"I really could n't, I could n't—oh, I wish I could.! Mary never lets me touch them. They were Aunt Julia's, her mother's. Is n't it selfish? I have often asked her to let me wear them."

"She will never know."

"Margaret would tell her, and if ever you saw

Mary Fairthorne angry, you would n't advise me to wear her pearls.''

"My dear child, if she saw you now she would give you the pearls. After all, you lovely morsel, they can't eat you alive. If I were a man I should simply fall at your feet.''

Kitty looked again in her glass, which told as sweet a truth.

"Well," she said, "Mary is not at home, and—''

"Yes, dear, and you can ask Mrs. Swanwick not to tell.''

"That is a good idea," said Kitty. The mirror and Lucretia won for vanity the battle against fear.

"It will make a pleasant little fuss if the big cousin ever hears,'' thought Mrs. Hunter, as they drove to the Swanwicks'; "and of course Mrs. Swanwick will tell. I would, any one would. The girl will never ask her not to mention it. What a lovely fool she is!''

XVIII

WHILE this debate took place, and Kitty was preening her feathers before the cheval glass, too pleased to anticipate disaster, Margaret was trying, in her nursery, to get away from the "just one more kiss" and the "do tuck me in, mudder."

"Ah," she said, hearing the front-door bell ring, "that is Harry's ring." She ran down-stairs in haste. He had been absent nearly a fortnight. It was like her, amid the joy which set her heart to throbbing, that she reflected on the individuality of the pull on a bell. She dropped the train of thought as her husband lifted the little woman and kissed her.

"Do set me down, Harry," she cried, as the bell rang again. "Oh, that must be Mary. I am sure it is Mary. She is just from the seashore, Harry, and is to be here a week. Is n't it delightful!" It was a noble fib, for just then she would far rather have been alone with her husband.

It was the travelers who entered. Jack had been ordered home after a week's delightful digging in the sand and the accumulation of a fortune in shells. Mary, very tired of the hotel life, was happy to be with her sister, and was made warmly welcome. She went at once up-stairs to her room to dress, Margaret having said there were, as usual on Saturday night, people coming.

Harry Swanwick threw himself into an easy-chair in the library, and Madge, on a cushion at his feet, rested an elbow on his knee. No, he was not tired, and had had some kind of a dinner; but what a bore to have people coming! Madge said it was sorrowful, but that he had set Monday for his return.

"Yes," he laughed, "that is so, but I had three reasons for haste—two up-stairs, and one here. Are they asleep?"

"I fear not, dear. If you go up now my little witch will be awake half the night."

He rose.

"No, no, please not," she said.

"Well, I must wait, I suppose." In little and large things he was more governed than he knew. At times the unsuspected taste for rule went beyond the line of wisdom, and his wife's interference became too much for the comfortable, disorderly ways of man. Once, when Mary had criticized her sister, he had quoted something about intelligent despotism and its value. Mary had replied that he was not very clear, and he, in turn, that what he meant was that his wife was generally right, even when she bothered him—which was true.

"Now," she said, "you must have ever so much to tell me. Your letters were exasperatingly short, and as for home news, I have a horrid budget with which I did not want to distract you. Oh, nothing serious. But first about your cases. I saw by the law reports that you won both. About the coal-lands I was not so sure. Uncle will like to hear."

"Yes, Madge," he said, "you were right about the bridge case. The point you made concerning the tolls and who received them and the date of their cessation was difficult to prove, but when I found the former toll-keeper his evidence settled it."

Madge's face lit up.

"It was a great triumph for you, and against a man like Leslie."

"Yes; he congratulated me later, and so did the judge, and when I told them you had suggested the point they were rather amazed, and Leslie said you ought to have half the fee. It will be large—quite five thousand."

"Oh, Harry! You ought not to have mentioned me. I really did not—"

"Did you not! I am not entirely and always the fool of love. You shall have all of the fee."

"I would rather have a kiss." It is probable that she got it. "And the coal suit? I had nothing to do with that," she cried, gladly.

"Perhaps not, and for a chamber counsel your fees are moderate. I won it easily, but the lands need care and Luke Pilgrim ought to be sent down there at once—he or some other mining engineer. Your uncle is being robbed right and left. I found one of my old rebel friends on the Kanawha, and put him in charge; but, really, Mr. Fairthorne must be getting very inert and it is not like him to let things go as he has done."

Madge became grave.

"Well," he said, "what is it?" He knew her ways. "You have something to tell me."

"Ye-es, Uncle John is slowly failing. He is more irritable—"

"More!" he cried.

"Yes; it shows in many ways. He is becoming a little careless about his dress, and that for him is— Dr. Archer says it is really a bad sign. He has days when he is just as clever and cynical and pessimistic as ever, but it does n't last. His love of method has become a sort of mania."

"Well, all this, Madge, is more or less an old story."

"Yes, I know that; but the change of late is very marked. He is feebler, and sleeps more in the daytime."

"But he is nearly eighty, Madge. Is that all?"

"No, it is not all. That Mrs. Hunter, whom our silly mischief, Kitty, picked up I do not know where, has got more and more of control over the girl, and now she has contrived to make herself apparently indispensable to Uncle John. She is there every day, all day, and she calls herself his secretary. Probably—oh, of course, he pays her."

"Well, that ought to greatly relieve Mary and Kitty."

"Kitty—relieve Kitty! But Mary was being by degrees set aside—being set aside before you left. And since Mary has been absent Mrs. Hunter seems to have completely taken her place. Worst of all, this woman sits and holds his hand, and really,

Harry, in the last month she has seemed essential to his comfort. You know how he craves attention and flattery and the woman is handsome and intelligent.'' Then she mentioned the fact of his asking Mrs. Hunter to look over his schedule of property when Masters was present.

Harry whistled low. For the first time her account disturbed him. He knew that Fairthorne had always been secretive about his affairs and kept his own accounts. He had often urged him to have some secretarial aid, but always in vain. Fairthorne said it was a needless expense. He had all his life been penny saving and dollar lavish, hesitating at nothing where a book or an autograph was to be had; a complex nature, now undergoing the radical changes caused by age, which strengthens some habits and weakens others.

''What you tell me,'' said Harry, ''is serious. Is it money or ease she is after, or does she want to trap this old man into marriage? Such cases have been. I must talk to Archer.''

''Marriage! I never thought of that. That is awful. Now, run and dress; I must go down-stairs. Ah, there is the bell.''

''Hang the people!'' he said.

''Be civil to her, Harry. My uncle has made me ask her here—I mean Mrs. Hunter.''

''Of course, Madge.''

Margaret had made up her mind that she would be gracious to Mrs. Hunter, and would also talk to Mary as to the wisdom of prudently dealing with the situation, the peril of which she saw better than did her sister. The girls were both of them possessed of moderate fortunes, and until of late Margaret had found it needful to live with care, and to remind her husband, who was apt to be now and then extravagant, as he had been about her ruby ring, that what John Fairthorne might do with his very large estate no one could say. Indeed, once, in a moment of irritability, he had said he would leave it all to Jack, who must take his name and arms. Harry had told him that that was un-American nonsense, and the old man had sworn outrageously that he would do as he blank pleased.

Soon after Margaret entered the parlor Mr. Knellwood appeared. He had a gentle gravity of manner which went well with his large proportions. He sat down with discreet care as to his chair. Madge, who respected him and rather fancied people who held distinct opinions, wondered, like Mary, why she did not like him better. She desired always to be able to give reasons for her attachments, and this man was of the best. He never spoke of things professional unless led by others to do so. He very honestly believed that his increasing love for needlessly added forms and ceremonial had a purely historical and logical foundation, not realizing that emotionality and taste for the mystical were controlling his opinions. Few who knew him only in his church ritual, or among the poor who loved him, would have supposed that he would have instantly turned to look at Madge's old Dresden china. He amazed her by his criticism of the Dresden, and by his knowledge of the marks of her old Delft plates.

When, after service as a war chaplain, he took to improving the ritual and to a life among the poor, he sold his father's collection and turned himself and his income to more serious uses. An old Wedgewood plaque of Franklin, given by the philosopher to the beauty, Tacy Lennox, attracted him, and he was talking agreeably of the great man when Tom Masters came in. The men shook hands.

"I do not see you as often as in the old war days, chaplain."

"I am glad to forget them, Masters. But not," he added, "my old army friends." He rarely spoke of the war. It was a dream of horror, of blood, griefs, wickedness. The service had been a painful duty admirably done.

"I," said Masters, "think of the war with regret. It is all I was ever fit for."

"There is a place for you, though you may not have found it," said Knellwood, as Harry entered and fell into chat with the ex-chaplain.

"Sit down, Tom, and amuse me," Madge said. "Isn't your chaplain handsome? I wish I liked him better."

"Not like him! Ah, we called him the reverend colonel. He was always close to the rear of the regiment in a fight ready to help the fellows that were hit, or to keep the men up to it when they got rattled. If there was a break in the line he was sure to be in it, and—good gracious, Madge, you can't imagine how splendid he looked when he forgot that his business was peace."

"He is two men, I suppose."

"Yes, most of us are."

"Tell me more of him. You know Harry never talks to me of the war, and I like war-talk."

"The chaplain and I were with the Forty-fifth at Cedar Creek when the rebs broke our line. The Ninth Vermont lost and recaptured their colors three times. It was a bloody mob fight, and what part the chaplain took he does not like to hear. That night, after Phil Sheridan won his big fight and we had had our turn, some one chaffed the chaplain, and declared he swore and was in the thick of that fight for the colors."

"Swore—and did he really?"

"I do not know. I hardly think he could even have remembered what he said or did. Certainly he was in the fight, and repented so painfully that we never spoke of it again."

"I think I shall like him better," said Madge. "Those were horrible and splendid days."

"And are over, alas!"

"Oh, Tom, don't say that! Ah, here are Kitty and Mrs. Hunter. Oh, and Mr. Grace. How good of you to come early. Mrs. Hunter, may I present Mr. Masters? Ah, I forgot; you know him." Kitty looked about her, uneasily conscious of the pearls, and joined Harry, who by and by left her with Knellwood, and, a little curious, went to sit with Tom Masters and the new secretary.

Mrs. Hunter, dressed in black satin and lace, was at her best.

"A striking looking, well-preserved woman," thought Harry. He was, like most of us, unobser-

vant of the features of his kind. Now he was
more watchful. No, there was no rouge, and the
peculiarity of the eye was that the whole of the
large, dark iris was visible, and not, as is common,
partly hidden by the lids. It was strange and not
quite pleasant. She dropped the gay talk about
Newport and people, and said:

"Miss Morrow tells me you have been absent,
Mr. Swanwick, arguing cases. You are greatly to
be envied."

"You would not envy me if you had had to live
two weeks in the hotels of West Virginia. Hog and
hominy and soda-raised, sour bread, sour women,
and sour children."

"Ah, but to have your training and work, and to
see results. If a woman is ever so able, what is
there she can do? She can't even kill things, Mr.
Masters."

"Well, she can always get married," said Tom,
lightly.

"Can she, indeed?" she cried, laughing. "And
you, Mr. Masters, who were complaining to me that
life had left you only ducks, grouse, and tarpon,
why not try your own remedy?"

"Thank you. Not I. What physician does that?"

"If I were a man I should go mad over Miss
Morrow. How winning she is!"

Tom looked at the damsel in question, as perhaps
he was meant to do. The shot had gone home. Lucretia had inexplicable satisfaction in stinging people and how hard he had been hit by Kitty's rejection
Mrs. Hunter guessed. Tom said, quietly:

"Miss Morrow would trouble the prayers of a saint." In a far corner, she was just then engaged in this very same business and was reporting to Mr. Knellwood the contents of a letter from a friend who had married a clergyman and was settled near Lenox.

"And now, Mr. Knellwood"—it was no longer Father Knellwood—"she says she is so glad to be both useful and happy, and I am happy and not a bit useful, except to uncle. Helen got her account of her roses and her babies so mixed up. Do you ever get mixed up? I do. If ever I marry, it will be a bishop. It is delightful to talk to you about getting married, because you know—you know—you are a priest and what Mrs. Hunter calls—oh, I forget! It was something out of St. Paul."

Cyril Knellwood knew that this child-woman was silly. He felt, rather than thought, that she might be insincere, and men said of her bitter things; but a vast tenderness welled up in the heart of the man as he looked down at her. He answered, with his usual gentleness: "I cannot think what verse of St. Paul could apply to me." He might have thought of more than one.

"I always do forget quotations," she said. "I will ask Mrs. Hunter, and write to you." Kitty was forever writing trivial notes.

"Do not trouble yourself." She looked up at him with lucid blue eyes.

"How can you think it a trouble? I like to write to you. Mrs. Hunter says it does so clear one's head to put one's thoughts on paper." Kitty was a dangerous person. An indefinable lure was in all her ways and movements, some note of sweetness in her slight lingering over any tender word. She had none of the chaste remoteness of her cousin Mary. She always seemed near. Margaret once said, with unusual savagery of criticism, that there was too much physical charm about Kitty. The man felt it as his look turned from the blue eyes. She leaned toward him as she spoke of liking to write to him, and added: "But I do not like to write to everybody, Mr. Knellwood." Then he said a strange thing for him, and was instantly sorry to have done it: "Miss Morrow, why do you no longer call me Father?"

The girl's eyes fell. This beautiful, half-trained animal was feeling the fatal power that lay for her in the stalwart man beside her, in a physical being as attractive in his way as she herself, and she was troubled into unusual embarrassment of speech.

He had asked why she no longer called him Father. Her head fell a little, as with slow affirmative movement she murmured, slowly and distinctly: "Because I cannot. I cannot any—any more."

Her meaning was plain. There were a dozen things he might have said. He knew very well next day what he should have said, but for the moment his moral mechanisms were in confusion, and his mind refused to assist him. He had been foolish, wrong, impulsive. That was the first thought which leaped to consciousness out of the vertigo of a passion on the boundary of uncontrol. He rose abruptly. As he looked down at her, the girl's face,

12

a moment before bent, regarded his set gaze. Her eyes were full of tears. She said: "Do not go."

He made no reply, but quietly moved away. She looked after him.

He will never come near me again, never." She made a desperate effort to recover her self-command. She saw the forms about her as if in a dream. She heard voices, but knew not what was said. In a moment she began to try to think of what had passed.

For the first time in her life a man had troubled her, and, she knew, might trouble her again. Or had she troubled herself? Yes, she had gone far, and perhaps too soon. Was this man really unlike other men? for Kitty regarded his well-known advocacy of celibacy as she did the rest of what Mary called his performances—lavations, chasuble and amice, the wafer and genuflections. In her mind, beliefs and their ceremonial attendants were of equal importance. Her own creed was the offspring of habit and education and could hardly be said to affect conduct. Margaret had once remarked that Kitty's religion was thin. She shrank back into her corner, and for a time was alone.

Mrs. Swanwick had urged Archer to bring Blount to one of her Saturdays, promising that she would take care of him. Archer, rather in doubt, had consented. In their previous intercourse Mrs. Swanwick's tact and evident interest had quickly set Blount at ease. She had been full of useful sympathy and had begun to make him feel that intellect and hard work obtain their triumphs more easily when aided by qualities which Blount's life and edu-

cation had never taught him to value. He was, however, by nature an observer, and once assured of a
need was almost absurdly ready to imitate the ways
of these pleasant people. The process of assimila-
tion interested Margaret.

The young man had been somewhat unwilling to
face what he feared might be a large number of people, but Archer, without more thought, had said:
"Nonsense! Put on a white tie and a black coat."
Mrs. Swanwick, too, was not to be lightly disobeyed.
There would be two or three pleasant people. The
rest she did not speak of.

Blount entered the room in a white tie, which gave
evidence of having been with difficulty adjusted, a
black cutaway coat, and gray pantaloons. Dazed
for a moment and shy, he looked about him with a
sense of shock at the bare necks and arms, for three
or four women, having dined elsewhere, were in full
evening dress.

Seeing Blount enter, Mrs. Swanwick came forward, and, after a moment of reassuring welcome,
looked about her. Observing that Knellwood had
left Kitty, she said, "This way, Mr. Blount," and
presented him to her cousin.

The young woman, still vexed and disturbed,
was glad of the company of a stranger, and said,
as he sat down: "I think we met at Miss Markham's." Talking disjointedly of nothings, she kept
thinking of what she had said to Knellwood, and
why he had asked her a question so strangely unlike
the man to ask. Herself a creature of impulse, she
was far from seeing that he, too, had been for the

moment the prey of an impulse. At length she began
to find in the abruptness of his retreat an evidence
of what she most desired to believe. Until her vanity had found for her this little crumb of comfort,
Miss Kitty's talk had been more than usually vapid
and disconnected; but now, with her habitual readi-
ness, she recovered from the shock of self-discovery.
Something Blount said amused her. She turned to
him with the satisfaction such women find in the
last male creature.

She soon put him at ease, and he, in turn, began
to exercise his normal powers of observation and to
ask questions not always easy to answer. When at
last she missed Knellwood from the room, and knew
that he had gone, she drew from this further en-
couragement and gave her whole attention to Blount.
He said: "I must be pestering you with questions."
Kitty said she liked it. He had asked, as Knellwood went by them: "Who is that?" She told him.

"I don't see why a preacher dresses like that and
wears a big cross. It looks like an advertisement,
as much as to say, 'Look at me. I am an up-and-
down righteous man.' "

"Oh, you must not say such things, Mr. Blount.
It is the sign of his—his high calling."

"But other people have high callings."

"But not like his."

"Do you think, miss, people's dress should always
in some way represent their business in life?"

"A clergyman's should."

"I don't see why. And the women," said Blount,
"and the doctors?"

This bothered Kitty.

"I do not quite understand."

"I was thinking Sydney Archer is quite as much a man of God as that big preacher."

"Oh, hardly! Of course, he is a very nice man."

"I should n't describe him that way, miss. Who is the lady in the corner?"

"Mrs. Hunter, a friend of mine. Is she not beautiful?"

"No. She is n't beautiful. I saw her once. I was trying to think where it was—in some hotel. She don't ever have her mouth quite shut—like a rabbit, you know." It was true.

Kitty laughed.

"You are too critical. I shall suffer next."

"You, miss! Why, any one would say you were beautiful."

"Good gracious!" cried Kitty, and they went on, the woman amused and not ill pleased, the man at his ease.

Presently Archer took an unoccupied seat beside Mrs. Hunter, and an old admiral whom she had been delighting rose.

At this moment Mary Fairthorne entered the room and looked about her. Seeing Kitty, who was not aware of her return, she went over to speak to her. As she approached, Kitty drew a light scarf over the white neck, but not quite in time. Mary saw her mother's pearls, and, seeing, grew pale, as was her way when one of her rare storms of anger was rising. She said, with distinct articulation: "Good evening, Katherine," and swept by.

"Now, that 's a right splendid creature," said Blount. "She looks like a Greek goddess."

"Oh, she is well enough; she is my cousin, Mary Fairthorne. I think she is too tall. Mrs. Hunter says she ought to live out of doors; she is too big for a house." Kitty was frightened and cross, foreseeing a scene with Mary.

That lady, compelling herself to a state of calm, spoke to Mrs. Hunter as Archer rose at her approach. She was still a little paler than common. Mrs. Hunter hoped she was quite well again, and Mary, thanking her, asked Archer how her uncle was. She observed that he spoke with some caution, saying that Mr. Fairthorne was much as usual.

Mrs. Hunter said: "Of course, you know best, but he seems to me better. I shall be glad to resign my place as nurse. To be Mr. Fairthorne's secretary is quite work enough."

Margaret had refrained from writing of this promotion to her sister, not desiring to trouble her while absent.

"Secretary!" exclaimed Mary, surprised out of her usual calm.

"Yes; Mr. Fairthorne thought his nieces were quite overworked, and I need not say how very glad I am to assist him and you."

"Indeed!" said Mary, glancing at Archer, who said nothing. "I cannot say I have felt overworked."

"Oh, but Katherine!" Mrs. Hunter knew she was worrying the tall girl, and liked the sport.

Mary made neither reply nor comment, but, turning to Archer, said quietly: "Harry seems to have had a brilliant success. He thinks he may soon have to return to Virginia, unless Mr. Pilgrim can very soon go down and take charge of the coal-mines."

Martin Blount, who was but a short distance away, in talk with Mrs. Swanwick, said suddenly:

"What is the matter with Mrs. Hunter? She is going to faint." It was true. She was white, and had fallen back in her seat.

"Oh, are you ill?" said Margaret. "What can I do for you?"

Mrs. Hunter replied, with evident effort: "No; I was—I am a little faint—a glass of water, please."

Margaret fanned her, the water was brought, and in a moment she was herself, and laughingly apologetic. Archer led her into the back room, which was cooler. There, at a window opened for the minute, she said: "I am subject to this annoyance at times. I am apt to suffer in close rooms." Then she asked him to find her a carriage. As his own was at the door, he put her in it, and, promising to excuse her to Miss Morrow, returned to the front room to reassure and chat with Miss Kitty.

He found her less agreeable than usual. She was thinking of Knellwood, and, too, was disturbed as she caught her cousin's eye upon her. Kitty rarely controlled her moods, and now she made Sydney Archer uncomfortable, saying how much better Mrs. Hunter cared for her uncle than Mary had ever done, and how good a thing it would be if that lady could be induced to come and live with them.

Of late Mrs. Hunter had more and more interfered
with him and now he rather unwisely lost his temper, and said: "Miss Katherine, I do not agree with
you. Mrs. Hunter seems to think that her place as
secretary gives her the privilege to meddle with Mr.
Fairthorne's treatment. I think her most meddle-
some."

"I do not like to have my friend abused," said
Kitty.

"What I say to you I shall say to her. It has
become necessary to speak positively. I am sorry
if it annoys you."

"Then you had better not have said it."

"But," he returned, "how can I possibly fail to
speak as I do? Miss Mary is away; Mrs. Swanwick
is not available; and I naturally turn to you for
support against influences that are plainly hurtful."

"I really know nothing about it, and if I did I
should leave you and Mrs. Hunter to settle your
own quarrels." Miss Kitty, still cross because of
a deep humiliation, was half-consciously revenging
herself by rudeness where rudeness was stingingly
felt.

Archer made no reply, but looked at her in mute
amazement. This Kitty was new to him. She rose
as she last spoke. When Margaret declared, as Masters had done, that Kitty was sometimes a little
common, she was correct. For the time Sydney
Archer was a disenchanted man. He, too, made no
comment, and was relieved when Swanwick came up,
saying: "There is a little supper in the back room."

Soon after the guests went away, and Kitty bade

a hurried good-bye, eager to escape her cousin. But at this moment she heard Mary behind her.

"Come up to the library, Katherine."

"No. I must go home. It is late." They were now in the hall.

"You must come if I have to carry you."

Kitty whimpered: "I knew you would be angry, but Mrs. Hunter said you would be glad to have me wear them." Mary made no reply. When they were in the library alone, she closed the door and said:

"Give me that necklace."

Kitty obeyed, saying: "I would never treat you so."

"Kitty," said her cousin, "you have hurt me more than I can say. Never do it again. I have never yet been able to wear my mother's pearls."

"Oh, I know. But then I might. I don't see why you are so—so particular about your pearls, Mary. You might wear anything I own. Mrs. Hunter said—"

Then Mary lost her temper.

"Mrs. Hunter is a servant of my uncle. I do not permit her to meddle with me. I shall say to her what I think of her and of this piece of insolence."

"Oh, Mary, please not. She will be so angry with me."

"Do you think that is of the slightest moment to me? My uncle will have to choose if this sort of thing continues; and as for you, never, never again let this woman come between us. Remember!"

She set her hands on Kitty's white shoulders, and repeated: "Remember!"

"You hurt me. You are rude."

"Rude! You are unbearable. A little while ago you insulted me about that letter. Now you wrong and hurt me and have not even enough decent sentiment to understand why I am angry."

"What is the matter, girls?" said Margaret, as she stood at the door.

"Mary has pinched me," said Kitty.

This queer statement and the drop from what to Mary was serious seemed to her so comical that she laughed, as she said: "Kitty has been wearing my mother's pearls by the sage advice of Mrs. Hunter, and I have been angry. Go home, Kitty; I am sorry I said so much."

"I will never speak to you again."

"Yes, you will," said Margaret. "You were wrong. There, now, don't say any more. Goodbye," and Kitty went away.

Then Mary said: "It is intolerable, Madge, perfectly intolerable! That woman! I told Harry she was dangerous. I am going to bed. Good night. Do not tell Harry, Madge. I shall if I stay up."

"No, it is not worth while."

"Plumbers or no plumbers," said Mary, "I shall go home to-morrow."

"I would," said her sister; "but we shall be sorry to lose you."

When Harry joined her a few minutes later, and sat down for his pipe, he said:

"Madge, that queer Dick Sydney Archer brought

here amused me. You told me before I left that Archer had asked you to take an interest in him, but I have been so long away that I have lost touch of you and your menagerie. What about this new animal? We had a few words together. You had better take his costume in hand.''

She laughed. ''All in good time. That will come.'' Then she told how Archer had asked her to help the young man. ''He really is worth it, Harry. Imagine the son of an old-fashioned Andover professor thrown at ten on the mercy of rough farming people, and left to grow up a mere farmhand. He somehow scraped together enough to give him two years at Amherst. Then he kept hotel books two summers, and did lumber work in winter. Archer will tell you the rest. Mr. Grace is helping him through his medical course, and our dear white mice, at Archer's request, are lodging him. It is easy to see how rough he is and how entirely without social training, but Clementina says he is thoughtfully kind and considerate. I told you that he comes of good stock.''

''Yes, you did. I often wonder how much of us is breed and how much training. And so you are to be the lapidary of this rough diamond?''

''I am—Archer and I.''

''And how do you do it?''

''Oh, the man has a talent for taking hints. You need not laugh. I am not hinting at any one's failure to possess that talent.''

''How does his talent show? It is a good sign.''

''Well, the nail question. I merely mentioned

that Sydney Archer had well-made hands, and that I thought a doctor should be careful of them. Mr. Blount's fingers have been immaculate ever since."

"I see," he said. "You are a delightful woman."

"Am I not?" she laughed.

"Let me see the embryo doctor. I shall be glad to help you."

"I knew you would."

XIX

HEN Kitty met Mrs. Hunter next morning she said:

"Dear Lucretia, you look as if you had seen a ghost."

"I have, dear—in my sleep. Something disagreed with me last evening." It was true in a way. Conscious of defeat as imminent, she had lain awake busily weaving schemes of self-defense. At last she sat up in the darkness and said, aloud, "Yes, that will do," and fell into a restless sleep.

When, in the morning, she entered Mr. Fairthorne's library, he said: "You are late."

"Yes, I am not very well. A small matter. Here is your medicine, but I do not think I would take it; you are looking so well to-day." He was pleased to escape, and said so. She had urged that this constant dosing only served to make him believe that he was ill, to keep his mind on himself.

"Shall I open the letters?" She was careful to ask leave. She ran over them and read their contents aloud. "Ah, here is a man who writes that he has some letters of your grandfather's."

He sat up, interested. "The man in South Street? I wish you would see him, and find out what they are about."

She said she would. "And these bills?"

"Well, pay them." As he spoke she slipped an unopened letter into her pocket.

"What was that?" he asked.

"A letter for me, sir, to your care."

She went through the work of cataloguing with her usual skill and accuracy, and then, glad to escape, left earlier than usual—to see about the autographs, as she said.

When she was in the street she opened the letter she had purloined. She had instantly recognized the writing on the envelope. It ran thus:

"DEAR SIR: At last I am free to visit those mines. I shall be in Philadelphia in four days.

"Yours truly,

"LUKE PILGRIM."

She reread it, looked long at the large, bold signature, slowly replaced the note, and walked on.

"How long will he be here? I must go away for a while. It is getting tangled. What a lot of things turn up! Why out of fifty million of men should this one man cross my path? Let me think. Ah, my handwriting! It is horribly peculiar. No one can escape from that. He is not likely to see my memoranda on the autograph covers. And Kitty wanted my photograph. Not I, indeed! And he never saw Lionel."

She thought it all over, and, in fact, nothing escaped her. The same ability honestly used would have given her success in any one of half a dozen less hazardous pursuits, but, like some thieves, she enjoyed the risk of the game in which she was engaged.

She walked slowly, and at last, smiling, moved faster, as she said to herself: "I shall know from Kitty when he goes and of his return. And, after all, how the old man will miss me! It will be lively in that house. Ah, well!"

She went on toward South Street, pleased at her own cleverness and courageous as always. She soon found the little bric-à-brac shop and entered. It contained a dusty litter of cracked china, ragged books, and rusty, valueless arms. A pock-marked little crippled man on crutches came forward. Mrs. Hunter would like to see the letters of George Benedict Fairthorne. She came at Mr. Fairthorne's request.

"Here they are," he said, placing a soiled portfolio before her. "I don't guarantee autographs. I buy and I sell, but I don't ask questions and I don't answer none."

Mrs. Hunter took from her pocket a magnifying-lens and began to study the script. The few weeks in Fairthorne's library had not been wasted. She closed the portfolio. "How much do you want for the lot? There are thirty-seven letters."

"Two hundred dollars, if Mr. Fairthorne takes all."

"I offer you one hundred."

He said, "No," and she promptly rose and left him. At the next corner he overtook her.

"One fifty," said he.

"No."

"Oh, then, one hundred."

"Send them to Mr. Fairthorne for examination. He will decide. You know the address."

As she moved away she thought how easy to make that other hundred.

"He would give two hundred if I were to advise it. Yet, there is a better way," and she laughed aloud. "The letters are forged. But I must have money. Lionel is outrageous. It is too bad." She simply could not refuse anything to this idle, worthless young fellow.

That day, after luncheon, Mary appeared, and despite the pervasive plumber settled herself in her own rooms. Well as she knew Kitty, it was a surprise to her when that young woman threw herself into her arms, saying:

"You were so unkind! but I forgive you, dearest Mary. Don't think for a moment that I don't forgive you."

Mary, vastly amused, kissed her, and the affair of the pearls was at an end, for Kitty at least. Whether or not she should speak of it to Mrs. Hunter, Mary did not then decide. She went down-stairs to her uncle's library, and, coming in, found him very full of excitement over the letters of her ancestor. She was equally interested. He hardly noticed her kiss, and said: "They run over many years, Mary. Here is one about the Stamp Act. The last is in 1780. Where did the man get them? They are addressed to several people. What do you think, Mrs. Hunter? How much was it he asked?"

"One hundred. But they are forgeries. There

are traces of the pencil alongside of some of the letters. See, sir?''

He said, peevishly: ''My eyes are too old.''

Mary, using a lens, saw that the secretary was right. He did not want to be convinced, and argued the matter until Lucretia said:

''Your grandfather dropped the name of Benedict after Arnold's treason.''

''He did,'' said Mary.

''I stopped at the library to look up the dates in Sargent's ''Life of André.'' The signature of Benedict is missing in these letters a year too early.''

''By George! That is clever,'' said Fairthorne, and Mary began, perhaps for the first time, to appreciate justly the secretary's ability. She was too honest not to say what she thought, and after a little more discussion of water-marks and what not went back to her room.

Mrs. Hunter closed the door and said: ''Here, sir, is a letter, come by the noon mail.'' She read aloud Luke Pilgrim's note. The old man was delighted that Lucretia should know Pilgrim.

''An unusual man; an able engineer; odd sort of talker; believes in this country.'' He ran on, garrulous, at times saying shrewdly cynical things and then other things of no moment. She waited, seeming to hang on every word. When he ceased, she said: ''I should like to see him, but I must lose this pleasure for the time. I have to go to New York in a day or two on a little business.''

''You must not,'' he said, taking her hand. ''You won't leave me.''

13

"I have to go. It is only for a few days. You will write to me when I am gone, and you will have Mary and Kitty."

"But they are not you. You will have to come and live here."

"Oh, no! That is out of the question. Miss Mary does not like me. That would never do."

"Then she will have to like you, or I will know why."

"Don't urge it, sir. Some day, perhaps; and now I must go." She kissed his hand, and saying, "Don't worry," went away.

He rose and rang angrily.

"Send Miss Mary here." She came at once.

"What is it, uncle?"

"I have seen that you are making it unpleasant for Lucretia."

"Lucretia!"

"Damn it! I said Lucretia. She has filled the place you and Kitty ought to fill. I am a forsaken old man. Do you hear me? And don't tap that way with your foot. I mean to be master in my own house and I want you to remember that I can alter my will at any minute."

This was so unlike him that for a moment Mary was dumb.

"Why the devil don't you say something!"

She made no reply. Usually, despite his unstable temper, he was pretty sure to be sobered by her silent endurance and to apologize when he had gone too far. She did not fully realize how rapidly he was undergoing degenerative changes, nor how ably a scheming woman had fed his vanity and by degrees maliciously made trouble for his niece. At last she spoke, looking down on him from her height in grief and scorn: "You have not been neglected. That woman is an unprincipled intriguer. What she wants I neither know nor care. As to your money, sir, do as you will with it. But if this goes on, and you talk to me as unjustly again, I will go and live with my sister."

"Oh, Mary!" he said, of a sudden alarmed, "you would not do that. I—Mrs. Hunter—"

"Mrs. Hunter has nothing to do with it, uncle. It is between you and me alone. I love you,—I have always honored and loved you,—but this kind of injustice I cannot and will not endure."

"Well," he said, "we won't talk about it any more." He was terribly afraid that she would leave him, and, being a very conventional person, dreaded the gossip and the scandal such a desertion would cause, and what Harry and, above all, Margaret would say.

"You won't desert me. Mrs. Hunter is going away. Oh, only for a week."

"Indeed! I think you were very cruel, but I will say no more," and, still angry, she determined that now she should have to speak of the pearls to Mrs. Hunter, and would under no circumstances execute her threat of leaving. As she went to her room again, she murmured:

"Lucretia! Lucretia, indeed! Does she call him John?"

She had said very little to Kitty about her horse,

but even had not the mare been lame, it was late to ride, and she missed the relief which physical exercise brings to aid the cause of the lesser morals. She needed some mode of relief, for she felt, as she went slowly up-stairs, that anger costs too much and brings with it a painful sense of having failed in self-control. She sat down and wrote in her diary:

" To be angry leaves me feeling as if I had been ill, and then, too, I have the humiliation of having fallen in my own esteem. I must tell uncle I am sorry. No, I did say so, and before I was honestly sorry, but he was then afraid I would go away. If again I excuse myself he will turn on me and we shall have another scene. It is hard to do right. Finally, I must not desert him. As for his money, I told him the truth, but Madge would not agree with me.

" And so Harry says Luke Pilgrim is coming. I hope he will not bother me again. Once it seemed possible, but when I knew, when he told me his life—oh, then it would have been too horrible for me. Now, it is over and done with, and there are things I cannot discuss, even on paper."

"Or," she might have added, "with Mary Fairthorne."

XX

EVERAL things of interest happened in the week of Mrs. Hunter's absence. How long would be her stay she did not know, and she left her brother with doubt in her mind, since he had quite suddenly declared that he could endure Miss Letitia Markham's rules no longer, and had taken a small room next to his sister's at the hotel where Mrs. Hunter was living. It was his first signal of open rebellion, and was the more ungrateful because she had introduced him to Miss Morrow one morning after church, and Kitty had evidently been pleased with his good looks and his too open way of expressing his admiration. Mary, who was practically the only dutiful guard over Kitty, was vexed when the young man called next day. He was told that Miss Katherine was in. Mary, with various motives in her mind, went down-stairs and said to Mr. Craig: "The servant made a mistake. Miss Morrow is out." She did not ask him to sit down, and herself stood silent, noting his slightly Oriental type and expecting him to go at once.

He was, however, a little confused and disconcerted by the quiet of the tall girl who stood looking down to him. He said: "My sister was so good as to introduce me to Miss Katherine."

"Miss Morrow," corrected Mary.

He was too inapprehensive to accept the reproof. His sister, who had been convent-bred, had studiously acquired the forms of ordinary manners, but had been sadly defeated by his impatience in her effort to polish Lionel. He said: "Yes, Miss Katherine Morrow. I am sorry she is n't in, but I am very glad to see you."

"She is seldom at home," said Mary; "and, pardon me, I hear Mr. Fairthorne's bell." It seemed to her during Mrs. Hunter's absence to ring all day. Then he said: "I hope you will say I called." Mary replied that she would do so, and he went away. When she remonstrated with Kitty, that young person said, with truth:

"No; all I know is that he is Lucretia's brother. I could not help his being introduced to me." As to asking him to call, how did Mary know that? and she wished that people would mind their own business.

Mr. Fairthorne wrote daily to the secretary, bewailing her absence more and more. He wrote, too, that Mr. Pilgrim had been to West Virginia, and had returned to report and consult. He would go again in a week, and would this time be absent in Virginia for a month.

Mrs. Hunter wrote him clever and entertaining letters about autographs and the books in the Lenox Library. He read parts of them to Mary, and wished every one were as thoughtful.

Mrs. Hunter, careful about all things, had left for New York two days before Pilgrim turned up at the Swanwicks', where he usually stayed while in their city. They had long been his friends. He arrived to find them all out.

As it was too late to see Mr. Fairthorne, who napped late in the afternoon, he called on the Misses Markham, in whose house he had once lived for a part of a winter, returning in time to dress for dinner. As Mr. Grace dined with them he had no chance of intimate talk until late in the evening, when, about the fire in the library, he and Margaret were alone, Harry having gone elsewhere with Grace.

"You may smoke," she said.

"Thanks, Mrs. Margaret. I liked your Mr. Grace. A Pennsylvania Yankee, he called himself. I suspect that I may have amused him."

"Why do you do that sort of thing? You are not really a Buddhist."

"I don't know. I have had a variety of creeds. It is intellectually interesting to put yourself in an attitude of faith as regards a religion not your own."

"I cannot conceive of that as possible if you honestly possess a creed by which you live."

"No one lives by his creed."

"No, only by what it pledges one to. I try to live by mine, and so, I am sure, does Mr. Grace. You do yourself injustice."

"No," he returned; "you think of your religion as definite. Nothing is less so. Every one, as life goes

on, evolves a religion which is, at last, personal.
It is the man plus the creed. In every church are
thousands of religions.''

"You are, as usual, puzzling. I think I could
logically confute you. It is n't worth while, but, I
will add, as fatal, that I know what you will do or
not do in every conceivable human situation. If you
were a Buddhist or a Mohammedan I should not. I
never know what you will say, but always what you
will do—oh, that I know, and I know it because I
am sure that certain well-defined principles control you."

"And so you honestly believe that you know me?"

"Yes—I do."

"Do you think I could ever be tempted to murder
any one?"

"Yes, tempted—no more. I do wish that you
would not make a man like Grace think you are—"
she hesitated.

"Well, are what?"

"Never mind what. He was comically surprised
when you turned to talk of mining and the paleon-
tology of the coal deposits."

"I did not mean to surprise him by any of my
talk. I fancy him a man so trained to a regular
conventional business life that he may take too seriously the vagaries of a man of another type. A terribly earnest person, I should think."

"Yes, he is that," said Mrs. Swanwick; "and, too,
he is a man who is learning many things just now.
The American of his class has a queerly open mind.
Where did you go to-day? You saw Uncle John?"

"No, it was too late. I called on the Markhams. Miss Letitia was as delightful as usual. She still indulges in a kind of fiction as to their not keeping a boarding-house. It is rather pathetic. Why would I not come and stay? Now that Clementina was older, having young men in the house was less embarrassing. I was flattered by the classification. Clementina said, 'Quite so, Letitia,' but was slyly amused. One of their young men, Clementina complained, was not at all a nice person—in fact, ill-bred. 'And gave us notice, Mr. Pilgrim! He really gave us notice!' Letitia thought well to reprove him. 'We are glad that he has gone.' 'Yes, we are glad, sister.' I assure you they were charming, as they sat up on the high chairs of Peter Markham, under the portraits, model little dames, with legs too short to touch the floor.''

"But what did our dear Letitia say to that sad young man?"

"Oh, I forgot that. She said, 'Mr. Craig, you are quite free to go when you please. People do not need to give us notice.' "

Madge laughed merrily.

"What a terrible reproof! And then—what then?"

"Clementina said, 'He guessed we would n't make any money if we ran a boarding-house that way, and then we both walked out of the room.' "

"Our dear white mice! They will not let Tom Masters help them. When they need new silk gowns Tom goes to Harry, and Harry recovers some mysterious debt out of their father's wrecked estate. I

have a fancy that they understand it. I am sure
Clementina does.''

''I saw their young man,'' said Pilgrim. ''He
had forgotten something and came back to get it.
A pretty young man, and would look well in petti-
coats. They have another young man besides old
Wilson, who, you know, has all the rest of the house.
By the way, he is going to leave them.''

''Indeed, I am sorry to hear it. That other is *my*
young man!'' and she narrated Dr. Archer's strata-
gem, and her education of Blount.

''You are as good as always, Mrs. Margaret. How
is Miss Fairthorne? She, too, was out.''

''Very well,'' she said; ''but, like all of us, rather
troubled about my uncle. Kitty took a fancy to a
Mrs. Hunter, whom she fell in love with at Newport,
and now—oh, it is a long story! Somehow this
woman has fastened herself on Uncle John and has
magnetized Kitty.''

''Is it serious?'' he asked. ''Does it really distress you?''

''Yes, greatly. One never can tell what may
happen.''

''I have known such cases. I shall be curious to
see her.''

''You will not see her. She is away, and Uncle
John is behaving like a child who has lost a nurse.''

Pilgrim was silent awhile, smoking quietly, before
he said:

''Mrs. Margaret, do you think time will have
made it worth while?'' She knew what he meant.

''No, I do not. It was a question of sentiment

with Mary, perhaps of what some people might call
excess of sentiment. It could not have been a matter of religious scruple on her part. But whatever
I do or say, you will ask again. You will hurt her
and yourself. That you were innocent does not in
the least affect her, and, indeed, I think she might
have cared for you once; but Mary has too much
imagination.''

"And if—if that woman were dead?''

"It would make no difference. At least not now.
Do you know, dear old friend, anything of her?''

"I do not for these last four or five years. She
still draws the income I set aside for her. I did not
mean her to be tempted by want of means. Ah, but
this is an unkind world.''

"Yes, and most unkind to her best.''

"I may not be that—I am not that, I fear; but I
was so constructed as to suffer more keenly than
many would. I do not know where she is. I do not
want to know. We are farther apart than two who
have never been married. I hope others do not suffer as I do, for I cannot realize, I never have realized, the completeness of the divorce. She still seems
horribly to belong to me, to be mine.''

"But surely, dear friend, you do not love her.''

"Love her! I hate her as I hate no other thing
on earth. It is some devilish combination of hate
and loathing. I asked you if you thought I could
ever murder—''

Madge looked up at the stern face.

"Do you understand?'' he said.

"Yes, I understand.''

"What she did was worse than that. She murdered life, hope, and the innocent chance of love unborn." He was silent.

Madge glanced at him again, oppressed to silence by her vast pity over this lifelong calamity. She thought sadly of the folly which, in his green youth, had cursed his life. She knew very little of this marriage, only the bare facts. He was a reticent man, and to her alone had ever confessed himself. But a man will say to a woman friend what he will never say to a man, and the outer world knew little of the life of the eminent engineer. They were both silent awhile, and then she said: "I do wish I could help you."

"No one can help me. I am a little child crying for the moon."·

"And if it be the moon, you cannot get it, and so would it not be wise—a little—to forget?"

"Ah, that is the curse of life, to be unable to forget. Perhaps that will be the best gift of the other world."

Pleased to turn the talk aside, she said: "I am very materialistic in my hopes of that other world. I want Harry and Jack and the baby, and I cannot dream a better world than ours if I could leave out of it a few minor discomforts—a few."

"I sometimes think it rather stupidly constructed," he said.

"Well," she returned, "my uncle is much of your opinion. He says that, considering the ingenuity of nature and her unlimited resources, she seems to have blundered a good deal."

"Perhaps. When as a youngster I was thrashed, it appeared to me outrageously stupid, a very complete blunder."

"My sister answered uncle by quoting, 'Imperfection is the noblest gift of God.' "

"How like her that was!" he said. "Ah, here is Harry."

XXI

T HE days ran on in the home of John Fairthorne very quietly, save for the uncertain temper of the master, who querulously complained of Mrs. Hunter's absence. Mr. Luke Pilgrim was there daily. He had plans to discuss with Fairthorne, on whom such matters acted as a tonic. The legal questions connected with the settlement of boundaries involved also consultations with Swanwick, and thus it was that a fortnight passed and they were well on into December before Pilgrim was able to return to West Virginia.

During this period, as Mr. Fairthorne was kept excited and more or less busy, the house lost the uneasiness which in some ways even the servants had felt so long as Mrs. Hunter's rule prevailed. Where Mary Fairthorne governed there was patience and a certain sweet serenity. Things went along tranquilly and the domestic machinery worked smoothly, as the best machines should do.

Kitty was devotional and attended evensong, and sometimes, by chance, was met by Mr. Craig after the services. But, except that he was a man, he did not please her as did most new male acquaintances, and this she herself recognized and put down to all causes but the one which was giving rise to the nearest approach to an honest heart-stir her life had as yet felt. When, again, this irrepressible young woman sent notes asking to consult Mr. Knellwood he did not reply in person, but wrote rather short answers. When she begged that he would again allow her to confess to him, he wrote curtly that it was impossible.

The retiarius was tangled in his own net. Kitty became pale, and went less and less to dinners and balls, longing for Mrs. Hunter's return.

But even after she knew that the engineer had gone, Lucretia lingered in New York. Soon, however, the excitement of business being over, Mr. Fairthorne began to insist on her return. Then she wrote that she had an offer to assist in the management of a school in the West, at a salary so large that it seemed folly to decline. Nothing but her recognition of the advantages of constant contact with a mind like that of Mr. Fairthorne made her hesitate. He groaned a little, but replied at once by offering her twenty-five dollars a month in addition to her present salary. Lucretia wrote him a note of thanks, and the next day took the afternoon train to Philadelphia.

It was one of Fairthorne's evil days. Archer had insisted that he must not drive. When Mary said that in this case she would use the carriage, he said:

"No; it must go to the station for Mrs. Hunter."

Mary, learning thus for the first time of her coming, flushed a little, and said she could do her errands afoot.

For a while this December, Mrs. Hunter, being in a good humor and seeing all Mr. Pilgrim's letters, was at ease and, for her, amiably disposed. Except that her brother had again been taken severely to task, she would have felt that the world was at last treating her well. When, however, he confessed, a few days later, that Mr. Grace had told him that in a month he must leave, she was in despair. He bewailed in a childlike way his sad fate as she caressed him and sat thinking what she should do. Kitty had not been captured, as she had foolishly hoped. That rather wild idea she had at last deliberately given up. It was plain that Knellwood not being attainable, Kitty was again playing with Archer. Her she could manage, but what about Lionel? Then she remembered.

Next day she turned from reading the morning paper to Mr. Fairthorne and said: "May I take a great liberty, sir?"

When he said: "You never take liberties, but you sometimes say damned queer things. What is it?" she went on to tell him that a friend in New York had asked her if the Republic Trust Company were in sound condition. Fairthorne was too little his old shrewd self to see the absurdity of Mrs. Hunter's being thus consulted.

"I saw," she went on, "in your property schedule that you hold a large amount of the stock."

He at once was alarmed. "Mr. Masters asked my advice about it some time ago. After that I forgot it. I forget everything nowadays. Thank you."

"May I be permitted to suggest that you consult Mr. Grace about it? He would, I am sure, come here if you wrote to ask him."

When he said Harry Swanwick could see Mr. Grace, she urged that he would not be as competent, and so, the letter being written, the banker, rather pleased to be consulted, came next day. He had meant to call about this very matter.

Mr. Fairthorne said nothing of his secretary, and simply put his question as to the stock. Grace replied that it had been badly managed, but was now, he learned, doing better and being better taken care of. Then he said that the finances of the country were in a critical state, and that he himself held a large amount of this stock. It was now down to par. If he or any one were to throw on the market a large block of the stock it might cause a serious fall, a run on the deposits, and possibly bring about a failure. He assured Mr. Fairthorne that on the whole he himself had decided not to sell, but he did not so advise Mr. Fairthorne. He thought he must judge for himself.

The old man hesitated a little, and when Grace saw this he said at once:

"If you determine to sell, I will take the whole of your stock at par. So large a sale, if made in the usual way and reported, would be calamitous. I should prefer to accept your stock, as I have said, even at a loss."

Fairthorne, who had no very good opinion of any one who dealt in money, became at once suspicious of an attempt to get the better of him, and replied with his old-fashioned manner that he was greatly

14

obliged, but would hold his stock and hoped it would rise to what he had paid for it.

Grace, satisfied, rose, when Fairthorne said:

"By the way, you have my secretary's brother, Craig, in your office. I hear that he has not done well, and that you have told him to leave."

Grace smiled.

"Why, yes, Mr. Fairthorne. He is really quite worthless. He is careless and lazy, and frequents billiard-rooms and is seen with people who are known to be disreputable. I try to know about my clerks."

"That is all very bad," said Fairthorne; "but may I ask, as a favor, that you will give him another trial?"

Grace, rather pleased to oblige John Fairthorne, said:

"Oh, certainly; it is a small matter. He shall have his chance."

Fairthorne rose with his guest, saying:

"Come in again when we have no business. My nephew-in-law told me they had declined to send you the Assembly book. I will speak of it to Masters and Winwood."

Grace flushed a little at being thus patronized, and at the disclosure of his social ambitions.

"It is of no moment, sir. I beg that you will not trouble yourself."

When he had gone, Fairthorne said: "What the devil does that dollar-grubber want with society? These people ought to be kept in their places."

Mrs. Hunter, well pleased, thanked him; and

Lionel, thoroughly scared at these revelations and his own danger, for a time kept better hours and was altogether more attentive. Roger Grace, partly from kindness and partly because he was gratified to oblige Mrs. Swanwick's uncle, had done a thing which, although seemingly of no moment, was to entail consequences of the gravest nature. He brought about a battle between character and circumstance, of which we shall learn more.

XXII

ELIEVED for a time by Mrs. Hunter's renewed services and by her rather too watchful amiability, Mary Fairthorne began to notice Kitty's paleness and want of gaiety. At the same time she saw that Dr. Archer was apt to be left by Mrs. Hunter to give his daily orders to Kitty, who was always near at hand upon these occasions. Why she was lamenting the loss of one man and using her chances to make another unhappy it would have puzzled even Kitty to say, and it is to be remarked that of her longing affection for Knellwood her cousin knew nothing. She was worried about Kitty, and troubled through all her nature with something akin to dismay by her own self-revealments; for this woman was too honest to escape self-confession.

Very little was made of Christmas in John Fairthorne's house, and it slipped away, as usual, quietly.

On the 15th of January Mary wrote:

"DEAR MADGE: I will call for the children to-day, unless Mrs. Hunter takes the carriage, which is rare of a morning. But in any event you must have me to dinner. I cannot stand Lucretia every third day. I am not in good enough spirits to keep up with her clever talk, and Kitty is as melancholy as an autumn day, and what for I do not know. She used to tell me always. Now I presume her confidante to be Mrs. H., and, dear Madge, I love Kitty. You insist that your affections are always reasonable—mine are not. No matter, I shall dine with you."

When Mary arrived, a little before dinner, her sister said that Harry had wished her to be told they would have two dull men to dine. When Mary knew them to be Grace and Martin Blount, she said: "Ah, this is your social kindergarten. How glad I am that I came!"

People as unusual as Grace interested Mary, and Archer's account of young Blount's energy and industrious persistency pleased a woman appreciative of all forms of honest human effort.

"Dr. Archer insists," said Madge, "that I am really helping the young man when I give a tired fellow the chance of an hour's talk. I like him, but, my dear, he is terribly direct. After he had taken and used practically a hint or two as to nails and soiled cuffs, he blurted out, 'Dr. Archer said it was an education to know you'; that is me, dear—or I should say I; and he went on to say that now he knew what his friend wanted, would I not just as leave say, 'You must not do this,' and 'You must do that,' ending with 'I won't mind. I 'll like it.'"

"Rather startling, that," said Mary.

"I meant to have had you here alone to-day with Mr. Blount, but Harry wrote me he had asked Mr. Grace. As to my young man, well, he does n't eat with his knife now, but he does say queer things, and he is what the doctor calls a natural observer.

I call that a very dangerous animal. As to Mr. Grace, I think of turning him over to Kitty.''

"Don't, dear; she is out of tune, and just now she is—''

"What?''

"Oh, no matter.''

"Is it Sydney Archer again? He is too good to be hawked at by Kitty. She is neither true woman nor true lady; and as for the man, don't you know, dear, the old posy—

> "There is always a fool
>   In the court of King Cupid,
> And sometimes he is clever,
>   And sometimes is stupid.''

"That is quite too true. But why this common malady should so cloud men's wits has always puzzled me. I might love a man to distraction, but I do not think I should cease to reason.''

Madge smiled.

"Amor furor brevis est.''

"I wish you would not use Latin quotations to me. As for Dr. Archer, he will never marry Kit. I am sure of that.''

"Well,'' said Madge, "we have only a friendly interest, but I wish he were not such a fool. It lowers one's opinion of a man to see him caught by such a girl as Kitty.''

"I do not think him a fool, but after all— Oh, here is Harry.''

A moment later she rose, as Grace and Blount entered. Archer had insisted that the young man should have a dress-suit, and how it was managed, against Martin's inbred views on economy, neither revealed. As he entered, Mary saw that this test was well stood. The strong, rugged face looked its best in the clothes to which fashion has so changelessly adhered.

Mary, very happy to be out of the forced gaiety of Mrs. Hunter's society, enjoyed the evident pleasure which the two male guests found in the little dinner-party.

Grace, a man of large views and national interests, was anything but dull. He talked well, and the chat dealt not too heavily with the strike on the railways of the year before and on party questions. Blount was silent, but listened, and noticed automatically what went on. He began to appreciate the skill with which his hosts kept the talk going even when to his mind a good deal of it seemed silly. The gay folly of well-mannered chat was almost as fresh to the banker as to Blount. The latter began, as was his way, to try to analyze it. How did they do it? And, above all, the goddess, Mary Fairthorne!

During an unlucky pause in the talk, Blount said:

"You have dropped some gravy on your shirt-front, Mr. Grace."

Mary said, quickly:

"I know a man who gets his whole menu there when he dines."

"What is a menu?" said Martin.

"What you eat and what you do not," laughed Harry. And while the banker, a trifle disconcerted, repaired as much as was possible of the mishap, Margaret said:

"I saw you well splashed in the park last week, Mr. Grace. You are hardy to face this weather."

"Oh, I must ride daily. I learned to ride after I was thirty, and I am too timid to break the habit. I should lose it altogether."

"I ride at least thrice a week," said Mary, "but always on the Neck-roads, as you know. You must ride with me some day."

"Yes, with pleasure."

"Why are you too timid to break a habit of riding?" asked Blount.

"I mean I am afraid of horses, Mr. Blount. Are n't you ever afraid of something? No; I ought to say, have you any real fears? We all have some unconquerable terror. What different people dread is interesting."

"Yes," said Blount, grimly; "I am afraid of being hungry. I mean really half starved."

Mary knew at once that this was autobiographic, and said:

"I trust you run no risk just now."

"That is so, miss," he returned, while the banker, too keenly curious, asked:

"But were you ever half starved? Some people dread a repetition of an experience, and some fear what they have never known."

Blount looked grim enough as he replied:

"Yes, I was once about half starved for a year."

Mary longed to ask him how this chanced, but Madge, a little fearful of some too frank autobiography, promptly invited her husband to confess his special terror.

Harry, laughing, assured her that his utmost fear was lest he should forget a dinner engagement and arrive with the fruit. To Blount, who was reflecting on a past of meager diet, this appeared trivial.

"And you, Mary?" asked Margaret.

"I am most afraid of—I decline to say of what. You may guess."

"Of illness?"

"No; of pain. That I do fear."

"You don't look like realizing it," said Blount, who had carefully partaken of his first champagne, and felt the effect more than he liked the taste.

Then Grace said: "I once asked a man this same question, and he replied, 'I am afraid of myself.'"

Madge wondered a moment at the gravity of his tones, but Mary knew instantly that it was Grace who had asked, and he who had answered.

"What can such a man fear in himself?" she thought. The serious, clean-shaven face gave to her glance no explanatory comment, as Harry cried, gaily:

"I, too, am afraid of myself—that is, of my better half," and the talk again becoming too gay for Blount to follow, he retired into his own mind to guess at what Mr. Grace could have meant.

Then, as chances at a dinner, the chat ceased to be general. Harry and Mary talked horses. Blount listened, watched every one in turn, was at last brought into the horse talk, and finally, he hardly knew how, brought to relate how he had for a winter

worked in lumber camps on the lakes and later carried the mail on skates over the lake to Mackinaw.
His description of the moonlit solitude of the great
lake and of his swift flight on ringing skates over
the ice, driven by a wild norther, was attractively
given. He had the gift of words. While the others
listened, Mrs. Swanwick and Mr. Grace talked in
lower tones of the large national questions which she
liked to discuss. Grace, like her husband, was a
steady Republican. She was as distinctly a Demo-
crat, and was now having what she dearly loved, a
grave argument. At last she said:

"I can stand in men anything but indifference to
these great questions. Mr. Knellwood thinks that a
clergyman should keep out of politics altogether.
When I told him it was wicked and a neglect of
manifest duty, he replied that the Master of us all,
the Christ, never meddled with politics."

"Did he say that? Were you not tempted to ask
if there were any such things as politics in a modern
sense in Roman Judea?"

"No; it did not occur to me."

"What did you say?"

"I said that there was no more sure way to injure
religion than to take a too narrow, a text-cramped,
view of what Christ taught."

" 'Text-cramped' I like," said Grace. "But no
one will move that man. He is anchored and makes
no voyages; and yet, for all that, what a great, big,
good fellow he is! Between fasting and close living, that he may give to others what he ought to
spend in feeding his bigness, I really think he half

starves himself. He is the most amazing beggar I ever knew. I simply get out a check-book and say, 'How much?' Then he says I am wrong to give without knowing why. I say again, 'How much?' and he takes it and goes away.''

"Yes, I can see him, with that pathetic smile. Even my uncle gives him money, and he is apt to hesitate. Now and then he comes to dine with us, and, to speak mildly, enjoys it.''

"No wonder," said Grace. "I should like you to take me as what they call a 'mealer' in Maine. I am at the mercy of my cook, or cooks, and usually I am driven to dine at my club, which I hate. The fact is, my servants have not enough to do and that is fatal. My cook, the last one, has aunts and god-mothers, and I am, no doubt, robbed famously.''

Mrs. Swanwick said:

"Why do not you take Miss Markham's house? Mr. Wilson has gone abroad. He had all of one story. They are in great need. You would be more comfortable than ever you were in your life.''

"What, those two little ladies you call the white mice? It seems a reasonable idea. I will think of it. How good of you to mention it!''

Mrs. Swanwick looked at her husband as she rose, and the men went up-stairs to the library to smoke. The women they left drew up to the fire in the parlor, and settled themselves for a talk about Jack and Retta.

"I sent you word I could not come to-day," said Mary. "Mrs. Hunter had the horses out. No, dear, it is useless to complain. When our old Israel told uncle that the horses were being frozen, and he 'just could n't stand it no more,' uncle said, 'well, he could leave whenever he liked to go'—and he has been with us thirty years, dear. The woman is cruel.''

"And how will it end?" asked Madge, as she poked the fire.

"I do not know. It will never end. I have simply given up. Ah, Dr. Archer,'' and her face lit up as she rose to make room.

"There is a fire," he said. "The Grant Hotel is in a blaze. That is Mrs. Hunter's hotel. They told me the fire was well in hand, and that every one got out."

The matter did not much concern them, or so it seemed; but, having named Mrs. Hunter, Archer said:

"I do not want her scorched, but I do not think I can stand that woman any longer. I am never sure that what I order will be done. She has some queer ideas of what she calls mental healing, a new Boston fad, I believe."

Mary turned to him, and said:

"You must not desert us. I beg that you will not. I know well how you must feel, but— I thought Kitty received your orders since I was set aside."

"Yes," he said, "but Miss Morrow is—"

"A fool," broke in Margaret, who was at times outspoken. "Any one who trusts body or soul to my cousin will repent soon or late." She had meant to warn her friend, and now had done so. As soon as she spoke she repented, but not very deeply.

"You are hard on her, Mrs. Swanwick," he said. "She is young and, perhaps, thoughtless. Are you not hard on her?"

"No. She has no sense of duty. Kitty is gay, what people describe as artless, and, Sydney Archer, she is cruel, as a cat is cruel, from mere instinct— artless and heartless. What I have just said I have said to her. It impressed her for five minutes. But I was talking of my uncle in relation to Kitty, and went beyond what I should have said even to a friend like you."

Mary, who doubted the absolute honesty of this explanation, remained silent, staring in the fire, a little ashamed that she felt pleased. Then as he, too, was silent, Madge said:

"You must not give up."

He returned that he would not unless he were dismissed.

"Not even then; but that is out of the question."

"That were to promise too much," he replied. So saying, he went up to join the men. What Margaret had so bluntly and of purpose said of Kitty had hurt him, and yet he knew it to be true. He knew, too, that he was being played with, and that what attracted him in Kitty was the mere woman. It was this as much as Mrs. Hunter's interference that furnished a part of his unspoken reasons for really wishing to give up her uncle's case.

And this other woman? There was no one on earth who so completely realized for him his ideal of the true woman.

Could a man love two women? The one basely,

the other nobly? Mary, in her dignified reserve, seemed to him remote, and the other perilously near. He stood a moment at the foot of the stairs, deep in thought.

"There may be two fools," he murmured; "the fooler and the fooled." He went up the stairs.

"Give me a cigar, Harry. The Grant House has been on fire."

"No one hurt?" asked Grace.

"No," and they fell to talking politics.

XXIII

ABOUT nine o'clock on the same night in January, Mrs. Hunter went up in the elevator to the fifth story of the Grant House. She talked to the boy in the lift, and spoke a pleasant word to the maid she met in the corridor. She was liked in the hotel, as she was apt to be by people who saw but little of her.

She found the room unpleasantly warm, and what she called "stuffy." She threw up a sash, cast a shawl over her shoulders, and, refreshed by the inflow of cold air, sat down. She liked to sit in the night at an open window, and now looked up at the sparkling stars over the snow-covered roofs, felt the crisp dry air, and heard the murmur of city life. The stars seemed far, the world of men and action near and familiar. Again she fell to day-dreaming of the life she desired. These imaginative anticipations were becoming more efficient as supplying motives than Lucretia knew.

She shut the window, made ready for the night, and, lying down at ease in dressing-gown and slippers, fell under the spell of a clever novelist. But after a few moments she remembered something, and rose to get a forgotten essay by John Fairthorne

on "Colonial Finances." He ceased to write after
a historian had criticized this essay as wanting in
method and inexact. Mrs. Hunter had asked leave
to read it.

"He must once have been able," she thought; "it
hardly deserved the attack upon it."

As she heard her brother enter his room, which
adjoined her own, she half rose, and then, changing
her mind, lay down again, having certain things to
consider. Success had given new hopes of larger
success. At first Kitty was to be a profitable acquaintance, an introducer to opportunities. These,
as they came, proved to be of easy use. She had
thought of John Fairthorne more as a venture than
as a probably available investment for her powers
of capture. He was so easily managed as to make
her feel what a chance his age and peculiarities
offered. Of course, there had been and would be
obstacles.

She had not yet come directly into collision with
Archer. Was it necessary? No, not unless he
proved to be in her way, and she must not be hasty.
She knew that without cause she often crossed people.
Kitty she controlled absolutely, and twice had taken
her to a spiritualist meeting, where she had been impressed by the agreeable predictions of a very amiable spirit. Mary Fairthorne had remained haughty
and coldly civil, but, as Lucretia saw, watchful. If
only she were ill or could be worried into leaving a
clear field! She played with the idea of drugs and
chronic illness, well aware that she was a creature

of small devices without the courage of such crime
as involves dangerous consequences.

Meanwhile, John Fairthorne was generous, and
she at ease except as concerned Lionel and the future. Circumstance had so far done very little to
help her. She smiled, pleased at what her skill had
won. If only she could become so necessary as to be
more urgently asked to live in the Fairthorne house!
She had said no, with some politic fear of resistance
on the part of Mary, who had by degrees given up
to Lucretia much that she had hitherto considered
duty. Would she care to resist a larger invasion?
Mrs. Hunter had no liking for a stand-up fight.
Well, something might turn up to help her. Again
she rose. Why was Lionel so quiet? She opened
the door between their rooms, and stood still. He
was asleep. What was that? She stood listening.
Suddenly she heard noises, shouts, cries of "Fire!
Fire!"

Quick steps went by her room. A man beat on
her door, shouting: "Fire! Fire!" She ran to open
it. Two rats ran down the hall. Thin ribbons of
smoke crawled slowly out of crack and crevice, mysterious, gray, and soon with swift increase. People
passed by her, dressed, half dressed, carrying clothes.
A woman dragging a huge trunk out of a room
begged her to help. One pulled along two screaming
children. For an instant Mrs. Hunter did not credit
the danger. Of a sudden the smoke thickened and
swayed to and fro.

She ran back into her room, seized, as she passed,

15

a purse from the table and a little jewel-case, and
crying wildly, "Lionel! Lionel!" rushed into his
room. He was on the bed, dressed and asleep.

"My God! He is drunk. What shall I do?"
She shook him, and at last pulled him out of bed, so
that he fell heavily to the floor.

Meanwhile, without, the tumult of terror rose, and
the smoke crawled in the open transom and floated
in gray masses along the ceiling. Lionel moaned:
"What is it?"

She threw over his head the pitcherful of water.
He sat up, clutching at her, at the bed. Half mad-
dened and strong in her despair, she shook him
fiercely and aided him to stand. He lurched against
her, crying: "You let me alone. What 's the
matter?"

She tore open the door and dragged him, reeling,
into the corridor. It was filled with curling, dense
smoke, warm and suffocating. She stood an instant,
appalled. More people went past; a dog whined and
ran by her. The first breath nearly suffocated her.
She saw the gas-jets flaring in yellow halos. The
smoke, the coughing—something—sobered Craig. He
tried to get away. A man struck against them, and
all three fell. The man got up cursing and fled. For
a moment Lucretia could neither see nor speak. She
lay on her face gasping, stretching out vain hands
to find her brother. Lying thus the smoke was less
felt. She crawled about, groping, calling hoarsely:

"Lionel! Oh, Lionel!" Not for a moment did
she think of deserting him.

The smoke grew hot. She was alone. She stood

up and pitched against the wall, dazed and half blinded. She staggered here and there, voiceless, still searching, trying to call Lionel, the slave to one desire, lost for the time to all thought of self-preservation. An instant later she was aware of the staircase, down which she stumbled, clutching at the rail. She tried to go up again, but dropped on her knees. The smoke above grew ruddy, the fire, swooping up the elevator, flashed in scarlet tongues of flame overhead, along the floor she had left. And still she persisted trying to reascend the stairs, until fragments of window-curtains fell blazing about her.

"He is dead! He is dead! My Lionel, my boy!" she moaned in a hollow voice, and, beating out the fire on the burning edge of her wrapper, she went reeling, half choked, down the stairway.

How she got to the floor below she could never have told. The lower stories were already inches deep in the water which was pouring down the stairway. Her feet were wet, her hands, slightly burned, were tingling with pain. She was coughing and gasping for breath. The firemen ran to and fro. She fell over a great hose, pulsing with the throb of distant engines. A fireman picked her up on the first floor and carried her down to the flooded hall, where he left her on a lounge. The water was dripping through the ceiling in an irregular, yellow, ill-smelling rain. Most of the inmates of the house were already out.

Lucretia lay for a time, unable to speak or move. Then she sat up and looked about her. One or two people were distractedly refusing to go, and one, a woman, was held by a policeman, whom she struck in her anguish, screaming out:

"Joe! Joe! He is up there!"

A man ran to her and said:

"I am Joe! Look, I am Joe."

"No," she cried, "you are not Joe," and was carried out.

A police captain came up to Lucretia as she sat moaning and rocking back and forth.

"Come," he said, "let me carry you. Every one is out."

"No, no; Lionel—he is lost!"

A clerk came up, loaded with ledgers.

"Oh, Mr. Craig? He's out long ago. He got out among the first. I gave him a drink."

"Are you sure?" she cried, hoarsely.

"Why, yes. He said you were out, too."

"Take me," she said faintly; "a carriage—the Lapierre House. Are you sure he is out?"

"Yes; he is all right."

The policeman lifted her in his arms and went out. The sky was a dome of glowing smoke. The street, kept free by ropes and a line of police, was aflood with slush. The engines spouted black, spark-lighted smoke. She saw dimly a man on a ladder overhead, and the flare of scarlet on the red-brick houses and the icicles, for the cold was intense. She saw, but lay sobbing in the arms of the sturdy officer.

"It's all right," he said; "he's safe, sure enough."

Her one only thought for the time was:

"He deserted me. He left me to die. Oh, Lionel!"

They went under the lifted rope and through the crowd. The theaters were not yet out, and a carriage was easily found. The clerk had thrown a blanket around her. She drew it closer, shivering. Lionel was the only person for whom she ever made kindly excuses. He would never have done it, she said, if he had been sober. And he never was so— so—like this before. It was hardly true, but she believed it or made believe to do so, and was comforted. She began to think.

"Ah!" she cried, and, leaning out of the window, called to the driver: "No, not the Lapierre. South Fourth Street, above Spruce. I will stop you at the house." She was still giddy and coughing. At John Fairthorne's house she called out:

"Here, stop. Come back to-morrow. You shall have five dollars. Ring—ring the bell."

It was hardly ten o'clock. She leaped up as the hall door opened, and, running up the steps, went past the amazed old servant, and, seeing Kitty, said:

"It is I—Lucretia. The hotel took fire. I am—I am burned. I am cold. There was not a bed in the hotels. I had to come here." Then she fell on her knees and rolled over on the floor.

How much was real and how much of it acted were hard to say. Kitty was useless in emergencies, but the servants, putting her aside, carried Mrs. Hunter up-stairs and very soon supplied her with warm garments, a good fire, and, what most she needed, bed.

Kitty sat by her side, really sorry, and suggesting

a variety of means of relief for the lightly scorched hands. At last Mrs. Hunter, a strong and healthy woman, said hoarsely:

"Now go to bed, dear. I have lost all my clothes. You will have to keep me a day or two. Get me a doctor to-morrow. These hands will want something. No, not to-night; and no, dear, not Dr. Archer. That nice old man. Oh, Dr. Soper. Lovely name! And, dear, when you tell your uncle, do make him understand how it all was, and that I hope I did not disturb him."

"Oh, no. He never hears."

"Good night, Katherine."

When Kitty went down-stairs she met Mary, who had just returned from her sister's and was questioning the servants. She asked what had happened, and was told the story in a rather confused way.

"No room in hotels?" said Mary, reflectively.

"Not one. Wasn't it terrible? Wasn't it awful? And so embarrassing for poor Lucretia!"

Mary said it was, and went up-stairs.

"I believe," she said to herself, "that woman set the hotel on fire." Then she inquired with care whether Mrs. Hunter had a good fire and blankets on her bed. In her own room she sat down in her wrapper and wrote in her diary:

"January 30. Mrs. Hunter is burned out of her hotel and into our house. I am sure that she arranged it, and as to there being no rooms elsewhere, I should like much to know the truth. The woman will stay; of that I am sure. If she does, I must have a talk with her. Yes, she will stay."

Mrs. Hunter, unable to sleep and in a good deal of pain from her hands, was making use of enforced wakefulness to reach a like conclusion as to permanence of stay. She was in John Fairthorne's house and meant to remain. What she most wanted in life for a time was precisely the luxurious ease of her present surroundings. How neat it all was, how comfortable! And what next? Money, in some way. She might end by marrying the old man, but she knew him well enough to doubt if he would do that in a clandestine way, and if not and she could persuade him to an open marriage there would arise difficulties—a difficulty. No, that would not do. She knew his personal self-esteem, his pride of race.

"Well," she said, "I must wait and see. I have had a bit of luck, and at all events it is deliciously comfortable here." By and by she fell into a sleep troubled by dreams, in which she was trapped by fire and saw Lionel, far off, laughing.

XXIV

HEN Mrs. Lucretia Hunter, with the wisdom of her kind, chose for her physician Dr. Soper, it was not for her burned hands alone. They were painful, but were not deeply injured. She well knew what Sydney Archer would say if she were to ask him, "How soon can I be moved?"

Thomas Soper, M.D., was also LL.D. of some remote little Western college whose president he had once attended when that official was taken ill in the city. The doctor was a childless widower of advanced middle age, described by mothers as a safe physician and by himself as a man who kept up to the times but never tried experiments. Sydney Archer said he never did anything else.

He was plump, rosy, and lived behind a perpetual smile. At limitless ease about himself and all the problems of the medical life, he was a fair example of what an average mind, the amiability of selfishness, and fairly good manners may attain in a profession where men who are not of great force fail or succeed as they are judged by the voice of the nursery. Dr. Soper was not a man's doctor, but this did not trouble him. He was as busy as he desired to be, but had no hospital appointment and only one source of discontent: that, although of mature age, he was not called upon for consultations.

When he sat down at Mrs. Hunter's bedside and she said, feebly:

"How good of you to come early!" he returned:

"Do not mention it. I am heartily at your service. And do not dwell on the horrors of your escape. Miss Katherine has told me. Ah, the poor little hands! Bless me, how small they are!" He took out his watch. "Ah, the pulse is not bad; a little irregular; you are paying the cost which a sensitive organization exacts." This was a favorite and successful phrase. "Might I see your tongue? Good! And your throat? A trifle irritated, of course. Nothing serious; you will be up to-morrow."

Lucretia had no such intention. She murmured, in a husky voice:

"I fear not. My chest aches, and I have a pain in my side. Rest is always my best remedy."

"Certainly, you may be right. An intelligent woman's opinion as to herself always has weight with me—always. I should say keep quiet, and in a day or two we shall see."

"Thank you," she returned; "it hurts me to speak, and please come in this evening. It does make one feel so safe."

He said he would, and ordered a soothing cough-syrup and a dressing for the hands. The latter she used. The syrup she did not. She had no belief in doctors, bad or good. At her rare need, she took certain of what she called Indian remedies, or credulously intrusted herself to what she had learned in

New England to call "mind cure." In fact, even about religion she had no honest belief, but cherished a number of superstitions which she kept carefully hidden.

Mary was decently grieved at the grave account Dr. Soper gave, and was therefore a little surprised when, on the fourth day, Mrs. Hunter, reclothed, appeared with still bandaged hands in Mr. Fairthorne's library. Lucretia, despite her vigor, had suffered too gravely from physical and emotional shock not to show it.

Mary rose as the secretary came in, gave her a chair, and said something of her recent escape. She was struck, as she looked at her, by the pallor of her face and the still reddened setting of her dark iris. It added to the singularity of her gaze, which had the steadiness of the unwinking eyes of babyhood. It meant little, but some people disliked it.

Mary had been busy with her uncle's morning mail. When she expressed civilly, but coldly, her pleasure at Mrs. Hunter's prompt recovery, she was graciously thanked in turn. John Fairthorne said: "I am glad to have you back again." He spoke very little of her peril and illness, but was certainly pleased to see her, having missed the incessant attention, the adroit flattery, the devotional attitude. No one else had ever so fully risen to the level of his self-appreciation, and Mrs. Hunter, unlike Kitty, knew when to be demonstrative. He said, with for him unusual want of courtesy:

"Now, Mary, you will have the freedom you like. Lucretia will go over the rest of the letters."

Mary flushed. She was hurt and angry.

Mrs. Hunter was about to say, "No, no," and to excuse herself for the time, but the liking to exert power overcame the wiser impulse. She said: "I shall be glad to relieve Miss Fairthorne. She has so many outside duties."

Mary walked out of the room without a word. She met Kitty on the stairs.

"Is n't it nice to have Lucretia well so soon?" said Kitty.

"Don't speak of her," said Mary. "She is an underhand sycophant. I should like to kill her!"

Kitty was shocked and passed up-stairs speechless, while her cousin went by her. Mary had meant to attend to certain household duties, but could not yet quiet herself enough to face the old black servants. She turned into the dimly lighted drawing-room, sat down, put her face in her hands, and began to cry, an uncommon thing for her.

John Fairthorne had been in the place of a father to her since her later childhood. He had been, in his better days, an intelligent companion, and, if not always kind, in the past had been courteous, if not considerate. When during the war Madge married, and after it their mother died, Mary had gone to live with her uncle. She was then a girl of fourteen. He had managed her modest estate with fidelity. That he was selfish she knew; that he exacted from her work which was often distasteful was also true; but she owed him much. As she said aloud: "I will not be driven out," Dr. Archer entered. She looked up, and hastily dried her tears.

"Oh, Miss Fairthorne," he said, "what is the matter?" The evident trouble in the face of this tall woman, usually so self-contained, affected him in a way he was unprepared for. There was more of the child than the woman in her reply, for tears sometimes make us very young.

"Ask Kitty," she said, and then, "No, no. Go away, please. I am a mere child. I let that woman hurt me. Me! Now do not say I am hysterical; I won't stand it." She was close to that state of unrule.

"Miss Mary," he said, gently, "we are old friends. Can I in any way help you?" A great tenderness came over him as he spoke. He understood how elemental must be the passion which so shook this wholesome girl. She was silent, now doubly wrought upon, and not yet in full command of herself. He took her hand and said:

"Please not to cry. You must not."

She drew away from him, trembling, and said:

"I wish you would go away."

"I will," he said, "if you wish it."

She was becoming afraid.

"Do you hear?" she cried, sharply. "Go and talk to Kitty. Go anywhere."

He stood still a moment, a little hurt, a little puzzled, and saying only: "I most honestly wish I could help you," left her alone.

MRS. HUNTER, in possession of pleasant quarters, was readily induced to stay, and took up again her duties as secretary. At first she was positive as to not remaining, but Fairthorne was as decided, and would not hear of her going. No one else was consulted. Kitty was pleased, and Mary, after one stormy talk with her uncle, was silent.

With her usual explanatory way of excusing Lionel, Lucretia accepted his abject apology for his conduct and for having lost her in the smoke. She said little, but was glad that the fright served for a time to keep him sober, so that he ceased to be a source of annoyance to Grace's head clerk.

Mr. Pilgrim was still in the Kanawha country, and, as he wrote, was likely to be detained there for a month or two. Fortune smiled on Lucretia, and the lost wardrobe had been amply replaced by the help of a check the size of which would have surprised Mrs. Swanwick and made Miss Kitty jealous.

XXV

R. GRACE, of late years a very deliberate man, usually acted with decision when once he had reached a conclusion. He had been kept a little uneasy by the financial outlook, but it affected him far less than the fact that his cook had announced her approaching marriage. This chanced a few days after Mrs. Swanwick had given him advice.

About five on a winter afternoon he rang at the door of the Misses Markham. He was by no means sure as to what he would do. It was a reconnaissance brought about by his cook's folly and Mrs. Swanwick's urgent counsel.

He was shown into the front parlor, and saw, in the dim light, two little ladies. They sat beside a small table, and by the light of what used to be called an astral lamp were industriously engaged. Miss Clementina, blushing, hastily concealed from the male gaze an undergarment which she was mending, Miss Letitia put aside her tatting, and both bade him good evening.

"I am Mr. Grace," he said, and then, with businesslike directness, "I hear, Miss Markham, that your house is empty. I am considering the advisability of taking the entire house, and of asking you to provide for me. I live simply, and my man-servant will wait on me. The terms are unimportant. I should like to come at once. May I see the house?''

Almost instantly on entering he had been attracted by the room, the women, the old-time serenity of the place. It was unlike any boarding-house he had ever seen. He had decided.

The two ladies in gray silk listened until he ceased.

"Mrs. Swanwick has spoken of this matter, Mr. Grace," said Letitia. "Our old friend Mr. Wilson has left us, and it is true that we have been in the habit of receiving guests for a compensation.''

"We like to call them guests," said Clementina.

"Sister!" said Miss Markham.

"Excuse me, Letitia.''

"I will put on paper and send to Mr. Grace what it is pleasanter to say thus."

"Mr. Grace will comprehend," said Clementina, "that, being alone in an unfashionable neighborhood, we find it agreeable to have one or two gentlemen.''

"Single gentlemen," said Letitia.

"Well, I am very single," returned Grace, smiling. "I give no trouble. When I have one or two men to dine in my sitting-room I can order dinner from the club."

"I fear we could not allow that," said Letitia.

"No, we could not," added Miss Clementina; "it would hurt Susan's feelings."

"And who is Susan, may I ask?"

"Our old black cook. We really could not."

Grace began to understand. He was both amused and pleased.

"We shall not quarrel as to that," he said.

"Susan's terrapin," said the younger Miss Markham, "has always been considered remarkable."

"That is mere detail, Clementina."

"But, Letitia, we could not turn away Mr. Blount. He has an attic."

"On no account," returned Mr. Grace. "I know Mr. Blount. But I shall want the whole second and third stories, and to dine alone. My man will live elsewhere."

"Excuse us, but do you smoke cigars, Mr. Grace?" said Letitia, gravely. He said he did. Letitia thought that serious, but was of opinion that this might be passed over because he would be careful. Young men never were. And would Clementina show him the house? The order and cleanliness of the ample old paneled rooms, and, above all, Miss Clementina's modest depreciation of what they had to offer, delighted him, and, like Blount, he saw here the kindly promise of a home.

When that night he received Miss Markham's letter he at once accepted her terms and sent a check in advance for the first quarter. Miss Letitia said it was a liberty, but Clementina thought they might pass it over as it was the first time.

"What pleasant, old-fashioned folk!" he said to Margaret Swanwick. "I cannot thank you enough."

"Yes," she said; "they are gentlewomen, and have suffered sadly."

"But why," he asked, "does Miss Clementina dress like an old lady? She cannot be over thirty, and Miss Letitia is at least forty-five and quite gray. Miss Clementina is pretty. They both look tired."

"Yes, the dear little lady thinks that it is, as she says, nice to dress like Letitia, and makes Letitia feel younger. I often tell her I should like to order her gowns. I did not say to you how very poor, and yet how touchy they are as to being helped."

"I guessed it. I have told them I always burn wood in my rooms, and ordered enough to last all winter."

"You will have to be careful. They won't like it if you begin in that sort of lavish fashion."

"I saw that. And they have no gas in the house. 'It is unhealthy,' said Miss Letitia, 'and dangerous.' I had to yield."

Mrs. Swanwick laughed.

"You will be mildly and firmly governed, and I do assure you it is good training for a future state."

"A future state?"

"Oh, yes. Not there—here on this earth—here."

"Not I," he said.

XXVI

ONG afterward Mary Fairthorne declared that the only thing which kept her sane that winter was her afternoon rides. These the constancy of cold with sunshine favored, and indeed they were much needed. In February Mary wrote in her diary:

"Mohammed was right when he said, 'Good humor is the bride of the rider.' It helps me wonderfully. Kit is lost to me, and more than ever needs me. I have hardly any home duties left. I live a narrowing life of fretful complaints from Kitty, and reasonable complaints from the servants. The house is full of unrest and suspicion. It is hard to see my way. I know only this: I will not be manœuvered out or driven out. The woman is astonishing, and I am simply a boarder."

It was true. She was almost without influence or power of control. Lucretia had become more essential to Fairthorne than any of his family. The machinery of the old man's subjection was simple. Miss Mary made it "hard" for her, said Lucretia. How could she bear it, when she could so easily find work and peace elsewhere? On this he was sure to become excited. Should he speak to Mary? No, no; it would make things worse. Then there were tears. No, she would never leave him.

As time went on, Mary retired from useless battle.

Margaret brought Jack to the house no more than she could avoid, and Harry came only on business. Their friends, resentful of this alien rule, unwisely ceased to visit the old man, and he was left more and more to the society of Lucretia. He made no complaint. She was amply, patiently competent to keep him amused, and might have rested at ease except for the inexplicable pleasure she found in petty tyrannies which were really detrimental to the ultimate plans she never ceased to keep in view.

As Mary ceased to resist, she turned upon Archer. She had driven out the nieces; she had narrowed John Fairthorne's world to the few who could not or would not be denied access. Her success had been all that she could wish, but Lionel had failed her. Kitty's mind was elsewhere, and for once was stable. Beyond the attainment of comfort and ease, Lucretia had been disappointed. Mrs. Swanwick would none of her, and the staid society of the old town, with its set ways and indifference to wealth, surprised her. She was socially inclined and at her best a gay companion, but here the houses she would have liked to enter were closed to her. She bitterly resented it.

What Mary Fairthorne thought of the situation she now and then confided to her diary:

"This woman disturbs me. She has, I think, some silly idea that those queerly set eyes affect me. I met her suddenly at dusk yesterday with Felisa, the cat, on her shoulder. Certainly she looked like an evil witch. She was evidently posing. I laughed and said I hoped I had not startled her. She did not like it. Why does she dress in black and yellow? I wish I knew her history."

She was walking her horse as she thought over this record and was wondering how it would all end. Hearing hoofs behind her, she turned and saw Sydney Archer, also on horseback. Her face lighted up with welcome as he joined her. He rarely rode during his busy winter, but, as he now said, the glory of the winter sun had tempted him. "I am twice rewarded, Miss Mary." She was joyously happy to have this man at her side.

"What luck!" she said. "I was gloomily busy, thinking over what you know too well—the distracted state of my uncle's house."

"Yes," he returned, "I do know it well. I have seen this sort of thing before—oh, more than once. But what can you do? If Mr. Fairthorne were worse we could simply take command. He is more excitable and is slowly becoming weaker, but mentally he is as clear as ever, with an intensification of all his peculiarities—his half-hidden pride of race, his dislike of contradiction, his closeness about little expenditures, and, what is rare in age, his willingness to give away money in larger sums. Really, he is a singular character. But age is fast changing him. He is not the John Fairthorne of middle life."

"Yes, that is true. Mr. Pilgrim once said that he wondered which of us would wake up in the world to come."

"Which?" he asked.

"Yes; shall we awake old or young? We are in life several people. That is his wisdom, not mine; but the thought of what my uncle was and is recalled it."

"It was like Pilgrim. In fact, the situation is full of danger. Do not underrate this woman. She is no common schemer. She may marry him."

"Good gracious!"

"I do not think she will. When last she asked me if he were likely to live long I said he might live ten years—and he may, but he will not. It made her thoughtful, I saw that. She was reflecting upon the prospect. Something is worrying her."

"Do you see through everybody in that way?" asked Mary.

"Oh, it is a mere guess. You put yourself in the place of another, and 'there you are.'"

"You are dangerously clear-sighted," she said.

"Oh! The art has its limitations. If I should try now to think of what is in your mind I should fail." The woman turned her face away, feeling herself flush, and touched her horse with the spur. In a moment Archer was cantering at her side again. She laughed as she called to him:

"Have the kindness to keep your insight for Mrs. Hunter. Is n't this lowland country interesting?" They were now on the road which led to Greenwich Point. "Over the river yonder is Red Bank, where the Hessians and Count Donap failed, and this in front is League Island. You must see it in the spring. It is like Holland then, and only needs a few windmills." She went on talking more rapidly than usual, while he watched her with a certain discomposure he could not have explained. She went back to the question she had asked.

"To see through people must be valuable in your profession. I envy you its science, its variety of human contacts, the feeling that you are helping people.''

''Well,'' he said, ''Miss Mary, it is as I see it the best line of human endeavor.''

''And you give,'' she said, ''so much to the hospitals, to the poor—not as others give, mere money, but hours and days of life, of thought.''

''Oh, as to that,'' he returned, ''it gets to be too habitual to afford nourishment to a fellow's self-approval.''

''But that is the finest thing about it,'' she cried. ''I hate to hear a doctor complain, like old Dr. Soper.''

''And yet,'' said Archer, ''he has had success.''

''But men on the front bench do not complain; or do they?''

''No; but he is not on the front bench,'' laughed Archer. ''By the way, talking of these matters reminds me to say that Miss Morrow's rector, Knellwood, is ill. Grace asked me to see him yesterday. He was in a second-class boarding-house, in a room that would make you shudder. There was hardly space to move in it. The furniture was shabby, the floor and chairs were littered with books and papers, the whole place was incredibly uncared for. It was cold, with a feeble escape of warm air from a register, and really the man had not blankets enough to keep him warm.''

''How dreadful! Harry says he has a very good property. I suppose that he actually starves himself that he may feed and help the poor. I do wish I liked him better. It seems really wrong not to like him.''

"If you are at all like me, Miss Mary, you will have long ago ceased wrestling with your likes and dislikes."

"I never can. But what can we do for him?"

"Ah, Mr. Grace always asks and usually answers that question. He carried him off at once to the Misses Markham's. You should have seen their dismay, and then how Letitia and Clementina went down before Grace's decisiveness. Miss Letitia confided to me that she should not mind, except that Clementina was so easily influenced, and really, his religious views, and so on—you can imagine it all. I represented that even a mild attack of typhoid would render him harmless. The fun of it is that Roger Grace, who likes the big preacher and thinks his doctrines abominable, vows that he will keep him there and feed him like a decent Christian."

"I tremble for Clementina," laughed Mary. "Let us gallop; here is a good bit of road."

As they turned their horses for a homeward walk, Archer said:

"A word more about Mrs. Hunter. I am being endlessly pestered by her interference. I shall fight it out, of course; I said I would. I see that you are troubled; let me, as an old friend, ask you not to conjure up all manner of things not likely to happen."

"I do, I do," she said. "I sometimes think her wicked enough for anything. Margaret is never tired of quoting what Mr. Pilgrim said, that people with too much imagination pile up mountains and then have to climb over them."

"Rather elaborate, that."

"No; it is true as far as I am concerned."

"A queer type of man," said Archer. "So practical in action, so efficient, and so—what shall I say? So fond of the mystical."

"Yes, his talk is often too indistinct for me. I hear they are having trouble about those coal-mines. Harry showed my uncle yesterday a letter about them and Mr. Pilgrim's difficulties."

As they rode up Swanson Street and past the old Gloria Dei Church, he said:

"Miss Fairthorne, you are very fine medicine for a busy man. It is good to be made to forget for a time. But I must make haste now."

"Thank you. I ride nearly every day, and always here." As he rode away, she said to herself:

"I wish I had not said that."

XXVII

IF Miss Fairthorne was troubled in mind and heart, Mrs. Hunter had, too, her share of anxieties. Lionel had been so good of late that she had begun to feel there must be enough wrong to make him afraid to confess, for usually when it was a question of money he was anything but reserved. She was right. He had, in fact, been speculating in a small way, and had had the usual first luck of the fool. He was living in the center of a vast business, and was getting used to seeing this enormous flow of checks, notes, and gold. The abundance and the seeming ease of it all might have tempted a man whose only honesty was the child of fear, had it not been for the perfection of the safeguarding mechanism, which, even to his small mind, seemed to be perilously certain. Just now he owed an importunate broker a small sum of money, not over two hundred dollars. His sister had recently been less indulgent than usual, and had told him that he had thrown away chances. He had said in reply that Kitty Morrow did not "amuse" him, and that it was "all no good." In fact, it had never been otherwise. He was essentially vulgar, and even

Kitty's uncritical taste could not stand it. At this time the devil set for him an easy trap.

Mrs. Hunter had invited him one afternoon to Mr. Fairthorne's study at a time when its owner was taking his afternoon nap. Lionel, who drew a little and sang a little and did no one thing well, was shown the musical autographs. His sister set before him with pride the catalogue she was making, and then the large portfolio in which were the autographs of Gluck, Mozart, Handel, and others.

"This will please you," she said, "you who love music. You may look them over. I will be back in a minute. I left my desk unlocked."

He turned over the collection in a languid way. Nothing interested him until he noticed the cost prices set down on the covers. One, an autograph of Beethoven, surprised him, as he was absolutely ignorant of the absurd value attained by such manuscript. He read:

"Bought of Donaldson & Co., London, June 9, 1855. See Annesly's Catalogue, No. 73, 1849, p. 9. Value, $700. Sold at Van Glück's sale for £110."

A thief of intelligence would have reflected before taking a document which must have been so well known to collectors. He had hardly a moment of hesitation. Neither he nor his sister had the moral mechanism we speak of as conscience. In her its function was partially replaced by a variety of constraining or restraining motives which had nothing to do with the act in question's being wrong or right.

Her brother was the unintelligent slave of impulse, and had too little imagination to serve him by predicting unpleasant results. He had been guilty of small thefts when at college and had escaped detection. The dog who steals a chop gives no more thought to it than Lionel Craig gave to his theft when he buttoned his waistcoat over the precious autograph of Beethoven's Ninth Symphony. He closed the portfolio, picked up the nearest volume, and was glancing at the sketches of trees in old Gilpin's delightful book "Remarks on Forest Scenery," when his sister returned.

"I thought I should find you lost in those Schubert songs, you who sing so well. I should not have thought you would prefer a book. That is a favorite of Mr. Fairthorne's. He is fond of trees. You must go out with me some day and see the country place."

He said that would be very pleasant, and, uneasily desirous to get away, rose as she replaced the portfolio.

The fourth day after Lionel had stolen the autograph Mrs. Hunter and Mr. Fairthorne were reconsidering—and he reconsidered a great deal—a novel method of arranging the musical autographs. In his youth he had played the flute a little and ever after believed himself a good musical critic. Suddenly, looking up from the portfolio, he said:

"The Beethoven Symphony is out of place."

Mrs. Hunter reflected.

"Miss Mary was showing the autographs to Mrs. Vincent yesterday. It must be here."

"Find Mary," he said. "I will not have my papers meddled with. Mary has no sense of order."

When his niece appeared, he said: "You have lost my Beethoven autograph. I want it understood once for all that no one but Lucretia is to handle my collection. Where is it?"

"I do not know. I did not show Mrs. Vincent the musical autographs. She wanted to see the writing of Blake and Poe. I know nothing of these musical papers."

"I suppose," he said, "I must believe you; and now, I desire to repeat—"

"What! Stop, sir! One word more like this, and I go to Margaret's. You will apologize at once—at once." She stood before him, tall, erect, and flushed, with anger in her steady gaze.

Mrs. Hunter hesitated. A word would complete the mischief and drive out this troublesome girl. She waited a moment too long, for as Mary, turning away, said, "Good-bye, sir," John Fairthorne rose to his feet, and exclaimed: "I was hasty, Mary. You won't leave me. You must pardon the ill temper of an old man. Do not go."

Any admission of age or failure was so foreign to his ordinary habits that Mary's anger of a sudden fell away to pity.

"That is enough, uncle." She would have said more had Mrs. Hunter been absent.

Lucretia spent an unhappy day in search of the lost document. When at last Mr. Fairthorne, dissatisfied, asked who of late had been allowed to see the autographs she suddenly remembered.

After leaving her uncle, Mary went up to her room, saying, "Could she have taken it?"

This was unjust, both to Mrs. Hunter's intelligence and her habits. The margins of the distinctly criminal she knew well enough, but there temptation ceased, subdued by the fear of results. She was cold-blooded and passionless, but if she loved at all, or if what grief she now felt were the outcome of attachment rather than affection, Lionel Craig was the only man or woman who possessed for her even this slender claim on her heart. There are women capable of keeping up one such relation at a time, and no more.

She waited that night in Lionel's room until he came in. He had moved again, or rather had been ordered to move, and was now in a shabby hotel, where he could afford a small room on the third floor. He had a fear of fire which haunted his dreams.

The room was dirty and ill kept. On the walls were pinned photographs of actresses and others, some signed affectionately. In the corner were half a dozen canes. The wash-basin was still full of water. The room smelled of patchouli and tobacco. On the unswept carpet were cigarette ashes.

Lucretia, a clean, neat creature, saw it all with disgust. She opened a window and wondered whether it were worth while to try any longer to help him. He was startled to find her in his room. She lost no time.

"Give me those autograph sheets you stole. My heavens! what a fool you are! You might as well

steal the Koh-i-nur or a great Raphael. No one
who knows its value will dare to buy it. Any one
who ventured to advertise it would be caught and
would tell. Give it to me.''

"I did n't take it," he said.

"You cannot even lie cleverly. You are suspected, and will be arrested.'' He turned pale and
sat down.

"I have n't got it. I sold it to that man on
South Street. I let him have it for eighty dollars
because he said he would sell it in Chicago. He
would n't give any more. I did the best I could.
I had to have money.''

"Oh, Lionel,'' she cried, "you will ruin us! And
to rob a man who is so good to me and who made
Mr. Grace keep you! It was wicked.''

She did not herself honestly feel what she was
saying, but perhaps Lionel would. He said he might
get it back, but that he owed altogether three hundred dollars, and how could he pay it? The fear
of arrest was her best argument. She repeated it,
and at last said that in the morning she would send
him a check. And—no, she herself would try to
recover the autograph, and hoped to be able to warn
him in time if the police suspected him as others
did. She left him in a state of abject terror.

When, next morning, Lucretia found the little
cripple in his shop on South Street she was not less
direct than she had been with Lionel Craig.

"Let us talk in the back of your shop, Mr.
Peachin.'' He went before her and dusted a stool.

"No,'' she said, "I will not sit down. You tried

to sell Mr. Fairthorne forged letters of his grandfather. They were well done, but as I urged on Mr. Fairthorne that you were poor and perhaps yourself the ignorant dupe of another he did not take any further steps.''

''I did n't guarantee—''

''Quite true; but you did them yourself, and he could have very seriously troubled you and utterly ruined your business. No matter. We did not follow it up. Now some one has stolen from him a musical autograph. It has been traced to you as the receiver. Give it to me.''

He said he had sold it.

''To whom and for what?''

When he declared that he could n't tell she knew that he was lying.

''Very well; you say that you paid eighty dollars. I am prepared to repay you and ten dollars over. No? Then, good-bye; you will hear more of it.''

When, as had happened before, she was a block away, the cripple hobbled after her. She had of purpose gone slowly. He said:

''If you will say one hundred you may have it.''

She said, ''No,'' and at last he agreed for ninety dollars, and they went back to the shop. She looked the sheets ever. They were all there. The cover Lionel had not taken. She paid in notes.

''If,'' she said, ''you get any really valuable autographs, let me know. Here is my card. I will drop in now and then. But let this be a lesson to you.''

As she went out, he said: ''Are you any relation to the young man who brought me those papers?''

"Oh, it was a young man, was it? That is strange. We suspected a young woman."

The cripple looked after her. "They 're as like as two peas." He did not believe in the value stated by Craig, and was well contented. So also was Mrs. Hunter. But she kept her brother usefully uneasy for days.

When she found the missing music script in the large portfolio of autographs of the signers of the Declaration of Independence, her tearful joy at this discovery was a touching thing to see.

Meanwhile, she watched the mail, and knew that Mr. Pilgrim was still busy in West Virginia.

Kitty had long since given up all charge of her uncle and Mrs. Hunter was now the only person to whom Archer could look to execute his orders. It too often happened that what he wished done was not done, and at last he resolved to make a stand.

One morning, as usual after his visit, Mrs. Hunter waited in the drawing-room to receive his instructions. In place of standing for the brief time his purpose required, Sydney Archer closed the door, and saying, "Sit down, Mrs. Hunter; I want to talk to you," took a seat opposite to her.

"I am at your service," she returned. "What is it?"

"I am an old friend of the people of this house."

"They are fortunate."

"Pardon me, I want to say certain things without interruption. I am an old friend, and you are a newcomer. You have, no doubt, excellent intentions, but somehow you have been able to obtain a control over Miss Morrow and Mr. Fairthorne which, as I see it, is not wholesome. You will say, perhaps, that it is none of my business. As to John Fairthorne personally I do not care. Miss Morrow has relatives who should be able to see that no harm comes to her. But through Mr. Fairthorne's weakness you have been able and willing to set aside a woman who unfailingly carried out my orders. That is my complaint. This cannot go on, or—''

Mrs. Hunter smiled meaningly. He understood it, and, a little nettled, continued: ''It has hurt her, but what has happened is not alone her concern. It is in part mine. She is naturally the person on whom he should lean. You have thrust her aside, and now, in place of my orders being complied with, I find that you are giving him medicines of your own choosing, or that he is induced to drive out or in one way or another to disregard my wishes. It is useless to go into particulars.''

''Quite useless, Dr. Archer. I have no belief in doctors. It is only necessary for a man of Mr. Fairthorne's intelligence to believe intently that pain is not a reality, that we are spiritually powerful to decree the absence of disease. I cannot conscientiously stand by and see used what I believe to be hurtful methods.'' It is probable that she was dishonest in her statement; it is quite possible that she was honest. People who have no religion are very likely to feed the human love of mystery with one of the many unwholesome diets of folly.

Sydney Archer had heard this kind of talk often enough to know that argument was valueless, even had he been inclined to argue.

17

"Frankly," he said, "all these notions and the books on them are the very apotheosis of the vague. I have nothing to do with them or your views. I am Mr. Fairthorne's physician, and so long as I am I mean to be obeyed. No, wait a moment more. The thing is simple. I do not know your object in bringing misrule and unhappiness into this house. If you let me and my work alone I shall do nothing to displace or disturb you, or shall warn you if I do. But if you interfere with what I think my duty, take care! That is all." He rose, saying: "I have changed the treatment somewhat, and here are my written directions."

Mrs. Hunter also stood up and fixing upon him the gaze which some people thought unpleasing was still for a moment. She then said, in a low voice, carefully kept free of angry emphasis: "You mistake the situation. I have made no effort to live here, or to become Mr. Fairthorne's secretary. It was the accidental result of Miss Morrow's attachment. Mr. Fairthorne found that I was able to do certain work, and to do it well. Kitty was too young, Miss Fairthorne was incompetent and careless." Her voice rose; she hated Mary Fairthorne. "If I say that she neglected her uncle, it is his charge, not mine. She has made my duties hard and has treated me with insolence."

Archer wished this woman were a man, but he kept, to appearance, the calm of one used to self-command.

"We are a little off the track," he said.

"Yes; it is not easy to bear what I have endured

and to make no complaint. I shall refer these questions to Mr. Fairthorne.''

''Why not now, at once?''

''I prefer to consider Mr. Fairthorne more than you seem inclined to do. He is not at all well to-day.''

''Come up-stairs with me,'' he said. ''I am unwilling to let this matter rest here. You may follow me or not, as you like.''

''I shall do exactly as I please.''

Archer smiled. There was a vibrant note of vulgarity in the voice that was commonly soft and pleasant. He went up-stairs, she following.

It was, in fact, one of John Fairthorne's better days. Very little things affected him, for good or ill. Archer had amused him by an account of Martin Blount and Margaret's efforts to instruct him.

''By George!'' he cried, laughing in his old hearty way, ''that must be a comical trio, the Presbyterian Grace, that ultimate churchman Knellwood,—ultimate is a good adjective; the adjectives get worn out, used up; 'extreme,' Mary would say,—and your plow-boy Blount bothering to get an education. There is too much education—makes the masses unhappy. Damn education! It is a premium on discontent. It is very well for the upper classes.''

Archer had laughed. ''What class would you belong to if you had not a dollar? Martin Blount's plow-boy life was a cruel accident of poverty. His people were in eminent colonial place before yours landed in this State.''

''Is that so? I should like to see him.''

This talk had amused him, and he liked to be amused. It was part of Lucretia's unending attractiveness. She did what Mary had ceased to do and what Kitty could not, and was, in fact, a gay and clever raconteur, with no very lively scruples as to the character of her stories.

When the doctor reëntered the library John Fairthorne was at the window, studying an autograph letter of Aaron Burr. As he turned, Archer was struck with the look of interest in his handsome old face. He had the blue eyes which do not show, as dark eyes do, the signals of degenerative decay. He was saying to Mary, who had just given him the monthly account of household expenditures, "If you find it correct that will do." Mary was amazed. Never before had he failed to inspect it. She rightly took it for a bad sign.

"Do not go, Miss Fairthorne," said Archer. She waited.

"Mr. Fairthorne," said the doctor, "I have asked Mrs. Hunter to come back with me. I find that she is continually interfering with my orders. My prescriptions are given irregularly, or not given. It is of the utmost moment that certain things should be avoided, and that the heart be sustained by systematically given tonics. I am of opinion that—"

Fairthorne stopped him with a lifted hand.

"I do not want to hear about my heart. It always upsets me." He became at once excited. His head shook tremulously.

Mrs. Hunter said, under her breath: "I told you so, Dr. Archer. It is most unwise. Sit down, sir, do sit down."

Mr. Fairthorne obeyed her, saying, "I do not like these discussions."

"I did not bring it about. I warned Dr. Archer." Archer took no notice of her.

"The question is, am I to control a difficult case, or is an ignorant woman to do it?"

"You must not speak that way, Sydney," said the old man. "I—I won't have it."

"Will you kindly answer me?"

"What about?" He looked from face to face, as if puzzled.

"Dr. Archer thinks I neglect you, sir. He wishes me to go." She caught up a fan and used it, fanning him.

"I said nothing of the kind," said Archer.

"Mrs. Hunter—Lucretia, you won't leave me! And you will not desert me, Sydney. I don't want these discussions." With the childlike cunning of age, he took refuge in the appeal of weakness. "I cannot stand it; I am not strong enough."

Archer knew that it was at best a drawn battle. He said:

"Very good. We can talk of it another time. A word with you, Miss Mary. Good morning."

Mrs. Hunter smiled. Archer went down-stairs in silence with Miss Fairthorne.

"Come in a moment," he said. He closed the door. "Sit down. Well, I failed, as you saw. For your sake and his I am sorry."

"But you will not give him up?"

"Not if I can help it."

"Oh, you must not. I know what you feel. It is responsibility without power. But do not go. I am

getting what Kitty calls nerves. I never knew I had
them. This woman is—she has the unexpectedness
of a ghost. Suddenly, anywhere in the house, I find
her behind me. I think she follows me. And the cat
never leaves her. The servants hate her, and I am
in endless trouble. You won't leave us, will you?"
The evident distress and emotion of this strong and
usually tranquil girl again affected him.

"No. Rely on me. I do not think her dangerous.
She wants money. She will get it, no doubt. The
trouble is that I shall be replaced by some more
manageable man. Now it is open war. Suppose I
volunteer a little medical advice. Get on horseback
to-day. I will join you if I may. We will talk anything but Mrs. Hunter."

"With pleasure. At four?"

"Yes." He opened the door for her, and then
went away.

Mrs. Hunter made up her mind that Dr. Archer
must go; but when, next day, she approached the
matter, Mr. Fairthorne showed so much annoyance
that she made sure it was best to wait. She could
wait, and meanwhile would compromise a little and
seem to obey this unmanageable doctor.

XXVIII

"CLEMENTINA," said Miss Letitia Markham, one afternoon in the beginning of March, "we have a great deal to be thankful for."

The younger lady looked up from her darning of Martin Blount's socks.

"Yes," she said, "we have, indeed, much to be thankful for. Mr. Blount gives so little trouble. How much he improves! When first he came he was almost rude."

"And his nails, Clementina."

"And his cuffs, Letitia."

"I had reference rather to Mr. Grace, dear, when I first spoke. He is, so to speak, plain."

"But not common, sister. You surely would not say that of him."

"No, and very delicate in his kindness. One would hardly have expected it. But, dear, you will not mind, Clementina, if I say that after I retire you sit up rather late talking to Mr. Grace. You know, dear, we are single women, living alone, and we have to be careful."

A faint little blush, like the first signal of the dawn of some emotion, rose from cheek to brow, as Clementina returned: "He is often interesting, Leti-

tia, and we see so very few people who are that.''
As she spoke the darning-ball rolled out of the stock-
ing. She bent to pick it up.

Letitia went on: ''I should be sorry to have you
think that I really imagine there could be any impro-
priety, but last night it was quite eleven before—''

''He wanted to talk about Mr. Knellwood, and it
did not seem polite to leave him. After all, we are
his hosts, dear Letitia.''

''Are you aware that you interrupted me, Clementina?''

''Excuse me, sister.''

''We will drop the subject. I am sure you under-
stand me. Katherine Morrow was here to-day again.
I do not think it very nice that she should be inces-
santly sending Mr. Knellwood soups and flowers.
In my day young women were better looked after.
She appears to go her own way.''

It was late of a Saturday night, and at this moment Martin Blount came in.

''Come to the fire, Mr. Blount,'' said Miss Clementina; ''you look cold. It is still wintry.''

''Oh, no,'' he said; ''all I want is to sit down and
feel home. It is very nice to feel home.''

''What a curious expression!'' said Clementina.
''I suppose you mean at home.''

''Oh, more than that. Mr. Grace says you spoil
us all. And to think that some day I must leave you!
I ought to be glad, I suppose. I heard to-day that I
am to have the clerkship at Bedford Springs this
summer. I shall save a lot of money to go on with
next winter. Is n't it jolly, Miss Letitia?''

"Jolly seems hardly the correct word—satisfactory, I should say, Mr. Blount."

"What is satisfactory?" said Grace, as he distributed a pleasant greeting. "I want you to try the tea I sent to-day, Miss Letitia."

"But it is a whole chest," said Miss Markham, with a mild sense of injury.

"Were there some books came two days ago?" he asked. "Those were the books we talked about last week, Miss Clementina—'Cranford,' and 'Little Pedlington,' and the 'Religio Medici.' "

"Thank you," murmured the younger woman.

"Is Knellwood asleep?"

Martin said: "Yes." He had been up to see. Then Blount told his good news to Mr. Grace.

"Yes, yes," said Grace; "very satisfactory, very much so. You go in June, you say? In June?" As he spoke he seated himself at the fire. He took the fire-tongs and put a lump of soft coal on the smoldering hickory logs. It seemed a needless waste to Letitia, whom poverty had painfully taught to be sparing. Then, remembering that it was Mr. Grace's coal and also his wood, she fell into the lap of humiliation because of this lavish guest who sat assaulting the coal at intervals with the poker.

Miss Clementina cast now and then a furtive sideglance, wondering what was keeping him so quiet. Martin took up one of the books Grace had sent, and was soon absorbed in the "Religio Medici."

Only the candle-light, of late amply used, and the red flame of the fire lighted the dulled white paneling. From the walls a half-dozen colonial gentlefolk looked down on the new and urgent generation, the man who had risen and the man who meant to rise, the latter deep in wonder concerning the seventeenth-century doctor.

A little apart from the fire sat the gentle Clementina, pretending, in dress and ways, to be as old as her sister, "because, dear"—this had been said to Margaret Swanwick—"it does please her. I know it does." Beside her, with, for a wonder, idle hands, was Letitia, nursing the fiction that Clementina was still so young as to need supervision and a control which only love perfected made always endurable. She had said, earlier in the evening, to the younger woman:

"I have looked over those books, dear. One of them I cannot quite approve of. I mean as to its religious views, dear." Clementina had said that she would be careful not to let the quaint doctor do harm, and then, with modest approach to the humorous:

"I think you read it all, Letitia! You might ask Mr. Knellwood to have mass for the soul of that delightful old doctor."

Letitia had said: "You surprise me, sister." In fact, of late Clementina had seemed to her "volatile, quite volatile."

Just now, as I have said, Miss Markham was idle, her hands in her lap, her eyes tearful as she turned her gaze on the blue uniform of the boy brother who had said: "There must be another general in the family," and had gone away to die on the sad hillside at Fredericksburg. They were all unusually silent. At last Clementina said: "Kitty Morrow left fruit here to-day, a basketful, and fresh eggs from her uncle's farm, and yesterday soup. Dr. Archer declares that Susan's soup is better. He forbade fruit."

"Now," cried Martin, laughing, "I know why I have such splendid lunch-baskets. I thought Miss Clementina was extravagant."

"And the Easter lilies," said Clementina; "Mr. Knellwood ordered them taken away. He was almost cross. Mrs. Hunter brought them."

"I wonder where that woman came from," remarked Grace. "A singular face."

"I saw her somewhere once," said Martin, "but I cannot say where."

"I think Miss Mary Fairthorne and some others would like to know," said Clementina. "Tom Masters says she is making trouble for our dear Mary Fairthorne. I think he called her 'a vindictive cat.'"

Martin laughed: "That 's descriptive."

"She quite controls Kitty," said Clementina, "and has filled her with folly about spirit rappings."

"I think I would n't gossip, sister," said Letitia, rising. Martin, with freshly acquired courtesy, opened the door and the two little figures departed.

"Martin," said Grace, abruptly, "give up that clerkship. I want the books at my country house catalogued. Let us consider it a business matter. You will have time to study. I really need you."

Martin smiled in his grave, slow way. "No, Mr. Grace, I want to fight it out. I have been too much helped already. I—well, it humiliates a fellow. You will excuse me, but I can't do it. Dr. Archer says you are the most ingeniously kind man he ever knew. He says you ought to patent some of your ways of helping people.''

Martin was shrewd enough to understand the present excuse for helpfulness. Had he known the reason back of it he would have been astonished.

''Well,'' said Grace, ''I used to feel as you do. Think it over. I do not suppose that you will change your mind, but think it over.'' Then he rang for the maid to put out the lights and they went to bed.

Meanwhile, up-stairs Mr. Knellwood was slowly recovering, and regretting the time lost to his work. While he was very weak he had ceased to think of Katherine Morrow, but as his great frame was reclad with flesh and he was forbidden to read, time hung heavy on his hands, and he felt the moral relaxation left by serious illness. Miss Kitty, as we have seen, had material means of keeping her too seductive image in his mind. He was for a while as feeble to resist or banish thought as to control his appetite for food. The physical man was asserting himself, the spiritual being was in abeyance. His color came again. He recalled the cricket-field and his great scores. He saw the grim battle-fields, as he lay in the fairyland between waking and sleep, and, half ashamed, knew again the joy of danger when the fighting chaplain had steadied the wavering battle-line. He stretched his gaunt limbs and laughed to find himself too long for the bed. Again he had thoughts he did not wish to keep in mind, and recalled what Archer had said to the effect that illness may leave men in a condition which for a time lessens the power to control emotion, or to summarily dismiss unwelcome memories. He knew, however, that he was surely regaining normal capacity to rule the domains of mind and body.

There was seeming truce in John Fairthorne's house, while from time to time Mrs. Hunter read the business letters of Luke Pilgrim, and tried to forecast a dubious future. The people were hostile, he wrote. The decisions of the courts were not much regarded. Men were robbing the forests and ready to defend their ways with the rifle. He had no idea of returning just now and had bought a coal tract adjoining the land of Mr. Fairthorne. He wrote very briefly and with a certain caution, due to another correspondence with Mrs. Swanwick.

At last came a letter asking frankly if he, Pilgrim, should insist, in the face of inimical feeling, upon running the surveyor's lines. He was prepared to go on or to withdraw for the present, until the railways opened the country and made it worth while. His own interests were small, Mr. Fairthorne's large. It was a clear, practical letter.

This communication alarmed Mr. Fairthorne. He said to Lucretia: "No, I want him to be careful. I do not want things pushed. Please write him to that effect. Make it plain; if he can go on and run the lines, let him do it. Very likely he overrates the risks. Now I must lie down. No, I need not see it.

Send it at once. Of course, I do not want my rights ignored.''

Mrs. Hunter sat long over that letter. If she could so state things as to delay the engineer's return it was clear gain for her. She wanted time. What Fairthorne had finally said enabled her to send a not entirely untruthful statement, which was well fitted to put a brave man on his mettle. She kept notes of what Mr. Fairthorne said, and they lost no strength in her rendering. The missive went on its way.

The occasional letters which Luke Pilgrim sent to his old friends Harry and Margaret stated the situation more gravely.

"MY DEAR HARRY," he wrote: "I think every country requires a vent for the men whose talents during peace are buried in club reading-rooms or drowned in whisky for lack of relief to the lust of battle. That is the real value of Hindustan to England. That is why war will always exist. It is a latent disease and breaks out like the plague under favoring conditions. Mankind ingeniously breeds a cause, and thus excuses the natural needs of a nation, which are like those of a man, to kill something. It is only a generalized expression of the instinct which makes Tom Masters and quieter folk shoot ducks, or kill salmon, or go after grizzlies. Alas! for the unlucky ones who are uselessly stranded on peaceful days and to whom war was pastime, evolution, and opportunity. Ah, this is the place for them. It is purely medieval in sentiment. The women despise a man who cannot kill. There are fine middle-age vendettas, temporarily abandoned when the community turns out to oppose the civilization of outsiders who innocently trust to title-deeds. There are many old Union men and Rebs here and these are with us. It is the refuse, who were neutral in the war, who are the bad lot. I foresee a row, and I hate it. I have a dozen rifles, and am quietly training my men.

"I wrote Tom, before things began to look serious, to come up here and kill deer and bear. When I saw that we were soon to have trouble about the boundaries the engineers are running, I wired Tom: 'Do not come. We are going to have mischief.' I was a fool."

"I should think so," said Harry. "'Here 's a nice bone, little bulldog, but don't touch it.'"

"Tom replied, 'So glad; come at once. Hurrah!'"

"He might have known that," said Margaret; "go on."

"He came, and really, to see that neat little gentleman, bored with clubs, and pigeon-shooting, and with what he calls the accursed certainties of modern life—to see him, suddenly alert, interested, with every faculty raised to the nth power—and all because of the ferment called danger! My English has got tangled, but you will know what I mean, because you remember the mad sixties. For you and me the war was a business of mere duty. For Tom, too, it was this, no doubt, but it was also more. He is a born leader of men—one of those rare people in whom nearness to death-risks ripens talent into genius. He knew it then; he knows it now. But what to do with these fellows in peace! I am most glad to have him and tell him every day to go away. You should hear him laugh. There is n't room for a laugh like that in towns.

"I have written cautiously to Mr. Fairthorne, for really I do not understand his letters. He dictates to that queer secretary of whom you speak. He hopes I will not hesitate to resist if there is trouble in making the surveys. 'Force must be met with force,' and so on. When I took his final direction, he said, 'If the lines cannot be run and the mines peacefully examined, I personally do not care to push matters. I do not need the money and after all the returns will be remote and the present cost large.'"

"There is more," said Harry, "but the rest is purely as to those titles."

"Read it," she said. He did so.

"Ah, here is Mary. Sit down. The winds of March have given you a fine color. We have been reading a letter from Luke Pilgrim. Read it, Mary."

Madge returned to her sewing, and Harry lit his pipe. Both were thinking over the risks run by their friends. Mary took up the letter. She had once been nearer to loving Luke Pilgrim than she had ever been to loving any other man. He was, on one side, a highly educated man, eminent and original in his profession—in fact, an engineer of unusual powers; on his other side, he was fond of the mystical, sensitive, imaginative, without distinct creed or definite religion; a tender man, also—a man people trusted on sight.

Mary reflected as she saw the familiar back-hand: "How near I was to it! But knowing that ended it."

"Well, Madge," she said, "how does it strike you?"

"It appears to me plain; I think Mr. Pilgrim may have misunderstood uncle's letters; but one likes to see the text when statements as contradictory are made."

"Meanwhile," said Harry, "there are two good fellows put in danger that an old man may add to an estate already beyond his needs. I suppose he wrote in one of his irritable moods."

"No," said Mary. "I am surprised, Madge, that you do not see that my uncle never could have dictated the part about using force. For one of us, for a Fairthorne, he is strangely timid. Do you recall his state of mind during the strike last year? He would have had the railroad yield every point. No; Mrs. Hunter's hand is in that letter.''

''But why?'' said Madge. ''One must have a motive. It is not reasonable. The woman is not a fool.''

''That is what she is occasionally. I sometimes think that, like Tom Masters, she fights for the love of fighting.''

''That seems to me a little absurd,'' said Harry.

''No,'' she insisted. ''Mrs. Hunter is there in that letter. Why she wrote all that I do not know.''

''My dear Mary, your imagination does sometimes carry you beyond the boundaries of proof,'' said Madge.

''Good gracious! You dear little logician! What else is it for? I should like to show this letter to uncle, but I believe that it would be useless.''

''Let us wait a little,'' said Mrs. Swanwick. Harry, as usual, acquiesced in her view of the matter. Mary shook her head in dissent. She thought that her uncle ought to see this letter at once, but as Harry sided with his wife she unwillingly ceased to urge the matter. Presently Madge asked what had become of Kitty.

''You must inquire of our dear Lucretia,'' said Mary. ''They seem to be largely engaged in attending to the physical wants of their spiritual director.''

''Indeed, Mary, that is too true. Kitty is a source of some amusement to the young man I am polishing. Miss Letitia is in a state of chronic disgust.

18

Kitty is being gossiped over as none of us ever have been. She really kept Mr. Blount a half-hour last Sunday while she asked all kinds of questions about Mr. Knellwood. It was like poor Kit's small cunning to think that the 'country-bred lout' (that is Kitty's, not mine) would not suspect. In reality, he is what Mr. Pilgrim described as 'too ingeniously inferential.' Blount said it did seem as if Miss Morrow and Mr. Knellwood 'must have been keeping company.' Don't look so shocked. It was his way of saying what we should put some other way.''

''Don't laugh, Madge,'' returned Mary. ''It is too dreadful, too humiliating. What could you—what did you say?''

''Say, dear? There is a refuse-heap in a corner of that young man's mind into which I am sweeping a fine collection of these country phrases. Wait a little, and see what I shall make of him. Let us thank God that Mr. Knellwood is a gentleman, and for his own sake a celibate.''

''Well that is small comfort. Are there other letters, Harry?''

''Yes, one other—no, two. Pilgrim says that, being in some doubt, he wrote to uncle more freely, and that uncle was in return even more positive that Mr. Pilgrim was right as to his determination to have the lines run and his legal rights enforced.''

''It is all very strange,'' said Mary.

''Here,'' rejoined Madge, ''is a letter from Tom Masters to Harry. I have not heard it. Read it to us, Harry.''

"DEAR HARRY: Pilgrim kindly wired me that there was a small war on. A man brought the telegram out to my boat. I was in Tampa Bay, and fast to a tarpon. I cut the line, came in, got a sloop up the coast, and so across country on a horse to the rail, baggage to follow. We may get off without a fight, but these fellows want it. They are fools enough to think it will end this matter of boundaries; as yet we have had no serious difficulties. Meanwhile, the people are rude and hostile, and for fear of what may come I am giving the young engineers a few lessons as to how to take care of themselves. By Mars! they need it. Luke is engaged in diplomatic efforts at some kind of compromise; it won't work; the trouble is the squatters and their women. One of them told me to-day I was 'a nice little man,' and her Bill would fetch me home to be 'a doll for the children.' She was a handsome devil. I said Bill would never get near enough. I put up my rifle, barked a gray squirrel on the top of a big papaw-tree, and said, 'Take that to the children, and let me off.' She 'guessed I could shoot,' but that the squirrel 'did n't have no rifle.' I said I had been shot at a good deal, and that I had a charm and could n't be hit. By Jove! I think she believed me.

"My worst trouble is with Luke. He wanders about in the hills alone, cracking rocks with his hammer. If things get worse here, some one will shoot him. When he gets away from the engineer party I am all the time uneasy. Next week the lines will be run through Bill's farm. Then look out!

"I am very well and enjoying myself. Send me down the last-pattern Winchester, 45-caliber, and two hundred cartridges.

"Yours as long as I last,

"TH. MASTERS.

"P. S. Some fool shot at Luke yesterday evening. It was, we think, a woman. What could one do against a brigade of petticoats? The sex down here is well advanced. I see in the papers one or two rather disquieting things about the Republic Trust Co. I suppose so long as John Fairthorne is satisfied I may be. I got out of it. I wonder has he sold?

"Yrs.,

"T. M."

They agreed that it was very confusing.

Late that evening Archer came into Swanwick's, as was his frequent habit, to smoke his only cigar of the day before bedtime. Mr. Swanwick was out.

"Sit down," said Margaret; "you look tired."

"I am more weary than tired. I had an annoying bout with Mrs. Hunter this morning; my out-clinic, which I like to run myself when I have time, was unsatisfactory—just a series of cases of the poor needing all kind of things which no man can give, or else hopeless incurables. And then I had to discharge from the wards three honest mechanics. They are well, but yet weak, stranded, penniless."

"How can that be helped?"

"Helped?" he said. "Ask the rich. Every man discharged from a jail is cared for, but the man who leaves a hospital, who cares for him? Sometimes it saps one's faith to see so much misery you cannot help."

"It must be trying in many ways."

"Yes; if a man wants to have his manners, his patience, and his charity tested I advise a heavy out-service for the poor. There are days when everything goes wrong."

"I know," laughed Madge.

"As if to complete things, old Soper stopped me at the foot of your steps just a moment to describe an interesting case. It took ten minutes. At last he said he was in a hurry, and had to go at once to see Mr. Jackson. Then he reported a Mr. Thurston's case at length, as if insomnia was as rare as Morvan's disease."

"What is that?"

"Pardon me, that is shop. You do not know his variety, the Bore Medical. He said at last he might have to ask my counsel. He never will. And Thurston's brother-in-law was ill, quite a remarkable case, and so on."

"Are not both of them officers of Harry's company, the Republic Trust?" asked Mrs. Swanwick.

"Are they? I might have regaled him in turn with the fact that two of Thurston's directors are out of sorts. That might have seemed even more remarkable. The coincidence is a little queer, though. May I have some whisky and soda? Let us talk of pleasanter things. You will admit that I never talk shop."

"No, not enough. I like it. I mean intelligent, impersonal shop."

"That is all well enough for you, who are only a rare customer. I like at times to put up the shutters. If I am tired of it—oh, very tired—I get my fly-books out. They are 'big medicine.' "

They talked of the children or of books until Harry Swanwick came in with a telegram in his hand.

"I found a boy, Madge, ringing as if he would pull the bell out. I pulled his ear, and that stopped him."

"I sent the servants to bed," she said.

"Well, shall we guess what it is about?" He held up the yellow missive.

"Open it, Harry; I have never yet become used to them." He obeyed.

"Oh, Madge!

"'Luke Pilgrim has been badly wounded. Send Archer down at once. See letter. Will wire again.'"

"How dreadful!"

"Get me the evening paper," said Archer, rising. He looked it over in haste, and then at the clock.

"I can catch the twelve through train from New York. I have just time and no more. I shall have to lie over in Baltimore. I will write and settle my own affairs from there. Give me some money, Harry. Thank you; good-bye."

They went down to the door with him.

"You will be careful about yourself," said the little lady. "You know how much we care for you."

"Oh, they don't shoot doctors," he said, laughing. "I shall be friends with every scamp of them in a week, and doctor all the children. Good-bye."

"Don't cry, dear," Harry said, for Luke Pilgrim was the friend of many years, and to be the friend of this house meant more than the word friend commonly implies.

They talked long of Pilgrim and how soon they might hope to hear. Just before Madge went upstairs, she said:

"There is one other thing, Harry, that I ought to say, and it is of moment. Uncle John, who lives in a world of his own, holds a very large amount of Republic stock. If he relies on any one, it is on you."

"Well, dear? You look serious."

"Yes, I am serious enough, and when I explain myself you will very likely laugh at me."

"I never laugh at you." It was true.

"Then I will tell you. Mr. Grace has resigned; the president can't sleep," and she related the doctor's talk; "the vice-president is ill and two directors. Put it all together and you will see."

"But Grace continues to hold his own stock."

"My dear boy, cannot you see it? Here are four directors ill. Mr. Grace may have good reasons for not selling."

"And your uncle?"

"He should at least be warned."

"I will talk to him, but your reasons are rather queer."

"No; and, Harry, you are still their counsel. There is something wrong, or else they would never secretly consult another lawyer."

He said in reply that it still paid him well; how would it do to consult Grace about resigning? Madge said: "Perhaps. Let us think it over to-morrow." She stood still a moment, reflecting. Mr. Grace might or might not be willing to advise on either question, and meanwhile Harry, with his occasional difficulty in coming to a decision, might delay too long to advise her uncle. She saw it all very clearly, and the possible disadvantage of representing as counsel a company within the risk of a discreditable failure. She had seen in the papers comments as to the fluctuations in the price of an unnamed trust stock and knew very well that this implied doubt and suspicion. She wanted her uncle made safe, but she was far more sensitive as to the fair name of Jack's father.

"He shall make uncle sell and he shall resign," she said to herself. Then she turned from it. She had settled the matter, and was equally ready to deal with the case of the unlucky engineer.

"As soon as he can travel, Harry, we must have Luke Pilgrim here. He could have your room, and you might use the hall room."

"My dear," he cried, "it may be weeks, and God knows what we may hear to-morrow."

Like most women who have the logically gifted mind, Madge was not apt to hurt herself with anticipation of disaster.

XXIX

HE next day Harry Swanwick left his wife and the children at breakfast, and went out earlier than usual, intending to see Mr. Fairthorne before he went to his own office. He met Roger Grace at the corner of Broad Street, and wondered what brought the banker up-town at so early an hour. Grace said, as they shook hands: "I was on my way to thank you for your kindness. I think I shall enjoy the dining-club. The list of members seems attractive. I meant to write to you, but I like better to speak my thanks." He was very much pleased. "What good friends you are!"

"We try to be."

"If Mrs. Swanwick will see me thus early, I have something for her."

"She will if you make the servant take your card to her. We had bad news last night. I am on my way to tell Mr. Fairthorne." Then he went on briefly to relate what had happened, and to add that Archer thought Mr. Knellwood might not now require a physician, as he was sitting up, but would write and advise whom to send for in case of need.

Grace said he would tell him. The banker did not know Pilgrim, but he clearly understood the situation in West Virginia, and thought it would have been wiser to have delayed active operations until the new railroad opened the country.

When Margaret came down to meet him, he said: "I have brought you a little money for the home. We wound up a rather prosperous real-estate transaction yesterday. I made two old fellows who never give anything to anything open their purses. They tried hard to get out of it, but it was hard to refuse a man who had made a lot of money for them."

"I suppose," she said, as she thanked him, "that some men have to learn to give. It is an education, and at last a pleasure."

"Yes; to be frank, at first I found it difficult to break too economic habits, when economy ceased to be needed. The habit of useless accumulation is not easy to shake off. Your uncle is interesting to me about that. He gives in large sums, and never in the way of small helpings to people in real need. Knellwood says if he asks aid for an individual Mr. Fairthorne invariably says no, and yet he likes Mr. Knellwood—why, I cannot imagine. No two men could be further apart in all ways."

Madge knew very well but held her tongue, and contented herself with saying that her uncle's likes and dislikes were past comprehending, and then asked: "But why do you yourself like him?" for she was really curious. Grace smiled.

"I don't wonder you ask. How rarely one puts that question to one's self! I like Knellwood for his utter disregard for money, for his entire honesty of purpose, and because—you will laugh—because of his completeness of self-control. Here is a great big man, built for battle, for field sports. Every bit of him must hunger for action, and yet, because he has certain absurd beliefs, he lives an ascetic life, starves himself to feed the poor, and fusses over ceremonial trifles.''

"I can comprehend all that, but cannot yet see why you like him. I do not. Respect does not insure affection.''

"I fancy, Mrs. Swanwick, that to like him you must know him well. Back of all his nonsense is a kind of sweet goodness, something one could trust in time of trial. If ever I wanted to confess to a man I should choose Knellwood.''

Madge looked up at the strongly marked face, with its look of power, and felt that there was an element of the comic in the idea of this man's confessing to the narrow-minded priest of St. Agnes.

"I ought to feel answered, Mr. Grace, but I do not. Let us drop him. I want to ask you—may I say as a friend?—a grave question. I will not go into my reasons for it. Do you not think my husband ought to resign from his position as counsel of the Republic Trust Company?''

The banker was somewhat startled. He had been hearing quite too much of that company in the inner circles of finance.

"Mrs. Swanwick, I do not like their ways. I hold a large amount of their stock, and I shall continue to hold it for reasons needless to discuss. I do not think it will go to the wall, and I am now endeavoring to sustain it in case of need. If the present state of things gets worse, that and some other institutions may break or will need assistance. Frankly speaking, I believe that in case of disaster its management would be savagely blamed.''

"And Harry?" she asked, anxiously.

"Oh, he is as much outside of their affairs as I —oh, even more so, but no matter. To answer you, yes; on the whole, he had better let it go. Tell him to resign quietly, and tell him too that this is all in absolute confidence. I meant to advise him to resign.''

"Will you?" she said, quickly. "I should prefer that.''

"I will. I will write to him within an hour.''

"My uncle is a large stock-holder. Should Harry advise him to sell out?'' The banker did not like it. He had urged Fairthorne not to sell. Between them they held a fourth of the stock. Since then things were, as he knew, going from bad to worse, but a large sale would precipitate trouble and the horizon was already darkening.

"Mrs. Swanwick,'' he said, "I long ago advised your uncle about his stock. In an interview which he sought, I offered to take it off his hands in such a way as not to disturb confidence and yet insure him against serious loss. The offer was not unselfish. I hold to it. I will say all this to your husband, but I do not believe Mr. Fairthorne will sell to me or to any one.''

"Thank you. I am out of it altogether. It is really not a woman's business—not mine, at least.''

"I will see Mr. Swanwick.'' He was beginning

to comprehend how much of the good sense and effi-
ciency of Harry was due to the female member of
the firm.

As he rose she opened the envelope he had given.

"My dear Mr. Grace! You were hard on them."

"It will do them good," he said, laughing, and,
after a few words about Pilgrim, went away.

Harry Swanwick found that Mr. Fairthorne was
still abed. Desiring to see him in person, he decided
to return later in the day. At his office he met a
clerk who said he had been charged by the banker
to place a letter in his hands. There was no answer,
he thought. Harry read it.

"No," he said, "there is no answer. You may say
that I will call at eleven."

At that hour he had a talk with Grace, who said
to him finally:

"On no account must Mr. Fairthorne throw his
stock on the market. At any time I will take it at
par." Then the banker advised him to resign as
counsel.

He went to his office, wrote resigning his place
as official counsel to the Trust, and gave no explanation. When, after the directors' meeting that
week, it was simply accepted, he said to Madge: "I
think they might have said a decent word of regret,
or, as is usual, requested me to reconsider it." He
was a little annoyed.

"No, no, Harry; you were an embarrassment. I
am glad you saw your way to take Mr. Grace's
advice."

When Harry left Grace's office he went to Mr.

Fairthorne's house, and was shown into the library. The unavoidable Mrs. Hunter was busy at one table, with the cat Felisa in her lap. Mr. Fairthorne, who was near-sighted and never wore glasses, was holding a book on surnames as close as the Fairthorne nose permitted.

"Good morning, Uncle John. How are you, Mrs. Hunter?"

Mr. Fairthorne looked up. "Oh, how are you! Fine March weather."

"I should like to talk to you a few minutes."

"Well, talk."

"I wish to see you alone."

Mrs. Hunter rose and went out. Harry shut the door.

"There has been trouble at the mines. Pilgrim has been shot, and I fear is dangerously wounded. Tom Masters is there and wired us last night. Archer went South by the night train. I hope to hear by letter to-night."

"Very bad—very bad, indeed!" said Fairthorne. "Don't see through it. I wrote to Pilgrim not to get into trouble about squatters. Until the court decided I could very well wait."

"I thought you were anxious, sir, to run the lines and open the mines; at least, so far as to decide on their value."

"Nonsense! I wrote nothing of the kind. I wanted Pilgrim to look it all over and report. I gave no orders to push things."

Harry was naturally puzzled as he recalled Pilgrim's letters. He knew Mr. Fairthorne's memory had been failing, and yet he seemed just now to be both clear and confident.

"I want Mrs. Hunter." He rang his table bell. When the secretary returned he said at first no word except as to what interested him most, his own accuracy.

"Have you copies of my letters to Mr. Pilgrim?"

She said she had, but somehow the letter-book could not be found. Mrs. Hunter explained that besides the daily care of the room Miss Mary insisted on a more serious weekly dusting. It had just taken place.

"Oh, very well," he said; "it must be found." He would have blamed any one else, but Mrs. Hunter he never blamed.

"Find it to-morrow, Harry. Some mistake. Yes, I will write to-day and set it all straight. They must all come away. I do not suppose it is very bad. Let me hear when you get your letters. You said Archer had gone down to take care of him? And now I am left without a doctor."

"May I ask," said the secretary, rising up from unrewarded search, "may I ask what is wrong? What has happened?"

"Happened? Everything has happened. Archer has gone off and left me without a word. It is most inconsiderate."

"But what has happened?"

"What has happened," said Swanwick, "is that Mr. Fairthorne's wishes have been misunderstood, and that there has been serious trouble with squatters. Mr. Pilgrim has been shot."

"Good heavens!" She sat down as she spoke. "Not dangerously, I hope?" If ever she lied it was then. Her command of her features was entire, and yet never in all her life had she been so disturbed.

Harry replied that as yet they had no particulars. Mrs. Hunter, eager to get away, asked if she were still needed. On the stairs she paused and stood still, deep in thought.

"I would have fought it out," she murmured. "Now there will be time and to spare—to spare, and perhaps—perhaps—" She turned and went upstairs slowly, heavy-footed with thought. She would be free for a time from a great fear and have leisure to do something more than merely to secure a temporary home. She sat down by the window and watched Felisa, who was in the garden playing tiger in the jungles of dead flower-stems.

"Ah! That will do," she murmured at last. "Yes, that will do; but there is no hurry, and now I shall get even with that sharp-eyed doctor. Decidedly we shall want another physician." The chance of annoying a man who had ventured to oppose her so pleased Lucretia that her face lighted up with an evil smile. "He won't like it."

While she was seeing her way through her game, Harry was discussing the affairs of the Republic Trust. He spoke with the utmost caution, but repeated Grace's offer, and also the banker's request not to sell in open market.

Fairthorne returned: "I do not think it is any one's business but my own, nor why this damned dollar-lord should dictate." Evidently, as happened when anything excited the old man, he was becoming testy and unable to use the power to think reasonably on matters of business which he still retained in calmer moments.

"You may tell him I am not to be made the fool of any broker's ring."

"I shall tell him nothing of the kind, sir; and you must not say this sort of thing to me. Roger Grace is my friend. I won't stand it."

Again, as usual, Fairthorne took refuge in his feebleness.

"I am too weak for these discussions. My temper won't bear it."

"So I perceive. I came here to do you a service, and you thank me by insulting me."

"Is n't that rather strong language to use to an old man? But no one respects anything or anybody nowadays. I suppose you want me to say I am sorry. I am not, but I apologize."

"That is quite sufficient," said Harry, shortly. "I will send you whatever news I get."

Fairthorne was easily beaten. He was not very much afraid of Harry, but he had a wholesome dread of Mary, who was unrestrained by any terrors of the use he might make of that deadly weapon, an old man's will. He had, too, a minor dread of Margaret's way of gaily putting him right. Moreover, as he well knew, any slight to her husband she never pardoned. Her mode of punishment consisted in keeping Jack away, and as Fairthorne was proud of his namesake he was never long in coming to terms when deprived of Jack's society. The cat was less

19

fond of Jack, and Mrs. Hunter stuffed the boy with bonbons, to Margaret's horror.

The letter-book was lost until other matters caused Fairthorne to forget it. The day after the coming of the telegram which disturbed so many people, a letter arrived from Tom Masters. It ran thus:

"DEAR HARRY: I inclose a simple statement of what happened, and of Luke's condition, and, not to keep you in doubt, I may say that he is doing well.

"Pilgrim came down with orders from your uncle to run the boundaries of his lands, test the outcrop of coal, and to avoid, at present, collision with squatters. Later Mr. Fairthorne wrote very positively that the boundaries were to be run and blazed, and his lines established, whether the squatters liked it or not. Pilgrim swore he would obey orders, and got together a lot of ex-Confederate engineers. It was a foolish business. The wood losses are really small, and the mines are useless until the railways get in.

"Pretty soon these fellows began to think their wretched little clearings in peril. They threatened, and Pilgrim went on in his grim New England way. Then I came up and saw what we had to expect. Luke said he was sent there to study the coal and run those boundary lines; he meant to do both. I set to work to take care of him. Two days ago a man named Springer came down to our camp and said no man should run lines over his farm. Pilgrim talked to him; it was useless. Next day I made half of the engineers take their rifles, and went with them myself.

"When we got on to the clearing, Pilgrim, who would not arm himself, walked toward the house. I was fifty yards behind and well to left. He called to the men to wait a bit, that he must talk to Springer. As he spoke, the man, who was out of my sight, within his doorway, fired, and Luke went down with a ball through his right lung. Several of our men fired into the doorway. Being at one side I saw Springer run out back of the house. As he climbed over the snake fence I fired. I am glad now I did not kill him. Queerly enough, my Winchester ball went through his right lung from back to front. It was good Hebrew justice—eye for eye—except that Pilgrim was hit by the smaller bullet. When Springer crumpled and fell, I ran up and took his rifle. It was a long-barreled old-time piece, a muzzle-loader.

"Pilgrim is doing well, and Springer is likely to die. I am anxiously waiting for Archer, for certainly both men are in peril. Springer's wife is comically suspicious because I want the rascal to get well. This is not the custom of battle here. I cut out my bullet with a penknife. It was just under the skin. Springer, half dead, cursed me, but they had to hold the man's wife. I am the third man in danger, and I am advised of several doctors learned in the law and practice of the vendetta, to seek a more wholesome climate. Mr. Springer's sons, æt. sixteen and eighteen, are in the mountains with guns. Mrs. Springer assures me that they will 'git me for certin, specially Bill.' Between nursing Pilgrim and fussing over Springer and running the lines through his farm, I am well occupied. Those boys bother me. Calf game is not to my taste.

"Meanwhile I am more alive than I have been since that mournful day at Appomattox, when I felt worse than Robert Lee. I fell out of the only business on earth for which I am fit. Tell Jack we will come here some day and camp in the yew-pines and kill bears. I never forget that I am his god-father. It is an awful responsibility. My love to his mother. Pilgrim sends his something or other—it was not very clear. I think he is going to pull through. There is, in my rooms, a double-barrel express-rifle. Send it down to me in a box, and label it 'fishing-rods' or 'tracts.'"

Harry Swanwick left a note at John Fairthorne's to the effect that Pilgrim was doing well, and went home to give Tom's letter to Margaret. She read it twice, and said at last that they would not have any satisfactory news until Archer wrote, and that things about the boundaries and her uncle's wishes in regard to them seemed to be in a queer snarl. When Harry mentioned the mislaid letter-book she became silent, and then said:

"That woman is at the bottom of it. Mary was right. I should like to know what it all means."

XXX

WO weeks passed by, and March was nearing its close. Archer had written that Pilgrim was slowly mending, but suffered a good deal. Springer had become the sworn friend of Tom, who had promised him that he should have a legal title to his farm. The boys had come in, and Tom was off with them after bears. Mrs. Springer had a new gown. Tom and the doctor had come to some kind of an agreement with the mountain men, and there was peace for the present.

Mrs. Hunter was at ease, and began to spin more spider-webs, and Mary to make arrangements for their annual moving to their country home in April. She had new cause for annoyance. Her uncle had told Margaret that the rooms she and her children usually occupied at Edgewood would be needed for Mrs. Hunter. In fact, he did not see how he could take them at all. But he would like to have Jack and his nurse.

Madge said that where she went Jack must go, and with difficulty restrained herself from warmer speech. She was less impulsive than Mary, and perhaps, too, was less indifferent as to what her uncle might be driven to do in regard to his estate. To do her full justice, it was less the thought of herself than of Harry and her children that kept down the angry answer with which her sister received a like statement from Mr. Fairthorne. Mary knew that not to have her summer home at Edgewood would be a sad loss for Madge and an inconvenience as concerned expenditures. She said as much to her uncle.

She had learned that to find fault with Lucretia only excited him; of her, therefore, she said nothing. When she mentioned that it would hurt her to lose this summer company, he replied:

"Well, why don't you go with her to the shore?" adding that he was willing to pay expenses.

Then Mary, vexed beyond endurance, said: "No one shall drive me out of my home, neither Mrs. Hunter nor you. If you insist on this banishing of Madge, and really desire to get rid of us, I will go; but you must say so plainly, and I shall go and never return. But as you sometimes change your mind, I should like you to say distinctly on paper what you want."

Upon this he declared that he never changed his mind and that when he wanted to talk things over he was always misunderstood. Perhaps later, in July, they might come. He was getting confused.

"Then I remain, uncle, and I trust that you will see that you are going to give occasion to a good deal of gossip if you persist in allowing this woman to drive us out and to rule your house."

He began to state in an elaborate way how essential to his work Lucretia had become, and wandered on until he forgot and repeated himself endlessly, while the girl listened sadly as she stood by his chair and saw that he was losing all that had once made him an attractive companion.

At last she said boldly: "Well, then, I am to understand that Madge and Harry are to go to Edgewood as usual?"

"I will think about it," he said. "I am always misunderstood."

"Then I will talk it over with Mrs. Hunter, uncle."

"Yes, yes; I wish you would. That will do." He was tired, and willing to accept terms. Mrs. Hunter had for the first time found him a little hard to manage. He had yielded when she suggested that Jack and the nurse might come.

Mary went at once to Mrs. Hunter's room and knocked. Mrs. Hunter laid aside her study of the pleasant figures in her bank-book and rose.

"So glad to see you, Mary."

"No, I will not sit down. I have already twice reminded you that I am Miss Fairthorne. I am Mary for my friends."

Then Lucretia knew that hostilities had opened. The "Mary" was pure insolence and meant to annoy.

"Pray pardon me, what can I do for you?"

"Nothing. I come from my uncle to say that my sister will, as usual, have her own rooms at Edgewood. What you have to do with it I cannot see, but as my uncle wished me to speak of it I have done so."

Mrs. Hunter was for the moment disconcerted and silent. She was not easily routed, but something in the cold quiet of the erect and dignified girl who spoke confused her wits. She said: "Of course, of course. I will speak to Mr. Fairthorne."

At this Mary lost her temper.

"You will speak of it! I have endured from you, Mrs. Hunter, more than I could ever have believed I could bear. I think you a designing adventuress. You have separated my cousin from me. You have fooled and flattered a weak old man and made endless mischief. I trust that some day you will suffer for it. If we were men I should long ago have laid a horsewhip across your shoulders." She advanced as she spoke, tall, flushed, and angry.

Mrs. Hunter stepped back in honest alarm, and, tripping over a rocking-chair, fell on the bed with a faint cry. She was on her feet in a moment, reassured and furious.

"I shall lay this whole matter before your uncle. I am not a servant."

"Pray omit nothing," said Mary, as she went to her own room.

Mrs. Hunter sat down. She had been thwarted by the will and sagacity of a girl. She felt that she would have to live in an atmosphere entirely hostile if the Swanwicks spent the summer at Edgewood. She had definite views as to what she desired, and had recently worked out conceptions as clear of how she would bring her plan to a successful issue. It would evidently be desirable to act sooner than she had meant to do. Her brief anger cooled quickly.

Not so that of the larger nature. Mary went to her room still feeling the effects of recent passion. It would leave her physically weak for a day, as she knew full well. She took herself to task and, while she threw out anchors of good resolutions against future occasions, she was not altogether displeased at the defeat her diplomacy had brought about. She had other cause for satisfaction. Archer had written to her on his way South that her uncle might need advice, and had asked her to suggest Dr. Miller. Mary replied, thanking him, but although she wrote no more he continued to send her letters. She told Madge how interesting were his descriptions of the mountain people, but did not offer to show his letters. He rarely and never willingly talked of himself. Why did he write of his life and ambitions, of the strain the war had brought?

When, after her talk, Mary was calm enough to use a pen she wrote to Madge that the summer plans were not to be disturbed. She sent off a servant with the note, and went back to her uncle's study. Mrs. Hunter was writing at her desk.

"Uncle," said Mary, "I have written to Madge that the misapprehension as to your summer plans is over, and that you desire her to occupy her own rooms as usual."

He looked up from a French catalogue of autographs and said:

"Why, yes, of course. What was it I said? Oh, about rooms. Mrs. Hunter must be taken care of."

Pausing in her work, Mrs. Hunter said:

"I hope not to be in the way or to incommode Mrs. Swanwick or Miss Fairthorne." She turned to Mary as she spoke. Her eyes, commonly wide open, contracted to a narrow slit. For the first time since she had known Lucretia, Mary felt a touch of something akin to fear.

Mrs. Hunter had not fulfilled her promise of complaining to Mr. Fairthorne. She did not now mean to do so. Mr. Fairthorne looked about him as if bewildered, and said, ''What, what!''—a way he had.

''Do not trouble yourself further, sir,'' said Mary. ''Mrs. Hunter and I are quite at one about it.''

''Ah, just so, just so,'' and here the matter rested.

XXXI

RS. HUNTER took care that Mr. Fairthorne should not have cause to complain of the loss of his daily visits from Archer, and for a week there had, indeed, been no real need for a physician. Meanwhile she kept the letter-book out of view, and in the face of family criticism and curiosity Fairthorne got into the mental attitude of being wronged by what was certainly the fault of his own much amended instructions. Swanwick had been very insistent in his desire to see the letters. Margaret had been inquisitive. Mrs. Hunter, equal to the situation, assured Mr. Fairthorne that all this inquiry into his private affairs was an impertinence, and he made this plain to all concerned, dismissing as usual all that might cause discomfort. The husband and wife felt that there was nothing to do except to wait for the chance of seeing the letters Pilgrim had received, and were in fact too far from guessing the truth to make a further struggle for the production of the letter-book. Enough was hinted or said frankly to trouble the old man, and he swore they wanted to kill him, and as usual complained of his heart. Mrs. Hunter insisted that he had only to exercise will-power to be stronger, that he must do a little more each day and that all doctors were both needless and costly. If, however, he felt relieved from the despotism of Archer's common sense, he soon missed the fresh air of the active outer world which the physician brought to a house into which nowadays few interesting persons came. Mrs. Hunter, with all her surface cleverness and manufactured gaiety, was too much with him to be constantly what Archer was for the hour—a wholesome mental tonic. When he complained of his heart Mrs. Hunter assured him of the value of her own means of relief, until one afternoon, when she had allowed him to double the length of his usual walk in the garden, he suddenly exclaimed that he was giddy and that his heart hurt him. Mrs. Hunter with difficulty succeeded in getting him into the drawing-room. He sank on a sofa and said he was going to die, and they must send for Archer at once. His death was the last thing in the world Mrs. Hunter desired just yet. She rang the bell, and then stood still a moment with her finger on his pulse. When the servant came a little brandy was brought and given him, and he felt better. He asked for Mary. She had gone out. He said he "must have a doctor." Mrs. Hunter, saying she would get a physician at once, left him with the servant and wrote a note summoning Dr. Soper in haste. He arrived within an hour and found Mr. Fairthorne, as he told the doctor, "quite well." A little rest and the stimulant had set him right for the time, and he was in the condition of rather agreeable excitement which often follows relief from pain and alarm.

The benignant doctor sat down, considerately grave, and with a finger on the pulse and a large watch in his hand, smiled reassurance. His presence puzzled the old man.

"I suppose you could n't find Archer, Lucretia?"

Dr. Soper said: "He is away in Virginia. For a time I fear you must put up with me."

"Yes, yes," said Fairthorne, "of course. I was quite well aware of that." He was troubled at his own lapse of memory.

"These attacks upset me. What is it? What 's wrong? Is it serious?"

He had not the least desire to know any too positive truth about his heart. He guessed at its gravity, but did not want it to be put before him with the emphasis of a physician's words. Soper understood. He went through the usual forms of examination with, "Ah, sound arteries! What a chest! Wonderful Fairthorne constitution! No cause for uneasiness! Not the least!"

Mr. Fairthorne knew the doctor well, and now, more at ease, began to take humorous interest in his ways, as Soper again expressed his regret at Archer's absence and his own pleasure in having, even for a time, the care of Mr. Fairthorne. Yes, perhaps it was only a little indigestion; might he suggest milk in place of cocoa? Fairthorne said he hated milk, and Soper retired from this idea, and would in that case advise his cocoa being taken weaker. Fairthorne, much pleased, replied that it was too weak already. Soper fell back on an inquiry into the diet of the preceding day, and finally thought a little calomel desirable. Fairthorne said it never agreed with him and was deuced old-fashioned. The doctor, who knew that the patient really needed nothing, and yet that, being called and a doctor, he must of course do something, said: "Quite true; an interesting idiosyncrasy. It will perhaps be as well for the time to continue the heart tonic Dr. Archer has been giving, and I will drop in to-morrow." Then he complained a little of the overwhelming nature and amount of his work, and went away, his watch reminding him of an important consultation.

He was hardly out of ear-shot when John Fairthorne exclaimed: "Why the devil did you send for that old humbug?"

"Why," said Lucretia, patting his hand as he lay on the lounge, "because he will not insist on dosing a man who is not ill. He does not know even his own stupid business. What is needed is to know you, sir, your vitality, your will-power, your recuperative energy."

It was silly enough, but it pleased a man who was losing both will and ability to examine the grounds of flattery; for, alas! it is dear to age, as a greater than Fairthorne once honestly confessed.

He said in reply that she might be correct, that at all events he had no belief in dosing, and that a doctor who was a fool was next best to none at all.

"How clever!" said Mrs. Hunter, rapturously. "How very clever! I must remember that," and she let her long fingers stray over his gray locks until he fell asleep.

She had future need of this pliant, self-satisfied

physician. That afternoon late, when Mr. Fairthorne released his secretary, she went out with much
upon her mind. She walked fast, an upright,
strangely handsome woman, one of whom observant
people were apt to say, "What a striking face!
Who is she?" She was tired of John Fairthorne and
the autographs and the books she made believe to
like. In fact, she was bored, and longed for a gayer
and less dignified life. If she had made her way
through the inner gates of the old town she would
for a time have been satisfied with what its social
welcome implied, rather than with what it gave, but
the air was inimical. She made no agreeable acquaintances. She was merely John Fairthorne's
handsome secretary. People smiled or laughed, and
she was left to her loneliness and her constant fears
for Lionel. She walked on and did a little shopping, and charged things needed or not to Mr. Fairthorne's account, aware that he would pay without
inconvenient questions. She had many ways of man-
aging him. To be in her room a day with a headache was effective, or to find in a catalogue a desired
autograph. She went on devising, planning, thinking, and, above all, stoutly facing the one terrible
embarrassment—Luke Pilgrim.

A homelike quiet blessed the house on Pine Street
where formerly lived that rector of St. Peter's
Church who thought it his duty to point out to Washington the need to betray his country. The rector
lies near by in St. Peter's graveyard; the accomplished mischief-maker who carried his letter rests
at peace close to the wall of the mother church. Of

the generations who had since gone in and out of the house none could have furnished so strange a group of people as were here met on a Sunday evening.

The two little ladies fitly represented the colonial folk who looked from their walls. Martin Blount illustrated the force of a breed which no accidents of fate could permanently subdue, the Puritan blood of a succession of ministers, colonial governors, and Indian-fighters. The chances of life had brought this last of them down to the plow-handle. He was on his way up, shy of being helped, hating money obligations, resolute, conscientious, a little too sure of himself, rapidly acquiring the manners and habits which, under kindlier social conditions, he would not have needed to be taught. He was pleased, in his good-humored fashion, with his double acquisition of knowledge and the courtesies of life. Moreover, he was conscious of the generous quality of these people who had busied themselves with the rough New England boy. In some ways he resembled the man who had found it pleasant to help him.

Roger Grace represented another type of our people. He came of the sturdy Presbyterian Scotch-Irish who very early settled the hill country of Pennsylvania and protected the Quaker scalps of the lower countries. From a little community of small farming folk he had come to the city with five dollars and a genius for finance. He held sturdily to his religion, and had, as we have seen, other qualities and undeveloped tastes which he was agreeably discovering with all the zest of an explorer, and learning to educate with the assimilative capacity of the American.

And last there was the gaunt form of Knellwood, now convalescent, the offspring of one of those families which for generations found in the navy the life they liked best. He had amazed them, after his recovery from a long illness, by resigning from the Naval Academy at Annapolis and entering the church.

On Sunday evening they were accustomed to collect in Miss Markham's parlor to talk or read, as best pleased them.

Miss Letitia looked about her at the two men, who were now silent. How comfortable it was to feel at ease as to her rent and much beside!

Her sister was watching the face of Roger Grace. He had looked serious of late, and to-night was almost austere. What was it that troubled him? He had talked to her with such glad freedom as he had never used before to man or woman. What could have disturbed his almost proverbial good nature, which had so often brought peace into boards of directors, and restored to men the power to consider matters calmly? He was gazing at the fire and now and then moving as if uneasy. His partners and clerks well knew the mood which sometimes came in the spring and dreaded the accompanying irritability which set every one on edge. He said it was the gout, and was pretty sure to decide that he must go to Saratoga or Bedford, and to return in high good humor and perfect health; but of this Miss Clementina knew nothing.

20

Mr. Knellwood sat still, with a copy of the Apocrypha in his hand. He smiled as he turned to the banker, saying: "You should quote contexts, Mr. Grace, when you knock down a clergyman with a text." He was very pleasant, this big man, when he let himself be natural, and now he was experiencing that exhilarating sense of returning vigor which makes convalescence delightful.

Grace sat up, and, conscious of effort, shook off the captivity of the mood he had learned to fear.

"What is it?" he said.

"Miss Clementina shall judge. Mr. Grace has had me at his mercy, and lectures me daily as to what he calls my wicked neglect of my health. I think it is merely an unfair mode of revenge for the dull sermons he has heard from his youth up."

"And what is it now?" asked Clementina, while Blount reluctantly laid aside his book to listen.

"Oh, he quoted for my benefit this advice, this text: 'But this again did even forget his own strength that the righteous might be nourished.' "

"I do not know it," said Clementina.

"It is in the Wisdom of Solomon," said Knellwood, "and was dreadfully misapplied. At first I did not recall it."

"No," laughed Grace; "you clergymen rarely know the Bible as do our divines."

Knellwood laughed quite merrily. "It applied to Jehovah, not to man." He rose as he spoke, adding: "I must go, I suppose, and have my bedtime diet."

"Let him groan," said Grace; "we shall soon have

him fat. I promise to hear your first sermon, Knell-wood.''

"And I," said Martin. "Miss Letitia takes me to Christ Church.''

"And ought to be ashamed," said Clementina, "to mislead an innocent Presbyterian youth." With this mildly humorous statement she slyly eyed her sister, who said: "Clementina, that is not quite respectful, nor is it correct.''

Clementina excused herself, and Martin said: "Oh, we are Congregationalists, not Presbyterians.''

Miss Letitia thought it very bewildering, and how much better it would be if they could all see their errors and come into the only true church!

"That is good ultimate advice to go to bed on," said Knellwood. "How well you have made me, you dear people! Good night.''

Grace followed him. In the hall he said: "I will send my coupé for you to drive to-morrow at noon if it is clear. I want a few minutes' talk with you before I go out in the morning, say about ten.''

"I am at your service. I wish there were any-thing on earth I could do to make you know how grateful I am, and shall ever be.''

"There is something. Good night.''

"Ah, Martin," said Grace, meeting him on the stairs, "have you still your mind made up not to oblige me?''

"Please don't put it in that way, sir." He spoke earnestly. "No, I cannot. I go to Bedford in a week.''

"In a week?" said Grace. "Well, I am not very

much disobliged. This is the third of May, is n't it?"

"Yes, sir."

"I am very much in the habit of going to Bedford Springs some time in April or May. It is uncertain. We shall have some rides, I hope."

"I don't have much time, what with accounts and the way women ask questions. A hotel clerk is everybody's slave. Good night, sir."

XXXII

LITTLE before ten next morning the banker sat in his library. The room looked to the south, over brick-paved walks and vine-clad walls. The day was somber. An east wind shook the swaying vine branches and thin rain fell softly on the opening leaves of early May. He gazed at the rows of books on finance and political economy, and then for a moment at what usually pleased him, a fine old "Burgomaster" by some unknown Dutch artist, and a Vandyke lately bought, a resolute-looking soldier in dark velvet. He was learning to love art, and, above all, the great portraits, but just now they failed to interest him. He lit a cigar and sat down, with his head in his hands; he had passed an almost sleepless night, though usually he had the priceless power to sleep serenely, no matter what trials or disasters the day had brought. His cigar went out. He threw it away as Knellwood entered.

"Sit down," he said. "I have made up my mind to do what it has always seemed to me I could never do. I want to speak of myself. I am in deep waters, in despair."

"Whatever I, as a priest, can do for you—"

"Oh, I want a man, not a priest. You are a man.

Why I am telling you what I mean to I cannot fully explain to myself or to you. I know it will not help me—it cannot help me. You cannot help me."

"But God may."

"Do you suppose I have not gone there for help?"

"Pardon me," said Knellwood. "Knowing you, I ought not to have said it. I should like you to feel how, with all my heart, I long to serve you who have done so much for me. Perhaps out of the desire I have to assist you a way will open."

"It will not, and yet I mean for once to lay bare my trouble. I am a straightforward man, and shall speak plainly. Hear me to the close. Then you will see."

He told his story clearly, and without emotional emphasis.

"Before I was born my father and grandfather died drunkards. I never knew it until I was a man. I had no inclination that way. I never have had the usual form of this temptation. I can to this day take without risk, at dinner, my glass of wine. When I was about thirty I had a commercial disaster and lost heavily. This was in May. I was seized with a sudden desire to drink—oh, to put it brutally, to get drunk. From that day to this it comes again once in two or three years. Sometimes, as last spring, I can overcome it. This year it is on me like—oh, nothing I can liken it to will let you know its power. When it comes as it does this year I am gone. I yield. I give up."

"But, dear friend, are you not over-stating it? How can it be? You, of all men!"

"I am impotent when it comes. I use all the brains I have to defend my good name. I go away to some remote little town. I calmly arrange to be cared for, not as Roger Grace; then I drink and drink. When I am through with it I go to some spring and cleanse myself of the consequences. I return at last, feeling physically well and clear in mind."

The barren simplicity of this statement appalled the good priest. How bewildering was the thing he had felt so hopeful of assisting with some one of the many kindly formulas he had been wont to find of value! For a moment neither spoke, until Grace went on:

"I need not say that I have been in constant terror of exposure. I am a more sensitive man than you would think it possible for one like me to be. I have lived, I think, an upright life. I have tried to be all a man ought to be. In my own church, in hospitals, and financial boards I am, I believe, useful and respected. Of late years I have learned how to enjoy what my youth never knew, the social contact with men and women whose happier chances have brought them refinement and cultivated tastes. I made friends—you, the Swanwicks, and others. My God! Knellwood, if this were ever known I should simply give up and go away for years."

"Is that all?" asked Knellwood. "And may I now say what I in my poor way think?"

"Not yet. There is worse. I know I shall yield, give up, go some day in a week or two or later, shall

go as a man on an avalanche goes—helpless. And
this year we are on the verge of a financial crisis.
Personally I am safe; but I am bound to protect by
money and counsel many interests. There are weak
institutions to be upheld by me and others. I ought
to be here, and yet at the hour of need I may be
lying senseless and mindless. One word more, the
saddest of all, and over it I hesitate. I have been
a lonely man, Knellwood. I have had, until I came
to this house, no real home, no serious thought of
the possibility of a wife and children. Pity me, my
friend; I have learned that the little lady, Miss
Clementina, may in time be willing to share my life.
Poor fool that I was! It made me happy. But
now, with this anguish of guilty craving on me, how
can I? How can I? Last spring I mastered it, and
rather easily. That is—that was—my sole excuse.
It would not be right now, would it, Knellwood?''

He was at last growing emotional, and sat with
flushed and working face, drumming nervously on
the table. ''One word of excuse for troubling you.
No, do not speak; let me finish. I said I did not
know why I was willing to open my sad secret to
you. It was not quite correct. It was because I
trust you to answer honestly the one question which
most pains me: if, having so nearly committed myself as I have, I am not still right to refuse to ask
a woman to share a stained and ignoble life?''

''No, a thousand times no. You are wrong.''

Grace shook his head.

''I hoped you would agree with me. I did hope
you would. If you could only see it as I do.''

"I do not. Think it over."

"It is useless. I should have felt strengthened for an inevitable duty had you agreed with me. Let us leave it. I thank you. I am a lost and a most unhappy man."

Knellwood put out one of his large hands, the hand of an athlete and a gentleman, took that of Grace, and pressing it gently dropped it. It had seemed so easy to say to a penitent, Do this, or that, and the like, but the strength and the spiritual force of this man forbade the use of what had often seemed to him helpful. What could he say, who was himself in the grip of a maddening temptation! With anguish at the thought that here was a case for which, yearn as he might, he had no available remedy, he spoke:

"Mr. Grace, as a priest I have no suggestion to make. You know as well as I what to do. I shall pray for you to be delivered from this temptation."

Grace smiled the curious smile which Margaret had described as pathetic.

"I am not disappointed."

"But I have not finished," said his friend. "You overrate the effects of a possible exposure. Were it known it would be your duty to remain and fight it out."

"Never! I could not! I should flee like a leper."

"Let us drop that just now. This seems to me a case in which a doctor, a man like Archer, might be worth something. Have you ever asked him or any one?"

"No. If I asked any one it would be Sydney Archer. He is absent, and Mr. Pilgrim, I hear, is worse. He will not leave him, so he writes. I can fight for a while, but then I am gone all of a sudden, like a dismasted ship on a lee shore."

"May I not go with you?"

"No, no. I should like you to know only Roger Grace sober; and let no thought of helping me through another tempt you to speak of this, not to Archer, not to any one."

"Surely not," and yet he felt sorry thus to pledge himself. "But if Archer return?"

"He will not be in time." He stood up, looking at his watch. "I have to meet some railroad people. You must now, and in my absence—in fact, always— use this as your study. Over there is your table, as you know. You will not go out, as it 's raining."

When Grace had left him Knellwood sat down and gave himself to thought of his friend. It was useless. He set it all aside, sorry and hopeless. Now that he could drive out, it was absolutely necessary to thank Miss Morrow for the constant kindness shown him. Although the wine, the game, and the flowers left at the house were nearly always accompanied by John Fairthorne's card, he knew very well that when his carriage brought these luxuries it was Miss Kitty who asked in person how he was. Since that evening at Mrs. Swanwick's he had been able to avoid her, and then had come his illness. Was it sent in kindness? More and more, with the return of health, he feared her and feared himself.

He most earnestly believed that no priest should

marry, and began to wish that some unbreakable vow of celibacy armed him against a temptation of which he felt ashamed. He resolved that opportunity should not add to his peril and that he would go in person and thank Mr. Fairthorne. Miss Kitty's notes, which now came often, he had not answered. They were tender inquiries, really needing no reply. He had written thanking her, saying that he was forbidden to write much and begging that she would not tax him further. It was a cold note, and when she showed it to Mrs. Hunter that lady, to whom Kitty had at last confessed herself freely, said that Knellwood was a priest and not a man, and that it was hopeless. Kitty cried a good deal, and waited, confident and unused to defeat.

With the instinct of her kind, she ceased to seek any form of communication with the man for whom she would have made any sacrifice. She gave up writing him notes or speaking of him, so that Mrs. Hunter, accustomed to listen and console, became uneasy at what she did not understand. She trusted no one, and was at once suspicious. She herself had no femininity, and did not see through Kitty's commonplace game, but she meant that no one should marry Kitty, and that some day they should travel together abroad. As to Knellwood's views on celibacy interfering between him and a pretty woman, well dowered, she laughed.

XXXIII

"MARGARET," said Swanwick, one day before dinner, "all sorts of things are happening. Here is a letter from Archer. He will be back in three days. What a friend he is! Think of the confusion and loss and sacrifice for a busy doctor to give a month to a friend."

"Yes, it is fine. He is an ideal friend. Do you remember that some one called the poet Donne 'the priest of friendship'? It is the harder for Archer, because he needs all he can make. Ah, I wish I were he for a month!"

"Why, Madge?"

"I should marry that sister of mine. Kitty is out of the game, thank Heaven! Why do men want her?"

"How do I know?" But he did.

"Well, what else?"

"Oh, nothing. Pilgrim will not come to us. He has rooms at the Continental. I am sorry—"

"You spoke of all manner of news. What else is there?"

"Oh, there is mischief brewing in money matters and more rumors about that confounded Republic Trust."

"You were wise to insist on giving up as its counsel."

"Was I not? I went in to see Grace on my way down-town, because, now more than ever, he wants Uncle John to hold his stock or to let him take it in block at par. It is down to ninety. Your uncle once refused his offer, and, I fancy, believed that Grace—Grace, of all people—meant to take some unfair advantage."

"That seems incredible."

"No. He thinks honor is not found outside of a small number of people who have great-grandfathers. I wanted to get Grace's advice and then talk again to Mr. Fairthorne."

"He is getting to be very dull-minded, Harry, and very cross. I never before saw him fail to take notice of Jack. Mrs. Hunter used to go out when I called; now she does not. Mary is never with my uncle. She was driven out, and is not to be blamed for absence."

"That is all true," he returned; "and the old man is obviously breaking up. Now and then he is his old self for an hour."

"But what happened, Harry? What did Mr. Grace say?"

"I did not see him. Mr. West, his partner, said he had left town for New York yesterday and would be absent two or three weeks, and at such a time that seems strange. When I pushed West a little, he said, 'Mr. Swanwick, about once in a year or two Mr. Grace gets so unreasonable and so irritable that we are driven frantic. It is gout, I suppose;

he says it is. At last he declares he can stand it no longer, and goes away, usually to Bedford. He orders that no letters be sent and disappears. He comes back, and is pleasant and well. Every one here knows his way, but just now it is serious. Of course I shall wire and write in case of need.' Then he asked me, as their counsel, one or two questions, and I left. On my way out of their office I met that insufferable cub Craig. He said, 'How are you, Mr. Swanwick? Getting hot in Wall Street, they say.' I said I had no interest in stocks or Wall Street. 'Well, the boss has gone. He was past standing. I tell you, Mr. Swanwick, if it was n't for—well, no gentleman ought to be addressed, sir, in the terms he used to me.' I think he had been drinking. I said that this concerned me still less. He probably had got a sharp wigging from some one.''

"Is n't there something singular about Mr. Grace's being away just now?"

"Certainly, my dear. You are quite right. As things look, nothing but grave illness could explain or excuse it; and to order that no letters be sent!''

"Oh! I presume Mr. West will disobey that; you said as much.''

"Of course," and they talked of other matters. The woman, however, continued to wonder, having herself noticed that Mr. Grace had lost his spirits.

The day the banker left, Knellwood received a note stating that he had gone to New York and elsewhere. It said simply:

"I go because I must. I go to the neglect of plain duty. No one who has been in the clutches of a temptation like mine can imagine the almost mechanical certainty of its action. It is like a machine. I have an awful joy in having yielded. I look forward and can hardly wait. Burn this."

The rector sadly obeyed.

XXXIV

HE day was warm and pleasant, a May morn of sunshine. Felisa sat on the window-ledge, sole inhabitant of the study. Mary Fairthorne entered and looked about her, surprised to find her uncle later than the hour of ten. She sat down at the window and patted Felisa. Mrs. Hunter came in, followed by Dr. Soper. The cat walked across the room and leaped on to the table. Lucretia set her on her shoulder, while the fat doctor said:

"Good morning, Mary. Quite remarkable, the attachment of animals, quite. I find your uncle unusually well, unusually well. I have just left him."

"But, doctor, he seems to me to be far from well."

"I think you should be very careful," said Mrs. Hunter. "The least hint of that kind depresses him."

"How he is to hear it except through you," said Mary, "I cannot imagine. Good-bye, doctor," and she left the room.

"You see, my dear doctor," said Lucretia, "what I have to endure. Nothing except my attachment to this dear old man enables me to bear it."

He said that it was sad—very, and they talked

awhile of Mr. Fairthorne. He had desired Dr. Soper to continue in charge when Dr. Archer should return. The doctor was distressed, but if Mr. Fairthorne really insisted he would of course see Dr. Archer or write and explain. When on his way out he met Mary and said how deeply he regretted this unfortunate whim of her uncle, Mary was a little indignant and a good deal amused. She failed to conceal her feelings altogether, and said that it would at least relieve Dr. Archer; how soon would her uncle desire to change his nieces?

"If," she added, "you would kindly arrange to have him change that gipsy witch you would oblige the entire family."

The doctor said: "Quite so, quite; very good joke, Mary. Can't be helped—very hard," and went away, well pleased with himself. Soon after he left the house Harry Swanwick came in.

"I want to see Uncle John," he said to Mary.

"He has just come down, I think. I will go up with you. It is getting rather dramatic here. Archer is dismissed."

"Indeed!"

"And Soper promoted. The gipsy—"

"Gipsy, Mary?"

"Yes, I have found her out. That is where the Oriental look comes from. Try her in Romany. I wish I knew it."

"How absurd, Mary! Anything else new?"

"No. Sometimes we cross swords. If it gets past endurance I talk firmly to uncle. He is fast failing, but to-day, when I saw him in his bedroom, he was

21

gay and sarcastic—his old self; I suppose only a doctor can explain that.''

When they entered the library Mrs. Hunter was at the window, looking over papers.

"Halloa, Harry," said Fairthorne. "How are you? Sit down. Show him the new autographs."

Mrs. Hunter rose.

"Here is a rare letter of Cranmer and one of Martin Bucer."

Harry had not the most dim idea who Martin Bucer might be, but he said it was immensely interesting.

"I have to thank Lucretia for it; a fellow in South Street had it."

"I want, Uncle John, to talk over a matter of business." As Lucretia made no sign of retiring, he continued: "I must see you alone."

"Well, Mary may go."

"I said alone, sir. Pardon me."

"Lucretia knows where everything is. I can't do without her. Go on, what is it?"

"Then I must write to you." He rose.

"Oh, damn it! Every one bullies me. I never get my way."

Lucretia, rising, said:

"Mr. Swanwick, you are quite right. Mr. Fairthorne is wrong." She had sat still only to annoy Harry and knew very well that she should hear all that might be said. Mary followed her out of the room.

Then Harry told, with some reserve, what he knew about Grace's absence and the state of affairs in regard to the Trust Company.

"Well, sell it," said the old man. "I suppose Grace got away to avoid keeping his promise to me." This seemed to Harry so absurd as to be hardly worth disputing. To his proposition to sell in small amounts, Mr. Fairthorne said testily:

"No. Sell it all, at once."

"At any price? You will ruin the market and lose a good deal of money quite needlessly."

"Sell it, I said; sell it! No banker shall control my private affairs."

"Very well, sir. Write me an order to sell." He did so.

"Archer will be at home in three days and Pilgrim will go to the Continental Hotel. I fear he is in a bad way."

"Well, I am sorry. He bungled things badly. As for Dr. Archer, I have been mending ever since he went away. Soper listens, and gives some weight to my opinion. I shall make no change. Mrs. Hunter says that the difference is surprising."

"I think you are making a mistake, but it is your business and not mine. I will see if the firm has any order about the stock."

It proved that they had no orders, and were still absolutely ignorant as to where Grace could be found. After ten days from his departure letters would find him at Bedford. Those were his final directions. The stock was sold at sixty-five, and the timid began to draw out their deposits from the Trust Company.

After Swanwick had gone Mrs. Hunter reëntered the library with a letter in her hand. Mr. Fairthorne was walking to and fro in the large room, his hands behind his back, his head a little bent forward. The habit and the attitude had been frequent with him in health but rare of late, and Lucretia was surprised by the quick way in which he turned to say:

"File with the autograph of Luther the correspondence and vouchers."

"Yes, sir."

"That is a good idea of yours to put in one portfolio forged autographs of interest. See that scoundrel in South Street, and buy one of those forged letters of my grandfather—only one."

"He promised to burn them, but it is not likely that he has done so. I will see him."

"What is that letter?"

"It is for me, but as it involves a very grave question, I come to you, sir, as to a friend, as to one who has brought peace and almost happiness into my life."

"What is it? Don't talk twaddle."

"I do not see how I can leave you."

"Leave me? What's all this? You can't leave me. Sit down and explain yourself."

She dropped on a cushion at his feet and kissed his hand.

"Take it, read it. It offers me release from care, a sufficient income, and a future of far-reaching usefulness. If I say yes, I must leave you in the autumn, and lose—oh, I cannot bear it, and I must— I must—"

John Fairthorne had preferences, but not affections. He liked Lucretia for a variety of selfish reasons, and more and more he disliked change. He was alarmed.

"Where are my glasses? Read it to me."

Lucretia let fall the hand she had taken in her grief, and wiped away what stood for tears.

"Ah!" she cried. "If I am like a hurt child at the thought of leaving you, when it comes to a final separation what shall I do? I—I—will try to read it."

"Do," he said. As to her life and her grief, he considered neither seriously.

" 'DEAR MRS. HUNTER: The trustees of the Wellsburg School for Young Women—'

"Those are the people who wrote to me before. Oh, it is long, sir; I can tell you the contents. It is a largely endowed institution. They speak of my success in New England. They offer me twelve hundred a year and a prospect of more. There are other details of no interest." She looked up. "What am I to do?"

John Fairthorne began at once to use his intelligence quite coldly.

"Are you satisfied here? You get twelve hundred a year, and"—the old man smiled—"a few trifles over."

"How could I be other than satisfied, but—"

"Yes, I know. If I die? That is where the but comes in. I want you, and I am willing to pay. I don't want affection. I don't object to it. I want attention, company, intelligence. You give them, you make yourself agreeable. If I were an impressible old fool you might expect more. I am too old to make an ass of myself. My advice is—don't! I will make a codicil to my will and leave you thirty thousand dollars. Will that do?''

She said he was "more than just," but felt that he was bargaining; and how keen he was, how definite! She rose and thanked him effusively. It was less than she had meant to get, but, after all, she had not yet exhausted her resources. He had made plain that he was not enough of a fool to marry her; nor was that desirable if she could buy autographs for him, and pocket a part, and live a year or two as she was doing. These thoughts went swiftly through her mind as she sat by him and varied her thanks, until he said: "Well, we are going to Edgewood shortly. I will ask Swanwick to draw a codicil to my will. I will write to-day."

Mrs. Hunter did not like this.

"I think," she said, "that your family will not be pleased. Perhaps some other lawyer?"

"Nonsense! What has my family to do with it? Do you suppose a man like Swanwick babbles to his wife about wills? Write now. Ask him to come and see me."

She was far from comprehension of the legal code of honor, but she knew when not to persist and saw too that Fairthorne was tired. When presently he took up a book she sat at her table and caressed the cat, wondering how she should deal with the risks that awaited her on Pilgrim's return.

By and by he looked up from the book he had

been reading, and said: "I want you to understand that this closes the matter. I leave you the money, and you promise not to desert me. It will take effect only if you are with me until I—until something happens."

This was not meant by Lucretia to be in the bond, but she promptly replied:

"I so understood it, sir. You are more than good to me."

Next day Harry Swanwick received Mr. Fairthorne's order to add the codicil. He made no comment, but sat down quietly and added it in due form.

"It will need, sir, two witnesses," he said. The old man rejoined that of course he would see to that, and the will was replaced in the safe in the far corner of the library.

When from time to time Lucretia reminded Mr. Fairthorne that the codicil was unsigned he showed a certain amount of annoyance and said there was time enough. Yes, Dr. Soper would be a proper witness. Mrs. Hunter began to be uneasy, and the more so because once he appeared to have forgotten it altogether, and was growing less and less his old, satirical self. At last he left the will in a drawer, but would do no more. Anything that involved anticipations of death for him was disagreeable.

Mrs. Hunter resolved upon a definitive move. The will, in a sealed package, still lay ready in the table drawer. Until recently such carelessness as to leave it out of the safe would have been strange to its maker. The days went on, and one morning, seeing him in good condition, she said:

"Mr. Knellwood will be here to-day at noon, and I have asked Dr. Soper to come in at that hour. They will be able to witness the codicil." He was apt on alternate days to be in better possession of his faculties.

"Well," he said, "get it out of the safe. I am tired of it."

"It is here," she returned, putting the package on the table. It was now close to twelve, and, to Mrs. Hunter's annoyance, Margaret Swanwick and Mary came in. They spoke to Mrs. Hunter, and began to talk to their uncle of the children and the country. Yes, he was going in two or three days. Kitty was to put the house in order. This amused Margaret, as Kitty had a talent for disorder which was very well recognized in the family. She laughed as she said:

"Who is to put Kit in order?"

"Not I," said Mary. "Madge will not come to us until June, uncle."

"Is that so?" He expressed no regret. "That fellow Grace has bought the Gray house next to his farm. They wanted too much for it. He has altered it, I hear."

"An agreeable neighbor," said Mary. "Ah, here is Mr. Knellwood."

He spoke pleasantly to all, and sat down, a large figure in his clerical garb. Mrs. Hunter, a little apart, was eager for the women to go.

Fairthorne began to talk in his better manner, glad of all this company, and especially of Knellwood's visit.

"Well," he said, "are you fit to go back to what you call work? By the way, here is a letter of Bucer's. He had a good deal to do with your prayer-book of 1549, or was it 1552? What a mess you fellows are making of it! I try to twist up Katherine's wits about it, but she says I am wicked and that you know best. You can't tangle Kitty's wits. She has the simplicity of the mindless. A woman wants to cushion her faith comfortably on a church or a man. This time it appears to be a man. Take care, rector."

"Miss Morrow might have—I hope has—wiser counselors than I."

"Apparently she thinks not. I asked her yesterday to clear my head about 'the godly consideration of election' and that XIIIth Article. I hope she has read them, but you seem to have sadly neglected her education."

Knellwood laughed. "You are not enough in earnest to get a fight out of me to-day."

"Let him try me," said Madge.

"Not I. You are disappointing, Knellwood. I am in fine order for a battle and my spiritual neutrality ought to make me logically valuable to the positive. I am an indifferentist."

"For shame!" cried Mary.

"Not even an agnostic," he went on, unscrupulously pleased to shock the rector of St. Agnes's.

"But why, uncle," asked Madge, "do you keep your pew in Christ Church?"

"Because—I was predestined by my great-grandfather."

Knellwood shook his head.

"Ah, the letter interests you. Here is one of Luther's."

"We had done far better without him," said Knellwood. "We owe him nothing but confusion."

"Did you ever notice," said Margaret, "the resemblance to Luther in the face of young Blount?"

"No," said Knellwood. "I like the boy, and I should be sorry to think he looked like Luther. By the by, he has gone to Bedford for the summer."

"Yes," said Madge; "and with Mr. Grace away you must be quite lonely in Pine Street."

"I miss them. I came here to thank you, Mr. Fairthorne, for all manner of kindnesses. I should have come before, but I have not been very strong."

"I fancy Miss Kitty has been the more active agent," said Fairthorne.

"I exact my share of thanks," said Mary, quickly. "You look far better than before your illness. Dr. Archer should be proud of you. He has been delaying his return, but now we may look for him at any time, so Harry says, or was it to you he wrote, Madge?" She, too, had heard from him, but of that she said nothing. Mrs. Hunter's knowledge of the mail matter which came to the house made it needless to pretend to conceal such trifles from her. But the ostrich attitude does at all events satisfy the ostrich.

Dr. Soper failed to come as he had promised, and when, after further chat, Knellwood and the rest went away together, Mrs. Hunter had lost another chance.

XXXV

TWO days later Sydney Archer came home, and having arranged for Pilgrim's comfort at his hotel found time to consider his own affairs. He wrote a dozen notes or letters to thank the friends who had cared for patients and hospital wards during his long absence. He saw one or two people who called for immediate attention, and left himself free for the rest of the day to pick up and arrange the many threads of the life of a man who was a physician, a teacher, and an investigator. He found time at length, after luncheon, for a visit which he felt he must make, and would very gladly have avoided. Among his letters was a civil note from Dr. Soper, expressing his regret at Mr. Fairthorne's decision to insist on the continuance of his, Soper's, attendance, etc.

Archer was a little relieved to escape the constant battle with Mrs. Hunter and the sense of being responsible and yet without control. But, being human and a doctor, the idea of having been displaced by a man of as little intellect as Soper was unpleasant, and to owe defeat to Mrs. Hunter made it seem far worse. Mary had written very forcibly of the state of things in John Fairthorne's house, and had

asked what was to be done, since Mrs. Hunter managed Dr. Soper and there was no longer an interested intelligence at hand to stand between a failing
old man and a woman without scruples. Archer
smiled as he recalled his last important interview
with the secretary. And now he was out of the fight.

He found Dr. Soper at home, and was cordially
welcomed. Archer began:

"I had heard of Mr. Fairthorne's desire to change,
and on my return found your note. I might as
usual say a civil word and drop the matter, but these
people are old friends, and—"

Soper interrupted:

"Pray do not trouble yourself. It was quite inconsiderate, quite. I fully enter into your feelings,
but, after all, what can one do? These things happen to all of us."

"The old fool," thought Archer. What he said
was:

"You misunderstand me. I want to say that Mr.
Fairthorne is under the control of this Mrs. Hunter.
You must have seen it, and perhaps know, too, that
to order anything for Mr. Fairthorne is one thing,
to be sure that your directions are carried out is
quite another."

"I cannot say that I have experienced that difficulty. I have never made the least suggestion that
was not received, I may say, with enthusiasm. A
very remarkable woman, very."

"On that I think we may agree, but I wish to
say, also, as a friend of the Fairthornes, that you
ought to know how most of his relatives feel in re-

gard to Mrs. Hunter. If my long knowledge of Mr.
Fairthorne's case will help you, that too is a part of
my purpose. It is in some respects an unusual case.''

"I cannot say that it so appears to me. When
did you get back, and how is Mr. Pilgrim?'' He
did not refer to the family question or ask about
Fairthorne's case. Archer saw that, if needed, he
certainly was not wanted. He rose, saying:

"I shall call on Mr. Fairthorne to-day. I must
tell him what Pilgrim cannot as yet do about his Virginia lands. Is he well enough to talk? Clear
enough?''

"Clear enough? He is as well as you or any one.
He has been improving most remarkably. He is
buying autographs and books and even changing his
will.'' When the doctor said this he suddenly remembered that Mrs. Hunter had asked him not to
speak of having been asked to be a witness. Conscious of indiscretion, he babbled on, talking rapidly.
Archer ceased to listen. He had seen the conscious
look of embarrassment. Had things gone so far
that Lucretia was influential and interested in
changes in the old man's will? What did this mean?
How far would it go? For here was a woman without conscience and here were possibilities of unlimited mischief.

Soper went on, relating at length "a most curious
case, quite unique, quite.'' Archer was aware of
assisting with "yes" and "indeed," but his mind
was elsewhere.

"Pardon me,'' he said, as he rose, "do you really
think Mr. Fairthorne competent to make a will?''

Dr. Soper replied:

"Competent? Yes, of course; but perhaps I should not have mentioned the matter." He forgot to ask Archer not to repeat his imprudence.

Sydney Archer was a man apt to act with decision. He went from Dr. Soper's to the Fairthorne house, and stood a moment in thought on the white marble step. Then he rang, and had a cheerful welcome from the old black servant. He went into the parlor, and was about to send up his card when Miss Fairthorne, hearing his voice, came in. There were the ordinary greetings which disguise so much, and Miss Mary said: "Yes, come up-stairs. My uncle is not very well, but he will be glad to see you. We are all more sorry than I can make clear to you that Mrs. Hunter succeeded in putting Dr. Soper in charge, but we are more powerless than ever."

As they entered the library Mrs. Hunter quickly threw a portfolio upon the mass of papers on the table. The doctor, in this hostile atmosphere, became instantly curious and observant, and noted the haste of Lucretia's movement. That lady retired to a corner and appeared to be deep in a journal, while Mary, excusing herself, left Archer to talk with her uncle.

"Last night I brought Luke Pilgrim back with me. He is in a rather critical state."

Mrs. Hunter sat still. At last it had come. The codicil was not signed; Mr. Fairthorne's mind was uncertain; he would and would not; was she strong enough to face boldly a possible disclosure? What would he do? She listened intently as Archer went on to mention where Pilgrim was staying, and then all that the latter at present desired to have said. Masters meant to remain for a time and would look after Mr. Fairthorne's and Pilgrim's interests. In a week or two Mr. Pilgrim might be able to spend a few days in the country at Edgewood. He could then put Mr. Fairthorne in fuller possession of his views as to developing their joint properties.

Long before he had come to an end Archer saw that Fairthorne had ceased to attend, and therefore cut his statement short. Mr. Fairthorne sat up, and said: "About joint properties—what is that? We have no adjoining lands. And speak louder, Sydney. Your voice is indistinct. You Southern people never half open your mouths when you talk." The old man was fast losing his hearing. Archer began to explain. "Oh, confound it! Don't roar at me. I am not deaf, or what Pilgrim calls 'deef.' "

He was puzzled by Archer's statement of the cause of quarrel with the squatters and said it was all a mistake, and that Mrs. Hunter knew about it, and must see Pilgrim and get it cleared up.

Archer, having done his best to make matters clear, got up to go, grieved at the mental failure of his old friend. Mr. Fairthorne said: "Why, Sydney, you have not felt my pulse."

"It is not necessary." As he passed the table he said he wanted a bit of blank paper, and lifted the portfolio to look for it. What Lucretia had desired to hide he saw—the will of John Fairthorne.

Mrs. Hunter knew at once that he had seen the will, but not, of course, what Soper had revealed.

He took the scrap of paper and wrote on it: "I want to talk with you. Meet me at my house at four." She took the paper and read it as she followed him, about to say no, when she reflected that it might mean a message of moment. It would be best to have it out, whatever it was. She said she could be there at four, as Mr. Fairthorne was unable to drive—yes, at four—and left him as he went down the stairway, smiling. It was war. She had used his absence to effect her purposes; now it was his turn. Why had she agreed to meet him?

"There is something wrong about the woman's past. What is it? She should have asked me to call here if I desired to talk to her. She did not. She rose to that fly."

When, that afternoon, Mrs. Hunter found herself alone in the little library, which was also his consulting-room, she looked about her with a momentary curiosity. The crowded book-shelves, the accumulation of journals on chair and table, indicated the student, and the spurs, whips, hunting-crops, guns, and rods told how the man amused himself in his days of leisure. A few books of verse, two or three etchings, a rare volume or two, the book-lover's cherished record of good luck, might have added knowledge of the man who had asked her hither. Mrs. Hunter sat for the few minutes of waiting deep in thought.

"I am a little late," said Archer, as he entered. "Pray pardon me."

"Oh, it would not be difficult to amuse one's self here."

"As a substitute I fear that you will hardly find me that—I mean amusing. I asked you here because we are assured of freedom from interruption as we are not at Mr. Fairthorne's."

"Certainly, I so understood it. Pray go on."

He remained standing by the mantelpiece.

"I did not know clearly, or did not until of late suspect, what you meant to secure during your stay at Mr. Fairthorne's."

"And you think you know now?"

"Yes, I do. From the time you got a hold on Mr. Fairthorne you very needlessly antagonized me. I say needlessly because if you had merely flattered and made comfortable a weak old man I should not have cared what reasonable or more than reasonable pay you got out of the business. But to see my orders canceled or changed was a thing no conscientious physician could endure."

"And yet you stood it pretty long."

"I did, and for good cause."

"Before we go on, Dr. Archer, allow me to say that I have a real affection for Mr. Fairthorne. I owe him much. Thinking as I do, how could I see him the victim of useless drugs, when I felt that I could insure health by simpler means?"

"You can hardly expect me to believe you," he said. "Frankly speaking, I do not believe you; but if you think this answers me personally, let me ask why did you continually go out of your way to harass and annoy Miss Fairthorne? You have with as little reason made her life unhappy."

"If," she said, rising, "this is all you can give to

22

explain your very singular request that I meet you here, I may as well go.''

''No,'' he returned, ''that was mere introductory matter. You were quite right to decline to answer me. It was idle curiosity on my part. I am, however, as a man—may I say as a psychologist?—interested in you. The problem is why an able woman, wanting something, should take pleasure in putting obstacles in her own way.''

Mrs. Hunter, at ease, well dressed, handsome, was never so near to liking Archer. She was grateful for being classed as peculiar. She smiled as she resumed her seat. ''Perhaps some day I may tell you. But what next? You are interesting; you never were before.''

''Thanks. In my little battle with you I have been worsted.'' He laughed.

''People who cross me do, as a rule, get the worst of it. Dr. Soper is far more manageable. My views are his views.''

''That is certainly convenient, but whether in the end you will be as well off as if you had let me alone may be doubted. You have made a friend of small value and a foe of some force.''

Mrs. Hunter, toying with her parasol, said:

''Will you kindly explain? You did not bring me here merely to sympathize with a doctor who has lost a valuable patient or to ask my pity for a young girl in whom he is, shall we say, interested.''

''Stop, Mrs. Hunter. I cannot keep you from saying whatever ill-bred impertinence you may choose to bring into our talk, but what I hold in reserve concerns you alone. You will do well to listen. Mr. Fairthorne has made arrangements to alter his will. Dr. Soper was to be one witness. Mr. Fairthorne hesitates. You are the person who will profit.''

A part of this was pure inference. The resolute stillness with which she listened strengthened his belief that he was correct.

"What next?" she said.

"Only this: if John Fairthorne has been led to leave you any very large amount of money, you will never get it.''

"Why not?" she cried, sharply.

"If," he continued, "you are left a moderate legacy you may be allowed the plunder.''

"Really! This passes belief. If I was impertinent you have matched me.''

"No," he said; "this is pure business and very pertinent. Come now, frankly, how much are you to get?''

She saw by this time that more was meant than a verbal duel. The buttons were off the foils.

"Suppose, first, you show your own hand," she said, quite coolly. "This may be pure bluff.''

"Well, we stand thus: if you are to have too much, enough to injure others, I can easily show that Mr. Fairthorne is now unfit to make or mend a will. Dr. Soper will desert you when the family make a fight. If your plunder be moderate I will be silent, and no one will interfere. Of course, I speak only as to probability.''

"You might not find it easy.''

"No, quite true; but a searching history of your

life in that house would be part of the proceedings, and a little study of your past life might make things uncomfortable. Am I clear?"

"Yes, perfectly. I expect Mr. Fairthorne to leave me thirty thousand dollars, and little enough."

"No, it is rather large, but may pass. It pretty nearly reaches the limit."

"Indeed!" she said, and stood up. "The limit, indeed! And you set a limit to what Mr. Fairthorne may do! He will be amazed! You, and the family which has treated me with contempt. Me! I, who am not good enough for their miserable little provincial, antique, claw-toed society! They should thank me for what I do not take. You think this time I am beaten. Shall you feel so when you see in the papers, 'Married, on blank date, Mrs. Hunter, etc., to, etc.' What will they give me not to do it?" She threw up her hands and laughed outright, in evident enjoyment of the situation. Archer said quietly: "Admirably played, Mrs. Hunter, but I think we understand one another. I am grieved that there yet remains much that concerns you which I cannot at present deal with, and do not want to if I can help it." He wished to leave with her the belief that there must be in her past that which he knew or could learn.

"Let me in turn congratulate you, Dr. Archer. That was fairly well done," she said, languidly, as if tired of the discussion. "At any time I am at your disposal for a dull account of a New England school-teacher."

"Thank you," he said; "you and I, Mrs. Hunter,

The Sherrods –

The Yellow Van –   Whiting

Blount of Breckenhow – Dix

A Forest Hearth – Major

Dorothy South

A Carolina Cavalier

are enemies. As you are a woman, what I really think—all I think of you—must remain unsaid. Certainly, Mrs. Hunter's account of herself might be entertaining. I hope to find some franker biographer.'' As he spoke she stood facing him, something sinister in the wide eyes' fixity.

''Poor me! How important I am becoming! A comparative biography by several authors would be novel and interesting. Add, then, the autobiography. I wish you joy of the search.'' She was aware how perilously near he had been to one who knew her thoroughly, but she never had lacked courage, and she meant at once to front this new danger and to learn where she stood.

Archer smiled as he played with his watch-chain. A duel of words amused him. He could not resist the desire to retort, sometimes an unwise desire.

''That idea of a comparative biography strikes me as promising.''

''Thanks for the rather adulterated compliment, Dr. Archer, and good afternoon. We seem to have got to an end.''

Archer opened the door, and saw her enter John Fairthorne's carriage. He went back to his library, feeling that he had not been eminently victorious. What did her threat mean? Was it merely an idle one? John Fairthorne was a proud man, unlikely to marry in haste an unknown woman, but then the power of a woman over a man is always an unknown or incalculable factor in the equation of life. There was, however, the mere fact of the outspoken threat as against the chance of occurrence of the thing feared, or as against the probability of its being seriously entertained. If this contingent event were probable she would have kept it to herself. He was wrong. Mrs. Hunter liked the show of power almost as well as the reality of power. She had been thinking of marriage as being still a possible move in her game until Fairthorne had spoken so plainly. Time was all essential to her now, for the codicil remained unsigned, and in two days there would be the dull country life of Delaware County, and more or less separation from her brother, who had lately been drinking enough to show ill effects on the pink-and-cream tints of his face.

Perplexed by the needless difficulties this man's weaknesses put in her way, she again asked herself why she did not abandon him. She had in no other case failed to put her own interests first. Had she troubled herself with self-analysis she might have learned that when, as a young woman, the care of the boy brother fell upon her she became the slave of an instinct which was as near to that of maternity as was possible for Lucretia Hunter. His personal beauty pleased her as time went on, and she dreamed ambitions for him and for herself; but of late years the wilful boy had become the weak and wilful man, and a certain cunning often seen in the feeble invited to acts of which his intelligence could not predict the results.

XXXVI

HE household of the Fairthornes removed to the country with far less friction than usual, as Mary reluctantly confessed to Madge. Kitty was here and there, apparently busy, but in every one's way, as useless and persistent as a housefly in August. No one of the distracted household was entirely pleased at the change, least of all its master. He went because it was his habit, but such changes are like too evident mile-stones to please the old; they mark the passing of relentless years. The ample house of his grandfather at Edgewood contented Fairthorne, a man always averse to altered conditions in his surroundings. He had long since satisfied his personal wants by building a library on the second floor, next to his bedroom, and by enlarging the wide two-story veranda on which these apartments opened. The number of books he took with him and the quantity of valuable autographs, as to which he troubled every one, usually made this annual exodus a source of exasperation to all concerned.

"She is certainly capable, Madge," said Mary. "And do you know, dear, I sometimes think Uncle John is afraid of her, just a little afraid?"

"Why should he be?" said Madge, thoughtfully. "Harry has terrified me with the idea that she may make him marry her. You very heroic people think money of no moment. What are you laughing at? When you have children of your own you will not laugh about money."

"I assure you I was not thinking of Uncle John's money. I was laughing at the idea of Aunt Lucretia. Oh, don't be alarmed, dear. Dr. Archer thinks it will never be."

"Oh, Dr. Archer 'thinks'?"

"Yes," returned Mary, somewhat reluctantly. "He has had a rather singular talk with that woman."

"Indeed! What was it? Do tell me all about it."

These two sisters were so near to one another, so habitually intimate, that each at times found it hard to safeguard thoughts she did not mean to reveal; a word, a phrase, a little hesitation, the least appearance of want of the customary frankness, was enough to betray her. They understood this, and preserved at need a respectful appearance of lack of interest or of inability to apprehend.

When Mary spoke of Archer, Madge knew that her sister had said more than she meant to say. When her curiosity had a little overcome her discretion, Mary had replied that of course she would tell her all about it, but that now she really must go out and attend to certain requirements of summer costume.

"I shall stay here to-night, dear. Then we can talk."

"I think I can wait so long, but I hate to starve

my curiosity.'' Madge did not question Mary, and, although very curious, said no word of Archer. As Mary prepared to leave, her sister said:

''Kitty was in town to-day. I was sure that three days at Edgewood would satisfy her desires for the country.''

''I shall go out to Uncle John to-morrow. I do hope you will not wait until June to join us.''

''Ask Harry, dear.''

''I wish you could come now; together, we should rout that woman.'' She went out, distinctly recognizing the fact that Madge had been kindly discreet. For Mary to have been entirely frank with her sister would have been to admit an increasing intimacy with Sydney Archer which she hesitated to confess even to Mary Fairthorne.

The day before the Fairthornes left for the country Mrs. Hunter secured Mr. Fairthorne's signature to the codicil. She doubly enjoyed her victory. Sydney Archer had called to report once more upon Luke Pilgrim's condition, and to say for him that very soon he would be able to set a time for his visit to Edgewood. He hoped then to arrange for the permanent management of their coal property. Mrs. Hunter was unprepared for this new embarrassment, or rather for its nearness. She had hoped for more time, and was aware that she could not let Pilgrim come to Edgewood without some preliminary arrangements.

Fairthorne said he should be glad to see the engineer, and the sooner the better. Archer thought it certain he could come in a few days; it was purely a question of health. As Archer rose, Mr. Fairthorne, pleased to have seen him, said:

"Do not go, Sydney. I miss you. I am pretty lonely at times." There was that in his voice which moved Archer. He sat down again, and began to amuse Fairthorne with his experiences on the Kanawha. Next, they fell to discussing Pilgrim's singular mingling of theoretic mysticism and practical common sense. The old man said shrewdly that Mary Fairthorne was not unlike that, and added:

"I used to fancy there was something between Mary and Pilgrim, a kind of transcendental flirtation, I suppose, or—was it Katherine? I cannot remember anything nowadays. Who was it, Lucretia?"

Lucretia said, smiling, "perhaps both," but that she had not been there then, and no doubt Dr. Archer would know. He made no reply, and Fairthorne said:

"You have been here very seldom of late, Archer. You do not ask how I feel. Doctors are getting to be too scientific. Dr. Soper comes, but he is soporific." He laughed applause at his well-worn joke on the name and repeated the jest over and over.

Mrs. Hunter listened, a little anxious, and Archer with more than a little pain. He checked him by saying that Pilgrim would himself write and set day.

a "Well," said Fairthorne, "tell him to come soon. I am pretty feeble myself; leaves falling, falling; sort of damned unpleasant personal autumn. Mrs. Hunter shall nurse us both."

"Yes," said Mrs. Hunter, "I will nurse him."

There was something in her tone that made Archer turn a quick glance upon her face. It changed as Dr. Soper entered with his perennial smile, and distributed an affluent greeting:

"Ah, how do you do, Archer. I am sure you must be gratified to see how well our patient is getting on."

Fairthorne considered the stout little doctor with a look in which there was both pathos and comedy.

"Soper," he said, "when you are ill let them come to me for a diagnosis. I will tell you now in confidence what is the matter with me. I am losing my wits."

"No, sir," returned Soper, "no, sir; he will have his little joke, Archer. People who are losing their wits never know it. Hope I may find them when you lose them."

Archer, shocked and sorry, rose.

"Kindly wait a moment," said Lucretia. A malicious opportunity was here. Bending over Mr. Fairthorne, she said:

"Dr. Archer and Dr. Soper could act as witnesses." She coolly took his will from a drawer, opened it before him on the table, and went on: "Now, sir, please."

He looked up with a face suddenly emptied of intelligence. Archer, surprised at his expression of dumb, questioning puzzle, waited. This abruptness of change from power to reason into bewilderment was recent. Fairthorne said:

"What is it I am to do? What is it about?"

Lucretia said:

"Your will, sir."

"I am not making a will."

"Yes, the codicil, you remember."

He seemed to comprehend, and said:

"Whereabouts?" when Archer spoke:

"Not yet, Mr. Fairthorne. I do not mean to be a witness, to be used as a witness. Good morning." Fairthorne said:

"Why not? What 's the matter, Sydney?" The cloud was passing. "Sorry you must go. Come in again. We will have a consultation on Soper." He did not insist upon Archer's being a witness. As the physician passed by Mrs. Hunter, he said:

"Did you think I would do this thing?"

"I?" She laughed. "No, indeed; but who could resist it?" He had a slight suspicion that he was being laughed at, and replied:

"Some jests are costly. Good day."

She knew very well that she had made a mistake, but the temptation to trap or at least to annoy Archer had been too sudden and too great.

"I was a fool," she murmured. She went downstairs behind him, neither speaking. When he had gone she found her brother waiting, by appointment, in the parlor. In a few minutes the codicil was signed, witnessed, and returned to the safe. Mrs. Hunter was at ease, and now, before Pilgrim came to pay that visit to Edgewood, she resolved with her usual courage to seek the unavoidable peril rather than to abide its coming.

The day after this, as has been stated, they moved

to the country, where Mary soon joined them. Here, three days later, she wrote in her diary:

"This habit of confessing to paper is sometimes inconvenient. Once the habit is made it seems to exact more than one could have anticipated. To fear to face one's honest thought on paper seems silly, but it appears very definite when it looks up at you and says, 'This is you.' I wonder if the habit be a wise one?

"Mrs. H. has become to me an interesting and is always a disagreeable problem. S. A. has written me of her having induced Uncle John to leave her money—thirty thousand dollars. I do not tell Madge. Money means more to her than to me, and—yes, to tell the truth, I cannot talk about what S. A. has told no one but me. Are all women like me? We come very near on paper. And now, of late, when he deliberately makes time to see or ride with me we seem to move apart. I recoil mentally, and—yes, physically. I am sure to say no and to be sorry, and to say no again. L. P. comes within a week. I do not think that now he would interest me as he did when I was younger. It was well for us both that he told me. Imagine a man base enough to hide it, and then to marry—and for the woman to wake up to that knowledge! I hope L. P. has lived out of remembrance of it all. It was dreadful."

As she ended Kitty came in to show a new frock, and then together they went out to look over the flower-garden on the slope leading down to Cobb's Creek.

Seeing them in the garden, Lucretia set out on what she called a tour of inspection. Miss Morrow she knew and governed, but nevertheless she now looked with care over Kitty's disorderly writing-table and read a few valueless notes. Thence she moved into Mary Fairthorne's small sitting-room.

Her eyes lighted up as she saw for the first time lying unlocked and wide open Mary's diary. On the page was a small paper-knife, apparently as a marker. Lucretia walked to the back window, and thus enabled to make sure of overlooking the two women, gave herself up to keen enjoyment as she ran over this record.

"It is as good as a novel. And so L. P. was an old love affair, and the man was fool enough to tell. I wonder did she care? I do not make it out clearly. Is she really in love with S. A.? It is droll reading. Am I what men call cold? I am not in the business at all. I have no machinery for grinding out any understanding of the passion of love. Oh, this is immense! I could advise the said S. A. what to do. I might sell him this page. That would be an autographic treasure! This description of me is not bad. 'A gipsy face, ivory complexion, eyes too large, vulgar habit of staring.' Thank you. 'Good figure and well dressed.' Thank you again, Miss Fairthorne. 'Has unpleasant hands, the thumbs are too long and they are always cold and damp. The brother is like a red, vulgar barmaid; not a man, an incredible little wretch.'"

Mrs. Hunter stood still.

"Ah!" she cried, "if I do not make you smart for that, my lady, my name is not Lucretia. But it is not!" she exclaimed, laughing; "and still, she shall catch it. I 'll give it to her hot." Mrs. Hunter was angry, and well-mannered wrath requires breeding.

The book was replaced, and soon after was locked

up in haste by its owner, who was well aware of Lucretia's taste for domestic inspections.

When next day, on her return from the city, the servant failed to meet Miss Fairthorne at the station she good-humoredly walked the two miles to her home in the rain. At the stable, where she went at once, the groom explained that Mrs. Hunter had taken the horses for some country errand. When Mary said, "But I left an order to come for me," the man replied that Mr. Fairthorne had personally given directions for Mrs. Hunter to have the carriage, and that Miss Katherine had the dog-cart. When Mary inquired of Mrs. Hunter concerning this matter, Lucretia said that it was impossible to contradict Mr. Fairthorne, that he had insisted on her doing certain errands and that she regretted it deeply. There was enough of truth in all this to make her excuse seem plausible, but Mrs. Hunter's regrets were of purpose overdone, and Mary haughtily retired from an unequal contest, sure that the slight had been arranged with malice which she had nothing in her own nature to explain. She went away vexed and puzzled, saying to herself:

"How will this sort of thing appear to a stranger, and how long will it last? Oh, if I only could; that would end it. But I cannot."

Two days later, Mrs. Hunter said to Mary:

"I have to go to the city this morning. Your uncle will need you."

Mary, flushing a little at what was close to an order, merely said:

"Very well, I will sit with him."

Mrs. Hunter dressed herself with unusual care, but with great simplicity, and went away with Kitty. At the city station, it being then about ten in the morning, she parted from Kitty, making an appointment to meet her in the afternoon, that they might return together.

Luke Pilgrim, comfortably convalescent, lay that morning on a lounge in his sitting-room. The journals of the day were on a chair beside him. The "Ledger" of the morning had just told him of the rise in interest, of the scarcity of money, of the disappearance of the president of the Republic Trust Company, and of the general sense of alarm. A little lower he saw an assurance that Mr. Thurston was to be at home the next day. It did not interest him. He had the long-trained endurance of the newspaper which is a part of our education, and the usual belief that its to-morrow will contradict to-day. Archer had allowed him one cigar daily. He sat up, very pale in his dark velveteen jacket, a large featured man from whose square forehead the hair was beginning to retreat; a very interesting face, with a certain steadiness of feature, the look of the habitually thoughtful. He decided for the after-breakfast cigar, for he had risen late and had for the first time since his wound enjoyed the meal. As he stood up there was a timid knock at the door. He cried: "Come in, come in." To his surprise, a closely veiled, rather tall woman entered. She shut the door, and, putting a hand behind her, quietly turned the key—a mistake, as at a later date she reflected. Pilgrim moved forward, and said: "Pardon me, but have you not mistaken the room?'' Lucretia threw her veil aside, and ran forward, crying:

"Luke, Luke, it is I! It is Inez!"

The man fell back. She dropped on her knees, and seized his hand.

"Oh, these bitter years! Will you not forgive me? I was so young, so foolish! And, Luke, I have suffered! Oh, won't you believe me?''

As he drew away, releasing his hand, she looked up, moving a step or two on her knees.

"Pity me, Luke! I am so unhappy!''

Seeing no visible sign of emotion on the face of stern judgment which looked down upon her, Lucretia staggered to her feet and cried: "Oh, my God! He will not,'' and fell into a chair. "My God! I am punished.''

Pilgrim stood still, speechless. He had never expected to see his wife again. Six years had passed since their divorce, eight since she had left him. He knew something of her life up to an uncertain time; then he knew too much, and wished to know no more. She had wrecked his young life, and brought disaster on him after they had been long years apart. There had been a time when to have killed her would have seemed right. All this and more went swiftly through his mind as he stood without a word, while the fire of a long-buried hate flashed up through the gray ashes of forgetfulness. She was sobbing, as she sat in the arm-chair, her face in her hands. Her parasol and gloves dropped to the floor. It seemed to him hours as she sat, brokenly muttering:

23

"Luke, Luke! I am so unhappy!"

At last she sat up and lifted face and hands in dumb appeal, to which her large eyes lent all but tenderness. The man's strange silence troubled her. Suddenly she had a revealing inspiration, such as comes to the greater actresses of real life. She ran forward and caught his arms as she cried:

"Do you want the truth? You shall have it. What rack is so cruel as silence? I never loved you. I was poor, in want. They said you would be rich. I married you—yes, you did not marry me, and then I got tired of everything. Your uncle came and ended the dream of wealth. I went away—" she paused. He spoke his first word:

"Well, Inez?"

She let go her hold, and as she stood hid her face in her hands and moaned with low-toned distinctness:

"It is horrible, but I must say it. I love you now, Luke. It came to me amid shame and anguish. It has cursed me with the thought of what might have been. That has been my punishment, that I have learned to love you."

For one brief moment the devil of self-esteem which is in all men rose up and preached belief. Then he knew that she was acting, and asked himself first, and then her, in a voice which was absolutely calm:

"What is it that you want?"

"Want? Want? How hard you are! I want what in my folly I threw away. I want what you will never give."

It was beginning to overtax the man, but he answered slowly:

"I do not think I can bear much more of this. You are not a woman to come here without some object. I have helped you in the past. If in any reasonable way I can help you now, for Heaven's sake say plainly what it is, and let me have done with it. You are as you were; no one can sift your lies from your truth. It would not concern me if I could. What is it you want?"

"Yes, I want something which you can give me."

"Well, what is it?"

"I want your silence. I am Mr. Fairthorne's secretary."

"You—you his secretary? I confess I was not prepared for that." He was indeed amazed. "You the woman—who— Well, no matter. Tell me what you desire and let us get done with it." She noted the way in which his voice and manner lost what little indulgent yielding had been in them. She said:

"Oh, I am so unhappy, Luke. Don't say you will not help me. You think I have lived an easy life on your money. Indeed, indeed it is not so. It was not spent on me. It went to help, to educate my brother. I have worked hard. At last I have found a home and peace, peace! I can even save for a rainy day. And now—you come and— How can I bear it?"

He said, quietly:

"Sit down," and as she obeyed he himself took a seat. "Mrs. Hunter, or—well, Inez, if you like,

I know well that you did not love me, also I know
that you do not now love me. It is pure fiction.
What you fear is that I shall tell the ugly story of
your life. You are a woman whom I utterly distrust.
You have left behind you a trail of ruin. You are
now in the house of my friend in a place of importance. What little I have heard, and I have been too
ill to hear much, has not been pleasant. I do not
know what to do. I do not like to be in the house
with you, and yet I do not mean that you shall shut
me out of that house. If Mr. Fairthorne is well
enough I have to make arrangements with him which
will require hours, even days, of consultation. I do
not mean to be shut out of this because it is unpleasant for you or awkward for me. What else I may
or may not do I decline to state. All of this is too
unexpected for decision; I must give myself time to
reflect.''

"And is that all?''

"Yes.''

"And you do not believe me, Luke? Do you
think I invented my love? Ah, if only I were free
from that bondage. Do not say that you do not
believe I love you.''

"I do not.''

"I am at your mercy. Be generous! You simply cannot say, 'This woman was my wife, take
care of her; she is bad, dangerous.' And it was
years ago. Do you not think a woman may
change?''

"You have not changed. I make no terms. We
will meet as strangers. You will be my old friend's

secretary, and beyond this I do not pledge myself. Pardon me, you have forgotten your parasol.'' She had risen. He picked up her gloves and handed them to her.

''And this must content me?''

He made no reply, but, preceding her to the door, perceived as he tried the handle that it was locked. He turned the key.

''You were deliberate,'' he said, bitterly.

''Good-bye, Luke,'' she said, with her head bent, a slight break, a certain humility in her lowered voice. Then, for the first time he was angry. He said:

''That is not my name for you. We are further apart than are other people. The law has built a wall between us. I am Mr. Pilgrim, and you, I suppose, are Mrs. Hunter, or God knows what name.''

''I will remember,'' she said, faintly. ''Luke— pardon me, Mr.— Oh, how can I? I will try to remember.'' As she spoke she stood as if for support leaning against the door he had unlocked. His hand was on the knob; he was faint in body and tortured in mind, but resolute to end it.

She repeated her last word—''remember, remember''—and reeled against him. This physical appeal, as of one about to fall, only angered him, but as by instinct he caught her on his arm. She looked up at him.

''Oh, kiss me, Luke—once, only once—for good-bye.''

The man started as if stung. He pushed her

from him. "You devil!" he cried. "Do you want me to kill you? By Heaven, for this second time you have been near to die—"

She fell back, and knew, as he threw open the door, that he had spoken truth. He was no longer a man to be played upon or tempted.

"Will you go?" he said.

Again she looked and saw that in his face which she never quite forgot. She turned in haste and, passing him, walked down the corridor with bent head. Once she staggered, as if weak. He watched her and closed the door as she turned a corner and was lost to view.

Once out of his sight, Lucretia drew herself up.

"I think that will do," she said; "he will not tell. I know him. It would seem mean, a revenge. I am sure he will not speak."

Pilgrim was not yet strong enough for so severe a test of strength as this had been. He threw himself down exhausted, and, wiping the sweat from his forehead, said to himself:

"That was terrible. What are ghosts to that? Oh, God help me, I was near to murder. Oh, that white neck! I wanted to hurt it, to silence the cursed tongue. If—if ever a man had done me as great a wrong, surely he had died for it."

For a long while he lay outwardly at rest, while the storm within subsided. Then he began to consider the practical features of the situation. He knew that he must not betray Mrs. Hunter's identity if it were possible to avoid it. He could not now refuse to make his visit, but certainly he must wait until he felt better.

"And by George!" he added, aloud, "I will make it short."

Archer, who more than suspected Pilgrim of having been in the past strongly attracted by Miss Fairthorne, had been, for a double reason, indisposed to talk of that lady to his friend. Thus it came about that at the time of this painful interview Pilgrim knew little of Mrs. Hunter's true relation to either John Fairthorne or his nieces. Tom Masters had spoken of the handsome secretary whom he had found agreeable, and Margaret Swanwick, during Pilgrim's brief former stay, had spoken and written far otherwise, but as he did not then dream of who Mrs. Hunter really was he had taken little interest in what he had thus learned.

He thought, as he lay still, of the fatal influence this woman had exerted upon a life which was assuredly both brilliant and successful, and as certainly most unhappy. Then, being the firm master of his own mental and moral processes, he resolutely put it aside, saying to himself:

"I made no promises. What wonder that as a young fellow I was the fool of this woman? What an actress!" After this he took up a report on the lighting of mines, and forgot for a time the scene which had so gravely tested his returning strength.

XXXVII

IME had run on and while Third Street and Wall Street were disturbed and anxious, the house of Roger Grace & Company had also its especial trouble. The doubtful condition of more than one institution was discussed, and the long absence of Grace became the subject of comment when it grew clear that radical measures must be taken to sustain this or that crippled bank or trust company. Usually, after seven or eight days of absence Grace had found his letters upon his arrival at Bedford, but now over twelve days had gone by, and where he was no one knew. Swanwick began to be uneasy about his friend, and said to his wife one morning after breakfast:

"This absence just now is very serious. No one has the courage and the clear head of Grace. I learn from his partners that thrice before, but not last year, he has declared he was gouty and gone away abruptly, telling his clerks not to bother him with letters, to send them all to Bedford; he would be there in a week or more. This year he went away in haste, and to-day I have a letter from Blount from the hotel at Bedford Springs. Here it is."

"Read it," she said.

"Dear Sir—There are a dozen telegrams here and no end of letters for Mr. Grace. His partners wired the hotel keeper about him. He told me to reply that he has not arrived and that we have not heard from him. He is well known here. His partners seem uneasy. Is it the state of the stock market, or is there possibly any cause to be personally anxious about him? You know, sir, or perhaps do not know, what I owe him. Before he went away he had become unusually grave, and seemed to me to want to avoid every one and to be alone. Perhaps Mrs. Swanwick would write and let me know if he is heard from—or, can I do anything?

"Yours truly,
"Martin Blount."

"That is a good-hearted fellow," said Harry; "and I, too, am anxious. I do not see what else can be done. His partners seem to me to think this absence mysterious. Certainly it is just now rather unfortunate."

"Do you often see his partners?" asked Madge.

"Yes, daily. They are really worried. It is like a general officer missing in a big engagement. Of course, they must be presumed to know why Mr. Grace is absent."

"They can make it seem too mysterious, Harry, and that is just what it is; but they are unwise to show their anxiety."

"Yes, I think they show it too much."

"They should not," said Madge; "they should seem confidently to accept it as usual."

"I will say a word or two of warning as I go down street." He did not even suspect that he was being advised to do this very thing. His mind was a capable instrument, but slow; that of his wife rapid and very decisive. She said, as he was leaving her:

"Wait a moment; do not forget to see Mr. Pilgrim to-day. I sent him some trifles this morning. See if he is well fed, our hotels are so bad."

"Anything else?" he asked, smiling. Margaret said: "Yes. Has any one asked about Mr. Grace at Miss Markham's? I shrewdly suspect the little white violet may know."

"White violet?" he queried.

"Yes, dear. Perhaps you may recall that a century ago, when we were lovers, we found white violets on the upper Wissahickon Creek."

"Thank you, madam. I remember, and am still your lover. Is it Clementina that is the white violet? And who was so sentimental as to call her that?"

"Roger Grace."

"Indeed! That is funny."

"I do not think so."

"Then where is your sense of fun, Madge? Is it a mildly conducted flirtation? Imagine it! Grace as the passionate lover, and Clementina primly responsive! She is still pretty, but imagine it!" He laughed merrily.

"My dear Harry, when we were young lovers some one was laughing at us. There is an element of the ridiculous in all love affairs for those who are still outside of the net. What if I were to say to you that the white violet in her pale silks is a self-subdued, passionate little woman?"

"I should say that that was one of Mary's charac-
terizations and utterly nonsensical."

"It is hers. I should never have put it just that
way, but Mary has curious insight."

"I did not answer you, Madge. Mr. West, Grace's
partner, did go to Miss Markham's to ask if Grace
had left any direction with them. They said no. Is
that all? I must go."

Madge was silent a moment. "Has any one asked
Mr. Knellwood, Harry?"

"Why, how on earth should Knellwood know?"
He was getting impatient.

"Perhaps not. Oh, by the way, wire Mary to
come in to dinner on Sunday."

"She won't. She plays the organ at St. David's.
Mary's duties are always in the way of her
pleasures."

"Try for Saturday."

"Very good. Anything else? No," and he went
away to say good day to the children and thence to
his office.

As soon as he had gone Mrs. Swanwick sat down
and wrote, asking Mr. Knellwood to drop in at five.
Knellwood was glad to receive her note. He, too,
was deeply distressed. Perhaps because he was not
a man of quick mind or large intellect the vital
alertness of Margaret Swanwick's nature and her
intellectual sympathy, even where her beliefs failed,
pleased the man who, whatever else he lacked, was
humbly appreciative. More positive than her sister,
she had less charity for opinions which both women

felt to be extreme and hurtful to their church. But, being a kindly woman, she never yielded to her constant temptation to have a bout at logical fence with the rector. The man she liked with a reserve of varying doubt; the priest was unexplained to her by any reasoning of which she was mistress.

When her note came the clergyman was distractedly turning over the pages of the "Guardian." Roger Grace, his temptation, and his long absence, were troubling deeply the tender heart of the rector. Archer had forbidden work, and had laid remorseless orders upon him as to diet and times of rest. In this enforced leisure the image of Kitty rose insistent, "as in a dream adorned," because these things no man can altogether set aside; but his beliefs were honest, and while Kitty was absent the more terrible power of the mere woman was in abeyance. Like Roger Grace, he feared and distrusted himself, and prayed with a humble heart to be delivered from temptation. It may seem strange, but a nobler woman would have tempted him less. He was glad now of Kitty's absence in the country, and thought with joy of the summer city, empty of his richer friends, and of a return to his poor and his clerical work. Meanwhile, he was a little bored.

Mrs. Swanwick was alone when he was shown up to the library. She meant to admit no one else save this invited guest, and was visibly pleased to see him. He said, as he picked out with care a sturdy chair for his big frame:

"I am so glad you thought to ask me. I am hedged about by Sydney Archer with things I must or must not do. Society is not forbidden, and, you know, you have what Miss Fairthorne calls 'the gift of welcome.'"

"That is very nice. I like that. Sit down. Jack wished to be told when you came, but he is out. Is there any news of Mr. Grace? Really, he is a bit inconsiderate to be away when everybody wants him."

Knellwood said:

"No, I have not heard, but I could not expect to hear. He likes to run off and get clear of work. Cannot you understand that?" He was needlessly explanatory.

"Yes, but not now." She knew as well as any one the treacherous state of the money market and the probability of the collapse of the weaker banks. She chose to quote her husband as her authority, and went on to state what Harry thought of the peril, how sorely Grace was wanted, what doubt and suspicion his absence created, the fact that he had meant to assist in sustaining certain institutions, and finally how unlike him it was to abandon his post at such a time.

The statement was made so clearly that it left Knellwood more and more uncomfortable about his friend. He felt that this acute little woman knew or suspected that there was something not quite right or usual in this unexplained neglect of duty. He began to feel it as an appeal to himself, and to fancy it rested on her belief that he knew something which she did not.

"It is a sad pity," he said; "but I suppose he will turn up soon or late."

"Yes—or late. That is the trouble. If any one knew where to find him it would be a great relief."

"I do not know. May I have a glass of water?" She rang and, as she sat down, said:

"Mr. Knellwood, we care very, very much for Roger Grace, and so do you. He is a noble-minded, generous man. Why he hides just now we do not guess, but it is very serious. You can have no idea how he is wanted."

Knellwood was disturbed both by her persistency and also by the fact that for others and for his own sake Grace should be at home.

"Mrs. Swanwick, I cannot help you. All I can say is that young Blount writes me that he must expect soon to be at Bedford, because a huge mail awaits him there. He mentioned also that year before last, as the landlord says, Mr. Grace came from Carlisle to Bedford."

She had heard enough, and turned the talk aside on matters of less personal import. As soon as Mr. Knellwood had gone she sent a note to what Philadelphians call the "Old Club." Her husband usually stopped there for an hour on his homeward way. He read it, said, "I must go, Masters," laid down his cue, and hastened home. Madge said at once:

"Harry, can you go to Carlisle? I think Mr. Grace may be there. But there is something very wrong and we must be careful. I am sure Mr. Knellwood knows," and she related what had passed and what Blount had said.

Harry replied that he could not go, at least not

for two days. "It seems to me, Madge, that you—that we are a little absurd. It is none of our business. How persistent you are! Grace is a well-known man. He cannot be ill; if he wants to stay away no one can prevent it, and he knew better than we why he should not have gone just at this time."

"It is just that which makes it grave."

"But Carlisle—why, of all places, Carlisle?"

"Well, of course my opinion is of no value, but if I were West or you I should at least wire Mr. Blount to go to Carlisle and inquire. Make him see the need for care and of course use no names in your telegram."

"My dear Madge, I dislike this way of thinking for other people." He did not like to hint to his wife the suspicion in his male mind as to there being a woman in the case. He had no least reason to think so, except that no other theory seemed tenable.

His wife replied to his general statement by saying:

"Yes, you are right; but I am so sure there can be nothing to be ashamed of in his absence that I am troubled. Do wire Martin Blount."

He reluctantly yielded. "I suppose it can do no harm. Give me a blank. Will this do?

"'MARTIN BLOUNT,

"'Hotel Stanton, Bedford:

"'Go to Carlisle. Find owner of letters to G. Be prudent. Wire me, but use no name. Very private.

"'H. SWANWICK.'"

"That is right, Harry. I can't but feel with you that all this is full of risk. I can't explain it, but one must do something and those partners seem rather at the end of their resources.''

''That is true enough, Madge.''

It had never occurred to Knellwood that the letter from Blount and his mention of Carlisle could be of any consequence. Much as he longed for his friend's return and great as was his anxiety, he knew as no one else did the cause of this absence, and had meant jealously to guard that knowledge.

When, however, Swanwick, after his talk with Madge, mentioned Carlisle and what Blount had said to West the latter replied that it was quite vain to do anything further, and would only annoy Mr. Grace. Later in the day, however, he had to make up his mind to sign for Grace two important papers which closed a difficult financial affair. He hesitated to act; the amounts involved were large. Feeling that Grace ought first to see the papers, he had sent them to Bedford, assured that as usual the banker would, after a week, find them at the springs. But now time had run on; his accustomed stay had been much exceeded. West hesitated until the safes were locked and most of the clerks gone. Then he looked to see who could best be spared, and called to Craig, who went back with him into the private office.

''Mr. Craig,'' he said, ''you have been doing better since Mr. Grace last talked to you. I want you to take this letter to the landlord of the Bedford Springs Hotel. If Mr. Grace has not arrived there he will give you two large sealed packages addressed to him. Ask when he is expected. Return at once. Keep an account of your expenses. Take the first train, and lose no time. There is a formal order to the landlord.''

Craig, well pleased to be thus used, promised due despatch, and went away in haste that afternoon. It was a mere accident which caused him to be thus chosen. He had spilled ink on his clothes, and, lingering late to rid himself of the stains, chanced to be the only messenger at once available for the purposes of an indecisive man.

Delighted to get a holiday, he left early in the afternoon, and reached Bedford Springs next morning.

Blount had had no difficulty in being set free for a time, as he was very faithful and the fuller season had not begun as yet. When he had explained to the landlord that he was going to see Mr. Grace the former asked him if he was sure to find him. Blount, who was on his guard, said:

"Why, of course." Why else should he go? The landlord, with the indifference of the American, suggested that he take with him Mr. Grace's letters and telegrams, and thus freighted, Blount went away, passing out of the station as Craig's train entered it.

Full of his own importance, Craig asked for news of Mr. Grace. Failing this, he delivered his letter and desired to receive the documents described in it. He heard, to his amazement, that these and all the other letters had been carried off by the landlord's request in order that they might the sooner find Mr. Grace at Carlisle. Craig was indignant on a large scale for the firm of Grace & Co. It did not seem to trou-

24

ble the landlord, but when he said that Blount had been charged with this errand Craig began to have a vague notion that it might be worth while, and certainly excusable to follow him. But what could make a man like Grace remain in a little town like Carlisle? Perhaps of all in the banker's employ this red-cheeked little scamp was the only one who surmised anything wrong in the fact of Roger Grace's prolonged absence at a critical time. Now he concluded, with a chuckle, that there was very likely a woman in the business. This was enough to send Craig off by the next train to the pleasant, old-fashioned town which the Presbyterians built in the hills, and where Benjamin Rush helped to found a college.

In the afternoon the two men in turn inspected the registers of the three hotels. Craig sought lodgings at one of these inns, and abandoning the search found some one to take a hand at pool, and spent an agreeable and profitable evening. After nine o'clock he lighted a cigar and strolled out to see the town and to find Blount, and to secure from him the papers West had desired him to bring back.

Meanwhile; the other young man had found for himself a room in one of the more modest of the inns, where he talked a little with the landlord and became sure, as he had done elsewhere, that the great banker was unknown to all of them. Just before bedtime, being of that temper which is hard to satisfy, he turned back over the register some two weeks and began to inspect the names. He, too, had been made to feel by Swanwick's telegram that there was something to be known about this good and kindly man which was not merely that, in pure freak or because of gout, he had so hidden himself that no one could find him. Thus musing, he read over the names, and came on that of James Rogers. No date of departure was recorded. He stood, disquieted.

Grace did not write what is known as a business hand. When Fairthorne saw his signature he said of it critically, as an expert:

"He writes a large, round, patient script, and loses no time on flourishes." Martin had seen on many kind, personal checks that honest, clear, round hand. The "Rogers" was penned exactly as Grace usually wrote Roger. Blount stood still in wonder, almost fearful to go on into something which his benefactor clearly meant to hide.

He went out and sat down with the landlord on the porch, declared it was a fine night, and, after the fashion of his host, set his feet on the rail. He talked agriculture, crops, and cheese-making, and at length said, as if it had just turned up in his mind:

"I was looking over your books. There 's one man I 'd like to see, name of Rogers—Jim Rogers. I see he has n't gone yet; old friend of my folks."

"I think I sort of remember him," said the landlord; "sandy-haired man; travels in dairy fixin's. He 's been gone a week. Ain't his goin' set down? Well, like enough."

Then Blount thought he would go to bed. At the door he turned, and observed that his host was looking after him. At this moment he heard:

"Halloa, Blount!" and, to his surprise, was

greeted by Lionel Craig. That young man, desiring later company, had sought Martin in the only inns of the town and had thus naturally come upon him.

"What brings you here?" said Blount, not over-pleased.

"Oh, I 'm sent up by the firm to find old Grace."

"Hush," said Martin.

"Guess you are after him, too. Any luck? He 's wanted, I tell you."

"Look here," said Martin, "don't talk, you 're a little drunk." Did this man know anything? He would learn. "Come up to my room. Lord, man, don't talk here."

"Got a cigar, Blount?"

"No. Come with me. I 'll get you one."

"I 'll come; want to talk. I 'm not drunk—not bad, anyway."

They went up a rickety stair to the second story, and passed along the hallway, which was dimly lighted by a suspended lamp.

"My room is No. 27," said Blount. They went on, looking at the numbers. Suddenly a door opened, and a man in a dressing-gown staggered out, fell against Lionel, and then lurched heavily on to a settee.

"By George!" cried Craig. "It 's old Grace, and he 's drunk."

Then Martin understood.

"Hush!" he said. "Help me if you can."

"O Lord, what a joke!"

"If you say a word more I will kill you," cried Blount. "Stand aside if you can't help me."

Craig kept silence, while Martin said:

"Mr. Grace, it is I, Blount. Try to get up."
Grace cast the unmeaning look of the deadened mind
upon him, but, seeming to understand, stood up, and
was helped back to his bed, where he lay breathing
heavily and fell asleep.

Martin's first thought was of deepest grief. His
next was of the need to keep for Grace this wretched
secret. Lionel had followed him into the room. He,
too, was thinking. A candle on the bureau dropped
grease, and dimly lighted the disorder of the chamber. Martin spoke:

"Look here, Craig, you and I alone know about
this. We can keep it so that no one else will ever
know it. I want you to promise."

"Oh, I 'll keep it, sure enough," said Craig,
lightly. "There will be you, and the old man, and
me. We 'll keep it, but he won't boss me any more.
Oh, I 'm safe, you bet on that."

Martin was sure he was not, but what more could
he do? As he spoke he had been seated by the bed,
a finger on Grace's bounding pulse. He rose, and,
facing Craig, said:

"If you are sober enough to understand, do you
listen to me. If ever you tell of this, as I live, I will
thrash you so that you will never get over it. If you
tell it you will ruin yourself, and I will spoil what
there is left of you. You lied to me, of course you
lied. You can't help it. This time it is awfully
important."

Craig said feebly:

"I did n't lie. Can't you believe a man?"

"Well, perhaps I was hasty," returned Blount; "but you know this has got to be a secret. I can't explain it in a man like Mr. Grace, but I know this, that for it to get about and get known would almost kill him. If I was rough with you it was because of the way you took it, just as if it was an every-day affair."

"That 's all right," said Craig; "when a gentleman apologizes that ends it, of course."

"Some day," thought Blount, "I will lick this little beast." He said earnestly: "Then it is clearly agreed between us that what we have learned by accident no other man is to know?"

"Yes, that 's all right; but what shall we do now?" That question had from the first been next to the need of concealment in Martin's mind.

"I think you ought to go to Philadelphia at once. You might say that Mr. Grace had been taken sick here and would be at home in twenty-four hours. You will get credit for tracing him."

"But they 'll ask such a lot of questions." Craig evidently distrusted his own power to stand cross-questioning. "Why, that man West, he 's like a terrier with a rat; he just shakes the life out of you. He 'd know right away." Had Lionel been quite sober he would have been confident of his power to hide facts.

"Perhaps you are right," said Blount. He hated the idea of sending this unmanly weakling to tell a string of lies. But what to do? Craig settled the matter.

"Suppose I go back, and say I went to Bedford

and the old man was n't there. I won't get any credit out of the business.'' .

Blount ignored the regret.

"That will do," he said. "I will stay here."

"Well, I 'll go; but I was to bring two packages back with me if Mr. Grace was not at Bedford. They are large and sealed, not like letters."

"Oh!" said Blount. "Here they are. You need not say I gave them to you."

"I guess not. But suppose I was just to stay and help you?" The uncertainty of an undecided nature, increased by slight intoxication, came upon him as he reflected upon the obligation which his aid would impose on Grace. Here was a fine chance.

"A good dose of spirits of hartshorn helps 'em," he added. "We 'll give him that. I 'll go and get it right away."

Blount replied:

"Craig, you go now, at once, out of this room. Get to town as quickly as you can. Mr. Grace must never know you were here. He will not remember. Now go, and don't forget—Bedford." He took the reluctant clerk by the arm and to the head of the stair, Craig protesting but yielding to the superior will. Here he halted, dully obstinate.

"And so you 're to get all the credit?" he said.

"Credit! You little animal! If you were ever scared you ought to be now. If you do not go at once and do as we agreed, and if ever you tell it will be the worst day of your mean little life. That 's all of it. Off with you now, and keep a close tongue."

This time the savage emphasis of the grip on his arm and the anger of the tones frightened Craig. He went as he was bidden, without further words, but humiliated and revengeful, feeling that he was being set aside and cheated out of an opportunity to better himself. He left Carlisle at early morning, with a head heavy and aching. No one questioned his statement, and for a day or two not even to his sister did he tell the story. It was a valuable possession. How should he use it?

XXXVIII

HEN sure that Craig had gone, Martin closed the door, lit a second candle, and sat at the bedside of the friend who had so unaccountably fallen. It would have been hard for his most familiar acquaintance to have recognized Roger Grace in the uneasy sleeper over whom Blount kept a watch almost as uneasy. Life had dealt harshly with Martin, but his sharp New England training, his own sobriety, and all his ideals of life made the banker's strange downfall a personal affliction to this debtor of his kindness. What to many men in the world of ease would have seemed a trifle to be heard and forgotten assumed for Blount a sad and very grave importance. Tears were rolling down his cheeks as he sat and thought of the man's generous goodness, of the little ladies who honored him, of what Mrs. Swanwick would think. The door opened and the landlord entered.

"What are you doing here?"

Blount related what had happened, not speaking of Craig, and said how queer it was he himself should have been in the entry just at that moment, and that, as he had said, Mr. Rogers was an old friend, and why had the landlord deceived him?

The landlord was somewhat embarrassed, but answered at last:

"Well, he's an old customer, and when he gets this way he gives me his money and it goes on a week or two. He likes it kept quiet. Then I help him to taper off. You just leave him to me; he ought to have a good nip when he wakes up. I'll leave it here. Are you minded to stay? He does n't care to have anybody know. Me and my man look after him."

Blount was not to be moved, and said he was a kind of doctor, and he would see to the liquor. The host, rather uneasy, but glad of a relief, for Grace had been harder to manage than on former occasions, went away.

The night passed, and the watcher saw the gray light of dawn. Suddenly Grace sat up, and made evident effort to recover his wandering faculties.

"I want a drink, Ulrich." Blount brought him iced water.

"No, drink this." He did not recognize Blount. "Mr. Grace, you cannot have any liquor." Eager cravings stirred the dull mind.

"Give it to me. I want it."

Martin said:

"No, not a drop." He crossed the room, opened the closed shutters, came back, and wiped the man's face with iced water. It revived him, for liquor had been allowed him in lessening quantities for several days.

"My God!" he said, "it is Martin Blount! What brought you here?"

"A good chance," said Blount. "Now take this cold water and go to sleep again. Don't talk, not yet."

Grace fell back and slept once more. At seven he sat up, with his head reasonably clear. He prayed for more drink, threatened, and got up to look for what he failed to find. The bottle was gone. Blount locked the door, and was not to be moved, until Grace gave up, and submitted to the will of his attendant.

By nine o'clock he had been made to bathe and dress and to take his breakfast. He was silent, obeyed like a child, and now and then cast mournful looks of pleading or humiliation on Martin. The lines of enfeebling ravage, the heavy, swollen lids, the slackened look of lost energy told their wretched story; but the brain was recovering, the immense vitality of the man was seizing again the fallen reins of self-control. He uttered a sentence from time to time, brief, disjointed, and then was long speechless. At last, seated on a creaking lounge at the open window, he said, with a faint smile: "May I have a cigar, Martin? Look in my case on the table."

"Certainly, sir."

"It tastes good. You must not let me drink any more. By evening I shall not need it, not for a year. I must get away to Bedford at once. How long am I here?"

"About thirteen days."

"That is terrible! Two weeks! That is longer than usual."

"Than usual?" asked Blount, surprised.

"Yes. This comes once in three or four years, and then I am lost, damned, gone!"

Blount looked the amazement he felt. Nothing in his own nature or experience explained this inexorable appetite. Archer could have told him that it was a form of the drink craving which, though rare, is in a very few an almost uncontrollable form of alcoholic temptation.

"Please, sir, not to talk of it now. I have with me all your letters and telegrams. You may like to see them. If you are at all able I think you must go to the city. We will drive about to-day, and to-morrow—"

"Let me see a paper—yesterday's." He was at once anxious. Martin came back with New York and Philadelphia journals. Grace turned in haste to the stock-list, tore open letters and telegrams. No alterative could have been so potent, no drug so tone-giving. He stood up and said: "We must go to the city at once, to-day. Get me a time-table."

"Certainly," said Martin; "but think a little. You cannot be fit, or be made fit, for instant work. And it is too late now. Let us get on horseback this morning, and walk about in the afternoon. We can get to Harrisburg to-night, and home with ease in the after part of the day, to-morrow."

Grace refused, until he found that to reach the city that night was impossible. "Very well, have your way. Please to wire Mr. West and Archer in my name to meet me at the office at 6 P.M. to-morrow. Wire to these three bank presidents to be there. Stop! I must write the names. You will leave me at this station to-morrow. I have been ill—add that. You had best go back to Bedford.''

Blount was amazed at this swift revival of capacity. He hesitated, as he said:

''Pardon me, sir, but are you—safe?''

''Yes, I am safe. No wonder you ask.''

The ride and the walk were taken, and at evening, when James Rogers settled his account with a liberal hand, the neat, clean-shaven gentleman with whom Blount walked to the station was a metamorphosed being. As they rode or walked during the day Blount answered his questions as to how he had chanced upon him. Of Craig he said not a word. He meant at some time to do so. He knew how it would disturb Grace, whose sensitiveness about this masterful appetite had become painfully apparent in the repeated cautions he expressed to the man who needed none. He would wait and see.

The more he saw of Grace the more wise did it seem to let the matter wait. The banker should go back without this added trouble. He was of opinion that soon or late Craig would betray his trust, but meanwhile it was well not to be too sure of this, and if Craig could be kept in order Grace would be saved a serious addition to the annoyances sure to arise out of a sad business.

That evening, when Grace parted from Blount, he said:

''I shall sleep at Harrisburg, and be at home to-morrow in time for my engagements. I think that now you may see your way to accepting my offer about my books.''

Martin said he would think about it. With Craig in his mind there seemed fair reason why this time he might for a double cause say yes.

Grace said: "Write to me, and come soon. I owe you a debt I can never pay, and, Martin, I have a long memory." Blount looked up at him. "The debt was paid long ago." They shook hands without other words, and the young man stood with a grave, set face, and saw the train pull out of the station and disappear through a gap in the hills. A little later he was on his way back to Bedford, reflecting on Grace's renewed offer and on the difficult problem of whether Craig would keep quiet. He settled the first question with ease, and was not long in deciding what to do. He wrote Archer that he had a good reason for not staying where he was—could he not get some work in town? Archer was puzzled. It was unlike Blount. He wrote in reply that he might help him in his laboratory, but that he was not able to pay an assistant. He spoke of it to Grace, who said:

"Let him come to me and arrange my books, as I once asked him to do. This would leave him at least the half of the day free."

Very joyfully Blount gave up his place. What he had declined before he felt that he could now willingly accept, since it would enable him to keep an eye on Craig and, at need, to consult Archer; but that must be a last resort, for this very practical young man had carefully listened to Grace's cautions and as carefully kept himself from any promise of secrecy. He was, however, much troubled, and not without cause, though he comforted himself with the idea that Craig could not afford to lose his place, that Grace was too formidable to offend, and that very likely Craig would prudently remember what had been said to him.

XXXIX

FEW minutes before six Roger Grace walked, smiling, into his own private office. His partners and Archer greeted him warmly. He gave no explanation of his silence and long absence. None was asked; he was a man whom people did not question. He had the habit of taciturn attention; men talked on and said to him things they had not meant to say. On his way home he had deeply studied the situation. Now he began:

"I see, Archer, that the Republic Trust has stopped payment, and that Thurston has run away. Let us deal with this first. It is a bad case, I fear." Pencil in hand, cheerful and competent, he made notes as his questions were answered.

"Did Fairthorne sell?" he asked his counsel. "What! And at sixty-five?" He noted the amount. "We must set it up again. This little panic will not last." He ran over a list of names and securities. "Among us we must help about half of these men." He went on, clear, confident, pleasantly decisive, until the bank presidents came. With their consultation, which lasted until nine o'clock, this tale has nothing to do.

"There is no one like him," said his partner to

Archer, as Grace left them. "But his absence has cost us dear, and where the deuce was he?"

"Ask him," said Archer.

"Not I."

Grace went home exhausted; he had gone since morning without food, and despite his rude health he was not yet the man he had been a fortnight before.

Miss Clementina met him in the hall, a trifle shy, a trifle red, glad to see him. He greeted her coldly, said he was tired, and asked for supper. He ate it in silence and went up-stairs, where he found Knellwood in his study. They shook hands, and Grace lit a cigar.

"Yes, I am back, and find that my absence has hurt many."

"But you could not help it," said Knellwood.

"No, but—the cost, the cost! It ends the only dream of my life, Knellwood. You really must feel by this time that I am right. I shall get away, go to the country—forget, if I can. I may have committed myself, but, whether or not, anything is better for her than to marry a sot. I thought for a moment that I would tell her."

"That would be best," said Knellwood.

"No, I cannot."

"You are wrong, altogether wrong, unjust to yourself, unfair to a woman. Let her choose."

"I dare not. She might— Ah! I cannot run even the small risk of her saying yes. And then, if this awful thing gets to be known!"

"How can it? Take my advice. You are too
25

near it all for thought to be reasonable. Talk some day to Archer. It is a malaria of the mind, of the morals. Go to bed now.''

''What a good fellow you are,'' Grace said, smiling. ''So Archer won't let you work? Come out to the farm.''

''Perhaps, after a while.''

''How is Miss Letitia? I did not see her.''

''As always,'' said Knellwood. ''Miss Fairthorne says she is like a dried primrose dropped out of one's grandmama's Bible.''

''That's pretty and gentle. Well, good night, Knellwood.''

The next day, at evening, Grace went away to his farm near Edgewood, saying that he would keep his rooms, of course; he might need them. He really meant not to return in the fall. When, at the end of a week he had not been near them, Clementina set herself to accept the disaster of her broken romance, and to persuade herself that, after all, it had been mere kindness. Life had not been tender to the little gentlewoman and now she was hit hard and felt it perhaps more than the rich or prosperous could have done. She was a woman of good mind, and as she prepared to accept a darkened life she tried to think calmly of what had caused his abrupt change. No! She was too feminine not to be sure of what Roger Grace must have wished. He was a reasonable, a kindly, and a good man.

''Not quite like us, dear,'' said Letitia; ''that needs generations. But a very nice man. One really might hesitate to say he is a gentleman, in our sense.''

"But would you say he is not one?" returned Clementina, a little hurt. What did she care? She loved him, and—oh, if she could only ask frankly what she had done, for to seek the blame there was as natural to her as to seek it elsewhere would have been to many.

Knellwood alone understood this simple tragedy, and watched its effects, pitiful and touched.

Meanwhile, the days went by as usual at Edgewood, no better, no worse. Pilgrim, now able to walk out, put off his visit day after day, hating to face Mrs. Hunter again. Blount, of whom Grace asked no further questions, was at the farm or in town, delighted to aid Archer in his laboratory study of South American arrow poisons, or to find time for a visit to Margaret Swanwick, and to see the pleasant people who to him were so new and so fresh. He had meant to keep some watch upon Craig, and had a young fellow's kindly dream of influencing the man for good. He did manage to meet him, but it was only to escape in disgust, or to hear him boast of what he could do with Grace, and that he was as safe as a bank, which just then lacked value as a comparison. It was impossible not to distrust him and his confident protests. Blount began to foresee trouble. Should he warn Grace, or tell Dr. Archer? An older man would have been less puzzled. But what, after all, could a fellow like Craig do? It was not in Blount to have imagined what did happen.

Of a Saturday morning Roger Grace, pleased at his recent financial success and at the better turn of affairs, sat looking at his correspondence. Of a sudden his face changed, as he read a letter, sealed with wax, and marked "Private." It ran thus:

" I know all about you in Carlisle. If you will send a check to bearer for three hundred dollars, to Cyrus Peters, General Post-Office, I will never tell. If you do not send it in three days there will be something come out you won't like."

Grace sat still, looked at the seal, the paper, the writing. He was terribly perplexed. It is hard to conceive how disastrous the chance of this revelation appeared to him. He seemed to see the sensational headlines in the Sunday papers, the dastardly phrases the baser newspaper employs to conceal the slanderer and without use of a name to make clear who is stabbed.

"Blackmail," said Grace; "if I send it that is only the beginning. If I set a watch and catch him, it will all come out from mere desire of revenge or in court. Yes, even if I convict; but how could he prove it? And who is he? I am lost! It is what I always feared. Who could know?" He dismissed instantly the idea that Blount could have spoken or that any one in Carlisle could have known him. His precautions had always been excessive.

But if it came out! Oh, if— He looked back over his life of purity and absolute rectitude, thought of John Fairthorne's sneer, of the regret of the Swanwicks, of Archer, of the men who, envying him, would fasten on this story with amusement. With all his positive business capacity, he was a man tenderly sensitive and deeply religious. Now, again reflecting, he said that he should be called a hypocrite. No, he must pay, but first he must talk to Martin Blount.

When that evening he sat with Blount in the parlor of the gray stone farm-house, he handed him the letter and said:

"Read that."

The younger man showed very little astonishment.

"Well, I never thought he would do as mean a thing as this."

"Who, Martin?"

"Mr. Grace, I see now I may have been wrong, although whether I was wrong or not this might have happened. Lionel Craig saw you with me at Carlisle. He alone could have written that letter." Then he related what had occurred.

Grace smoked quietly until he had heard it all, asked a question or two, and said:

"You should have warned me."

"At first I could n't; you were awfully upset, sir, over the telegrams and letters. I was on the point of speaking of it, and then—"

"No, you were right; but later—later—"

"Ah, he promised never to say a word about it. I did not believe him, but I never dreamed of a thing like this, and so I just waited, and at last I hated to talk to you about it. I was wrong. When things went on and nothing happened I just could n't."

Grace sat smoking as he listened.

"I see your difficulty. Had I known I should have bribed him to hold his tongue. Now he has asked to be bribed. Don't worry yourself about it. It had to happen. To know who it is does not help me. I simply cannot afford to have this thing get out."

"But you won't pay this beast? Why, sir, there is no end to such paying!"

"I know."

"But, excuse me, sir, it would be wrong—wicked."

"Yes, I know."

Martin was bewildered for a moment. He had expected an outburst of anger and swift, resolute reprisal. It seemed to him easy to arrest the man and finish the matter. He was sure, from what he knew of Craig, that the mere threat of arrest would end it. But Grace had said he meant to pay, after which they sat a long while, neither of them speaking, both busily thinking.

The two men had many characteristics in common, but the successful banker was by far the more sensitive person. Perhaps, too, he overestimated the value of the society which was pleasantly accepting him, and also the force of its opinion and the interest with which it regarded passing events. Either Archer or Masters could have told him that few people would care, and that those who did would forget it in a fortnight. Perhaps what most influenced his timid decision was the thought of the woman in whom he had developed a love which was a flower before he thought it could be a bud. He was an educable man, and she, in her refinements of person and manners, had innocently taught him much. He had come to value her opinion, to consult her tastes, and now what a gulf there was between them! He over-imagined her disgust, and what she might say of him.

As he thus sadly tortured himself, the younger man was more wholesomely busy. He looked at Grace, and knew that for himself, at least, to reason with the man would be vain. He was too young to have weight with him. The fact that this gnat could sting to madness of folly so noble a life as that of his generous benefactor aroused his anger. His wrath was the greater because of the promise Craig had made and broken, and because of his own feeling that he had been an idiot to trust him at all. He blamed himself for this and accepted the thought that he, as well as Mr. Grace, was injured. At last he said:

"I suppose, sir, this scamp will not draw your check before Tuesday, if," he added, "you send it." He still hoped for a better way out of it. In his trouble he ventured to say, "I do wish you would just arrest the fellow."

The banker rose, and, with a hand on Martin's shoulder, said: "I do not wish to discuss this matter further. My mind is made up. I shall mail my check to-morrow. Fortunately for you, you have nothing more to do with it. You acted as seemed best to you, and I least of all blame you. Let us drop it." For a moment he was silent, and then went on: "It is due to you, who wonder at my decision, to say that I have imperative motives and reasons about which I cannot talk. Most men would say weaknesses. I am ashamed, Martin, to recall for

you and myself what you saw. It is horrible! I
would, at need, bury it in gold. Never let us speak
of it again. It has cost too much, too much of things
better than gold; and now this is between us, never
speak of it. What are you doing with Archer at
the laboratory? It interests me." He discussed
Blount's reply with intelligence, and seemed able
calmly to dismiss what kept incessantly distracting
Blount. But when night came Grace lay awake, as
he rarely did, for not without pain of mind does a
strong man become the fool of fear.

As there was work to be watched in the laboratory Martin took an early train to the city on Monday. He had passed through the stage of anger
into a condition of stern resolve to settle with Craig.
He felt the necessity as he usually felt a debt. He
found that Archer had left directions which would
give him a full day's work. He said to himself that
Craig would keep, and gave him that day no further
thought.

On the morning of Tuesday he disposed of the
laboratory work very early. As he passed through
Archer's library he picked up a slim bamboo cane,
and, swinging it vindictively, went away toward
Market Street. When, in a third-class hotel, he asked
the clerk if Mr. Craig were in he replied that he was,
and that he guessed he would be all day. Blount
announced, without mental reserve, that he was
Craig's friend, and went up-stairs.

His knock was not answered, and he had to make
an unseemly noise before his louder summons
brought Craig to the door in a shabby dressing-

gown. He was sober, but red-eyed from his de-
bauch of the preceding night.

"Oh, it 's you," said Craig.

"Yes, it is I." He went in, and locking the door
put the key in his pocket.

"What 's that for?" said Craig, in alarm. His
mind at once reverted to the letter. Ever since,
with the cheerful courage of alcohol, he had sent it
and even after receiving Grace's reply it had been a
source of terror. He was now nervous and fearful.

"You get out of here," he said. Something in
the look of Blount seemed to threaten, and the rosy
little man was born a coward. Blount began at
once:

"Sit down, I want to talk to you. Oh, you
won't?" He thrust him into a chair and stood over
him. "Keep quiet and listen to me. You lied to
me, you miserable little wretch. You promised to
hold your tongue about Mr. Grace. I am going to
take it out of your hide. I said I would—I warned
you."

Craig cried out in vain:

"Murder! Murder! Please don't. I was tight.
I did n't think what I was doing. I 'll never, never
do it again. You hurt me."

"Do what again?" asked Blount. "It is no use to
howl. I shall be through with you before any one
can come." Then, seeing the abject terror of the
man, he had a bright idea. "If I don't beat you will
you tell me all about it? And mind you, I shall
know if you lie. You can't fool me this time. Now,
out with it."

Craig began to consider how little he need tell.

"Well," and the bamboo shook ominously. "You said you would never speak of it. You did talk."

"I swear I never told any one but my sister."

"Mrs. Hunter! You told her?" exclaimed Martin, astonished.

"Oh, she won't tell. She said I was a fool to talk." This was also Martin's opinion. He had heard enough of the secretary to know that she was disliked by Mrs. Swanwick. Was she, too, by any possibility concerned in the letter to Grace? He had heard Archer speak of her as an adventuress. He said, quickly:

"You are thinking, you cur, how little you must tell to get out of a bad scrape. Now, take care how you answer me. Was she in the whole of this business?"

"What business? I don't know what you mean."

Blount's patience was at an end. The bamboo fell cruelly across Craig's shoulders, as Martin cried out:

"You liar!" This time Craig was conquered. He whimpered:

"That hurt. I 'll tell if you—if you won't—"

"No, I will let you off if you speak out. I said I would, but you believe nobody. Now, perhaps you know I am in earnest."

"Well," said Craig, sullenly, "what do you want?"

"Does your sister know what you have done? Come, now."

"No, she don't."

"When did you do it?"

"Are you going to tell Mr. Grace?"

"I! No, indeed. When was it?"

"When was what?"

"I think you must be itching for the rest of that thrashing. What a fool you are!"

Craig looked up at the grim and lowering face. "I wrote it on Friday. I was n't myself. If you won't tell Mr. Grace I 'll swear I 'll never do it again." For a moment he was of a mind to hand over Grace's letter and the check to bearer which he had in his pocket. Then he reconsidered it; Grace would not know. For once he believed; Blount had declared that he would not tell Grace. "You promise me you won't tell Mr. Grace? You swear?"

"I never swear," said Martin. "I said I would not tell him. You may be sure." Then Craig determined to keep the money.

Blount let go his hold and sat down. The thought of securing the letter Grace wrote did not occur to him. He was otherwise occupied. He now knew all about it, and not alone from Grace. He was free to speak out to Archer, for he felt entirely assured that the man at his side would talk freely when again in liquor, and be still capable of doing mischief. How to provide against this he did not know. It was like dealing with a half-imbecile child. Archer might help him. He was sure, at all events, that the blackmailing had come to an end. But what of the sister? These thoughts passed rapidly through his mind as he sat. Craig, furtively watchful, said for a moment no word, but as Blount

rose he spoke. "You said you would n't tell Grace?
You won't go and tell any one?"

"I make no other promises. If you do not keep
straight and quit drinking I may have to see if
your sister can do anything with you." Craig's uneasiness was very evident. Blount continued: "Remember one thing: if Mr. Grace gets to know who
wrote that letter you will be in the penitentiary in
no time. I came here on my own quarrel. We are
quits." It was like him to turn back and, with
some sense of pity, to say:

"Why don't you quit drinking and behave yourself? If you would just try I would help you."

"Oh, you go away and let me alone. You 've
bullied me enough, and now you want to talk Sunday-school."

Blount's face grew hard; he made no reply, but
went out and down the stairs. It was now one
o'clock and, as he had expected, he found Archer at
home and about to lunch.

"Sit down, Blount," he said; "you are doing my
work very well. There is nothing like the laboratory
to train a man to exactness. Individuality must
always keep our work at the bedside more or less an
art. It never can have the precision of science so
long as one man differs from another. So long as
men so differ there will be the chance of our being
unable to foresee results with certainty."

Such talk usually delighted Blount; now he failed
to respond, and only said: "I came here to talk
to you about something serious. I am not sure that
I am right to talk."

"Then don't."

"But I must."

"Then talk. By St. Mayflower! You Yankees are queer folk. That ship must have carried a heavy freight of conscience. It has lasted long. What 's the matter, Martin?"

"I will try to state it. While Mr. Grace was away a very unpleasant thing happened. I was there and saw it. It concerned Mr. Grace, and it is a thing which ought never to get out."

"Indeed!" Archer took up a paper-knife and began to bend and handle it, a trick he had when attentive to a patient's talk.

"I made some kind of promise to Mr. Grace not to speak of it."

"You are not going to now?"

"Oh, no; but if you will just let me go on you will see why I want advice."

"Very good. Go on."

"I said it must not get out. Now, what I saw a fellow named Craig saw too. He 's a brother of that Mrs. Hunter and is a clerk in Mr. Grace's office. Do you know him, sir?"

"I think I have seen him. I cannot say I know him."

"Well, he is a pretty little man, without a shred of character. He gambles, and drinks, and gabbles. He swore he would never speak of this matter. But he did; he told his sister."

"Oh, his sister! And what next, Martin?"

"I went there to-day to lick him because he lied to me."

"The remedy was heroic."

"I did n't hurt him much, because he broke up and confessed the whole thing."

"Confessed what?"

"Why, that he had told his sister and the rest."

"What else? Let me hear it all. You are rather exasperating as a story-teller."

"Now, that 's where my difficulty comes in. You see, I myself am pledged to Mr. Grace not to speak of it. Then this man tells me to-day—oh, I made him—the whole story, and what he did. Now, I want to ask you if, after I hear it all from another than Mr. Grace, shall I do wrong to tell you?"

Archer reflected.

"Are you sure that to do so will be of any service to Mr. Grace?"

"I don't know. Unless some one is able to stop this fellow he will babble it out in every bar-room. He has done worse already. I think he is afraid of his sister, for he begged me not to tell her. I said I would not promise."

Archer got up and walked about, while Blount waited.

"Martin, years ago, when I was young like you, and pretty nearly penniless, I went to ask Mr. Grace if he would take as security a mortgage on a small property of my mother's in the South, and lend me money to secure me a year in Germany. He talked to me awhile, and said no, but that he would lend me the money on my personal pledge to pay when I could. He was not then as he is now, a very rich man. I took it frankly. If I can help him in any trouble I am at his service and yours. I think you may speak freely. I suppose it is a woman.''

"Oh, no, sir!" said Blount, much relieved. "Craig and I saw Mr. Grace at Carlisle drunk."

"What—Grace? Incredible!"

"Yes, sir, it is true. I think that it must be a very rare thing in him."

Archer had heard of the banker's unaccountable absences. He at once remembered two other cases of this strange form of temptation. "Well, go on. What next?"

"Craig had himself been drinking. I persuaded him to go away before Mr. Grace was able to recognize any one." He went on to relate what had passed, and Craig's confession of the blackmailing letter. Archer said:

"That is a queer tale, but the matter seems simple. Mr. Grace has only to arrest the man."

"He won't. He has paid."

"Not really!"

"Yes, and I can't explain it. He's like a scared girl about it, and he 'll go on paying if that fellow asks him; and, as if that is n't enough, the scamp will be sure to get drunk and talk. I said he had told his sister. Cannot you do something, Dr. Archer?"

"I think I can, Martin. I will try." He knew that he must not speak to Grace. He ought to recover the letter and check and have a more distinct confession. That would surely end it. Merely again to scare the young man would be useless. There was still Mrs. Hunter. Over this he hesitated

long. A part of his indecision was due to his difficulty in comprehending the motive which had influenced Grace. He had in himself nothing which
could explain to him how such a man could become
the easy victim of a drunken boy.

When at last he fully decided to act through Lucretia he believed that he was swayed alone by the
feeling that it was right to serve one who had helped
him, and that it was a wise thing to do. That his
intense dislike of Mrs. Hunter had any effect in
bringing about his final determination he was far
from apprehending. Nor was he yet sure that she
might not have had a hand in the matter, and if so
she would be in his power and must go. The
thought was one more proof of how little he understood Lucretia. Leaving out Grace, the most efficient motive which urged him to act through Mrs.
Hunter was Blount's unfaltering conviction that no
ordinary motives would permanently stop the tongue
of Lionel Craig.

XL

S we have said, on Sunday Grace had sent his check for three hundred "to bearer" to the address given in Craig's note. Reflection had only strengthened his desire to bribe the man to silence. He asked for Craig on Monday morning, and was told that he was absent and said to be sick. To the surprise of West, he made no comment, but plunged at once into the details of a difficult suit against a Chicago bank.

Since the Fairthornes had left town Archer had seen nothing of Mary, but she was one of the board of ladies who visited the children's wards of the hospital, and this and other matters served as an excuse for writing to her. He felt, too, as she did, that in a letter she got nearer to him than she ever did in personal talk. As he drove about he read her reply to a letter concerning a gift of books for the children's ward and other matters.

"DEAR DR. ARCHER," she wrote, "When next I come to town I will ask my sister to help me select the books. I am most glad to assist you."

Then she questioned about some of the little ones— whom to send to the seashore and how to manage it.

"You say that you are not always happy—who is? But your life surely ought to content you. It is so full, so complete; I seem to lead a life of trifles. I read, and sew, and garden, and ride. My duties and my pleasant hours with my uncle (for, despite his peculiarities, they were often pleasant) are over. My cousin has become irritable and dissatisfied. If I were but let alone I might endure it, but Mrs. H. does really seem to enjoy the game of opposing me.

"The garden has always been my special care. This woman cuts my flowers, and orders what changes she will. Yesterday the horse we use in the dog-cart was lame. She drove my saddle-horse. We had some sharp words, but it was useless. Most of the time she keeps a sort of guard over my uncle, who is, at times, almost childish.

"I am silly to pour out my woes to you, but" (here there was a careful erasure) "one must talk. When a child is hurt it cries. It has 'no language but a cry.' When grown-up folks are hurt, they talk of it. It seems to me only a form of crying. I ought to add that I do not talk much of my moral aches; to write of them seems—well, I leave to your charity what excuses you choose to contribute.

"It cannot last long. The poor old gentleman is fast fading. In his clearer morning hours he complains about Mr. Pilgrim's delays. I wish he would come out and settle the matter. Mr. Masters was here to-day, and stirred up my uncle, thinking to amuse him.

"Dr. Soper says he is getting better!

                    "Yours sincerely,
                              "MARY FAIRTHORNE."

Archer read this letter more often than so simple a document demanded, and at last put it in his pocket, reflecting on the improbability of the writer's ever speaking as frankly as she wrote. It had not lessened his resolution to see Mrs. Hunter. And yet he was in no haste.

The mischief for Grace had begun, and probably no new demand would be made, at least not until the money so easily won was spent. He was very busy, and must wait. He said as much to Blount, who was impatient of delay and wished to see the matter settled. He asked for Craig at Grace's office, but was told that he was absent and had written that he was ill. When West, who disliked Lionel, spoke of it to Grace, and of the utter worthlessness of the man, the banker said he would go to see him. This he was sure to do in cases of sickness among those he employed; but the partner was surprised when he went on to say that Craig was young, and Mr. Fairthorne had asked of him—Grace —not to be hard on him. It was unlike his senior, who was clearly indisposed to be severe or even just in a matter which seemed to require to be sharply dealt with. Grace did not call on the clerk. He was beginning to feel what a fatal noose he had cast about his own neck.

In the latter part of the day on Tuesday Archer, afoot, as he liked to be in the afternoon, was busily reflecting on Mary Fairthorne's annoyances, and with rather natural satisfaction on the prospect of paying her debt in kind.

He was hailed by the laughing voice of Masters, who, coming out of the club, joined him on Walnut Street.

"Busy?" he asked.

"Yes."

"Wish I were. May is a bad month. Nothing to kill but time. In June I am off to the Restigouche for salmon. I think this week of trying the drumfish down the bay. Halloa! Here 's the big chaplain, Syd. What a fine cavalry colonel was lost in him. He is going to Swanwick's. He 's like a stray dog—tries everybody's door-steps.''

''I have set him a double decalogue of things not to do. He is unhappy.''

''So am I, Sydney. I yearn for another good, honest war, where you cannot have a doubt as to which side to take. The last fellow gets me on the tariff or what not.''

''It was as you say, Tom; for my part, I loathed it.''

''But how the chaplain liked it and vowed it was horrible, and how he loved the battle-line. He 's a fine fellow, with all his fal-lals.''

''He had them then, Tom. Do you remember how fussy he was about his uniform?''

''Indeed I do!'' They joined him as they approached the steps of Swanwick's house.

''Good evening, Tom. No one is ill, I hope, Archer?''

''Oh, some small malady. Since the mamas have begun to keep thermometers the doctor has no peace. How are you?''

''So well that I am ashamed to be idle.''

''Perhaps,'' said Masters, slyly, ''the exercise of patience may absolve from that charge.''

''That does n't sound like your wisdom, Tom,'' said the big man.

''Well, who cares where the guinea was coined? If you are bored for a time, I am bored indefinitely. Come and kill drum with me, and fill up the vacuums between your ribs with soft-shelled crabs and sedge oysters.''

"No, I cannot."

"Ah," said Archer, "don't you wickedly yearn sometimes, chaplain, for another ride down the valley with Sheridan?"

"Or a rally on the firing-line?" said Tom.

"Go away, little Satan," laughed the chaplain, as he rang the bell, and they went, merrily chaffing one another, into Mrs. Swanwick's parlor.

"Mrs. Swanwick would like Dr. Archer to go to the nursery."

"I am to entertain you," said a stout lady, who rose as the servant delivered her message.

Masters said:

"Glad to see you, Mrs. Craycroft."

The rector bowed to the widow.

Mrs. Craycroft is of small moment in this story, but it is often the people of no personal importance who bewilder the lives of men or women, and have at times simply the confusing effect of displaced punctuation marks. She had a wide range of shallow knowledge, was as definite as a dictionary, and as sure of her facts as Tom of his first barrel when his hand was in and the ducks flying low. She was an uninventive gossip, and simply carried to and fro her freight of facts, social or other.

In five minutes she had assured Mr. Knellwood that he wore his chasuble wrong, and lectured Tom, to his delight, on the breed of Chesapeake ducking dogs. When, by and by, Archer returned with Margaret Swanwick, she instructed the doctor on the condition of one of her friends then under his care and advised a change of treatment.

Archer laughed and said it was an addition to medicine.

"Oh," she said, "you may smile. I have seen it tried. And, dear," she added to Margaret, "don't let them over-ventilate the nursery. The doctors will do it."

"Of course not," said Madge, while Knellwood and Archer exchanged smiles, and Masters contentedly listened.

The chat soon became less general, and the widow grew positive as to a variety of social items, and asked Margaret in an aside if Mr. Pilgrim were really engaged to Mary Fairthorne. Margaret, accustomed to a curiosity which merely collected facts and was free from malice, said:

"No; what a strange report! Don't repeat it, Sarah."

"Certainly not. I merely ask you. I never repeat things unless I am sure of their truth. Who is Kitty's last victim?"

"Herself," said Margaret, laughing. "That is a constant love affair."

After other talk the men went away, and Mrs. Craycroft began to discuss Mrs. Hunter. She had been out to lunch with Mary, and had thought Mary must find her such an interesting companion, so gay, so clever. It was well Mr. Fairthorne was not younger. But where did the woman come from?

Margaret said curtly that she did not know, and made it so plain that Lucretia was not a person she would talk about that Mrs. Craycroft retired from the subject, saying:

"Well, she is interesting enough to make one curious; but then, Margaret, you are so wanting in curiosity."

Madge smiled.

"Indeed, I am often curious to know why you are curious."

"Bless me, how complicated!" she cried, as Miss Katherine Morrow entered. Kitty kissed her cousin on both cheeks, asked how dear Mrs. Craycroft was, adding, "What a too lovely gown!" and "How are the dear children, Madge?" She was inwardly relieved to hear that Jack had a cold and Retta was asleep. The maternal instinct slumbered in Kitty; children bored her. If ever this instinct should awake in her it would be as despotic and as unreasoning as that of a panther for her young.

Mrs. Swanwick soon went back to Jack, leaving the two to the game of "Have you heard?" and "Do you know?" Kitty's facts were not accepted without critical examination. Presently the widow said:

"You missed Father Knellwood. He looked so well and so handsome! I had to correct him about his way of wearing the chasuble, and, really, last Sunday the incense was—oh, it smelled atrociously!"

Kitty, a little confused, said something incredibly silly about the odor of sanctity, which made the older woman, who had no full-blown sense of humor, stare at her with astonishment, and say: "I really do not quite understand you. Do you know that Father Knellwood is going to Europe? We shall miss him sadly."

"To Europe!" gasped Kitty. "Who told you?"

"I overheard him say he thought of it, and that Dr. Archer said he ought to go. Mr. Masters asked him when he sailed. I hope it does not mean Rome. He is certainly going."

Kitty had grown white to the lips. As the widow spoke she saw the girl's quivering lip, but had the good sense to go on talking. Kitty caught her breath and rallied, as she said: "I scarcely think it can be true."

"Perhaps not," returned Mrs. Craycroft, "but he is thinking of it; and now I must go, dear. Tell Margaret I could not wait." She had ignorantly done mischief.

Kitty, left alone, burst into tears. She had waited with her little traps set, and circumstance had not been her friend. Mrs. Hunter had promised all manner of things, and now—here was the end!

Mrs. Hunter had reconsidered her beliefs about Knellwood. She had reached the opinion that he did not now care enough for Kitty to break through the pale of denials he had set about his life. At one time she had thought otherwise, but there was, even for Lucretia's skepticism, something convincing in the man and his ways. She had for a time gone regularly to St. Agnes's, but had excused herself from church work on various pretenses. More recently, she had now and then attended some short service with Kitty. Her own church, which was that of Rome, she cared as little about, and the move to Edgewood agreeably relieved her of all need to keep up a tiresome pretense.

Knellwood had not been very long deceived as to Mrs. Hunter's religious earnestness. Despite what Mary Fairthorne called his omnivorous charity of opinion, he had begun to feel that there was something untrustworthy in Lucretia. He could not have explained what was more a feeling than a conviction; but the instincts of a gentleman are sometimes wiser than his intelligence. Of late he had heard too much of this once ardent seeker after truth and work.

Lucretia had no mind that Kitty should marry any one. For a time this longing for the love of a man who was apparently not of the world of those who marry had seemed to her useful, but a wilder passion than she had it in her nature to comprehend possessed Katherine Morrow with a power which swept away the barriers of conventional training.

Margaret, returning, surprised the girl in an attempt to wipe away her tears.

"Why, Kitty," she said, "what is the matter, dear?"

Kitty looked about her little mind for a plausible lie, and said:

"Mrs. Craycroft abused Lucretia."

"Indeed," returned Madge, puzzled, for the collector of facts never abused any one. "I rather thought she liked her."

"No, no," cried Kitty, decorating her invention; "she said she came from no one knew where. She said—oh, I could n't stand it! You all hate her." She made herself angry to relieve the fury of another passion.

"I certainly do not love her," said Madge; "suppose we drop her. Stay and dine; we can wire Edgewood and Harry will take you to the nine train."

"No, I must go. I never see you or talk to Mary without your getting on to this subject and abusing a woman who—who understands me as you have never done."

"But it was you, Kitty, who brought up this woman. I never mention her to you, and indeed we never see you."

"And will not soon again, I can assure you. Good evening."

This was rather too much for even Madge's well-trained temper. "You are both incomprehensible and ill mannered. Nothing was said to justify such words as you have just used. I shall leave you, and I advise you not to go out until you have quieted down a little. No; I will not listen to another word," and with this the little mistress of the house retired to the nursery. Kitty sat still in the parlor. In a moment Madge was forgotten, and her eyes began to fill.

Oh, surely this man must love her. It was a gift —this bliss of love which she had never before had to give. Could it be that this one man did not want it? Or was it really his principles which forbade avowal, or—and she sat up—was he fleeing from a temptation he dared not meet? She felt that only the chance of an hour was wanting; how happy she could make him, and how good she would become if he were but hers. As she sat still she flushed, her mouth grew dry, her heart beat in her neck and against her breast. She stood up, a woman in the toils of passion—a soul astray if ever there were one.

"If I could but see him! Oh, I must—I must!"

For good or ill her prayer was granted. Cyril Knellwood entered the room, and in an instant knew his peril. He made haste to explain his return.

"Is Mrs. Swanwick in? I forgot to ask her something. I want to see her. I came to ask her to receive at the farm school a little scamp who can be helped; it is very odd how one forgets." He talked on, speaking fast. Then the servant came in to say that Mrs. Swanwick could not leave the children, and must be excused.

Knellwood got up. "I am sorry. I must go."

"Just a moment," said Kitty. "You need not wait," this last to the servant.

The rector felt the danger, but the habit of courtesy forbade his insisting, when Kitty added, in a voice near to breaking: "I must see you for—for a moment."

"What is it?" he asked, and sat down, laying his hat beside him, while, with a hand on his cross, he waited.

Kitty's face fell for an instant, and then, looking up at him, she said: "Are you really going to Europe?"

Up to this time his voyage had been in doubt. He made an instant decision. "Yes, I am going; and, pardon me, but I am in great haste. Good-bye."

Then Kitty broke down. The poor, foolish little beauty had always had her way. It was she who denied. Now she caught the note of severe formality in his voice and saw his face set sternly. To his horror, she exclaimed: "You cannot go!" and caught his hand, looking up at him, as he stood appalled at her outbreak. She went on wildly: "You are cruel! Cruel! You have made me love you. You have ruined my life. Pity me! You cannot go away and leave me. Say you will not go! You know I love you!" She lifted up her charming, rosy face, raining tears on his hand. He was speechless before this wail of passion. Drawing back, he said:

"My poor child! May God be my witness that I have never done anything to make you care for me. Do you know what you are doing?"

"I don't care. I love you!"

"I pray you not to say this. I have never— never—"

She broke in: "Never—never? You asked why I did not any longer call you Father. Oh, what did that mean? I was sure it meant— Oh, you can't say it meant nothing!"

It was the one little joint in his armor. She had found it. He was too honest to say it meant nothing. It was not quite true that he had done nothing to betray himself. He was terribly shaken, and moved away as he said: "Miss Morrow, this must end—here and now. You are a young girl. You are doing a wrong and an imprudent thing." He looked down from his great height on the yellow hair, the face of pleading passion. His eyes filled. "I am pledged to Christ's work, and to it alone. I cannot marry. I never shall. I beg of you—"

"What do I care?" she broke in. "I want love—love. You have cheated me."

The rector said sternly:

"I must go, and at once. Some one may come at any moment. I beg of you to let me go."

"Who cares?" she cried. In her madness she stood resolute between him and the door.

"Either," he said, "you go or I must ring." His voice broke with the vast pity he felt for her, the fear he had of himself, and it was very great.

She passed him as he spoke, and, turning in the doorway, cried: "I hate you! I wish I could kill you! You have broken my heart."

She would never in all her life know how measureless was the temptation to the man who stepped by her, saying: "May the good God pity and help you," adding, in thought, "and me, his servant!"

He was sinning against nature, thinking so to serve God, and nearly lost self-control. To say "I love you" would have been so easy and so true, and, alas! so delightful. His hand clutched the gold cross till it broke in his grasp. In her, love had turned to anger and shame.

She ran down the steps, and walked swiftly away; while he, going back for his hat, was aware of the broken cross in his hand and the torn ribbon. Once outside he walked westward in the darkening twilight, sternly questioning himself. No! His conscience was clear, but for that one slip. He groaned. Had he shown her the love he felt? No, never! Was it love—a pure and honest love? And how had it come to life? The big man shuddered. "Ah," he thought, "how near damnation lies. And how piti-

able it was. All for me!—for me— Oh, what am
I? My God, what am I, that I should be the cause
of sin?''

He went out to the river, and, crossing at Market
Street, walked fast and far up the Lancaster Pike.
It was near eleven when he reached Miss Markham's.

He let himself in and went up to Grace's study,
once more the steady master of himself. There and
then he wrote to Archer that he had at last made up
his mind to take the doctor's advice and go abroad.
''I find that I can readily manage to get three
months in England. Pardon my long resistance;
but you, who are so good to all men, will find that
easy.''

After this he wrote to Grace, and then went to his
own room. When he spoke of his plan to the maiden
ladies they were troubled.

''Why, you are all gone, or going. Mr. Grace,
and Mr. Blount, and now you,'' said Clementina.

''But I shall be with you in the fall, and Grace,
too, I am sure.''

''Perhaps,'' said Clementina, ''perhaps.''

''There is no perhaps in our lives, dear,'' said
Letitia, wearily. ''Everything goes wrong at last,
no matter how fine it all seems at first.''

''That is not like you, sister.''

XLI

IN the middle of this week Archer wrote to Mary Fairthorne:

"DEAR MISS MARY: Thanks in advance for the books. Let them be, above all, picture books.

"Mr. Knellwood sails week after next. He needs it. There are who say Rome; I know better. He loathes Luther (fine alliteration, that), and thinks Cranmer hardly better, grieving for the way the saints with queer names were tumbled out of our prayer-book. But he thinks there was, and is, a Church, never the vassal of Rome, and, dear old chaplain, what kind of church he would evolve if there were no bishop in the background, I cannot dream. But to know him you should have seen him in the thick of it on Cemetery Hill.

"Mr. Pilgrim asks me to say to your uncle that he will come out on Saturday morning and remain until Monday. He has all the maps and plans ready, but both he and Masters advised that no mines be opened until the branch rail gets into the valley. Some one must meet Pilgrim at the station, 10.15 train, please.

"I shall go out to Grace's on Saturday, and if you so please, Mistress Mary, will ride with you on that afternoon. I may remain until late Sunday evening. I will call for you at Edgewood at five.

"I am rather tired and want a breath of country air. There are days when everything goes awry. This has been one.

"Save up some good talk for me, and believe me

"Yours truly,

"SYDNEY ARCHER."

415

On Thursday he made his daily call on Pilgrim. The engineer was fast mending, and his table was strewn with letters and plans. He said: "At last, Sydney, I can swing dumb-bells without things creaking inside of me. I suppose this apparently needless business means something. Lots of pain, weeks of loss to you and me. But what it means I do not see. I am no wiser and no better for that fellow's bullet. I have been patient, but I am not more so than I was. I know now what pain is. That was a new experience."

"Well, is not that a gain? It was for me, as a physician. All doctors ought to have a bout of several educational diseases."

"But not engineers, if you please. I am afraid that I shocked Knellwood yesterday. I asked if the Maker of the world could have felt pain. I said that logically he must have realized it. Knellwood has a very direct and limited, but not an imaginative mind."

"His goodness has no limitations," remarked Sydney. "What did he say?"

"He said, with curious humility, that he had not the form of mind to grapple with such questions, that faith was his form of reason. I was tempted to go on, for that did seem to me too absurd, but he looked so like a big, bothered child that I hesitated. Then he said, 'But as Christ suffered, and was God, we must feel that to be a sufficient answer.' When I replied that from his point of view it was an answer, he said, in his courteous way, that I was nearly as bad as John Fairthorne, who asked him if the Creator chose to decree that He should not have fore-knowledge would not that be possible for omnipotence.''

"I don't wonder,'' said Archer, "that he puzzled him. I have long ceased to reason on my creed, or to enjoy such subtleties. I used to like them. As for poor old Fairthorne, he is past all such games nowadays.''

"I cannot get away from them, Sydney. I have been wrestling in the twilight of recent experience with this question of pain. Nature seems to me to have misused her wealth of opportunities.''

"Were they limitless?''

"How do I know? Pain is for the most part needless. You once told me of a man who could not feel pain. What an example for nature!''

"There are worse things.''

"Yes, that I know. By the way, Sydney, as I am going to Edgewood, what kind of woman is that secretary, Mrs. Hunter? Tom Masters spoke of her as a remarkable woman, very handsome and clever.''

When Pilgrim thus questioned it was with a growing doubt in his mind. Knellwood, who had the reticence of a too lavish charity, had been so overcareful when Pilgrim spoke of her as to arouse his suspicions. Now the engineer was resolutely bent on finding out whether he had been right in letting a base woman work her will on a broken old man.

"By this time, Luke,'' said Archer, "you ought to know that for dear old Tom all petticoats are objects of worship. He knows little of Mrs. Hunter.''

"Do you know more?''

27

"Yes, too much."

Pilgrim sat up, attentive.

"I have reasons for asking you, Sydney. Now, if you may, tell me all about her."

"I do not see why I should not. It is a long story, and a queer one."

"Well, go on."

"An unknown woman picks up Miss Morrow's acquaintance, obtains absolute control over her, gets as complete possession of Fairthorne, induces him to give and leave her money—a good deal, too—breaks up the family, sets poor Miss Kitty against her cousins, and by degrees becomes unquestioned mistress. I do not complain that she drove me out, but the pleasure the woman takes in inflicting pain is something quite amazing. I think she has but one affection. It is for a girl-like, pretty young fellow, her brother—a drunken, dissolute cub. He is in Grace's office."

"A pleasant character, Sydney. And what of Miss Fairthorne in this cheerful household?"

"Read that," said Archer, "and you will see."

He gave him Mary Fairthorne's letter, hesitating a moment whether to read him parts of it or to let him see it as a whole.

"Thank you," said the engineer. He read the letter with care, and, slowly refolding it, replaced it in the envelope. "Thank you. That is enough, and too much! Too much! I might have known it."

"May I ask what you mean?"

"Yes; I hate it, but I must tell you." He rose and began to walk about the room, speaking as he moved. "I suppose, Sydney, I could do what is a duty and a hard one without explaining myself to you; but we are old friends, at least in events if not in years, and, above all, your great kindness has brought you very near to me. And yet, in our many talks I have never spoken freely of my younger life. Now I must do so, much as it hurts me. I am suddenly set face to face with a painful duty, or what looks like a duty. Some one should know why I act, in case at any future time there arise questions. Then, too, I want a man of honor to say I am right, for, believe me, Archer, it has not been easy to feel sure. Now, listen to me." He paused in his walk. "This woman, Sydney, is—I mean was—oh, damn the thing! She was my wife!"

"Your wife! Your wife!" exclaimed Archer. He was without more adequate reply than an exclamation. It seemed incredible.

"This, Sydney, of course is a surprise to you. You know my temperament. You know me through and through. I am a sensitive man. Even the careless words of people I love sometimes hurt me in a way that to them would seem absurd. Imagine, now, what a hell of memories I have carried with me for these last eight years."

"I see," said Archer. "Having known her, I can understand. If this be hard for you to speak of, why go on? It is sad enough for me, who am your friend. That woman must have left behind her a trail of misery for many. What a devil!"

"Stop, Sydney! Please don't. I would rather not hear even you abuse her." This remnant of protective tenderness seemed to Archer pitiable. The speaker went on: "Do not mistake me. It is not love. That is as dead as the years that knew it. I said why I must talk it all out. Now, please, not a word until I have done."

"Go on, Luke."

"When I was just twenty-two, and not very strong, my uncle sent me to California with John Percy, the mining engineer. It was supposed that I should inherit my uncle's estate, as I was his nearest relative and had lived with him since I became an orphan. We stayed some time at Sacramento, where I fell in with a school-teacher, Inez Quinones, the child, as she told me, of a Spanish ranchman, as to whom there was a neatly fabricated story of ruin and poverty and womanly effort on her part to help herself and a half brother, the only child of a second marriage. Percy, finding me troubled with a cough, left me in Sacramento while he inspected certain mines. To cut it short, I had a sunstroke, and then meningitis. When I became enough myself to understand things, I found that Inez, who lived in the same hotel with me, had been practically my only nurse. The doctor, whom she had charmed, thought that she had been of inestimable service. It was true. When I was able to sit up she was in and out, after school hours, reading to me, singing, bringing me flowers, writing my letters.

"At last, one day she burst into tears. People were talking; she would lose her place. Two or three days finished the matter. She was a perfect actress, and much older than I. It was simple enough—I had an ample allowance; my uncle was a well-known mine owner. I was sensitive, weak from illness, not even quite clear in my head. I was told that she had ruined her chances of self-support for my sake, had neglected her duties for me. She showed me, at last, her letter of dismissal received from the school board. It was forged, as I knew long after.

"Of course, I married her. A week later my uncle arrived. He saw her, went coolly into her story, asked me to give her up, and when I would not consider it in any shape left me to fight the world alone with her, and without a penny.

"Well, I won't trouble you with my struggles. It was hard, and harder as I learned to know her. Two years passed. I acquired some practical knowledge of mines and mining. About this time I bought on credit a small share of the Centre mine. I went to see it for the larger owners, who paid me in this way. On my return to Sacramento I found that she had left me without a line or a word of explanation. I was then about twenty-four. It was for her a question of luxury or of honestly borne hardship. She fled a day too soon. I was at ease so far as money went, as the mine proved to be valuable. I do not mean that I was rich, but I had enough. She had gone to the Sandwich Islands with an Irish mine owner, a rich, coarse, decrepit old man. There was no passion in it. She had always been a cold-blooded woman, with capacity to act the passion she never felt—a woman who loved a highly seasoned life. I will not tell you what I suffered before and after this flight. The man got tired and dropped her.

"Then, where she went or what she did I do not know, until she obtained a divorce on the ground of desertion. I did not resist. Meanwhile, I did what may seem even to you quixotic. I wrote to her that I would not leave her to the temptation of sin because of want of means; that I would make her an allowance of eight hundred dollars a year. She replied, calmly, that it was very proper. From that day to this she has had it. At times I lived scantily to save enough; one year I borrowed it.

"I know little of her life, except that she has twice broken up families, and has always been gifted with this power to win young women. I have reasons to believe that when the Irish mine owner got rid of her he gave her money—a good deal. She has changed her name, as you know, and has in some mysterious way been able to go to Europe or frequent our own summer resorts. Once, she went abroad as a teacher with some Canadian girls. You know how really accomplished she is. I am sure that she is unscrupulous, but how criminal or how far really dangerous I do not know. That is my story and hers, and now what am I to do? If she were not in the midst of my friends, if—well, I would let her alone. I ought to say that on my first visit here she left town, I suppose to avoid me. Now she is afraid to abandon her prey, is comfortable in a life of ease and even of luxury, and no doubt making money. She had to face me this time and either defy or cajole me. She acted with her usual skill and courage, and came to see me."

"Came to see you?" repeated Archer.

"Yes, to plead that I would not betray her. Really, it was well done, wonderfully well. I made no promises. How could I? Now I know more. How, after that letter, can I hesitate? Now, Sydney, what must I do?"

"A word or two before I reply. Of course, her story was not true."

"No; she was the child of a Mexican picador who had saved money. He came to San Francisco, speculated, and died poor. The stepmother also died. The girl, then quite young, was admirably educated in a convent school of French ladies of the Sacred Heart. The boy, a baby, was put in an orphan asylum. When about eighteen she ran away and got a place as a teacher. About the boy I know little, but she certainly did take care of him later, and he is the one person she really ever cared for—why, I do not know. And now do not ask any more, and again what am I to do?"

"You have no choice. You must tell your story to Mr. Fairthorne."

"Would it answer? Is he in a fit state to understand its force and me?"

"Perhaps not. How would it do to threaten her that you will tell it? Fairthorne is breaking up. His family will be justified in acting despotically. She might fight, but how could she? I have myself a matter to settle with her brother which will drive him away and perhaps help to make her feel willing to go. I think she will make some conditions and give up."

"But if John Fairthorne is as you say, why not

wait? He will die, and that will end it." Pilgrim
was clearly trying to find some mode of escape from
an unpleasant situation; it was natural enough.

"I will tell you why; the old man is slowly failing, but he still has, as I have seen in these cases of
senile decay, his hours of clearness of head. He
may again change his will, and so change it as
seriously to affect his heirs and make a contest necessary after his death. I fear this woman; and, after
all, Fairthorne may live for months. Harry Swanwick is unwilling, perhaps wisely, to move in the
matter. Meanwhile, Miss Fairthorne is and will be
kept wretchedly unhappy."

"I see. I must do something. I go out to Edgewood on Saturday early. I shall have an hour or
two with Fairthorne, and between that and Monday
find my chance to talk with—with Mrs. Hunter."

"I shall be at Grace's, Luke."

"Thank you; and now, as I am rather used up, I
will let you go. Good-bye. It is a relief to feel
that I can deal with the matter without having it
known to any one but you and her. She will show
fight, and I dread it. Good-bye."

When alone Pilgrim threw himself on the lounge.
"If," he thought, "the old cynic had been the only
one concerned I might have let things go their way,
or hers; but Mary! No!" He thought of the time
when, years before, he had come to know clearly that
he loved her. That his chance was worth something
he had begun to see. He had said then, "I must
not wait. She must know in time." He had frankly
said that he loved her, that he had hoped she, too,

would some day care for him, but that, as an honest
gentleman, he was bound to tell her that he had
been divorced, and that his wife was alive. Then
he had very plainly told the sad story of his young
life.

She had replied that whether or not she cared
enough for a man to be willing to marry him his
divorce would be an insurmountable objection. Yes,
she knew him blameless, but this she never could
face. It was a matter of sentiment rather than of
principle.

He, too, had the sad conviction, being as sensitive
as she, that to marry a divorced woman with a husband alive would have been as horrible to him. He
accepted his defeat, and, remaining something more
than friend, went his manly way through a lonely
life of distinction and usefulness.

Mary's letter to Archer had made up his mind for
him. She should suffer no longer.

"Dear old Syd! Did he know that I could read
between the lines of that letter? Ah, me, but life
is hard!"

XLII

ILGRIM had never been to Edgewood, and was delighted with the colonial home, with its vine-clad outbuildings, much like those of the too famous house in Fairmount Park to which Arnold took his bride in days gone by.

Mary Fairthorne met him at the door.

"You are most welcome. Yes, my uncle is pretty well, and blissfully happy over some autograph letters of Gray to Mason. A new autograph always arouses him. Come up. He wished to see you at once."

Fairthorne had become thin, and too shrunken for his clothes, but the outline of his handsome features came out even the more distinctly for his loss of flesh.

"Call Mrs. Hunter, Mary," he said. "Glad to see you, Pilgrim. Lucretia knows all about these lands. I want you to know her—remarkable woman!"

"Mrs. Hunter is out, uncle."

"Well, find her; send some one. I want you to know her, Pilgrim."

She was not to be found. Fairthorne grumbled, and then began to look over the engineer's maps, while Pilgrim talked. Soon he failed to attend, and, falling asleep, woke up as the voice of Pilgrim ceased to explain. At last he said:

"That will do. We need Lucretia. We will look at these things again. Show Mr. Pilgrim the garden, Mary."

Luke lunched with Mary Fairthorne, and afterward wandered off alone for a walk over the rolling hills of Delaware County. Mrs. Hunter had a headache, and did not appear all day. Archer rode over from Grace's farm, and then through the May afternoon with Miss Fairthorne, a happy man.

"Care leaves one on a good horse," he said, as they crossed the bridge over Cobb's Creek. "I hope it is as good a remedy for you."

"My cares are less easily dismissed," she returned. "I have made up my mind this last week to go to Long Branch. Mrs. Craycroft has taken rooms for me. I cannot bear it any longer."

He hesitated as they rode on.

"You will pardon me, Miss Mary, but will you leave your uncle alone with this woman?"

"He is that now. I am a cipher, outside of his life."

"Will you trust me a little?"

"We have always trusted you."

"Not we—you," he said.

"Yes, I do. What is it?"

"Do not leave him."

"I must. You do not know what you ask."

"No." He leaned over and touched her hand. "I ask you not to leave him, not now—wait."

"You are very mysterious."

"Perhaps; but once you asked me not to give him up. I obeyed you. There is nothing you can ask that I would not do. Do not question me, but silently trust me when I, in turn, say do not go away."

"I will do as you say because—well, because I trust you."

"Could you not trust me always—for life, Mary Fairthorne?"

"That is rather long," she said, laughing. "The spring is a time of promises. The summer might find me changed."

"But not the winter," he said.

"I do not know. Give my mare a lead over that hedge. Thanks!" she cried, as they galloped over the turf of the old meadow-lands. She kept him off the perilous subject, and they rode in at evening past the gray stone church of St. David.

"See there," she said, stopping her horse. "Yonder lies Anthony Wayne. The little church is curious. You enter the organ-loft by a stone stair from the outside. We shall go there to-morrow morning; I play the organ. The place will interest you. It is strange that you have never seen it."

"No; I have made visits of an hour to your uncle, and back to town in haste. Miss Mary, I want to have a talk alone with that woman—with Mrs. Hunter. How can I manage it?"

"She is apt to breakfast in her own room, and then to smoke horrid cigarettes, now that she is careless as to what she does. About ten she joins my uncle. On Sunday she is later."

"If, then, Pilgrim and you and I walk to church, and I leave you and return I may catch her?"

"Yes, very likely; but I want you to see the church. It is well worth a visit. Why not see her in the afternoon?"

"She will hide or get out of the way."

"That is not her custom."

"It will be what she will do."

"You are very mysterious again. What is going to happen? Oh, if it should be anything to get rid of her I would—"

"Well?"

"Be so glad," said the girl.

"Then wait."

"On Sunday afternoon she takes a long walk, always alone."

"I shall see her in the morning. In the afternoon we will look at the church. And now for a good gallop."

At dinner Mrs. Hunter was still absent and suffering. In the late evening Pilgrim learned from Archer how the day was usually spent by Lucretia.

"If she stays up-stairs," he said, "I shall remain here until I get my chance, if it take a week."

After breakfast on this Sunday, Mary sent up to ask if Mrs. Hunter were well enough to be with Mr. Fairthorne, as they were all going to church. Mrs. Hunter still had neuralgia, but as every one else was to be out she would, of course, make the effort and sit with Mr. Fairthorne. Mary handed the note to Archer.

He left Pilgrim and Mary on the hill above St. David's, went back to the house and at once up to

the library. Mrs. Hunter was reading aloud the
life of Alexander Hamilton. She read well.

"Ah!" said Archer. "Glad to see you up."

She rose as he entered. She was watchful, and
evidently uneasy at his return.

"Will you give me a few minutes?" he said, in a
low tone.

"I cannot leave Mr. Fairthorne."

"You must, or you will regret it, for your brother's sake."

She made an excuse and went after him, saying
she would soon return.

"Where can we talk?" he said.

"In my sitting-room." He followed her. "Will
you have a cigarette?" she asked, coolly.

"No. Sit down."

"You said my brother Lionel. What is it?" She
spoke very quickly, and fairly concealed her anxiety.

"Mrs. Hunter, your brother told you that he had
seen Mr. Grace at Carlisle intoxicated. You told
him to hold his tongue about it. He did not. He
wrote Mr. Grace an anonymous threat of exposure.
It was madness to try this with him, of all men. In
reply Grace sent a check to order in a letter. Your
brother is known to have taken it out of the office
and drawn it. This is blackmail, and means, if a
warrant be served, the penitentiary. Mr. Grace is a
merciful man. To arrest and try Mr. Craig would
ruin him forever. He has shown no desire to push
the matter." Here he stopped.

"Why did he not come himself?" She was suspicious. "Did he send you?"

"Mrs. Hunter, I did not come here to be questioned. If by Tuesday next that money is not returned and your brother has not written to confess that he had tried to blackmail, the question of more kindly dealing with a weak young man may be closed. If you are wise you will oblige him to do what I have suggested." He meant, if he failed, to go boldly to Grace and insist that he face a matter already known to four people, and perhaps to many. Lucretia met this attack with her usual courage.

"Will you swear," she said, "that this story is true?"

"No; I have said it was true. Accept it or not, I have done."

"Why did you not go directly to my brother about it?"

"Go to a drunken, conceited fool—a man not to be trusted for a day? No. That would be folly."

Then the woman broke down. She put her head in her hands, and, it is to be hoped, cried. She cared nothing for the sin and little for the shame of it. Neither, as such, disturbed her. She could have done, at need, worse things and felt no qualm, but through much of her life she had been struggling to keep this weakling straight, proud of his doll-like beauty, hoping always that he was about to be what he never could be. Was it love, or pride, or the fact of his long dependence upon her that made his life and acts so bitter?

A few moments went by in silence. She looked up, saying:

"I am beaten. You have your revenge."

"It is not revenge. I suppose that were I to tell you I am sorry for you"—and he was sorry—"you would not believe me."

"I would not, I do not, and I do not care. There is something in it not clear to me. The only thing I do believe is that you could not find him, and so fall back on me."

"You are not as shrewd as usual, Mrs. Hunter. I give you my word that no effort will be made to follow or to trap him if that confession be written promptly and the money returned."

"You shall have both. I said I was beaten. I am, but I promise you not to forget, and if I can ever repay you it shall be done, and with interest."

"Thank you. Kindly send the letter to me, South Thirteenth Street, you know the address." With these words he rose and left her.

She closed the door, and sat at the open window, deep in thought. It was a terrible reckoning.

"They do not want this to get out, but that does n't help matters. As between being bled for years or having a paragraph in some blackguard paper, they will choose the last, of course. Any one would. Should I care if some one said I took too much champagne? Lionel must go, Heaven knows where! He can't fight Roger Grace. Oh, what an idiot, to be trapped like this! Why could n't he have waited a few months? I could have gotten anything out of John Fairthorne, but if—if they use this letter I am lost. I never thought of that. Why does n't this tiresome old man step out? Lord! That would make my money pretty certain, and mourning is so becoming to me. Ah, my brother! I have too many things to think about. If it were only one at a time, but Luke—Luke. He goes to-morrow. Well, well, that will be one relief! He is very handsome, but about as great a fool as ever, and as shy of me as I am of him.''

As usual, her meditations ended in some practical way. It was Sunday. She would take her usual afternoon walk, for nothing was allowed to interfere with the exercise by which she kept a very sound body in perfect health. Just before dinner she would go to the city, and thus escape meeting Pilgrim. She must see her brother at once, and must feel secure about him, for now it seemed clear to her that if this blackmail matter should become public, and Lionel be arrested and tried, her own position would be untenable. Yet, to be just to a selfful character, less purely personal motives were uppermost in her mind, and she had no scheme of an unfettered life which did not involve the dream of more respectability for Lionel than was compatible with her own ideal of an existence away from these sedate, reputable people, with their unquestioning beliefs in themselves and their ancestors, of whom they said nothing and thought much.

For once Kitty had hidden her doings, and the day after her confession to Knellwood had decided to spend a few days at Chestnut Hill with one of the many young women she labeled ''friend.'' Her discontent, her recoil into shame, her general dissatisfaction with what she called life were all helpful to Mrs. Hunter's schemes. But of late this stage

manager had been too anxious to attend with equal
care to all her puppets. Just now the showman
Fate was relentlessly pulling the wires, and she, too,
must dance, whether she would or not.

On the other hand, she had a bank account which
would have surprised the heirs of John Fairthorne.
Even in her present anxiety she smiled to think of
it. If only she were secure of that codicil! Then
there would be Paris and the slack society of the
Riviera, or later Cairo and all manner of agreeable
chances, other preserves and other game, with
Kitty's income to pay the bills, for in a year or
less she would have control of the well-managed
accumulations of a long minority.

Lucretia's power to set aside care was remarkable;
her belief in her resources self-satisfying. Twice on
this Sunday morning she had been summoned to
Mr. Fairthorne, and had allowed him to await her
pleasure. At last she went down-stairs, fanning
herself and humming a Spanish song. The day was
warm and the atmosphere heavy. Mr. Fairthorne
gave up his intention to lunch with his guests, and
insisted, to the secretary's satisfaction, that she
should share his meal in the library. There were
others as well pleased.

Lucretia was never more agreeable. She talked
of Mexico and bull-fights, told the old man gay stories,
and, alas! it was the Sabbath or she could sing for
him, but "Oh!" she gaily pointed down-stairs, "I
should—oh, I should be socially excommunicated!"
Some day when they were alone she would dance,
just a little, a sketch of the real dance. He was delighted and cheerful.

After the luncheon they went out on the wide upper porch. She arranged his reclining chair and cushions with a display of tender care.

"Sing for me," he said.

"Oh, no! Not now, sir." She heard the broken hum of voices on the veranda below them.

"Sing," he said, "don't you hear me?" He was like a spoiled child.

"I cannot, Mr. Fairthorne. Indeed, I cannot. I never should hear the last of it."

"What is that to me? Do as I tell you. You have talked of this sort of thing so long that I am curious."

Lucretia stood up, a queer gleam in her eyes, a sense of joy at the freedom of an open door of reckless self-abandonment. As she would have said in other company, she let herself go. "Oh, you naughty man!" she cried, smiling, and, curtsying low, fell back a little and began to dance with slow movements and sway of body eminently graceful. Then she began to snap her fingers, and, in a low voice, to sing a love song of the muleteers of the Sierras.

By degrees, enjoying the performance, she was swept away on the current of her mood. The castanets rang out, the dance movement grew quicker, with growing pleasure she gave way to the temptation of utter unrestraint, and with wild laughter let her voice out to its full compass.

As she paused a breathless moment, the old man cried "Brava!" and clapped applause.

On the porch beneath them sat Pilgrim and Archer smoking. The engineer was of no mind to talk, and Archer respected his disinclination. At last Pilgrim spoke, as the song rang out overhead. "What a strange voice she has, so distinct, so entirely true. Listen! Do you know what she is singing, Archer?"

"No."

"As well not. And in this house! It is intolerable, Sydney. I shall go to my room; I have letters to write. Let me know when she goes out."

"I will."

He paused for a moment listening, caught in the meshes of a distant memory. The songs were not all evil. As he lingered, she was singing the lay the Mexican fishermen's wives sing to their children when the boats are coming laden to shore. He had heard it when she sat by his side, and kept time with her fan as she cooled his fever long ago, when she was for him an innocent girl who had risked her all for his love. He turned away, and went up-stairs.

After his friend left him Archer sat still on the porch. The music overhead ceased, and the hours of a sultry afternoon went by. He had much to occupy him. Unless he failed, he should have done Grace a material service, and it was pleasant to feel that the banker need not know who did it. Also, there were more things to think of, things still set about with doubts. The hours slipped away. At length he saw Mrs. Hunter at a distance, walking rapidly. She had gone out of a side door and escaped his watch. He made haste to find Pilgrim.

"Mrs. Hunter has gone out. I missed her. If you go at once you will overtake her on the road. If you do not or miss her, you had better return and wait in the churchyard. She is sure, I learn, to come home that way; otherwise she must go miles around to get back, and it is late. She walks very fast.''

Pilgrim said not a word. As he went out, Archer called after him:

''It looks a little as though we might have a thunder-storm.''

Pilgrim hastened on, making no reply, eager to get it all over. Archer returned to the veranda. Then Miss Fairthorne came down all in white.

''Mr. Pilgrim is off alone, I see. I thought we might have had him with us.''

''No. Which way shall we go, Miss Mary?''

''Oh, over the creek, across the fields. There is a view I want you to see. It looks rather threatening, does n't it? But you really must see St. David's; we need not be long; we will come back that way.''

''It will not rain,'' he said, decidedly. He was by no means sure. As for St. David's—well, Luke would in his evident haste be sure to overtake Lucretia. They would not come in his way. He was too anxious to give it more thought, only seeing that the sky was already clearing again.

They went away through the first roses of the old-fashioned garden rather silent, now and then letting fall a phrase. He was doubly distracted by the thought of Pilgrim and by what he himself meant to say to the girl at his side. She, aware of something unusual in the man, tried in vain to lead the talk into by-roads of the commonplace, wished herself at home, and was conscious of danger and of happiness.

She led him beside the fields of spring wheat, over rolling uplands and by forest ways to a hill-top, where they overlooked the peaceful vales and, not far away, the gray church among the graves. It was near to sunset, and the doubtful storm-clouds were changefully driven across the western sky. As they stood, he said:

"How very still it is here, and what tumult there." As he spoke the darkening cloud-curtains slowly parted, and in a minute there was between them a vast flare of crimson.

Mary's pleasure at this wonder of color showed in the look of joyful interest which possessed her face.

"How can people fear the lightning and thunder of a storm? When there is such a royal blazoning in the heavens one would expect some triumphant sound. A great sunset brings to me a feeling of expectancy of something about to happen."

"That is what I feel at daybreak," he returned. "Not now, not here."

The cloud-curtain closed in gray-green masses, and as she spoke a lance of lightning darted across the blackness and, as it were, shivered into splinters of violet light. Instantly a thunderous peal rolled resonant among the peaks and abysses of the vast mountain cloudland.

"You have your wish," he cried, "and more," for the great rain-drops began to fall.

"Come," she answered, laughing; "as a weather-prophet I will none of you in future. We can reach the church in time—perhaps." At first she thought of a cottage not far away, but the church was nearer, and at all events she was glad of the need for quick movement. She led the way, walking swiftly. The rain fell faster.

"This way," she called to him, as they crossed the graveyard. "The stairs to the organ-loft are sheltered."

"We are just in time," he said, and, merry over their escape, they sat down on the stone stairway under cover, while the rain fell in torrents. Except for a word now and then they remained silent. He was intent on the face of the woman. Once he spoke of the dance of the leaves as the drops fell upon them. She made no reply, save to look at him and to nod, smiling.

She had wholesome pleasure in what she saw as they looked out from the over-arched stair, and fearlessly enjoyed the drama of a summer storm. Meanwhile, the fast-coming clouds made a sudden twilight. Little gusts of wind fell here and there, and shook the spring leafage. Then a greater wind swooped down with patter of driven drops aslant on the gravestones, as the storm breath swayed the gray columns of rain.

Archer respected her wish to be silent in the presence of these elemental forces.

"Where," he thought, "can Pilgrim be—and Mrs. Hunter?"

Presently she spoke.

"I never want to talk when we have these great storms. It seems irreverent."

"I, too, have the desire to be still during a tempest. It is so terribly suggestive of unused power. I think it will soon be over.''

''Yes,'' she said, ''the storm is nearly past. The rain has stopped. Let us go.''

She rose and went down the stair and out into the glory of the second twilight, for now the clouds, piled in dim masses above the fallen sun, set free a glow of orange light to glorify the glistening earth.

''Is not that,'' she said, ''a thing to remember?''

''Surely, I shall not forget it.''

''Before we go, will you please to find my fan for me? I left it this morning in the organ-loft, on a stool to the left. Here is the key. Be careful; there is a step down, and it must be dark. I will wait for you here.''

Archer took the key and went up the stone stair which led, and still leads, from outside to the gallery. It was very dark and he had to move with care. He found the fan, and then something happened. He stood amazed.

When Pilgrim left the house of the Fairthornes Mrs. Hunter was out of sight, and, in his ignorance of the country, the engineer concluded to follow Archer's advice. He therefore went within the churchyard gate and waited. After fully an hour he saw Mrs. Hunter descending the hill. She must pass close by him. He stepped back a little and waited, not conscious for the time of the gathered storm. There was a vivid flash of light and a quick following crash of thunder. He heard Mrs. Hunter's exclamation of terror, and remembered her alarm at lightning. The rain fell in large drops.

"This way," he said, as she turned in at the gate, not seeing him.

"Ah!" she cried; "you here?"

"This way, this way," he repeated. "Perhaps the church may be open."

"No," she said; "I will go on. There are worse things than a storm."

He caught her wrist.

"I came here," he said, "to have a talk with you. I mean to have it, if I have to force you to stay."

Another blinding fire-bolt crossed the darkening sky.

"Madre de Dios!" she cried. "Anywhere—anywhere!"

He tried the church door. It yielded, and they went in.

"Sit down."

She sat down on a bench at the back of the little church, now in twilight gloom.

"If I must, I must. What is it?"

He stood before her, and for a brief moment was still.

"When we last met you asked me not to speak of you and of your life to these people, my friends."

"You promised. Do you mean to speak now?"

"I did not promise. Since then I have learned more than enough to make it my duty to see that they know you as I know you."

"Your duty!" she cried. "I like that! Your pleasure, you mean."

"I do not mean to have a contest of words with you. Listen! I will not say to Mr. Fairthorne or to

Miss Fairthorne one word about you if you will go away, not to return.''

''And if not?''

''Well, if not, I will tell them all.''

''All what? Do you think he will care? Nonsense! He would laugh at you.''

''Very good. There is my marriage, a forged letter, the life at Tahiti, the pleasant wreck of those kindly people in Montreal, the—oh! there is more of it and worse. Do you think the Swanwicks and Miss Fairthorne would leave you here a day after I have told my story? They would simply turn you out. Fairthorne would be made to yield. You would lose your money. Oh, at need, I will make it public. You must go!''

Lucretia would have given much for time to reflect, to decide. The man was coldly implacable.

''Let me think of it,'' she said.

''Not a minute. Yes or no—go or stay?''

''You are hard, cruel.'' He made no comment. She was dreadfully in doubt. If she stayed, all was lost. Even the codicil might, as Archer had said, be called in question. If she left, the family, on their uncle's death, might not disturb or dispute it. Perhaps they would think her absence cheaply bought. And there was Lionel, too. As she resolutely took time to think he stood in silence. The rain trampled on the roof overhead, and vivid flashes at times lighted up the darkening interior.

''If I go,'' she asked, ''will they dispute what he has left me? I earned it—honestly earned it.''

He smiled as he answered: ''I think they will not

dispute it, but I can make no promises for other people, or for John Fairthorne. But go you must, or I shall speak out this evening, and most freely.''

"If I go, how long will you give me? My brother is in trouble. If I go to the city as if for a time, and then—''

"No, you leave the city. As to how long you may stay here—you asked that, I think?''

"I did. Give me a week.''

He made a sort of compromise. "To-day is Sunday. On Wednesday you go.''

"I will go on Wednesday.'' As she spoke she rose. It was too much, first Archer and then this man. She stood still, helpless, beaten, and raging with anger fed by deadliest hate. She longed to strike him. He stood still, watching her.

At last he said quietly, "That is all. And now I shall leave you.''

"No, it is not all.'' Her voice rose shrill and high in anger. "You have driven me out, and never—''

"Hush!'' he said. "Hush, I hear some one.''

In the brief time of their silence Archer had found the fan. As Lucretia's voice rang out he stopped, astonished. Amid the roar of the rain he had heard slight noises below him, but thought it some sexton or other caretaker.

Lucretia mocked at the warning.

"Why should I hush?'' It was rare with her that wrath routed prudence. "Oh! You order me to go! As if I did not know why. You are more of a fool than you were as a boy.''

"Have you no sense? There is some one—"

"What is that to me? You don't get off that way. I will tell you why you want me out of that house. It would be rather awkward to make love to another woman with your dear, divorced wife in the same house."

"Do not dare to speak of her." He turned to go. She caught his arm. Without violence he could not release himself.

"Oh, that hurt you, did it? She will never marry you. I saw her diary. It was entertaining; rather careless, was n't it? I am now her confidante; it would surprise her. She is in love with the other man. Do you hear?—with the other man. Archer will cut you out. I suppose he will some day have the courage to ask her. Now, you may go. Advise him to write to her. Some women are very yielding on paper, and it is so nice to help one's friends." She laughed savagely. "I always did love to do things for you."

"I ought to have strangled you long ago," he said, and went out where the unveiled glow of the sunset lay on the early leafage and the gray tombstones. He walked away, across the graves and over the fields.

The woman waited alone, and, hearing Archer in the organ-loft, thought:

"There was some one. I must go. Three days— well, I made him uncomfortable. It was foolish, reckless, but—how he hated it! If I were sure about that codicil, I should not care. He will keep his word; he always did."

She followed him through the graveyard and up the hill a mile or more to Edgewood. There, somewhat later, she saw Miss Fairthorne, and said she was going to the city at once, as she had an appointment with her brother. She would return next day.

Archer went slowly down the steps, out of the organ-loft, to where Miss Fairthorne was standing in the lessening sunset light, "a daughter of the gods, divinely tall and most divinely fair."

"Thank you," she said. "I saw Mrs. Hunter go by. I wonder where she took refuge. How beautiful it is! I love this old church. Here is Anthony Wayne's tombstone, and there are some of the unknown dead who died at Paoli in the fight." They went to and fro, reading the love, the lies, the foolishness on the gray slabs, interested as we all are to see what the living have written of the dead.

They paused just outside of the gateway, as he said, looking back: "How like the little church is to one near our southern home."

"Have you heard from home lately?" she asked, and went on to inquire as to his own people, of the brother now at the University of Virginia, of the cousins who had at last consented to forgive his loyalty to his country. She knew how freely he had helped them when the means of helpfulness had been found at the cost of much privation. She was not beyond being influenced by the appearance of the physical man. As Archer moved ahead of her and turned, she felt a certain satisfaction in his well-knit figure, the look of strength in face and form, as of a

man who owned and was master of himself in mind
and muscle.

"Do you ever record your thoughts?" he said,
rather abruptly.

"Sometimes. What a curious question! Why do
you ask?"

"Why you, yourself, asked me just now as we sat
on the stairway if I kept note-books, and how thought
about scientific questions matured—how it was dealt
with. I said I had to think on paper. I wanted to
know if this were true of you."

"I keep a diary."

"Indeed! What gets into it?"

"Many things—notes about books, remarks, who
dine with us, all kind of trifles."

"Do you ever set down your opinions of people?"

"Yes; Mrs. Hunter's biographer would be en-
lightened. I wrote to-day that you had been mysterious."

"Ah, then I do get in sometimes. Do you ever
write of yourself?"

"Rarely. Not often—sometimes."

"Do you find, as I do, that to state a problem
on paper is the best way to approach it?"

"I have no such problems."

"I have one now."

"I am bad at problems. They are very disappointing. I hate them."

"But suppose you were ever to—well, to like a
man, would you write about it in your diary, and
would it help you to decide?"

"It might, if I were ever in so sad a state."

He laughed.

"I should like to know if ever by chance I have the honor to be in that diary."

"Certainly—when you dine with us."

"And nobody ever sees it?"

"No one. I keep it locked."

"Suppose I were to guess a little as to what is in it?"

She colored slightly: "If you knew, I should deny it."

"Ah, Miss Mary, it is your heart I should like to read."

"It is uncertain, variable, not worth reading."

"Well, then, your diary. Let us try. One day you wrote that you did care for a man. Oh, you put it more plainly than I dare to put it. Mary Fairthorne, he is here—here at your side. He has long loved you. Will you let him go on alone, without you?"

She was looking down as he spoke, and for a moment was silent. Then she said:

"I knew this would come. I have feared it for you, for myself."

"Was it only fear, Mary?"

"No." She walked on, not speaking.

"I have had a rather hard life, you know that; but not even my break with friends, my family, my home, in the war days, ever hurt as one little word from you will hurt."

"I shall never say it."

"That is not enough."

"But will you not wait?"

"No, not now."

"But if I am not sure? I really am not sure."

"We cannot leave it in this way. How can I make you more certain? You will never know me better."

She moved on without looking at him, saying: "Come away from these tombs."

He followed her as they passed out into the road.

"Well," he said, "I want my answer, Mary."

"I think I love you," she said, turning a grave face to him.

He leaned over and gently lifted and kissed her hand. Then she knew, and said:

"I think I know that I love you, Sydney."

"Say it, Mary."

"I love you," she repeated timidly, and among the gathering shadows they went up the hill in the faith of love's fresh childhood, hand in hand.

"God bless you, dear," he said, and she went up to her room.

In the evening, after dinner, the two men strolled about in the brick walks of the garden, between the high rows of clipped box. Here, omitting all that was personal to either himself or his friend, Pilgrim told him of what had passed in the church that afternoon.

"And now," he added, "you will be quit of this plague. I wish I could as easily blot her from my own life. She will go, and no one here will know why. I shall say good-bye to the Swanwicks and wander abroad. If my chest threatens me with trouble I shall go to Egypt for the winter, as you desired.''

"You will have no trouble," said Archer; "you are as well as a man can be."

"And now," said Pilgrim, "as you condemn me to early hours, I shall say good night to Miss Mary and so to bed. I feel as if I had had an illness. No, I have no pain. I am merely used up for the time."

Sydney went out on the porch and waited, reflecting, as he walked up and down, on the harsh punishment life provided for a man who, in the chivalry of a young man's love, had wrecked his fortunes and his life to guard a woman's honor. He realized the horror with which a refined nature must by degrees have discovered the true personality of this attractive woman. He tried to put himself in Pilgrim's place. It was a game of which, as a student of his kind, he was fond.

"Ah, I should have killed the man! Why did he not?" There seemed to him to be here something about his friend which he could not understand.

"I hope this patience," said Mary, when she appeared, "is a good promise of what you will have need of. Uncle John sent for me. He was in pain; now he is better and asleep."

What they said does not concern us here. It has been said before, and will be many times again. The man had come by degrees through friendship to love. The woman, long in doubt, was now in the bewilderment of one suddenly come ashore in a

29

new land. Fear, a gentle fear, interest, a new tongue to learn, were all hers.

"I thought once, Sydney," she said, "I mean I was afraid, that you were to be one of Kitty's captives. I did not like it. I suppose that was a form of jealousy. I do not think I knew why it troubled me. Was it love? Love in its infancy must be ingeniously prophetic. I am jealous yet."

"I should not be the man I want you to think me if I simply put that aside. Miss Kitty is a perilous person. She likes the pursuit, the game, not the final object of the game—a woman to whose eyes it is hard to say no, a woman whom to know more nearly is to pity, and at last to fear. I never felt for her more than that attraction which many have felt. I like to feel that all the past is clear between you and me. Is it not?"

"Yes. To a woman like me, Kitty is an enigma. Margaret says no, that I manufacture enigmas, and that Kitty is simple."

"Let us drop Miss Kitty. When you came out I was thinking of a man I know whose life has been unhappy. I was trying to explain him to my own mind, to realize him. I used to think him also simple, and in a way he is."

"Well, forget him too, Sydney. You ought to be ashamed to have been thinking of any one but Mary Fairthorne. I sometimes think no one is simple. I know that in a few hours I am become dreadfully complex."

"I think," he returned, "that I, on the other hand, find myself simplified. I have good news for you."

"As good as to-day's?" she said, in a low tone. "Or was it so very good, the news I gave you?"

"Ah, not like that. But good, worth—well, I am generous, Mary; I make no bargains. You shall name the honorarium."

"Please to tell me."

"Mrs. Hunter will depart on Wednesday, and go, never to come back."

"Mrs. Hunter! Go! Impossible, Sydney. My uncle will never, never let her go. And why does she want to go?"

"She must go."

"But why? Do tell me."

"I am not free to tell you, but go she will."

"Now, this was why you were so mysterious, but is it—can it be true?"

"Yes; but why she goes you may never know. It is not my secret. As for your uncle, she will, I fancy, make excuses and write to him, and, for very good reasons, try to keep him in a good humor. But of this rest assured—she will never come back."

"Thank God!" she said. "Oh, Sydney, no one knows what this winter has been to me, no one!"

"My dear love, are you crying?" She was sobbing like a child.

"Tears of thankfulness!" she said. "I have gone through so much—so much! And I am so, so happy. Let me be quiet a little. Don't speak to me." He was silent, respectful of her mood, until she said: "There, you see what a child I can be, how foolish, how weak!"

"There is weakness one could ill spare," he returned.

"Thank you."

"And my honorarium?" he said.

"Oh, not for that—that woman."

"Well, not for that. I want those dear lips to speak to me, to mine."

She blushed red, under the masking darkness of the night, but paid him honestly.

They talked far into the night, and, as she rose, he said: "I will walk over to Grace's now, and go to town early to-morrow. I shall see Mrs. Swanwick some time during the day. May I tell her?"

"Yes, and the little ladies, our dear white mice, and your mother, of course, you will write, Sydney. No one else just now. I shall say nothing to uncle until that woman goes—if she goes. It is too good to be true."

"She will, and now I must go."

When, on this Sunday night, Mrs. Hunter set foot in the city she had two errands; one was easy, and concerning the other she had the indecision of a woman who, having been more than once on the verge of serious crime, had always drawn back in the dread of consequences.

In the exaltation of alcohol, now an habitual indulgence, and, too, under the pressure of debt, Craig had written the letter to Grace. It was no sooner sent than he fell into the clutches of fear, and stayed away from the office, declaring that he was ill. His fears had not been lessened by Blount's visit.

He was out when Mrs. Hunter called on this Sunday evening. She took a room for the night, and sat down in his untidy apartment to wait for him. When she had decided on action she was apt to become impatient. She remained quiet for a while, and then walked to and fro, sat down again, and saw the hours go by, while she thought of this reckless brother or turned to think of the graver matter which so much concerned her.

Meanwhile Lionel, who had kept his room all day, was glad of the cover of darkness, and ventured out to wander from one bar-room to another, on the way to make more mischief and to be the ignorant, indirect cause of good.

Martin Blount was now living with Grace at his farm. It was from a strong feeling of loyalty, and with reluctance, that he had given up the self-support his clerkship offered. Now, reassured by Archer and by what he saw of Grace's ordered life, he began to regret his action. But Archer was very busy, and the laboratory work was important and interesting. He could not at present abandon it. Archer had asked him, at last, to take entire charge, for the time, of the mere mechanical labor which at this stage of the investigation was such as Blount could readily manage. To aid his labor, Archer wrote out with care the needed directions, and, Grace consenting to spare the young man for a week from his work of cataloguing, Martin determined to remain for that time in the city. Archer was glad of the relief. He was not himself in a condition of mind to give to experimental work that incessant thought which is one of the essential elements of success. He was about to conduct a far more absorbing investigation.

When Blount had arranged to his satisfaction for a week's stay at Miss Markham's, and had received Archer's final instructions, he naturally inquired concerning Mrs. Hunter. Archer said it was a long matter, and was so plainly preoccupied that Blount, who was slowly acquiring social wisdom, felt that he had better await a less busy hour.

On this Sunday, while Lucretia waited for her brother, Martin, having finished some needed laboratory work, at evening returned to Miss Markham's for supper. The ladies still adhered to the old custom of a midday dinner on Sunday. After supper he went up with Knellwood to Grace's library and was soon deep in eager talk of the lands Knellwood was about to visit, or had already seen when a lad. The younger man, in turn, spoke of Vienna, and how he must get a year there, when he had been graduated. He was already learning German.

"And then," said Knellwood, "after that— what?"

"Oh, I shall settle here or in New York. I shall get on." He was confident.

"And of course a professorship," said the rector, amused at an assurance which smiled at fate and took no account of circumstance.

He himself lacked this absolute trust in his own will, even in his own moral nature, and was now about to flee like a bird scared at the net of the fowler.

"Well, Martin," he said, "it is pleasant to see a fellow so securely confident of success; and yet, life will as like as not refuse what you expect to get, and give what you never dreamed of getting."

Martin looked at the speaker in some surprise. He had himself had hard work, but he had never failed to win what he wanted. Perhaps the note of sadness in the rector's voice made him ask with his occasional indiscreet directness: "Have you ever failed to get what you wanted?"

Knellwood smiled. "No, not to get what I wanted, but rather to be what I want to be."

"Oh, but that's in a man's own power. A fellow can always manage that."

"Can he, indeed! I hope that you may always be able to say that."

The talk soon fell upon English cathedrals, and the rector had a happy listener.

A little later Lionel Craig, reeking with tobacco and in the exuberant stage of alcoholic confidence, rang a double peal at Miss Markham's door. Why he went thither it would have puzzled him to say. The next day he hazily recalled having had something very important to say to somebody. Blount must have been associated in his mind with the house. He certainly had no desire to see him when he himself was in control of the small amount of wits with which nature in a sparing mood had endowed him.

"Mr. Blount at home?" he asked. "You say I'm here. Want to see him." He went past the old black woman whom his violent pull at the bell

had aroused from slumber, and entered the dimly
lighted parlor.

Clementina Markham, her finger in the book she
had been reading, was aroused from sad thought as
Craig entered. Somewhat surprised, she stood up,
in summer white, simple as a wild rose, and sweet
with many ways of gentleness.

"How d'ye do, Miss Clementina," said Craig;
"come to pay a visit."

She had no experience of intoxicated men, but this
was obviously a man not quite sober.

"What do you want?" she said, very quietly.

Craig held himself for a moment till the room
stopped swinging round. When it came to a rest,
he inquired:

"Old man in?" This might have borne some dull
reference to Grace.

"Who?" she asked. "I do not understand."

"Old man Grace."

"You are insolent," she said; "you have been
drinking. Mr. Grace is not here; he does not live
here. You had better go home."

He caught at the back of a chair to steady himself.

"I ain't drunk; just a bit set up. You need n't
make a fuss. Old Grace, he gets drunk, real drunk
—saw him at Carlisle. Oh, I ain't afraid of him;
got him safe enough. He knows me."

She rang the bell at her side, and rang again till
the bell-rope broke.

"What 's that for?"

The servant came in haste.

"Call Mr. Blount, Mr. Knellwood, quick—some
one!"

"Want to see Blount—you ask him 'bout it." He had the singular persistency of the intoxicated. "He knows 'bout old Grace. I say, you set down, and I 'll set down; we 'll talk it over. Don't you be afraid of Grace. I 'll protect you. He knows me— I 'm Lionel Craig."

Blount ran down-stairs and into the room. Miss Clementina, flushed, indignant, troubled as never before in all her too tranquil life, was standing with the broken bell-rope in her hand.

"This man, Martin—he is intoxicated. He says—" she stopped. "He says—some nonsense."

"What did you say?" cried Blount. Craig was far over the line of dread of consequences.

"She says I 'm drunk. I say old Grace he gets drunk. You and me saw him. We know—we saw him—we know, don't we?"

Blount caught him by the arm.

"Out of this," he said; "don't make a row here."

"You let me alone."

Blount, with no gentle hand, pushed him out into the hall, and, swinging open the street door, thrust him forth roughly.

"If you were not drunk, Craig, I would thrash you well. Off with you! By George, this is twice I have let you go! If ever I see you again, if it be even in Roger Grace's office, I will— Out with you!" He pushed him down the steps, and left him swearing as he clung to a tree-box on the sidewalk.

Blount paused, surprised, at the door of the parlor. The quiet little lady there had seemed to him always so tranquil, so dutiful, so far from the influ-

ence of passion or emotion in this side eddy of city
life. Now she was seated, her head in her hands,
sobbing. Martin, who loved her well, stood over
her, deeply distressed.

"But he has gone," he said. "Please don't cry,
Miss Clementina." He was puzzled by her grief,
and sorry for what he could not understand. She
sat with her face in her handkerchief, making no
reply to his embarrassed efforts to comfort her. At
last she sat up, hastily wiped her eyes, and said:

"Please not to tell Letitia."

"Tell what? Why, there is n't any harm in crying. I 've been awful near it, just watching you.
I 'll do whatever you say."

To his surprise, she stood up and said rapidly, as
she laid a hand on his arm:

"What he said, what that man said cannot be
true. It—is—very disagreeable to hear such things
said. Of course it cannot be true!" She paused,
as if for assurance of the untruth of this drunken
babble. Martin, embarrassed, made no reply. "Why
don't you answer?" she continued. "He said—he
saw—he said you saw Roger Grace at—at Carlisle.
Oh, I can't talk about it! You heard what he
said."

"Why, a man like that, Miss Clementina, will say
anything."

Blount looked down on the tearful, questioning
eyes. What honest answer could he make? She
hastened to explain her too evident anxiety. "He
has been so good to me—to us, and I should be so
sorry. But it cannot be true. You can't think it

is?'' The faint smile of an innocent hope was as the rainbow to these tears. ''Please tell me.''

How could he reply? He tried to escape.

''You can never believe what a beast like that says. I would n't worry about Roger Grace.''

Of a sudden she looked like the rigid little grandmother of the portrait above her. She shed the restraints, the prudence, the reserve of years.

''You should know better than to trifle with me. I insist on knowing. Is it true or not?''

He was yet more puzzled. Here was another Clementina.

''I cannot tell you.'' He was at his wits' end.

''Then it is true.''

He urged that she had no right to use his silence as implying an affirmative. She said:

''I know, I know. You are afraid to tell me. I thought you, at least, were my friend.'' Then she sat down, leaving Martin much discomfited, and glad to be enabled to glide quietly out of the room. He went up-stairs, mind-blind, as he said in after years, face to face with his first serious feminine problem. He thought:

''Is a secret ever kept? Here is one of the utmost moment, and Craig and I and Archer and Mrs. Hunter, and now Miss Clementina all know it. Grace would pay thousands to hide it.'' He could not help wondering why it so deeply troubled Miss Clementina. It was pretty bad, but if Grace had been her brother she could not have made more fuss. He passed Miss Letitia in the hall and to her question replied:

"Oh, it was only a drunken man. I put him out." The gray-haired lady paused at the open door of the parlor.

"Clementina!" she exclaimed. "Look at the floor, dear." The worn Turkey carpet was soiled with the mud Craig's feet had brought in from the street. Hearing no reply, she raised her head. "Why, my dear sister, you have been weeping. What is the matter?"

"That man Craig was here. He was intoxicated. He was disagreeable."

"But did that make you cry? You seem discomposed, Clementina, and for a creature like that! If we are to go on supporting ourselves we must take what comes. I have sometimes reproached myself of late that I had not enough insisted on the government of the emotions. When, a few weeks ago, that butcher was in haste to be paid and was inconsiderate and, I may say, abrupt, you were quite needlessly disturbed."

"I think I had better go to bed," said Clementina, who had the desire of the hurt creature to find a lonely corner. "I will send Susan to attend to the carpet."

"Do, my dear. An intoxicated person! It does seem to me, Clementina, that we are almost keeping a boarding-house."

"Or a tavern!" said the younger lady, sharply.

"A tavern! I would not quite say that, dear."

"Well, as you please, sister. But life is sometimes very hard, very difficult, very—worthless."

"Isn't that rather excessive, and I might even say irrelevant?"

"Oh, say what you like, I don't care. Let me go. I don't care what any one says."

"Clementina!" But Clementina had fled.

Miss Letitia raised hands of dismay and surprise, looked down at the carpet, and then at the general, and last at the Councilor of Penn. She took the miniature of Gerald from the mantel and kissed it. Her eyes filled with tears. She wiped them away with a quick movement.

"I am glad Clementina is not here," she said aloud, and stood still until the mud was in part cleaned away. "It will be dry to-morrow, Susan. Then you can brush it out. Be careful. You can always brush away mud marks if you wait until the next day, but not always—other things," she added, reflectively, unaware of being an heroic person or that, as often before, she was reinforcing endurance with memories of men and women long dead.

She went up-stairs automatically, wiping her tear-dimmed glasses.

"Perhaps I was too severe with Tina," she said to herself. Very rarely did she use the diminutive of her sister's childhood. "But of late she is changed. I suppose she is feeling the results of this uncertain life. It is hard on the young." For her Tina was always a girl, needing restraint and guidance. Yes, she had been severe. She remembered her merry, gay, pretty, and prosperous. It was not so very long ago, and now— She knocked at her sister's door. "Tina, dear."

"I am undressing. Good night."

"Will you have a little valerian, dear?"

"Oh, no! There is nothing the matter with me."

"Or my smelling-salts?"

Clementina laughed the self-mocking laugh of the wretched.

"No, no," and Letitia went to her own room, reproaching herself and unhappy.

Clementina sat on her bedside. "My poor Letitia!" she exclaimed. "Well, this is the end. What a life! What a life! I cannot even tell him how I pity him. And how can it be? A man like him! Oh, it is all a maddening puzzle." She laughed outright the laugh that is twin to tears. "Valerian for a broken heart!"

XLIII

NELLWOOD had gone to his room for a book before Blount went down-stairs. Martin, returning, found him again in Grace's library. The rector looked up, and said: "The bells seem to have gone mad below stairs. What was it, Blount?"

"Oh, nothing much. Craig came here drunk. I put him out."

"Indeed! I went down as far as the door of the parlor. He must have gone. I only heard Miss Clementina crying, and then you spoke. Of course I did not go in. What was the matter? A woman like that does n't cry merely because a drunken man comes in."

"Oh, women are extraordinary things!"

"Things! My dear fellow," said the rector, smiling, "you had better not classify them to Mrs. Swanwick as things."

"You never can tell what they will do."

"I have seen men to whom that would apply."

"I suppose so."

"I heard her ask you if what Craig said was true. What was it? I do not ask lightly. These people are now my friends. I owe to them kindness never to be repaid. If there is anything going wrong that

I can help to set right, I want to help. She was plainly in distress. If for any reason you do not want to speak I will ask her. Women like these are reticent, and hide things when sometimes a few frank words would enable one to help them.''

Martin felt, as he listened, that it was hard to know what to do. Here was Craig again drunkenly talkative. How many people had he talked to of this matter? More than ever the folly of an over-sensitive man became plain to Blount. Grace ought to know how little good his weakness had done. Again the ethical question arose in the young man's mind, but now it embarrassed him less. It was hardly to be called a secret any longer. Presently others would know it. He shared to some extent the feelings of Grace. If he himself had fallen like his friend he would have fled from all these kindly folk, ashamed. He hesitated before making answer. Knellwood waited. At last Martin said:

"That miserable sot told Miss Clementina that he saw Roger Grace drunk at Carlisle." He expected as he spoke to see the clergyman astonished. Knellwood showed no sign of surprise, and said, quietly: "Is that all?"

"All, sir? It's awful."

"Do you believe it?" Blount was again in the toils.

"I don't want to be asked any questions about it."

Knellwood understood at once.

"Pardon me," he said, "I shall say no more; but, leaving you out of the matter altogether, Grace should know what has passed here."

"I think so," said Martin. "Yes, I really think so." He was greatly relieved, but added, quickly: "Will you tell him? And you will not speak of me? I have my reasons."

"I will see Mr. Grace to-morrow, and I shall have no occasion to use your name."

"Thank you," said Blount. Then he hesitated, and said at last, with characteristic courage: "But if there is any doubt about it in Mr. Grace's mind, I don't want to shirk the matter, even if it might seem to him— Well, I leave it all to you."

"That is wise and right. One other question, and then we will drop it. Was Miss Clementina very much troubled?"

"I should say she was. Why, Mr. Knellwood, she cried like a baby. It was really rather strange. Of course we all care immensely for Mr. Grace, but why it should set Miss Clementina to crying is past my comprehension."

"Indeed! Well, Martin, women are a soft-hearted folk. You cannot always know what they mean. Poor little woman!"

He rose, and said as he took Martin's hand: "This has been a grave talk. You won't mind my saying that you have behaved with discretion and good sense. Good night."

"Thank you."

XLIV

HEN, late this Sunday night, Craig found his sister in his room, and not the more amiable for waiting, he was in no state to be dealt with. Early on Monday she settled matters with despotic swiftness, and about one of the same day found Dr. Archer at home. "No," she said, "I will not sit down. Will this do?" laying on his table an open letter to Roger Grace. "Read it. There are three one-hundred-dollar notes in this envelope. Be careful Mr. Grace gets it in person."

"Very good; it is as it should be." It amused him not a little, both the cool caution and the letter, but he kept a grave face and did as she desired.

The letter was in Lucretia's best style, certainly not Craig's, although he had copied and signed it in a rather tremulous hand, and written "Private" on the cover.

"Is that all?" she said.

"Yes, that is all." As she turned to go out the light fell full upon her. She was of a corpse-like yellowish pallor.

"She has suffered," he thought. "Is it that boy?" Her face was stern. There was a certain rigidity about her look. Where was it he had seen that coloring? It was like some antique marble. He went with her to the door. "Good morning." She made no reply.

She walked to Second Street, and took the street-car up to the shipyards of Richmond. Here, miles away from the center of the city, she entered a drug-gist's shop and had made up an old prescription of Dr. Soper's for a strong preparation of aconite. When she had once complained of palpitation of the heart he had given her this, telling her to be careful, as the dose was small, and a teaspoonful would be fatal. She had never used it.

The druggist warned her of its poisonous power. She said through her veil that she had used it often. The prescription was correct. He could not re-fuse it. The man's doubts troubled her. She started out, walking swiftly. In a few minutes she was lost. In what were known as the Northern Lib-erties, the yea-and-nay plainness of Penn's checker-board city is changed in the wildering confusion of streets crossing at all angles. She was made calm again by the need to find her way, but was so long delayed that she missed a train. It was late in the afternoon when she reached Edgewood, where she went at once to her room and began to pack up her clothes, unassisted, as was desirable, for the accumu-lations were many and valuable.

XLV

UST before the close of bank hours on Monday, Roger Grace received by a messenger a letter marked "Private." He had his hat in his hand, and was about to leave. He had been out most of the morning. A clerk reminded him that Mr. Knellwood, who had failed to find him earlier, would return at three.

"Thank you. When he comes show him in."

He sat down and read the letter, with a vast sense of satisfaction, of thankfulness, and also of surprise.

"RESPECTED SIR: I have not had a moment of happiness since I broke my word to Mr. Blount. I did worse to threaten you that I would tell what I knew if you did not send me money. I hope if ever you felt sorry for anything you ever did when you were young, you will feel sorry for me. I was in debt and did not know where to turn. I hope you will understand that I was not myself, and was tempted. I am going away. May I entreat, Sir, that you will forgive me? I enclose three hundred dollars, which I borrowed from my sister. I paid my debts with your money.

"Respectfully,
"LIONEL CRAIG.

"Dutton's Hotel, Market Street."

Grace sat still, the letter in his hand. He was in a mood to be touched by the plea and to be sorry for the man. He laid it on the table, and sat in thought, comparing his own case with that of this miserable boy, who had sinned and repented. What right had he to blame him? Both had alike been tempted; both had fallen; but this was a young man, not a man in well-disciplined middle age. Then, too, he himself had timidly shrunk from facing consequences, as this man, scourged by conscience, had found courage to do. He had reproached himself with cowardice, with failure to punish that meanest of crimes, blackmailing. His very great happiness at this relief made him uncritically charitable. He took a sheet of paper and wrote:

"Mr. Grace has received Mr. Craig's note. Mr. Craig may be assured that the matter will go no further. Mr. Grace feels deeply the penitent tone of Mr. Craig's letter, and hopes it may be the beginning of a better life. He returns the money in a check to Mr. Craig's order, and desires that Mr. Craig will consider it as a gift from one who, fully appreciating the motives which caused it to be returned, prefers not to keep it."

He sent his note at once to Craig's address. In his amazement at this windfall, Lionel forgot to mention it to his sister, and told her he had for reasons of prudence burned a brief, very kind note from Mr. Grace.

And as for Grace, he could have doubled his check. He was beyond expression relieved, and with the relief began to wonder why he had been such a fool. He had hardly added this letter to his sum of folly and sent it on its way when Knellwood entered. Although Grace was always pleasant, and

made you feel that you were welcome, Knellwood was
conscious that there was more than common pleasantness in his usual phrase. "What can I do for
you to-day, Knellwood?"

"Nothing; I want, for a wonder, to do something
for you."

"Well, I am amiable. Sit down."

"May I close the door?"

"Certainly. What is it?"

"When you honored me with your confidence I
felt that, as to a part of what you said, you were
utterly wrong. Indeed, I said as much. You went
away, and I, of course, knew why. You were seen
at Carlisle by that fellow Craig."

"Goodness gracious, Knellwood! Who told you
that? Surely not Martin!"

"The fellow came to Miss Markham's quite off his
head last night and saw Miss Clementina. He boasted
that he had seen you at Carlisle, and—"

Grace lifted a hand.

"That will do," he said, flushing. "Miss Clementina! Read that, Knellwood." He gave him Craig's
note.

"I do not think," said the clergyman, "that this
letter is altogether like the man Craig. It is too
clever. The hand"—and he smiled—"is the hand
of Esau. But no matter. It is a confession. You
are safe. So he tried to blackmail you?"

"Yes, and I yielded," said Grace, defiantly, as if
expectant of criticism.

"You were wrong, Grace. It was a thing to meet
with prompt courage. It was a wrong to the community, and, as you see, useless."

"I would do it again."

"No, never. But there is a graver matter. What you felt most was that you, a man cursed with this craving, could not with a clear conscience ask a woman you had taught to love you to give you her life."

"How could I?"

"How could you? Only see, my friend, how it has worked out for her. Now she knows too much or too little. You are in honor bound to let her know all—to let her choose, not choose for her. There is no other course possible."

Grace got up and walked to and fro in visible agitation.

"Did it trouble her?" he asked, pausing, a hand on his friend's shoulder.

"My dear Grace, she cried like a little child."

"Oh, my God!"

"Do you think that a woman feels as you do about a thing like this? What she wants is to comfort, to help, to watch over you. It will never happen again. It is not the common, constant temptation."

"No, it is worse." He shook his head mournfully.

"Nonsense! Go like a man and talk to Archer, and, above all, go and set yourself right with Miss Clementina."

"And suppose she is foolish enough to say she will marry me?"

"Then, thank God to-night for the gift. Now go, at once. Do not wait. What need to ask her to marry you? What I want is that, as an honest man, you let her know the whole truth, and why your sick conscience made you desert her."

"I will go. I will at least do that."

Knellwood smiled behind his clerical hat as he lifted it. "You will go now?"

"Yes, I will go."

The rector went away, amused at his rôle of matchmaker, paid a visit or two, and dropped in late at Mrs. Swanwick's. He found Archer, Margaret, and her husband.

"Well," he said, "I sail next week, but I am ridiculously well and consider it a wicked waste of time and money."

"We shall miss you," said Archer, "and, I fear, so will the Markhams."

"May I tell him?" said Margaret.

"No," cried Archer, laughing; "but you may tell him that Mrs. Hunter leaves on Wednesday for ever and ages, as the Russians say. We think of having fireworks."

"From all I have heard," said Knellwood, "Miss Fairthorne will not grieve. As to the rest—as to your secret, I may at least be permitted to guess?"

"No, indeed!"

"I am at your service for the trousseau in Paris. They say I am given over to church millinery; perhaps my experience may be of use."

Amused at the idea of Knellwood choosing a trousseau, Margaret said to Archer:

"I made no promises."

"Please don't."

"Well, we will mention no names," laughed Knellwood. "I am rather in that line to-day myself, but mine is—prophetic."

"How exasperating you are! Do tell us," said Madge.

"I might. I may exchange news, but I *guess* yours, and you cannot guess mine. My warmest congratulations, Archer. She will have the best fellow I know."

In the midst of it all Jack made a wild rush into the room and at once mounted on Knellwood's knee for a ride. The talk went on as to the mysteriously abrupt departure of Mrs. Hunter and what John Fairthorne would say or do, concerning which Mrs. Margaret was in doubt. As Knellwood and Swanwick talked together, Archer said to Margaret: "I wish you would go out to Edgewood and stay until she leaves." He had some unstateable apprehension, and urged his request so strongly that she said, speaking low: "Why are you so anxious?"

"I do not know. Are you never in that state of mind?"

"No, never, without a cause."

"But you will go. Perhaps because of Mary I am—well, absurd, if you like." He was haunted by that stern, sallow face. She said, at length: "I will go, but only because you wish it."

"Promise me."

"I do. I will go out early to-morrow."

At last Archer rose. "I shall be at Edgewood in the afternoon to-morrow I hope."

"Very good. We shall meet there. You are not going so soon, Mr. Knellwood?"

"I must. I am full of bits of business," and he left them.

"He was mysterious," said Swanwick. "I wonder what it was."

"Are you very glad for me, Mrs. Margaret?" said Archer. She had seemed to him to take his great news very calmly. She laughed. "I am not Mrs. Margaret. I am Madge now and always. How tall you are! I like nice fat little doctors nearer my own earthly level. Stoop down a little. I want to tell you something."

"What is it?" he said, as he bent over. Then she kissed him, crying: "That is how glad I am, Sydney Archer!"

"Oh, my!" said Jack. "I did n't know you kissed everybody."

"I do not," said Madge. "What brought you here, you little scamp?"

"I heard Mr. Knellwood," said the boy; "I like him. He 's got nice long legs to ride."

XLVI

IF ever mortal was afflicted with an ague of indecision it was the banker after he had committed himself to Knellwood. He concluded that it was better to write what he had to say. Next he recalled the fact that he had written one letter too many that day, and was in no mood to write letters. After all, what could he write? It was horrible to put it all in black ink, to be burned or not, as might chance.

Meanwhile, in automatic obedience to the idea which was in his mind on leaving his office, he walked toward Pine Street with the slow pace of a man deep in thought. Thus absorbed, he moved southward down Third Street, past the brokers' offices and the beautiful marble front of Girard's Bank. As he went by men spoke or touched their hats, and wondered that they did not receive the usual cheerful response.

On the step, with the bell-handle in his grasp, he still hesitated. "No, I cannot. Not to-day," he murmured. He turned to go.

Then circumstance, in the shape of Susan, opened the door. With the friendly familiarity of the old-fashioned black servant, she said:

"Why, Mr. Grace, we ain't seen yo' these weeks.

The ladies was a-speakin' of yo' this very mornin'
at breakfuss. Come in.''

He entered, saying: ''I am going up to the library. Tell Miss Clementina that I should like to
see her in the parlor. I will be down in a minute
or two.''

He went up-stairs slowly, and passed through the
open door of his bed-chamber. His library, a room
thirty feet wide, lay across the entire front of the
house. To it he had brought most of the books he
cared to have about him. He opened the door and
went in.

Perched high on the top of a step-ladder sat the
woman he had come to see. She was in gray linen,
her sleeves rolled up, and she wore a blue-check
apron to preserve her from the dust she had been
carefully blowing or brushing from a precious shelf
of daintily bound volumes of authors' proofs. The
long apron gave her slight figure a childlike youth-
fulness which Grace at any other time would have
been quick to observe. Just now she had paused to
note the changes which the hand of her best-loved
poet had made on a page proof of the ''Excursion.''
She looked up, and, coloring, dropped her skirts over
a pair of neat ankles, and came down quickly from
her perch. It would be hard to say which of the two
was most confused.

''I was dusting your books,'' she began; ''it is
quite impossible to keep out the dust. Pray excuse
my appearance.'' It certainly needed no excuse.
Without any word of greeting, he said: ''I came to
get a book, but I also wanted to see you.''

''What is it?'' she asked, and then, hastily: ''Can

I find you the book you want? I really think I know better than their owner where your books are. I was quite absorbed in your Wordsworth proofs. What book shall I find for you?''

"That can wait. I have an explanation to make.'' He drew himself up, resolute at last. "I want to say that what that drunken young man told you last night is true; but a half truth is often worse than a lie. This—this horror—this thing has happened to me five times in my life. I could not leave you in the belief that I am a common—''

She broke in: "Oh, don't! I do not want to know. You are very good to wish to say what must cost you so dear. I do not wish to hear it. I—a man's whole life counts for something, Mr. Grace, and I know what yours has been.'' She seemed, as she stood before him, to be a larger personality than he had known in the quiet past. She had the dignity which some little women possess. A beautiful tenderness was in her tear-filled eyes.

There was a moment of silence after she ceased to speak. The gentle truth of the excuse overcame the strong man. He had wondered again and again what she would say. He had never dreamed that she could or would be anything but shocked, or would fail to feel the disgust the remembrance had for him. He sat down, with his hand on his forehead. The woman stood before him. Boundless pity, born out of the first love of a restrained and limited life, rose up and captured her.

The man was as much a child as she had been the night before. He shook with the passion of an emotion he was unable to restrain.

She put out a hand and timidly touched his shoulder. She was on the verge of an equal loss of self-control. "Please not to—to do so," she said. "I can't bear it."

"Why are you so good to me?" said he, not looking up.

"I am only just, not good."

"No. Is it possible? How can I believe that! Oh, I cannot bear it! Your sweet goodness, I mean. I am not fit to talk to you. I must go." He stood up. She said, instantly:

"You cannot go."

"I must."

"But—" and she flushed and was silent, speaking only with her eyes.

"But what? You have not blamed me? Say what you will; I have deserved the worst you can say."

"How could I hurt you? How could I blame you? You, who are so good to me, to all—"

"You ought to wish never to see me again."

"No, no. I can say nothing like that. Oh, never —because—" Then he raised his eyes, and saw the truth in hers. He held her off, seizing both wrists and facing her.

"You love me? I ought to be sorry that—you love me. I see it in your eyes. My God! It is pitiful."

"Yes, I love you," she said, faintly. "Oh, what have I done? Let me go. How could I!"

"Never!" he cried, and he lifted her hand reverently to his lips, as Miss Letitia entered.

For the first and last time in her life she said:

"Great heavens!" and then, "Clementina, what does this mean, child?"

"It means, dear lady," said Grace, "that I have what no man deserves less than I. Miss Clementina has done me this honor."

Miss Letitia put up her glasses and regarded him as a farmer looks at the culprit boy caught stealing apples.

"I am surprised, Clementina. I think I should have been consulted. This is very unexpected. I was not prepared for it."

"Nor I," said Clementina, meekly.

"You will have the kindness, Mr. Grace, to follow me. I desire a few words with you," said Miss Markham, with severity.

Grace, embarrassed and also a little amused, said: "Certainly."

"You had better go on dusting the books, Clementina," said her sister. She went down-stairs, followed by Grace. It is improbable that Clementina returned to her interrupted occupation.

What thereafter passed between Miss Letitia and Roger Grace it is needless to state, but, as he went back to the library and found Clementina, it is to be presumed that Miss Markham was satisfied. Grace came out of the interview much the better for the mirth it aroused; but when, a few days after, he spoke of it to Clementina, she said: "You must not laugh at her. I never did. She thinks the Markhams belong to some angelic peerage. You must not mind what she said."

"I? No! I shall buy this house and give it to

her, or you shall, and we will put an end to all this work and worry.''

''She will not let you.''

''But it will be you, dear. Gracious, how pretty you are!'' It was true. The butterfly had emerged from the cocoon of a restricted life, and was shining in the light and liberty of the sunshine—love.

XLVII

VERY one, even Archer, had left Mrs.
Swanwick's that afternoon. Husband
and wife were about to dress for dinner when the bell rang. She ordered
the children to the nursery. Madge
made haste to say to the servant:

"Not at home." But Roger Grace was not to be
denied. He was in a state of effervescent joy.

"Pardon me," he said, "I insisted. I heard your
husband's voice." He had been, for a year or two,
a most valuable friend to Harry, and had by degrees
attracted Madge. Moreover, she was interested in
his slowly developing taste for society, pictures, and
rare books. He had been more than merely generous to her charities. She had learned to like him
and to respect him of course, for, unlike Mary, she
had no liking for those whom she could not entirely
respect.

She made him welcome. No, he would not return
to dine. He had missed Swanwick at his office.
There was a large bond affair on hand, and a rather
complicated lease of the Wilton and Detroit Railroad to be drawn. Thus he explained his visit.

"I should like to draw it," said Madge, laughing.
"Keep still, Jack; sit down." The boy looked on
Grace as his legitimate prey.

"You shall see it," said Harry.

"And the fee?" she laughed.

"It will be large," said the banker. "I came in to ask you to call on me to-morrow."

"Come and dine with Harry. I go to Edgewood for a day or two."

"Indeed! Yes, I will come. There is one other little matter. I came to speak of it, too. Not quite as important. Perhaps you may like to guess at it."

"It cannot be up to the news we have just had," said Harry. "Mrs. Hunter, that female Nimrod, a mighty hunter before the Lord—or the devil—departs on Wednesday."

"Indeed!" exclaimed Grace. "You are to be congratulated, and especially Miss Fairthorne."

"That is not all," said Harry.

"Hush!" said Madge. "My husband cannot keep a secret."

"No one can," said Grace, grimly. "I will test my belief. Here, Jack, I mean to tell you a secret. If you keep it five minutes I will give you a pony."

"And a saddle?" said Jack.

"Yes, and a bridle."

Grace whispered in his ear.

"Now, five minutes, sir." He took out his watch, laughing.

"Come here," said Madge. "You are only six. You are too young for a pony."

"No," said Grace. "Now we begin."

Madge laughed. "Tell me, Jack."

"No, mama."

"If you do not tell me at once," said Harry, "I will thrash you every night for a week."

"Mama won't let you."

"And I will sell your pony, Jack."

"You can't until I get him, daddy." He remained firm.

"Four minutes, Jack."

"But if you do not tell me," said Retta, "I will never love you again."

"You 're a goose, Retta."

"Time 's up," laughed Grace. "I have found the only fellow that can keep a secret. Go and tell mama. The pony is all right."

"Mama, the secret is somebody is going to marry Mr. Grace."

"I suppose so," said Harry, "some day."

"No, now-day," said Jack.

"Dear Mrs. Swanwick, I am like a child for the joy of it. It is Miss Clementina."

"Well, that is almost as good as the other," cried Harry. "Nonsense, Madge! I must. Archer is engaged to Mary Fairthorne."

"I told you," cried Madge, "I was sure he would tell."

"Well, you dear people, my belief is again justified. No one can keep a secret. I owe you much, Mrs. Swanwick; and this, too, in a way."

"Upon my word, Madge," said Harry, after Grace had gone, "I must have a bottle of champagne to-day. I hope nothing more will happen this week."

XLVIII

N this Monday afternoon Mrs. Hunter despatched her brother to New York, a thoroughly alarmed man, and he thus passes out of this story toward the sad fate of those who lack power to resist temptation.

Mrs. Swanwick, to Mary's great relief and somewhat to her surprise, appeared at Edgewood on Tuesday morning, and Mrs. Hunter, who had returned the afternoon of the day before, was not pleased with this addition of another and a too watchful witness.

Mr. Fairthorne kept his room on Monday. He was restless all day, complaining of sharp pains in his heart, and asked repeatedly for Lucretia. Dr. Soper had been sent for, and had advised quiet and turkey soup rather than chicken soup. He hoped the arsenical drops would be given punctually ten minutes before the meal, but if unfortunately forgotten then to be given ten minutes after the meal. Above all, there should be no excitement. He went away, as usual, optimistically at ease, leaving the nieces by no means reassured.

Mrs. Hunter had a late supper, having arrived after dinner. After a little more packing, she sat down in her wrapper at the open window. She was summing up her chances. If she went away, as she knew she must, she could keep Fairthorne in a good humor for a while by letters. But would they let him see her letters? She was a woman who found it impossible to guess what others would do except by asking herself what, under like circumstances, she would do herself. She decided that Mary Fairthorne would not hesitate to read and burn any letters she might write. She would certainly take care that they did not reach Mr. Fairthorne. As surely Mrs. Swanwick would stand implacably in her way, and no letter from the uncle would ever be mailed. She misjudged both women.

Archer had said that he did not think any one would try to test the validity of the codicil. That might or might not be the case. It was Mr. Fairthorne she feared. On condition that she remained with him and gave up the school appointment he had promised to leave her money. He had kept his word. Now, she was to be driven out and forced to leave him without reasonable excuse. What would he do? She was very sure what he would do. He would be furious. All the chances were hostile.

But he had a weak heart, and, Archer had said, was in constant peril. Dr. Soper was not of that opinion; it was latent gout. She smiled. What a poultice of a man! She had at last seen enough to believe that Archer was right; Mr. Fairthorne might die suddenly, but when? If he lived even a few weeks he would surely revenge her unexplained desertion by changing his will. If he lived? She had always faced impending disaster with resolution, and hesitated at no remedial means short of positive punishable crime. Again and again she had come near to it, and then had found some less risky resort. But here she saw none.

Pilgrim had written that he had put in trust for her in Boston enough to give her for life the annual income he had been paying by a quarterly draft. He wished to end even this slight relation. Why he had ever given the money she could not see, but now it would certainly be safe whether he died or changed his mind.

Then, too, her gains had been large, and the autograph business profitable. Would Mr. Fairthorne ever discover the share she had exacted? What if the man in South Street, losing her as an intermediary, should betray her to Fairthorne, or be forced to confess? What then? There was another risk, for other skilled autograph collectors came to see this collection.

She leaned on the ledge of the open window and looked out at the night. A dog bayed in a distant farmyard. Now and then an early katydid shrilled its sharp statement, "Katy-did, katy-did n't."

"If before I count nine," she said, "no, thirteen, that dog bays again, I will do it." As she spoke, Felisa, who usually slept in her room, leaped on the window-sill. It startled Lucretia. A moment later she repeated:

"Thirteen! No, thirteen will not do. It is my unlucky number. It shall be fifteen."

The night was intensely dark. She stared through

the open space and waited. Then she began to count, slowly: "One, two." As she said "thirteen" the long, melancholy cry of the dog broke the stillness.

"There," she cried, "I will do it! I wish it had not been thirteen."

The strange howl, or I know not what, disturbed Felisa. She sprang on Lucretia's shoulder and fled with a wild cry to the door, thence back to the window, leaped a few feet to the veranda roof, and was lost to view.

"Ye saints!" exclaimed Lucretia. She was startled by the hollow sound of her own voice, and strangely troubled by Felisa's flight. A vague fear came upon her. It was like a desertion of the one friendly thing in an unfriendly house. For a while she looked out into the unrevealing night. At last she called: "Felisa, Felisa." There was no response. Sitting down, she let fall the masses of her dark hair, and slowly ran her hands through it as she tried to strengthen her resolve.

Yes, she must make sure. There was so much she wanted—an unwatched life, the demi-mondaine freedom, the opera, the café chantant, the social Texas of Cairo or Tangiers, anything except the tiresome decencies in which she had patiently lived. And Kitty? She had promised to go with her.

She turned aside coolly, as often before, to sum up the danger. How much aconite was needed? Her time was short. She went to bed, and could not sleep. The dog bayed. She shut the window, and still tossed about, restless through the long hours of the night. She ordered breakfast in her room, and, making a careful toilet, entered the library before ten. Felisa left her chair and came to purr a welcome 'at her feet. Madge had tried to persuade her uncle to remain in bed for the day. Dr. Soper had said rest was desirable. The old man would have his own way. Why had they refused to let Archer attend him? Soper was a petticoat doctor. He insisted on rising even earlier than usual, and after breakfast went into the library. Here Mrs. Hunter found him seated.

"I will come back presently," said Madge, and left the room as Lucretia entered.

"Where have you been?" Fairthorne said to Lucretia. "If you neglect me I shall die."

She soothed him, stroked his gray hair, and gave a laughing account of her shopping and of the bad manners of the shop-girls. Had he taken his arsenic? As she desired to please Soper, she had given it steadily of late.

"No; no one looked after him." This was incorrect; Mary had given it before breakfast, but he had forgotten.

"I will give it," she said; "Dr. Soper wishes it given in a little sherry."

She went down-stairs and poured into the small medicine-cup a glassful of sherry wine. In her own room she added a teaspoonful of aconite and then a little water. She put the half-empty vial in her pocket and returned to the library.

On the stair she halted. The indecision of the unhabitual criminal was upon her. Was there no other way? Yes, she would tell him she must go away. That would do. She would try him.

"I will say Lionel is ill." Glad of her self-reprieve, she went on up-stairs. "If he is good to me," she said, "I will not do it. If he is angry—it will be he who decides."

She entered and set down the glass on his table. Then she knelt and took his hand. "Mr. Fairthorne," she said, "my brother is ill in New York. I must go to him. Cannot you do without me for a few weeks? I am in great trouble."

The old man looked around at her. "You can't go. You promised to stay with me. I am weaker every day. You won't leave me, Lucretia?"

"But Lionel is ill, sir. I—I have to go to him. Please to be good to me."

"You promised," he said, with dull persistency.

"But I must go. I have no choice. I will soon come back."

He was now, as always, excited by opposition. He pulled away his hand and sat up. "I won't have it. I can change my mind, too. If you go away and desert me you will suffer for it. I will not let you." His eyes filled, from the childishness of age; a tear rolled down his cheek. He was conscious of his weakness, and angered by this signal of loss of self-restraint. He cried out: "You are ungrateful, damn you!"

Lucretia rose. Her wide eyes narrowed to a line, and her face set hard. "I can't bear to have you threaten me. It is sad enough to leave you."

"Then, stay."

"I will write. I will see what I can do. I will try to stay."

"Well, then, give me my medicine." He put out a shaking hand to reach the glass.

She quickly anticipated his act, and stood up, again indecisive. Yes, she must! As she turned toward him, he said: "I hate that stuff. You have upset me with your cursed nonsense. Between Soper and you, I shall be poisoned. Why do you stand there staring at me? Let me get the stuff down and be done with it."

She stood like a statue, unable to move. It was only to put out her hand. She tried to do so. She could not. Of a sudden she broke into a profuse, chilly sweat.

"Give it to me," he cried; "I have pain in my heart. You look like a witch. Why do you keep me waiting? You have upset me, and even that ass Soper said I was not to be excited."

Lucretia was motionless. She rallied, saying: "The cup is too full. I—I made a mistake. I will pour some out."

"Nonsense! You look as if you were really going to poison me." He laughed feebly. "Case of antecedent remorse?" For a moment he was his former self; the fine, old, high-bred face lighted up, well pleased, as he added: "Lucretia is a fatal name. I never thought of it before. A name to hang any woman. There was the Borgia, and—"

She broke in abruptly, terrified:

"Why do you talk so? You frighten me." She moved a step away, the glass in her hand.

"Stuff!" he said. "Give me the medicine. What on earth is the matter?" He put out his hand.

"No," she said.

He stood up.

"I will have it."

"Please, sir, sit down. Take care. You will spill it. You are excited. You shall have it in a moment."

"I want it now. Do you hear? Every one bullies me." He caught her arm, and, being still strong, snatched at the glass, crying: "Give it to me." She pushed him back, and the wine fell over his shirt-front.

Suddenly he grew white. His face twitched, his eyes rolled from side to side. He exclaimed: "Oh, my heart!" With a low, hoarse cry, the final wail of pain, he fell back, shook all over, and was dead.

For a moment Lucretia stood appalled. Then she staggered backward, away from him, still looking at the changing face. She threw out on the floor what little was left in the cup, which she dropped into her pocket. Casting a look of horror at the gray, fallen head, the large, inert body, but a moment ago alive and angry, she seized the bell-pull and rang it violently.

As she ran to the door, she met Mary Fairthorne and her sister.

"He is dead! He is dead! I was reading to him! All of a sudden he cried out, 'My heart! my heart!' Oh, send for a doctor, quick, quick!"

"It is useless," said Margaret. "Oh, Mary, he is

gone! He is gone! He is dead! Stay here with Mary, Mrs. Hunter—''

"I cannot," she said. She had an intense terror of the dead.

"I will stay alone," said Mary. "Run, Madge, and send for Dr. Archer, Soper, any one. Send at once, but it is useless. My poor old uncle! Ah, how good you were to me!" The latter days were forgotten. She threw herself on her knees beside him, overcome with grief.

The scared servants came to the door, huddled in a group. Mary rose and gave some quiet orders. The dead man was carried into his chamber and laid on the bed.

Mrs. Hunter had gone to her own room. She threw herself on a lounge, limp and weak. Presently she got up, and, finding a flask, drank a long draught of the brandy. In a little while she felt better.

"What an escape! What an escape!" She got up, washed out the cup and emptied the half-filled vial of aconite out of the window. Next she carefully removed the label and rinsed the bottle. After this she lay down again, and, with a sense of entire relief, fell into thought.

"I must ask to stay to the funeral. That will be best—and mourning? I suppose I must. It is rather a waste, but, after all, it becomes me. What an escape!"

In the evening she wrote a note:

"DEAR MISS FAIRTHORNE: I had meant to leave on Wednesday not to return. I had not told your uncle. You and I have not been friends, and perhaps my own unfortunate temperament has been at fault. That I was useful and devoted to your uncle you know. May I not ask the privilege of remaining for his funeral?

"Yours truly,
"LUCRETIA HUNTER."

Mary read it and wrote in reply:

"I see no objection.   M. F."

When, three days later, they assembled in the little graveyard of St. David's Church, Lucretia, tall and handsome, in deep black, came last to the grave, looked down, threw in a handful of lilies of the valley and went away to the station.

Two weeks later, as Grace was on his way to dine with the Swanwicks, a quiet family dinner, he saw Archer on the far side of the street. He crossed over and joined him. As they went on, Archer asked: "What day did Knellwood sail?"

"Yesterday. He changed his steamer and has waited. I do not know why."

"It would be strange if he were to come upon Mrs. Hunter and poor little Miss Kitty in Europe."

"When," returned Grace, "I chanced to say to him that she had gone to join Mrs. Hunter and was going abroad with her, he said, 'I trust that we shall not meet.'"

"It has troubled Miss Fairthorne," said Archer, "more than it has Mrs. Swanwick. Harry went after Miss Kitty to New York, but she was very unpleasant and perfectly under Mrs. Hunter's control. It was useless.''

''I should think that a threat to contest that amazing codicil would bring Mrs. Hunter to terms.''

''Yes,'' said Archer, ''it might, but Miss Kitty has the obstinacy of the weak, and, besides that, the family would not willingly act against Mr. Fairthorne's will. On the whole, they are wise. You, of course, know that he left Miss Morrow, to our surprise, only as much as he left Mrs. Hunter, and then divided his large estate between Mrs. Swanwick and Miss Mary.''

''I heard as much. What becomes of his autographs?''

''Thereby hangs a rather queer story. They are left to the university. In making a valuation of them, the experts found that a good many of those lately acquired and set down at high figures were of more than doubtful authenticity, some of them obvious forgeries.''

''Mrs. Hunter again,'' said Grace, laughing.

''Possibly,'' said Archer, ''or probably. A word as to Blount, Mr. Grace.''

''Well?''

''Do not help him too much. Don't make life too easy for him.''

''I owe him much, Archer; more than you know.''

''And yet, I think I am right. He has a very stoutly held belief in himself.''

''That is so. I will keep it in mind. But the problem of how to help and not to harm is not always an easy one.'' For a moment he did not speak.

Then he said: "How strangely influential are the accidents of life, the circumstance that seems at the time so small."

"And character, as it meets them, and bends, or breaks, or stands fast," said Archer.

"True, true," returned Grace, "but here we are. There are Miss Clementina and Miss Mary on the steps. I thought we were late."

A few months later Grace received a letter from Knellwood:

"MY DEAR SIR: What you say of Archer's opinion and advice is very pleasant to hear. What little I can do for you I do every day. May it help you.

"I enjoyed our dear old cathedrals, and then wandered on to the Continent. At Monaco to my surprise I saw, unseen of them, Mrs. Hunter and Craig as they came out of the door of the gambling saloon. She was ghastly white. Had she lost money? I do not know. He was a bloated, ill-dressed, flabby wreck. Miss Morrow was not with them, and I left that evening. Can nothing be done to rescue the poor girl?

"I wish to be remembered to all who care for me.

"Yours truly,

"CYRIL KNELLWOOD."